CHRIS EVANS

OF BONE AND THUNDER

D1438477

TITAN BOOKS

Of Bone and Thunder
Print edition ISBN: 9781783297559
E-book edition ISBN: 9781783297566

Published by Titan Books
A division of Titan Publishing Group Ltd
144 Southwark Street, London SE1 0UP

First Titan edition: February 2015
10 9 8 7 6 5 4 3 2 1

A CIP catalogue record for this title is available from the British Library.

Printed and bound by CPI Group (UK) Ltd, Croydon, CR0 4YY

What did you think of this book? We love to hear from our readers.
Please email us at: readerfeedback@titanemail.com,
or write to us at the above address.

To receive advance information, news, competitions, and exclusive offers
online, please sign up for the Titan newsletter on our website:
www.titanbooks.com

OF BONE AND
THUNDER

For all the Vietnam War veterans I've had the great fortune to know.
You inspired me with your service and honor me with your friendship.

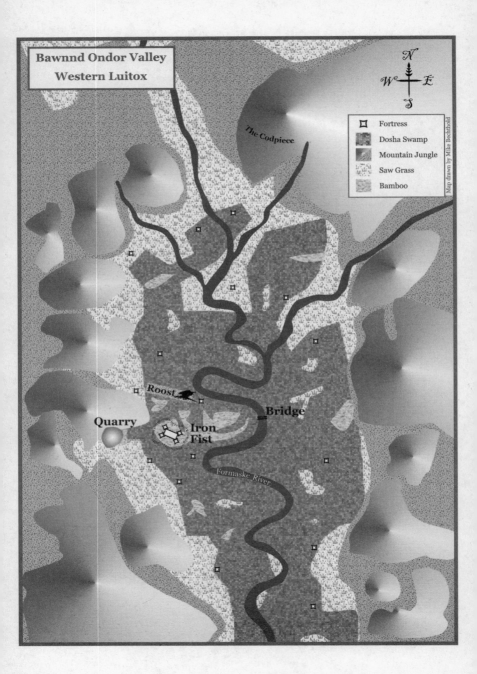

PROLOGUE

A BLACK CONDOR DIPPED her featherless head and flapped her wings, straining for height. Another vulture drifted in front of her, forcing the condor to climb higher in the crowded wheel of circling birds. The condor struggled, her body weak from having little to eat over the past month. The sun had yet to crest the hilly peaks to the east, but already, dozens of bald-headed condors had taken up stations high above the mist-shrouded valley below. The other vultures were hungry, too. The birds flew without calling to each other. Only the sound of their massive wings working laboriously in the humid air marked their passage.

Long-tailed shrikes darted between the condors, refusing to settle in as they twisted and banked among the larger, slower birds. When this sport became dull, a shrike ventured down to the roof of the mist, skimming along its rolling surface and kicking up a cottony spray in its wake. It darted to and fro wherever the mist churned and a hole appeared to open, but it was never fast enough to dive through before it closed.

Shadows passed over the condor and she turned her attention from the shrike. The wheel was breaking apart. The reason flew several hundred feet above. Three pairs of green-breasted eagles had been drawn by the waiting flock. The condor tensed. She was significantly larger than the eagles, but the birds of prey were aggressive and unpredictable. Hunger made the condor brave, and she kept to her course. The other condors settled in behind her and the wheel resumed its slow rotation.

When the eagles showed no sign of attacking, the condor allowed herself to look down again and quickly spied the shrike flying inches above the undulating whiteness. A large wave of mist surged upward momentarily before collapsing, pulling down the mist around it and creating a gaping tear in the otherwise uniform surface. The shrike chirped and dived toward the opening. It managed to penetrate several feet before the walls of mist closed in around it. The shrike's chirps grew frantic as it twisted and tried to fly back out. Its wingtips brushed the mist and were instantly tangled in wispy skeins that stuck to its feathers. The shrike flapped harder but only succeeded in becoming more enmeshed. Its wings were still beating as the mist closed over it and the condor lost sight of it. The condor kept an eye on the spot where the shrike had vanished, but the bird did not reappear.

The sky began to take on a rosy hue. Shadows cast from the eastern peaks drew jagged black teeth across the mist, reaching all the way to touch the peaks running parallel along the western boundary of the valley. Though the birds couldn't see it, they knew a thick, brown river surged through a fertile plain of lush green vegetation far below them. They could, however, smell the life that teemed in the jungle, but that wasn't why they had assembled so early.

It was what they heard, still miles away to the south.

It had happened three times before, over a month ago, in valleys to the south and to the east. In each case, holes had been torn in the impenetrable mist that walled them off from the life below, revealing the jungle and all its inhabitants, and beckoning them down. They had only to circle, and wait.

Whup-whup-whup.

It was faint and distant. A soft, rhythmic sound that carried like the coppery tang of fresh blood through the humid air. It was a sound foreign to this land, but one to which the circling birds had quickly adapted.

The condor dipped her right wing, allowing herself to drift beyond the wheel and out over the eastern ridge as she angled toward the distant sound. While the eagles continued to circle, the rest of the flock followed her, forming a descending spiral that eased into a single column as they leveled off above the ridge. The condor began to rise as she caught the heated air roiling up from the sun-warmed side of the ridge, but she ignored her instinct and tacked away from the updraft, continuing to follow the ridgeline toward the end of the valley.

Whup-whup-whup.

It was louder now, echoing off the ridgelines in a growing crescendo. She caught movement out of her right eye and tilted her head. The eagles were finally descending, coming straight down toward the sound instead of hugging the ridgeline.

The condor turned her attention forward. The mist at the very southern end of the valley stirred as seven dark shapes carved along its surface. She shuddered but kept flying.

The eagles screeched, tucked in their wings, and dived, aiming directly for the approaching intruders. Talons and beaks glinted in the sun as the birds of prey called out their challenge at full throat, meeting the interlopers at speed.

The screeching ended abruptly in sprays of red mist.

Brown and green feathers tumbled in the wake of the dragons as they flew on, their wing tips gouging enormous swathes of mist while their tails churned it into froth. Gossamer threads stirred up from the mist found little purchase against the dragons' scaly hides and did nothing to slow them down.

The condor, with the flock in tow, kept her course as the dragons closed the distance between them, their formation unnaturally precise. It unsettled the condor. Nonetheless, she kept to her path over the ridgeline. She had no concept of what "bravery" was, not that she needed one. Hunger made her fearless. Better to risk being eaten than to feel her insides being gnawed to nothing as her strength faded.

She took a chance and tacked toward the dragons, desperate not to miss the fleeting opportunity that would soon present itself. It was unnerving, but she had no choice. The dragons offered the only safe passage through the mist.

As the dragons came level with her, the closest predator flew only a couple of hundred yards away. The beast turned its head slightly and fixed a large, black eye with a gleaming red pupil on her. The condor's wingspan would fit inside this dragon many times over. Every part of the creature elicited fear. It was all pointed teeth, stone-hued scales, wings bristling with thorny spikes, and oddly shaped bumps astride the dragon's shoulders.

The four lead dragons, smaller and more agile, suddenly slammed their wings hard on the downward stroke, vaulting them high above the mist. Even at this distance, the condor was buffeted by the move. The dragons arced gracefully in the air until their momentum burned off and they hung motionless at their flight's apogee. As one, they flicked their tails hard left, pointed their heads toward the mist, and shot their right wings out in a sudden flare.

Grace became violent force.

The dragons snap-rolled onto their backs and plummeted toward the mist, each one tucking its wings in tight alongside its body. Their tails elongated as two small fins at the tip took on a rakish angle, imparting a rotation to the hurtling dragons. The wind whistled through their teeth and thrummed across the membranes of their wings.

When they were still fifty yards above the mist, the four dragons opened their maws and breathed fire.

The condor squawked and turned away as the heat washed over her. Shit and piss and feathers flew through the air as the flock broke up in wild panic. The mist crackled and sparked.

She turned back in time to see the dragons plunge through the smoking hole in the mist and disappear. A moment later, the remaining dragons, much larger than the lead four and sporting many more of the odd bumps along their backs, lumbered down through the hole.

The condor banked and flew after them, hurtling through the gap in the mist, which was already starting to close. Though the opening was polluted with the caustic odor of the dragons' fire, the blood of the eagles hung in the air and she opened her beak out of reflex. This was why she risked everything. Wherever the dragons appeared, death followed, and that meant food.

Turbulence buffeted the condor as she flew downward, but she splayed her pin feathers and kept herself away from the rolling walls of mist. She pumped her wings faster, determined not to become trapped.

She was still accelerating when she exited the hole and the entire valley stretched out before her like a vast, green sea. The wet, thick air with all its earthy smells filled her nostrils as if she'd dunked her head underwater. For a moment, the pangs in her stomach vanished. Below, the dragons were hundreds of yards away and angling toward the ground.

The condor splayed her wings and slowed her descent. She could easily track the dragons from here as they flew toward the valley floor. She began to circle well below the layer of mist, comforted as other birds came through and fell in behind her. The waiting began again and she became aware once more of the hunger pangs in her stomach. That pain would not last much longer. Already, a new scent was rising in the air. The condor opened her beak in response.

Deep in the jungle below, blood was spilling.

PART ONE

CHAPTER ONE

"**S**ON OF A POXY witch."

Crossbowman Carnan Qillibrin craned his neck to watch a rag race over the treetops and disappear behind the other side of the mountain. He made out crouched figures on the rag's back, but he couldn't see if any were hit by arrows. A billowing stream of gray smoke marked the rag's passage as a second barrage of arrows arced into the sky. The arrows' flight grew erratic as they passed through the disturbed air in the rag's wake.

It was the third rag flight over the mountain today, although only the first to be shot at. Carny thought those were decent odds, but he doubted the higher-ups would agree. With more and more flights coming into Luitox from the Kingdom every day, Red Shield, like all the other shields that made up the second of three javelins in Seventh Phalanx, were being marched ragged trying to find the elusive archers.

With the sun already beginning to fall, all Carny wanted was to get back to the relative safety and comfort of their camp down among the dunes. Being that close to the water and the big sailing ships constantly arriving with more supplies and reinforcements gave him a sense of security completely absent when they went out on patrol.

Tired, thirsty, hungry, and bored, Carny wanted this day to

be done. He lifted up the rim of his metal helm and said a silent prayer, hoping they didn't have to go back up. So a few natives shot a few arrows at a rag. The crafty bastards wouldn't be there if they went back up. They never were.

Silence reigned as Red Shield waited, strung out a third of the way down the mountain along the main dirt path. It was the one and only way the shield climbed and descended the mountain as the rest of it was a dense green tangle of palm fronds, vines, trees, and leafy plants.

"They're going to make us go back up, I fucking know it," Crossbowman Yustace Vooford said from farther up the mountain, spitting the words out. The lanky baker's assistant-turned-soldier carried a chip on his shoulder as big as one of his bragged-about loaves.

"Keep it down," Carny said, waving at Voof to lower his voice. "It was a few arrows at most."

"A few arrows?" Big Hog said, using his crossbow to point up at the mountain. "You might be about the only one of us that can read, but as sure as my crotch itches like a witch's in a ditch full of thistles, you can't count." The pig farmer—large, beefy, and forever red-faced and sweating—shook his head, rattling the chain mail curtain that hung from the back of his helm.

Carny tried and failed to get the image of the itchy witch out of his head. "Fine, more than a few," he said, lowering his voice in the hope that Big Hog would take the hint. "Still, the rag flew on, so we're good. Right?" He pushed his helm higher onto his head to allow the air to get at his scalp. The liner slid back, releasing a stream of sweat. Carny wiped his brow with the back of his bare forearm. *I might as well be wearing a damn forge on my head.*

Sighing, Carny bent over and wiped his arm against his dun-colored trouser leg and wished they could take the heavy linen things off. Trousers were too hot for this weather, and the cloth kept getting bunched up underneath the bronze greaves protecting his shins. An oozing rash now covered him from knees to ankles, the yellowy-pink liquid pooling in the bottom of his ankle-high leather boots. That in turn made his feet slip in his boots, spawning blisters on top of blisters.

"We ain't been good since before we got here," Voof said. "I didn't ask to come here and fight in this war. None of us did, but here we are. And why? I'll tell you—"

"For fuck's sake, Voof, leave it for one afternoon, would you?" the Weasel said, emerging from the side of the path while pulling up his trousers. Thin with sharp features and a sharper tongue, Crossbowman Alminga Meerz was the one soldier guaranteed to find the wrong thing to say at the exact wrong time to Voof.

"They'd fucking like that," Voof said, staring hard at the Weasel. "Mark my words, it's what they've always wanted."

Everyone in Red Shield and the Second of the Seventh knew Voof's views on the Kingdom's war in Luitox and the conscription of men into the army. The thing of it was, Voof's views were shared by most, but his seething rage made it difficult to agree with him at the best of times.

Carny didn't bother responding. Voof would rant until he ran out of breath or someone put a fist down his throat. Carny reseated his helm on his head by dropping his chin to his chest and letting the helm fall back into place. Anything that saved a few precious drops of energy was worth its weight in silver. He grabbed the front of his dark green aketon and pulled it away from his skin as he sucked down lungfuls of hot air.

The aketon was more agonizing than listening to Voof. The jacket's thick quilting filled with horsehair provided exceptional warmth, which in this land was like wearing a blanket of coals. Defying the army's dress code, the entire Second Javelin had cut the sleeves from the garment. It was either that or keep passing out from sun vapors. What remained, however, were the eighteen two-inch-by-two-inch steel armor plates woven into the linen casings, which were sewn into the aketon to protect chest and back. It was an additional twenty pounds that Carny would have just as soon done without, but high command would turn a blind eye to only so much defiance.

"Look!"

A single arrow wobbled into the sky from the top of the mountain, trailing a wisp of red smoke. Carny had seen it before.

"The slyts are ghosting," Big Hog said. "Ten to one says half of them will be back down at the beach by nightfall at their little stands selling us that piss beer and dog on a stick."

Carny reached for his neck. *Slyt* sounded like *slit*, which always made him picture a thin razor against his throat. Carny figured their nickname came from their greeting *I ga slyt*, which was really just "hello." Every slyt he'd met always started with *I ga slyt*. He called them slyts now, too. It was better than trying to learn their fucked-up names.

Carny took it as a cue and turned and started walking down the mountain. As the enemy had so kindly announced their intent to leave it seemed only fair that Red Shield do the same. Other soldiers started to move with him.

"Shield will remain in place!" Red Shield leader Wallseck Sinte shouted, bellowing like they were on a parade square.

"Fucking told you," Voof said.

Carny halted. The smell of the sunbaked jungle washed over him and he gagged. It was like breathing in hot dung. You didn't just smell it—you absorbed it. The heat of Luitox did something to the air so that every odor stuck to your skin like putrid honey. He breathed through his mouth and did his best to stand perfectly still.

Salvation, in the form of base camp with its white, sandy beaches; cool ocean waves; and all those eager, lithe whores camped just outside it was only fifteen hundred more yards down this path. Fifteen hundred precious yards.

Carny turned and watched as Sinte came to a halt. Sinte stood upright without leaning against the angle of the mountain. It looked unnatural and it bothered Carny. The rest of Red Shield's twenty-four soldiers, just one of six patrols from the Second Javelin combing the mountain for slyts, were sensibly hunched over as they descended toward the beach, but not Sinte. He wouldn't give the jungle the satisfaction. It was as if he feared one flaw, one deviation, would cause his whole world to crumble. He shaved his square jaw twice a day and his head once. From his polished bronze greaves to the gleaming steel shield marking his authority strapped to his back, he shone like a beacon announcing that wherever he stood, that dirt belonged to the Kingdom. And the Kingdom bowed to no one and nothing.

"Listowk, what the hell was that?" Sinte asked. He was six feet tall and muscled like a wild boar, and his voice reverberated off the foliage and set brightly colored birds to flight.

The second-in-command of Red Shield, Lead Crossbowman Ugen Listowk, shorter, wider, and quieter than their leader, shouldered his crossbow and ambled back up the path toward Sinte. He winked as he passed Carny. Carny offered him a weak smile. Where Sinte shined, Listowk absorbed. Leaves and other bits of foliage somehow always got stuck to the LC's helm and straps while dirt dulled his greaves and bare arms whenever they went on patrol. The man, ancient at forty-one and still only a lead crossbowman, was a slow, plodding bush. The joke around the shield was that if he ever stayed in one place for more than a few candles, he'd take root.

Listowk came to a stop a few feet below Sinte and saluted, or possibly scratched his head under his helm. Sinte stared at him, his eyes darting between the many different bits of flora.

"It was clear, SL, not a slyt in sight," Listowk said, leavening his voice with the exhaustion they all felt. "We scoured that mountaintop for a good quarter candle. We looked under logs, up in the branches, and peered through the bushes, but didn't find a thing."

Sinte used his crossbow to point back up to where the rag had flown over. The sun made the oiled ash wood shimmer. "Then where did all those fucking slyt archers come from? They flying them in on invisible rags?"

Listowk spit in the dirt and appeared to think before responding. He made it look painful. His nose scrunched up, his eyes squinted, and the mustache covering his upper lip curled like a furry caterpillar being roasted on a fire. "Well, I've heard tell them slyts way inland have some strong thaumics. That's deep, dark green out there. What I hear, army ain't ventured there 'cept for a few rag hops, so no telling what they got."

Sinte stomped his boot on the ground. "Druid's balls, Listowk, don't give me that mystic-slyt shit! They're nothing but savages that are a damned sight better at hiding than you are at finding!"

Listowk shrugged. "The slyts are crafty. You ask the boys, they'll tell you. We didn't see a damn thing," he said, pointing toward the eight men of the shield who had searched the mountaintop while the rest, with Sinte, patrolled just below it looking for new paths. "Carny, you see any sign of the little bastards when we was up there?"

Don't get me in the middle of this, Carny silently pleaded. Yes, they'd climbed to the top of the mountain as ordered, and yes, they'd looked around, mostly for snakes and spiders. Going up this damn mountain day after day had become one big grind. They'd been up it fifteen times in the past three weeks alone to clear of it slyts. The first few times, they'd actually spent a half candle hacking and crawling their way through the undergrowth in search of the bastards. They had to be hiding up there somewhere, but all the patrol came away with were bug bites and a growing sense of pointlessness.

"Couple of frayed bowstrings, a piece of arrow shaft, but not a slyt to be seen," Carny said, hoping that would be the end of it and knowing it wouldn't. "Even kicked around in the dirt looking for ash from cook fires, but didn't find any."

"Then you're as fucking blind as Listowk," Sinte said.

Carny looked at his shield leader and shrugged. Sinte knew everything. It didn't matter if it was what was in the stew or which slyt whore had the liveliest tongue—his pronouncements were always made with such conviction that everyone just agreed.

"Yeah, maybe," Carny said, turning his head to look at the beach and the water down below. *So damn close.*

"Fucking useless, the lot of you," Sinte proclaimed. "Do you know what kind of shit I'm going to hear when we go back down there and report that all we found was a couple of bowstrings?"

Carny smiled, then quickly frowned lest Sinte see it. *Sinte said when, not if!* Glory on high, they were not going to go back up.

"There's another rag!"

Carny turned. At first, he couldn't see a thing. Then he noticed a dark smudge low over the ocean.

"It's a seabird," he said, hoping against hope he was right.

"Naw, it's a rag," Listowk said. "Low and slow, but it's a rag."

Carny looked down at the beach before looking back out to sea. The dark smudge was bigger than before. *Fuck.*

"Any bets on what happens if this rag gets shot at?" Voof asked.

No one answered. Carny slammed his crossbow against his thigh and hung his head. *So damn close.*

CHAPTER TWO

"LOOKY, YAH? WE GOTS some rolly blues up yonder! Gone git mad-jiggin' afore we hits Loot-ox!" the rag's co-driver shouted over his shoulder. He raised and lowered his three-fingered right hand in the air for extra emphasis.

Jawn Rathim lifted his head and was immediately buffeted by a rushing wind laced with heat and sulfur. Strands of his long brown hair, no longer carefully combed and tied in the back, fluttered freely. He sneezed and squinted, looking around to see if anyone else understood the man's colorful patois. It was a wasted effort.

Two rows of military officers and crown representatives rode single file on either side of the rag's spine. They sat on saddles—really just leather-padded wooden planks affixed to the rag's scales with finger-sized spikes. Facing forward, all had their heads down to keep them out of the wind. In one amazing case, an officer appeared to be fast asleep.

"Choke 'em straps up an in, yah?" the co-driver said, waving his abbreviated hand around for emphasis.

Hope he flies better than he talks, Jawn thought. An assumption that at least the rag's driver would be of more refined material was wrecked on that man's fist-sized wad of chewing tobacco crammed into his right cheek. It was, as the driver had so eloquently informed Jawn before takeoff, so he could "enjoy ma vittles side by each wit' ma chaw."

The rag's wings began beating faster. Jawn instinctively flinched as the wings rose up like two sea behemoths breaching on either side of him before rumbling back down. The wind rushed past his head like heavy, invisible waves eroding him bit by bit. A not-so-gentle force began to push Jawn down into his saddle as the rag started climbing higher into the sky, her long torso undulating with the strain. She coughed, spewing out a shower of sparks that stung Jawn's face. That was followed by a billowing cloud of inky black smoke that temporarily obscured everything from view. Jawn closed his eyes and held his breath for a few moments. When he opened them again and inhaled, the air was clear save for the ever-present heat and smell of sulfur. The rag was coughing more frequently now. The scales beneath his ankle-high leather boots were getting hotter, too, but he couldn't tell if that was from the broiling sun high above his left shoulder or the rag's guts heating up from the inside.

Jawn craned his head around to check the position of the sun. He calculated they'd been in the air almost two full candles since taking off from Swassi Island on the second leg of their cross-ocean flight from the Kingdom to Luitox. Though it was correctly pronounced "Lew-tow," not "Loot-ox," as the co-driver kept calling it, Jawn was keeping his mouth shut. The crew might have been a pair of bumpkins from some deep, dark forest province where the sunshine had to be carried in by buckets, but they apparently knew how to control and fly a ten-ton rag. That earned them his respect.

Jawn winced as the rag dipped and then jerked back up. He clenched his fists as a searing pain lit his lower back muscles on fire. He'd debated staying on Swassi for a few days to rest and get used to the heat. The half day he'd spent on a different rag just getting that far had been painful enough. Besides, his orders to report to the Seventh Phalanx gave him another week to get there. Wandering around Swassi for a candle, however, had changed his mind and he'd taken the next rag out.

Barely rising above the waves, Swassi was a long brown

smear across the ocean. Its features could be counted on one hand: wind-bent palm trees, a rambling series of huts making up the naval way station, a hastily constructed canvas-tent sanatorium filled with sick and wounded soldiers evacuated from Luitox, and a huge burn pit behind the sanatorium that gave off a greasy, thick smoke the entire time he was there.

And I volunteered for this. It had been a rash decision but one he didn't regret. Life in the Kingdom for his kind wasn't what it had once been. The change had happened virtually overnight with the Bastard Revelation. A royal historian—no-good muckraker, as Jawn's mother put it—found proof that King Wynnthorpe and the two monarchs before him were descended from the pairing of Queen Arbara and the royal huntsman Kofery Dar Minkon. Every king and prince who followed was illegitimate. Instead of a monarch, chaos now reigned. In one fell swoop, the very notion of the royalty was called into question. "Rightful heirs" popped out of the woodwork like so many noxious bubbles from a witch's boiling cauldron and were just as appealing. In the span of a fortnight, five distinct High Councils emerged laying claim to leadership of the Kingdom and its many far-flung protectorates, arguing that until a true heir was found—if one ever was—they, in their wisdom and sense of duty, should rule in his or her stead.

There were no riots in the streets and no one was calling for a storming of the palace—yet—but in ways Jawn thought far more worrisome, society was changing. Town criers, until recently solely the mouthpieces of the king, were now paid men—and, shockingly, occasionally women—in the employ of the High Councils and an increasing number of concerned citizens and merchant guilds. Where there had been one official report of happenings in the Kingdom and beyond, now there were dozens. It was madness.

Jawn coughed, spitting out some black phlegm into his hand. He looked at the mess before wiping it on his trousers. Everything he'd believed to be solid and stable now had sand under its base. If the king wasn't the king, then what other lies were waiting to be revealed? He shifted in his saddle and groaned. One lie he knew he'd never believe again was that riding a rag across the sky was glamorous. All feeling in his buttocks was gone, while the pain in his lower back grew. This was no longer a flight; it was a feat of endurance.

"I did the right thing," Jawn muttered, hoping to convince himself that it was true. The Kingdom was at war abroad and tearing itself apart at home. The place for a young man was at the point of the spear, and that was out here. It's what men did, what they always did. They went to war because there was one. There was no better way to prove to yourself and everyone around you what you were made of. Jawn knew it in his heart even if his brain had had second thoughts.

All thoughts of glory had been put to the test early, however, during training. Everything the army did seemed tailor-made to numb the mind and weary the body. For all that, he'd ultimately come to enjoy it. Even the questionable food. It was amazing how good even the grayest hunk of boiled beef tasted after working up a real appetite. And outdoors, no less.

The physical demands had pushed him beyond any exertion he had ever attempted. He'd always been considered gangly due to his tall, thin frame, but now, instead of protruding collarbor and a washboard rib cage, he had muscles, actual muscles! was in the best shape of his twenty-four years. Not only he throw a punch, he could take one.

The rag lurched sideways, wrenching Jawn's attention back to his current situation. The agonizing monotony of the flight vanished in a series of erratic jerks and bumps, as if the rag were having a seizure. Jawn would have thought that very thing, but the co-driver's warning, however colloquial, finally made sense. "Rolly blues" must have something to do with rough air currents. Knowing the cause of the rag's distress did nothing to make him feel any better as she dropped vertically, leaving Jawn's stomach somewhere up around his ears. Men and women screamed all around him. The beat of the rag's wings increased, the huge leathery sails chopping the wind like two massive axe blades. Her entire body shook with the effort as she struggled to stabilize. She dropped again, then vaulted skyward as if a giant hand had scooped her up and tossed her like a ball.

As she reached the top of her climb, the rag flicked over onto her right side and began to roll upside down. Jawn experienced the sensation of hollowness as he floated in the air, his butt coming off of the simple leather saddle. The leather belts buckled around his thighs and calves bit deep through his canvas trousers and into his flesh but kept him from plummeting to the ocean some three thousand yards below. He risked looking down and saw more water than animal beneath him.

He chanced a look behind to where their baggage was strapped down. Happily, the crew knew their knots as the passengers' belongings appeared well and truly secured.

The rag twisted its body into a crescent shape and began falling back toward the water. Soot flaked off its scales as they slid over one another, revealing patches of the dull brown color beneath.

"Makes you wonder if two weeks in a ship's hold would have been better than this!" the passenger opposite Jawn shouted— although currently *above* was more accurate than *opposite*. The crowny had his arms wrapped tightly around one of the rag's triangular dorsal plates, which ran down the length of its spine from the top of its head to the tip of its tail, like a row of shark teeth. "At least you can see waves on the water. I don't know how those buggers see these rolly blues up here!"

Someone near the front of the rag wailed in obvious terror. The driver and co-driver, sitting strapped in forward of the rag's wing shoulders on a wooden yoke with their feet dangling in thin air, traded shouts. Jawn still couldn't understand what was being said. A moment later, the air carried the ringing crack of iron bar against scale. More shouts and more cracks followed. The co-driver was half out of his saddle and twisted around to face backward, swinging a four-foot wrought-iron bar up against the underside of the rag's right wing where it met the huge shoulder joint.

"Gone up, ya licey stoof!" he shouted, then looked back at Jawn and smiled. "'Tain't but a li'l tweekin' laek, yah? Ter rag done feel a ting!"

He went back to hitting the rag, each blow timed on the wing's upstroke. The rag began to pump her appendage a little harder in response. Droplets of steaming blood and small flakes of scale began flying off the leading edge of the wing.

The rag turned her head around toward the co-driver, but the driver sawed on the chains bolted to the cast-iron bit in her mouth and snapped her back. The speed of the wind increased as the angle of the rag grew steeper. *I can't die like this*, Jawn thought. Back in the Kingdom, criers had begun relaying tales of courageous acts in battle that often included the story of the fallen soldier who had died in its commission. *Jawn Rathim, twenty-six, fell out of the sky from the back of a decrepit dragon driven by two yokels* just didn't kiss the ear.

They'll get this sorted, he hoped, avoiding prayer because no matter how dire his situation, he wasn't about to call for a help he didn't believe in. Independence wasn't something you gave up the first time things got a little sticky. He chose to think of something pleasant.

Milouette. The smell of strawberries and the blush of excitement coloring her neck. Milouette of the small, perky breasts; freckled nose; and long, colt-like legs that wrapped firmly around his waist. Images of his mother's handmaiden brought a smile to his face. She'd been seventeen, he barely fifteen. The first stirrings of an erection caught him by surprise.

The rag lurched back to level flight, slamming him down into his saddle and ending all thoughts of Milouette. Lightning lanced his member as a sledgehammer drove his balls deep into his stomach.

"High Druid beyond!" Jawn yelped. His eyes watered and he gulped in a lungful of the foul air. He gritted his teeth until his temples throbbed and slowly counted to twenty until the pain began to subside.

Jawn took a few more breaths, then eased himself over to lean out and look down past the side of the rag. The whitecaps still looked small. Way too far to fall and survive.

"Done gone o'er the hills I reckon! Jus' li'l uns, yah?" the co-driver shouted. He sounded amused.

Any temptation to yell back at the man vanished as the caustic stench of vomit stung Jawn's nostrils. He ducked, feeling the wet splatter in his hair and on the back of his neck. He now had a new source of irritation.

"Hey! Quit puking!" Jawn shouted, sitting up and shaking his head in the wind. He unwound his right hand from the leather thong looped into the heavy iron chain running down the right side of the rag's spine. Reaching forward, he jabbed the man in front of him in the thigh with the knuckles of his fist. "Do that again and I'll heave you over the side!"

The officer twisted around to look over his shoulder at Jawn. The front of the man's uniform was a crusted mess of vomit; wet strings of the stuff hung from the corners of his mouth. One detached in the wind and flew back at Jawn, catching him in the cheek. The officer whimpered, "We're all going to die!"

"Fucking idiot officers," came the reply from the crowny on the other side of the dorsal plate.

Jawn wiped his cheek and came away with a hand covered in wet, black soot. Sighing, he rubbed it against his filth-covered tunic and turned to look at the man beside him. They'd barely talked the entire flight, not that the crowny hadn't tried to strike up a conversation more than once.

"He might be right," Jawn said, hiding his annoyance at the other man's use of obscenities.

"Aw, don't listen to him," the crowny said, wedging his upper half between two dorsal plates. He looked like he was bellying up to the local bar. "This old rag might be a clapped-out carcass not long for the rendering vat, but she'll get us down in one piece. Rags were built to fly."

"It's a long flight for one this size though, isn't it?" Jawn asked, reluctantly leaning to the left and grabbing the edge of the nearest dorsal so their conversation could continue at something less than a full-throated shout. "She's not exactly making this look easy."

The crowny smiled. He had the look of a jovial talker, one of those pudgy-faced, grubby bar patrons whose friendly smile hid a desperate need to talk when all a person wanted to do was to be left in peace.

"Not her fault. See the notches on her tail fin?" he said, pointing with his thumb toward the back of the rag. "They mark it every time a rag makes a long haul like this. One this size is supposed to be good for two hundred trips before they switch them over to shorter routes. Something about the muscles pulling away from the bones and their internal workings getting too hot."

Jawn turned his head and watched the rag's tail as it swayed back and forth. Her vertical tail fin looked as tall as him. As it swept far to the right and then back he did a quick count of the notches. His eyes widened.

"That looks closer to four hundred." He noticed the heat again emanating from the scales beneath him. It was more than the sun. The rag was definitely getting hotter.

The crowny's smile got bigger. "Yeah, ain't that a newt in the cauldron. Between the upheaval back home and the overthrow of the governing tribal council in Western Luitox by the Forest Collective, the Treasury's vault is more cobwebs than coins. And we haven't been there four years yet. So old girls like her are having to take the strain and fly farther and longer."

His pronunciation of *Luitox* was spot-on. It even had the slight hard click on the start of the second syllable that Jawn had only heard used by long-serving diplomats. Maybe he could have an intelligent conversation with this man.

"You jest. The war can't be costing all that much," Jawn said.

"It's bleeding us dry, is what it's doing," the crowny said. "Do you know what the single most unproductive use of a man's time and energy is? Fighting wars. You destroy the fields, maim the livestock, kill the farmers, and leave the women barren."

Jawn had never considered that, nor did he want to. "You're completely ignoring the moral imperative to wage war. We don't fight to fill our coffers—we fight for what's just. We defend the weak and vanquish evil." He didn't bother adding that they fought because it was an adventure beyond all others. Jawn could tell this fellow wouldn't understand that. "It's our duty to crush the Forest Collective and return Western Luitox to the peace-loving peoples that live there. If we don't stop them now, what next? We—"

"You're serious?! High Druid's balls!" the man said, his eyes wide. "We *absolutely* fight war to fill our coffers. Problem is, it's a terrible way to do it. Always ends up costing more than what we get. Hang my words from the highest branch: Luitox will not pay off."

"Perhaps they don't keep you up-to-date in the Crown Service with what's going on military-wise," Jawn said, not bothering to hide the disdain in his voice. "The army is confident that the fighting in Western Luitox will be over before the first autumn leaves fall. The Forest Collective are disgruntled peasants, not a well-trained army like ours."

Instead of being duly humbled as he should have been, the crowny grinned, his smile full of butter-colored teeth. "I didn't realize you were so up-to-date on things. But first, where are my manners? Name's Rande Cornalli Ketts, field inspector, Commerce and Taxation." He paused for a moment before continuing. "Most know me as R. C. Ketts, but *you* can call me Rickets." He raised his eyebrows as he pronounced his nickname.

Cute. Jawn obligingly nodded. He took the man's outstretched hand and shook it. It was surprisingly rough for a paper-and-quill jockey. "Jawn Rathim. I've been assigned to the Seventh Phalanx, Command Group." He hesitated to say more.

"Genuine pleasure to meet you, Jawn Rathim," Rickets said, still shaking Jawn's hand. "It's rare I find an officer who can hold a conversation on anything of substance. Not really the most enlightened, no offense."

"Why would I be offended? I'm educated," Jawn said, immediately regretting it. The last thing he wanted to explain to Rickets was who he really was.

"Of course you are," Rickets said, nodding seriously. "That's why I'm talking with you and not the rest of this luggage," he said, motioning toward the other passengers. "All the independent thought of a flock of pigeons. Not their fault though; most of them probably don't have much more learning than basic numbers and the alphabet. Not like us though. We've been schooled."

Jawn didn't like where the conversation was heading. He particularly didn't like the man's use of the word *us*. They shared nothing in common.

"So, back to the furtherance of my education," Rickets said, easily changing horses. "Why, pray tell, if we're so close to putting down these—what did you call them?—*disgruntled peasants*, did the king declare martial law? Why would he need to threaten con dodgers with prison and even execution for not reporting for service?"

Jawn was ready for this. "It was a momentary and necessary step to ensure calm and order."

"'Momentary and necessary,' I like that," Rickets said. "I'll have to remember that the next time I do something especially egregious. So, everything is sunshine and flowers in the Kingdom? That is heartening to hear, because where we're heading, it's raining shit."

Jawn lowered his head and massaged his temples with the thumb and middle finger of his right hand. "As this is my first trip to Luitox, I can't speak to the weather," he said, deftly twisting the man's words in hopes of ending the conversation. "What I can say, and any loyal subject would agree, is that the Kingdom will prevail."

"How?"

Jawn lowered his hand and looked up. "What do you mean, how? We're the Kingdom! Luitox is a dust mote. Our military might will crush this Forest Collective like a bug beneath our boot."

"Then why haven't we?"

Jawn opened and closed his mouth a couple of times. The

man was aggravating. "We have... I mean, we will. These things take time."

"To crush a bug?"

"It's not as simple as that," Jawn said, now wondering why it hadn't turned out to be as simple as that so far. His army instructors had seemed certain enough. In their robust vernacular, it was just a matter of putting your boot on your enemy's throat until his eyes rolled back and his tongue turned blue. And then stabbing out his eyes and pissing in his skull for good measure. Jawn thought the military took these analogies a bit far—at least, he hoped they were analogies. Then again, many recruits came from the peasantry and seemed to appreciate the more colorful renderings of Kingdom foreign policy. "There are other factors at work."

"Do tell," Rickets said. He rested his chin on a fist and looked up at Jawn with rapt attention.

Just smile and leave it at that. The more you talk with this horse's arse, the more aggravated you get. Smile, say something polite, and turn away.

Jawn drew in a breath, gagging on the hot, sulfurous taint of the air, and decided instead to wipe that smug look off of Rickets's face.

CHAPTER THREE

JAWN RAN HIS FINGERS through his hair and squared his shoulders. "I just don't think you're seeing the oak for the pine here. Tough times, my dear Rickets, don't last. Tough people—tough nations like the Kingdom—do."

The crowny's left eyebrow arched. "Armed with platitudes instead of reason, I see."

Jawn ground his knuckles into his thigh. The man was impossible. "I can see there's no point discussing this. You're not taking it seriously."

The crowny's grin vanished and he sat up straight. "This will be my third crusade in Luitox. I've been places you've only seen paintings of. I assure you," he said, leaning closer to Jawn, "I take this very fucking seriously."

Jawn knew his mouth was open and quickly closed it. "Your third crusade? But it's a hardship posting. A friend of our family is in the Crown Service. He said after one crusade in Luitox, he was exempt from returning."

"Guess I didn't get that scroll," the crowny said, slapping a dorsal plate. Bits of plate flaked off and were carried away by the wind. "Just like with this old rag, the Kingdom's having to squeeze a little more blood out of the acorn these days. Crownies don't grow on trees. We need training up just like you military types. It might surprise you, but when a fellow like me gets killed, it takes time and treasure to put a new one in my place."

Jawn squinted, looking at Rickets with practiced skepticism. "Killed? What are you talking about? They don't put crown reps in battle."

Rickets nodded. "They don't have to. The battle finds us just fine on its own. You didn't think the only fighting was in Western Luitox, did you? It's everywhere. The Forest Collective is *everywhere*. They blend right in. You can't tell a disgruntled peasant from a gruntled one until he's swinging a hoe at your head."

Jawn rolled his eyes. "Oh come on, you're exaggerating."

"Do you remember when it all started?" Rickets asked. "A quick little crusade and done. That was more than three years ago."

Jawn huffed. "That still doesn't change the final outcome. We just need to apply a little more pressure."

"Right," he said, giving Jawn a wink. "One final charge up that hill and before you know it, the natives will be back on their farms squeezing out litters of fruit pickers."

"Nice," Jawn said. "Look, a few more legions shipped over to Luitox and our army will be unstoppable."

Rickets's eyes widened. "Do you have any idea what that *costs*? Training that many soldiers means you need more barracks. Equipping that many soldiers means more cloth, leather, iron, bronze, and wood. And they have to eat, too. Every day. And don't forget the horses, either, not to mention these beasts," he said, giving the rag's dorsal plate a solid smack.

The rag shuddered and dropped twenty feet. Jawn reached for a dorsal plate and gripped it tightly. He held on, waiting for another lurch, but nothing else happened. Jawn slowly pried his hands from the plate and wiped his brow.

"That's not the only cost," Rickets said, continuing as if nothing had happened.

Jawn nodded, adopting a solemn tone. "I know. Soldiers die. Crownies, too. It's unfortunate, but it happens." He wasn't really that callous, but something about this particular crowny was bringing out the worst in him.

"I'm glad you at least acknowledge it's unfortunate, but that wasn't what I was referring to. Do you know what it takes to cobble together legions of conscripts? Cobblers for one. And farmers, grocers, potters, miners, clerks, smithies, carpenters, tanners, millers, masons, weavers, butchers, bakers, candlestick makers, and even young, educated fellows like you." He paused to catch his breath before continuing. "Every last one taken away from his village, his home, his family, and his job. Still think it's the best use of the Treasury? Who's plowing the fields and bringing in the crops? Who's building the bridges and filling in the wagon ruts? Who's paying taxes and tolls?"

Jawn sat silently, aware again of the slow, rhythmic flapping of the rag's wings and accompanying creaks and groans from her scales. As the son of a prosperous shipbuilder and an alchemist, he'd never had to worry about how things were paid for. Despite the obvious jokes that his mother simply made precious metals in her laboratory, from Jawn's perspective she might as well have. He'd never wanted for material things. That there were potentially troubling ramifications to the Kingdom's military intervention had never crossed his mind, either.

Very well, he conceded, *war isn't cheap, but this man's worried about who's going to bake the bread in some sleepy little village.*

"You make it sound dire," Jawn said, unable to come up with a better response. "Luitox is small, and this Forest Collective smaller still."

"I can see why it would look that way to some," Rickets agreed before tossing a new wrinkle at Jawn. "But even if that were true, what of all those tribes in the Western Wilds? Don't you think they'll have something to say about that big army of ours showing up on their doorstep?"

The Western Wilds. Jawn's favorite stories as a child were tales of adventures in that fabled place. Top among those were of the intrepid exploring duo Sir Wyse Morpaldo Oxlington and his faithful companion, Herm Crinkell. They climbed mountains, braved raging rivers, traversed gorges, and triumphed over every savage tribe they encountered.

"What of them?" Jawn asked. "The tribes of the Western Wilds stay hidden deep in the interior. If Ox and Crink could outwit them, I don't think the army will have much trouble."

"You ever meet them, these brave explorers of legend?" Rickets asked.

Jawn shook his head. "I wish. They're old men now, close to fifty."

"I met them three years ago, in Luitox actually," Rickets said. He didn't sound thrilled by the experience. "They were flown over to provide expert advice on all things Wild. The assumption being we would take a little foray into the Wilds, as dealing with the revolt in Western Luitox wouldn't take very long."

Jawn remembered when just a year ago there had still been talk of marching through Western Luitox and civilizing all of the Western Wilds. Over time, however, talk of the Wilds had died away. He had never thought to wonder why until now.

"So what are you saying?" Jawn asked.

"Not to disparage ol' Ox and Crink," Rickets said, "but their tales of simple tribes didn't comport entirely with what our advance scouts found. We call it the Western Wilds, but the natives that live there call it home. And they call the Luitoxese brothers, or at least kissing cousins. One day, they might get tired of us camping on their doorstep."

"Aren't you worrying over something that'll never happen?" Jawn asked.

The crowny looked at Jawn for several flicks before responding. "I figure you for an intelligent sort, Jawn Rathim, but merciful High Druid, you hide it well. Five years from now, we'll be lucky if we aren't neck-deep in a full-blown war with them. And if that's the case, we won't win."

It was a stunning observation by a crown representative. "You jest, sir, and poorly."

Rickets shrugged his shoulders. "Us being over here is like putting orphan lads in a monastery. We don't know it yet, but we're fucked, and we ain't going to enjoy it."

Jawn did his best to ignore the appalling imagery and

focused instead on the crowny's view. "We haven't lost a war in three hundred years—four hundred if you don't count the amalgamation of the territories." Jawn sat up a little straighter, ignoring the pain in his back. "We will win. We always do."

"Such faith," Rickets said, his tone mocking.

"I know what I'm talking about. My professors taught me well." Jawn placed his hand on his chest, his fingers instinctively spreading to match the crescent shape made by the metal runes branded into the skin over his heart.

"Oh, I *knew* it!" Rickets shouted, startling several of the other passengers around them. He leaned closer to Jawn and lowered his voice. "I thought I smelled a thaum. And no provincial, one-room-school-trained thaum at that. You're a full-blooded RAT, ain't you?"

Jawn's back prickled and he broke out into a cold sweat. He flung his hand from his chest. He'd given it away. He'd never been prouder than when he was accepted into the Royal Academy of Thaumology. His pleasurable if pointless existence until that moment had suddenly taken on a transcendent meaning. The forces of nature *could* be controlled by men, and he, Jawn Rathim, was such a man.

And then the very fabric of society began to unravel. Thaums, extremely rare and seldom seen—by design—were the very embodiment of power. Even now, each High Council and the King's Advisory Council had several thaums as members. But the people of the Kingdom, so long dormant, gave voice to concerns about the thaums. Why, they asked, as the realization struck that their ruler was a fraud, should so few hold so much power? "Because they can" no longer seemed a sufficient answer.

"Anyone can make that gesture," Jawn said, looking around to see if anyone else was listening. None appeared to be, but he leaned closer to Rickets so that he could keep his voice low. "You don't know what you're talking about."

Rickets winked at Jawn. "You'd fool most folks, I've no doubt of that, but you got that aura about you."

"That's just the rag," Jawn said, fighting to remain calm.

"So tell me I'm wrong then," Rickets said. "Tell me you're not a RAT."

Jawn could tell there'd be no convincing Rickets. The man was far sharper than he appeared.

"Fine, but I'd rather no one know," Jawn said, staring hard at Rickets with the faint hope that the man could be discreet.

"Not to fear. Your secret is safe with me. I'm a locked box wrapped in a sack and chucked into a hole. So tell me," Rickets said, lowering his voice, "what did you do to get put in the army? You're far too young to have completed the full circle," he said, pointing at Jawn's chest.

The crowny spoke truth. Each rune, shaped in the form of its symbol on the thaumic conductivity chart, took years to earn. Most thaums never completed it. Getting to silver, the most conductive natural element known to man for initiating a thaumic process, was rarely achieved, and not without taking insane risks.

"I don't want to talk about it," Jawn said.

"Aha. What happened? Get kicked out for turning one of your professors into a frog?"

Dolt! "For all the… thaumology is a key pillar of the natural sciences. It conforms to and amplifies the laws of nature. There's nothing mystical or miraculous about it."

Rickets shrugged his shoulders. "I thought thaumology by definition had to do with druids and miracles. Gray-bearded fellows in long robes calling down lightning from the heavens, turning water into mead and the like."

Jawn rolled his eyes. "Yes, but that's because people didn't understand what was happening, and so that's why it was called thaumology. They really did believe gods and angels were involved," Jawn huffed.

"So, you weren't kicked out for turning your professor into a frog?" Rickets asked.

Jawn flung his hands in the air, then quickly reached down to grab on to the harness chain. "No! That's the purview of witchcraft and wizardry," Jawn said, wrinkling his nose as he said it. "Just a whole lot of potions, elixirs, dried newts, and cackling."

"You still didn't answer my question," Rickets said.

Jawn ground his teeth. The man was relentless. "If you must know… I left of my own accord and volunteered for the army. I felt this was the right thing to do. Our country's at war and I wasn't going to let my privileged position keep me from serving."

"Mmm. How very noble of you," Rickets said, his voice thin like a stiletto.

Jawn swung around to stare Rickets down. "Mock me all you want, crowny, but I have nothing to be ashamed of." *I don't have to justify anything to him.*

Rickets leaned back. "Never said you did. Don't mind me, I'm a cynic of the first order. Spent my whole life serving a king who it turns out isn't one at all. What's a crowny to do? Figure I'll put in my time, make a little extra silver on the side, and live long enough to collect my pension. But you… well, you're a patriot, you are."

Jawn searched Rickets's face and tone for even a hint of sarcasm, but if it was there, the crowny hid it well. "I don't know how patriotic I am—I just felt I had to do something," Jawn said, knowing that was at least part of the truth.

Rickets leaned forward and reached out, giving Jawn a friendly slap on the shoulder. "I understand. You're young. I almost remember that feeling."

Jawn gave Rickets a halfhearted smile. The heat and the wind were combining to batter Jawn into numbing exhaustion. He couldn't sleep and didn't want to talk anymore but had no desire to be alone with his thoughts, either. Feeling at a loss, he twisted in his harness until his back rested against the dorsal plate. Slouching down out of the hot wind, he stared out at the ocean.

CHAPTER FOUR

"HERE, RICKETS SAID, handing Jawn a small metal flask between the dorsal plates. "This'll revive your spirits."

"I'm not really a drinker," Jawn said, deciding the distraction of Rickets was the lesser evil.

A moment later, a simple leather water skin appeared. "Here, try this instead. It's hot as tea and probably tastes like piss."

Jawn grabbed it and downed several mouthfuls. The water did taste like hot piss, but right now, it was as refreshing as a cool mountain stream. He handed it back.

"Thanks. I should have come more prepared." Jawn cringed the moment the words left his mouth. He didn't want to delve deeper with Rickets into his rationale for joining up. "You seem to know a lot about these rags," Jawn said, sitting up straighter and forcefully projecting his voice. "I've heard stories about fireballs seen in the sky—" he started to say, but Rickets finished it for him.

"That rumor about rags overheating and exploding?" The crowny nodded. "It hardly ever happens in the wild because they know enough to slow down and cool off. They aren't the sharpest arrows in the quiver, but they know not to get themselves killed by flying more than they should. That all changed once we tamed them. Now we fly the living shit out of them."

Jawn winced at the vulgarity. Government officials were supposed to be schooled, thoughtful... patriotic. He tried to console himself for having the great misfortune to sit beside the one exception. "So, are the stories true?"

Before the crowny could answer, the co-driver turned around in his seat and waved his hands to get their attention.

"Praise the maker an' sing on high! Loot-ox dead on!"

Jawn sat up straight in his saddle and looked past the co-driver. A dark line appeared on the horizon and grew larger with every wing stroke.

"Thank the High Druid," Jawn muttered, forgetting his oath not to invoke deities he didn't believe in.

"I wouldn't thank him just yet," Rickets said.

Jawn turned and looked at the crowny, expecting to see a wry smile on his face.

"Wait, you're serious?" Jawn asked, suddenly desperately hoping to see Rickets's yellow teeth again. "We've made it. Luitox is in sight. The old gal could probably glide in from here."

Rickets gave Jawn a nod, but it wasn't reassuring. Jawn wanted a better answer, but the noise on the rag increased as the passengers yelled their joy that their long shared misery was about to be over. Sighting land had done wonders for the mood on the back of the rag. There was no more talk of dying, and best of all, no vomit.

Perhaps sensing the end of her journey was now at hand, the rag picked up her speed. Her wing strokes cut through the air with far more purpose and the heat emanating through her scales increased. She was as eager as everyone else to land.

Jawn turned away from Rickets and began going through the checklist he'd made in his head before he left the Kingdom. This was his war, his adventure, and it started now. He wanted to remember every detail from the most mundane to the enormous. More, he wanted to find the words to commemorate the moments. Later, back in the Kingdom, he would be asked what it was like.

He looked up and green mountains stretched across the

horizon. It would all be over soon. Best of all, he'd be forever done with this rag and its crew. Not to mention Rickets.

He counted over a dozen large ships of war anchored far off the beach and another six merchant ships moored to makeshift piers. Troops were disembarking by the hundreds. There was no way the Kingdom could lose. He was tempted to point this out to Rickets but held his tongue, enjoying the relative silence instead.

"Weez claws dry!"

Mercy be, we've made it. The beach stretched inland for a good hundred yards before it gave way to swathes of tall, thin grass that followed a natural slope away from the water all the way to the foot of a squat, jungle-covered mountain range running parallel to the shore. The peaks were round and fuzzy looking, the tallest just a few hundred feet below the rag's current height. Judging by the rag's speed, they'd be flying right over the mountains in no time.

The rag's wings began to beat faster and she started climbing. Unlike in the rough air of a short while earlier, however, she had little power left. They gained maybe another hundred feet before her wings slowed and the rag started to drop again. The co-driver was half out of his seat with his iron bar but then seemed to think better of it and simply reached down and patted the scales on the rag's neck.

The co-driver turned and waved his hands again. "Burrow in laek youse a tick, yah?!"

Jawn let go of the heavy harness chain and raised both his hands in exasperation. "I have no idea what that means!"

The man just grinned and nodded before turning his back.

"You best heed his warning and tuck in tight," Rickets said, detaching from the dorsal fins and disappearing behind them.

"What… why?" Jawn asked, not seeing a reason to panic. The air felt smooth—none of those rough, invisible hills—and they would clear the mountaintop by fifty yards or more. Not a lot, but enough. It would give him a chance to overlook the land. He'd never seen jungle before. He wanted to experience every moment of this. This was living! All the agony suffered on the

42

flight was forgotten. "Our landing at Swassi was actually pretty smooth. We glided in like a feather. She might be tired, but the old girl should let us down nice enough."

The crowny's head popped up. There wasn't a trace of a smile this time. "We come in a bit steeper over here on account of the slyts."

"A... what's a slyt?"

Rickets never answered, ducking down again. The other passengers did the same. Jawn looked back toward the ground. He could make out a dirt path winding its way down the mountain wherever there were gaps in the foliage. He looked closer and saw black scorch marks around those areas, as if they'd recently been burned. Maybe the peasants were clearing the land for farming.

The smell of the jungle rose up and struck Jawn's nostrils for the first time.

He'd gotten used to the smoky aroma of the rag and the scouring, clean smell of salt water over the ocean. This was something entirely different. It was as if the scents of a hundred different animals, dead and alive, had been thrown into a bubbling vat of rotting vegetation and heated until the resultant steam stained the very air like a hot, moist mold.

"Ugh. That's putrid," Jawn said, trying to breathe through his teeth.

"Hah. Wait until summer!" Rickets shouted.

A gleam caught Jawn's eye. A group of soldiers were spread out on the path. Some of them waved and motioned toward the top of the mountain, but most of them simply looked up at him. One pointed his crossbow at the rag as it flew overhead.

The rag continued to descend, picking up speed as they approached the mountain ridge. He'd misjudged. They'd clear the top with less than forty feet to spare. It was a shame they were going so fast, though; everything would be a blur when they overflew it.

A movement in the treetops drew his attention.

"What are those in the trees?" he asked, then realized he was talking to himself. A moment later, the canopy of leaves in front of them began to sparkle as several small flames appeared in the crowns.

"What—" was all he got out before the rag nosed down. Finding a final reserve of energy, she flapped her wings and thrashed her tail, pushing forward even as she fell. Black smoke poured out of her nostrils and streamed back along her body. A shimmering heat seeped through the spaces in her scales. Jawn madly tore off his jacket and stuffed it underneath him.

Damn if, I should have taken a ship! A howling rumble built into a roar as the rag's scales creaked with the strain. Chunks of scale cracked and flew off from the area around her rib cage. Jawn ducked as pieces as large as two-foot paving stones cartwheeled past his head.

An orange glow grew in intensity forward of the rag's wings on each side of her massive chest. Jawn squinted and saw a large section of scales lifting into the wind stream.

"She's breaking up!" His innards contracted into a frozen block of fear.

"It's her air gills!" Rickets shouted. "I figured the old girl's would have seized up long ago, but I guess not!"

"Air gills?" Jawn cursed his limited lack of knowledge on all things dragon.

"Lets them suck in more air to feed their fire when they need the speed! Makes things exciting when they use them!"

"This is normal?!" Jawn shouted, gasping as the heat coming off the rag got hotter.

"If we survive, it is!"

They began skimming just above the treetops. A mat of thick green flashed by beneath Jawn as small black objects streaked into the sky all around them. Several trailed smoke and fire.

"They're shooting at us!" Jawn yelled, slamming his body forward so hard that he bounced his head off the rag's hide. He yelped, not from the impact, but from the heat seeping through the scales. They were close to scalding.

Jawn ducked his head again as a maelstrom of torn leaves

and shattered branches flew past his head, the rag now blasting through the treetops.

"Weez gone to tha weeds, yah?! Caterwaul if'n y'all want, might spook the slyts' aim a skosh!"

Jawn was desperately searching for meaning in the co-driver's rambling when the rag's wings stopped flapping and the spray of vegetation ceased. With a grinding of bone and scale, she tucked her wings in against her sides and bent her long neck straight down. After almost a day of living with the nonstop beating of her massive wings, the solitary sound of rushing wind was disconcerting.

That changed a moment later.

A rain of vomit and urine soaked Jawn, seeping under his collar to run down his back. He ignored it, turning instead to look over his shoulder at the mountaintop they'd just cleared. In a stunning reversal of the laws of the natural world, the mountain appeared to be hurtling upward.

Arrows peppered the sky in their wake. As the rag's tail swished into view, Jawn saw half of its vertical fin was missing. What remained was quilled like a porcupine.

More fluids splashed in Jawn's hair and plummeting to his death or not, he'd had enough. He faced forward and reached out to jab the sickly officer in front of him. His arm froze as he cocked it back.

The officer was sitting upright, his arms flapping above his head in the wind as if waving. A single arrow wobbled from his neck just above his collar. With each back-and-forth movement of the arrow, the gash grew larger as more blood spurted out in a dark red mist. His head lolled between his shoulders and then tipped back. The weight of his head and the rush of the wind widened the tear until the muscles ripped and his neck bones cracked, flopping his head to hang upside down between his shoulder blades. His sightless eyes stared at Jawn as blood surged up from the gaping wound.

Jawn hunched down as close to the rag's scales as he could stand, gritting his teeth as the heat burned into his cheek. He closed his eyes and searched for anything to replace the grisly image in his head. Unable to control his stomach, he vomited, which immediately steamed as it hit the scales. Thoughts of battles and poignant words fled his mind as his entire existence narrowed to a plummeting, blood-and-vomit-and-filth-covered moment in time. His war couldn't end like this. *Not like this!*

CHAPTER FIVE

"HOLY FUCKING HIGH DRUID!"

"Did you see that?" the Weasel asked, pointing at the black smoke trail. "They skewered one of the bastards on board."

Big Hog huffed. "What are you on about? That old rag was spewing out so much smoke you could barely see her when she went over."

Carny wanted to believe Big Hog was right, but he knew it wasn't going to matter. Command would have seen that from the beach.

"About time the manor born got a taste of what it's like for the rest of us," Voof said, the satisfaction in his voice dripping with malice. "Let their blood paint the whole mountain red."

"For fuck's sake, Voof, you're mad, you know that?" the Weasel said. "You keep talking like that they'll string you up by the neck until you're dead."

"Only if we don't stand up to them," Voof said, looking around.

Carny avoided his eyes. Voof said what Carny didn't have the courage to say, but this wasn't the time or the place.

"You have something to say, Crossbowman?" Sinte said, walking down the path.

Carny groaned. This would only end badly.

The sound of hooves galloping up the path heralded a new and most likely worsening situation. A gleaming rider on a bluish roan pony came into view. Hoots and catcalls greeted the Seventh Phalanx commander's crippled little messenger, Firl Bristom. His withered legs bounced off the sides of Gallanter like two twigs in the wind. A pair of wooden arms cushioned with leather padding like those on a chair rose up from the front of his saddle and wrapped around his waist, affixing him in place. Bulging satchels and water skins slung by leather straps draped over the pony's back.

"Hey, Squeak, when are you two getting married?"

"Did your mother have any children that lived?"

"Did you see any slyts this time?" Squeak asked, reining in his pony and ignoring the japes directed at him. He wore the simple, sleeveless, waist-length dark green cotton tunic they wore as an undergarment, although his was trimmed with silver, denoting he was part of the command group. He didn't wear an aketon, but perversely, he'd had half sleeves sewn onto the shoulders of his tunic.

He reached up with a hand to adjust his highly polished helm, which had slipped down over his eyes. When he lowered his hand, Carny could see his pimply face was flushed, though whether it was because of the ride or the taunts he didn't know. A nickname like Squeak certainly couldn't help.

"What?" Sinte said, glowering at the boy.

Squeak sat up straighter and threw back his narrow shoulders.

"No need to get snippy, just doing my duty. Commander Weel is kicking cauldrons. He saw the show and put the fire to all the field deputies," Squeak said. Carny could easily imagine the scene. Weel was forever yelling at the FDs who commanded the Javelins, who in turn blasted the shield leaders like Sinte. And Sinte was all too happy to keep the shit ball rolling downhill.

"And?" Sinte asked.

"And," Bristom continued, pulling a folded piece of paper from inside his tunic, "by order of FD Rhomy, Second Javelin, you are hereby commanded to turn around and march back up there and not come down until you have something to show for it… preferably slyt heads."

The shield groaned. Carny's stomach grew hollow and he felt homesick. Until that very moment he'd still held out hope that they'd make it back down to the beach before dusk.

"We don't have to listen to this little piece of afterbirth," Voof said, casually pointing his crossbow at Squeak. "He's just a mouthpiece for those that want to keep us down."

"Lower your weapon!" Sinte shouted, storming down the rest of the way to stand in front of Vooford. "Keep that shit up and you'll be for the stockade. When you're back in camp, you can piss and moan and scrawl notes home about how your worthless ass got conscripted and how unfair it is, but when we're out here you will act like a soldier. We only point weapons at things we mean to kill."

Voof glowered at Squeak, unwilling or afraid to look straight at Sinte. With excruciating slowness, Voof lowered his crossbow, letting the weapon drift in Sinte's direction. The motion was subtle, but Carny knew it wasn't an accident.

Sinte lashed out, punching Voof in the gut. The tall man crumpled to the ground clutching his stomach. "Why'd you do that?"

"The better question is, what lice-ridden harlot gave birth to such a horrid creature as you and why wasn't she put down?" Sinte said, shaking his head. He turned away and looked at the shield. "And what the fuck are the rest of you staring at?! We're still in slyt land here. Face out and keep watch for movement!"

Carny did as ordered, angling his body to face the jungle while still keeping Sinte and Squeak in sight. The chance of any slyts coming within a mile of the roaring Sinte seemed highly unlikely, but the idea of an arrow in the back was enough to keep his eyes peeled all the same.

Carny pulled his hewer from its scabbard and hacked away at some large, floppy leaves. The eighteen-inch-long and two-inch-wide rectangular blade had only one side sharpened, which Carny appreciated as he bounced it off of ironlike vines and hit his shoulder on the rebound. Unlike a sword, the end wasn't pointed, but instead widened slightly, sloping at a twenty-degree angle from the spine down to the cutting edge. A single, deep blood groove ran the length of the back on the left side of the blade, though the only blood it had tasted so far was his own.

"Ugh!" Carny shouted, backing away as a brown spider with yellow stripes the size of his fist tumbled onto a leaf near his face. He squeezed the grip of the hewer hard and brought it down on the spider, cleaving it in two. He carefully approached the leaves again, ready to attack should any more of them appear.

Sinte snorted and walked past Carny, stopping when he got to Squeak. He grabbed the messenger's pony by the bridle. The mare shied and tried to back away, but Sinte's grip was iron. "It's going to be dark soon. We've been out here since dawn."

Squeak leaned over the pony's neck, smoothing its mane before sitting back up. He twisted around and grabbed the pair of satchels and water skins slung across Gallanter's back. He grunted with the effort, finally tipping the water skins onto the ground, where Big Hog walked over and picked them up. Squeak motioned for Carny to come over and take the satchels, but Sinte grabbed them out of his hands. "Enough water and food to last you the night," Squeak said, looking over at Carny and motioning with his eyes at the satchels before focusing on Sinte again.

Sinte let go of the bridle. "Messenger *and* delivery boy. You're making quite a career for yourself."

Squeak ignored the slight. "Look, trust me on this—you'll be safer up there than down in camp. All the FDs are squawking about it. They don't think it makes any more sense than you do. Rhomy even said so to Weel. I was there."

That was rather surprising to hear. It was a wonder Rhomy still had his job. Carny couldn't remember the last time anyone had called out Weel.

"It's a lousy deal, but that's the hand," Squeak continued. "None of the FDs want to report back to Weel that they still haven't found the slyts. And believe it or not, Weel's getting serious thorns from higher up, too. Senior officers and other highborn creatures ride on those rags. Getting shot at upsets them. If any on that rag that just passed by wind up tarped, someone's going to pay…"

And Carny knew damn well it would be them. It wasn't their fault. They could send the whole phalanx up the mountain and they still wouldn't find the slyts. He'd been in the Lux three months now and he'd yet to see an armed slyt.

Sinte hung his head for a moment, then looked up. "How's Weel think our camping up there is going to help anything? The rags don't fly over at night."

"You see the ships?" Squeak asked, hooking his thumb over his shoulder toward the ocean. "Finally got us some mules, hundreds of them. Come first light, Weel's marching them up there to cut and burn every last tree down so the slyts have nowhere to hide. You've just got to keep it secure until the mules arrive."

"And if the slyts come back?"

Squeak pulled at the reins, backing his mare away. "The other shields have orders to stay on the mountain, too. Black Shield is on the other side of the saddle to the north and Gray Shield is due south. The others will be spread around lower down. If the slyts come back, a few heads would go a long way to putting Weel in a better mood."

Sinte stared hard at Squeak before finally waving him away. "Get the fuck out of my sight."

Squeak wheeled the pony around and started down the path without looking back. Carny watched him go, knowing there was nothing for it. They were going to march right up the mountain.

Sinte confirmed his fears. "All right, the sooner we get moving, the sooner we rest. I damn well don't want to be marching around here in the dark. Vooford," he said, pointing a finger at the soldier, who was now back on his feet, "you walk ST."

"Fuck that. I ain't walking spear tip. Slyts are all over that mountain now, SL," Voof said. His voice had the shocked tenor of a wronged man's.

"Go down and complain to Rhomy if you'd rather," Sinte said. He didn't yell. He didn't smile. He didn't even move his crossbow, but the entire shield held its breath. If Voof turned and headed toward the beach, he wouldn't make it two steps.

Voof stared at Sinte for several flicks. The noise of the jungle and beckoning rush of the waves over sand made the air seem crystalline. Carny's eyes began to sting, but there was no way he was going to risk blinking.

"Aw, fuck it," Voof muttered, cradling his crossbow in his arms and trudging up the path. The rest of the shield let out a collective sigh and fell in. Carny blinked and cursed as sweat washed over his eyeballs. Stupid bastard was going to get them all killed.

The four longbowmen in the shield stayed in the middle of the line. With jungle never more than a few feet away, their longer-range bows were of limited use. They wore the standard-issue heavy hewers and nine-inch hunting knives, but if the slyts got close enough that those weapons were necessary, things would definitely be in a bad state.

Sinte stood off to the side as they filed past. When Carny reached him, Sinte fell into step beside him. Without warning, he shoved the two satchels at Carny, who hurriedly grabbed them.

"I sent you up there with Listowk because I figured at least you had some sense." Sinte's face was inches from Carny's ear. "You got education. Numbers, reading and writing. You spent an extra three weeks in training in shield leader class before you came over."

Carny started to shrug but realized Sinte was too close to see the gesture. "SL, I'm trying.

"Try harder," Sinte said, moving his face even closer. "Listowk's losing what's left of his mind. Stupid bastard looks more like a slyt every time we come out here. You'd think he'd be able to spot 'em now that he damn near looks like 'em."

Carny glanced sideways at Sinte, then quickly turned back. "The slyts weren't there, SL. They must have sneaked back the moment we left."

They trekked in silence side by side for the next few moments. Carny was just about to offer a joke to ease the tension when Sinte leaned back in to him. "I was wrong about you," he said, picking up his pace and leaving Carny to stare at his back.

The sound of waves crashing on the beach trailed after Carny all the way back up the mountain.

CHAPTER SIX

"EASY NOW, YER GRACE, ya'll be purrin' laek a kitten with warm milk afor' long, yah?" the co-driver said, looking up from the ground. He held out a three-fingered hand to help Jawn down from the rag. Jawn blinked. They'd landed. He couldn't remember it.

The beast was sprawled flat on the ground, her wings spread out to either side in utter exhaustion. The grass underneath her smoldered as heat poured off her body in shimmering waves. Men wearing heavy leather aprons and elbow-high gauntlets ran forward with wooden water buckets and began dousing animal and passengers alike.

Jawn numbly took the man's hand, suppressing the urge to grimace as his fingers wrapped around the stump of the index finger. The scar tissue over the stump was coarse, like a hard crust of bread. He jumped to the ground and would have fallen over if not for the steadying hand.

"Takes a bit to git yer walkin' pegs under ya agin."

There was no detectable gloating in his voice. Jawn squeezed the man's hand in thanks.

"I'm covered in blood," Jawn said, looking down at his clothes. *And vomit.* He was a mess, but as bad as he looked, he felt even worse. The heat coming off the rag combined with the sweltering air of Luitox draped over him like hot pitch. His head pounded and he was on the verge of puking again.

"Bad luck that. Them slyts is gittin' right ornery when we flies o'er. Army kips sayin' they'll go up thar an' clear 'em out, but the lazy buggers 'tain't done it yet," the co-driver said, stepping smartly to the side as water tossed from a bucket cascaded over Jawn.

Jawn gasped. "Hey, a little warning!"

The co-driver smiled. "Fair 'nuff. Here come two more."

The force of the thrown water knocked Jawn back a couple of steps. An expletive died on his lips. The nearly decapitated body of the officer who'd sat in front of him was being lifted into a tarp. The men doing the lifting weren't gentle, but they weren't rough, either. They could have been handling sacks of fruit.

"Friend a yours?" the co-driver asked, motioning with the remaining fingers on his left hand.

Jawn shook his head. "Just met him." He tried to think of something more profound to say. "He threw up on me."

"More water, then? Puke's a bitch to git out," the co-driver asked.

Jawn backed away a pace. "No, thanks, I think I'm good."

The rag groaned and began exhaling in a series of short, ragged puffs. She started thrashing her legs and opening and closing her jaws as if she couldn't get enough air. The air gill that Jawn could see was closed again, although steam issued from spaces between the scales. Men began running away.

"What's wrong with her?" Jawn asked, aware that only he and the co-driver were now standing near the rag.

The co-driver shook his head. "Poor gal, musta blew a lung gittin' o'er the mountain. I tol' Ecker weez pushin' her, but when youse gittin' over a mountain, thar ain't nuthin' for it but to push, yah? Mountains down't git out a yer way."

"Isn't there something you can do?" Jawn asked, realizing he wanted to avoid finding out if there was something *he* could do. He was beyond tired, every muscle ached, and his thought process was mush. Trying to muster a thaumic process into something that could help the ailing beast would call too much attention to himself, even if he could think of something useful.

"They gonna try, but when they git lek this it's usually the chop for 'em. Cut up their parts. Peepers alone worth my weight in silver," the co-driver said.

A group of ten men came running up to the rag. Like the others before, they wore ankle-to-neck leather aprons and elbow-high gauntlets. In addition, their faces were covered in black swaddling so that only a thin strip revealed their eyes. The four largest carried two sets of heavy iron chains between them. Metal spikes hung from leather belts around their waists and sledgehammers were slung across their backs with rope.

The largest man towered over Jawn and was twice as broad at the shoulders. He carried a wicked-looking pickaxe with a three-foot-long pick on one end. Two others only slightly smaller held standard axes and the fourth had a man-length section of three-inch-diameter bamboo coated in a thick layer of clay on his shoulder.

"What's all this?" Jawn asked, backing away as the men approached the rag. Instead of dissipating, the heat emanating from the rag was increasing. Her thrashing was growing more intense, as well. If not for the long trip, Jawn suspected she'd be up on all fours rampaging. As it was, her claws were gouging deep furrows in the dirt and her wings were beating against the ground, kicking up small dust devils.

The men with the chains tossed them over the rag, one across her neck at the shoulders, the other at the base of the tail. As they used their sledgehammers to pound spikes through the chains into the ground, more men jumped on her wings and pounded U-shaped iron spikes directly through her wing membranes over the bones, pinning her appendages to the ground.

"Doesn't that hurt her?!" Jawn asked.

The rag roared and tried to swing her head around to get at the men, but even more had arrived and were pinning her head and neck between large metal poles sunk into the ground, effectively corralling her in place.

The man with the pickaxe stood off to the side, swinging the tool through the air with a master swordsman's skill.

Meanwhile, the man holding the bamboo pipe approached the rag. He set the pipe down and pulled a small cylindrical glass tube from a satchel at his side. Slipping a heavy cloth hood over his head, he pressed the glass against the side of the rag. He then leaned forward and placed his ear against it. He did this several times. He finally nodded and stood up, taking a bar of red clay mixed with copper from a pocket and marking an X on one of the scales. The bar melted as he pressed it to the scale.

Jawn's stomach sank. *They're going to kill the rag!* Jawn started forward, not knowing what he was going to do.

"Easy now, they's jus' makin' sure they don't hit her boiler," the co-driver said, laying his three-fingered hand on Jawn's arm. Jawn tried to shrug his arm away, but even with three fingers, the co-driver had an impressively strong grip. "We'd best be backin' up a bit, yah?"

Jawn found himself being propelled backward. "Why, afraid to get a little blood on you?" Jawn asked, spinning around to face the man and breaking his hold at the same time.

The co-driver slowly shook his head. A tear glistened in the corner of each eye. "If'n they miss an' hit her boiler or one of the main pipes, well, she could up'n furtle-eyes."

"What does that even mean?" Jawn asked.

The co-driver spread his arms wide apart in an arc, then wiggled his fingers as he brought his arms down. "Furtle-eyes a few 'undred yards in all directions."

"What, explode?" Jawn asked, remembering the rumors.

The co-driver nodded, gently reaching and grabbing Jawn's arm again. "She's hettin' up laek a coal pile that's caught afire. All the water in the world won't put her out now. Don't know all the whys and why-fors, but their innards gets thinned out when they gets hot, makes 'em inpredickable laek. And when they's keenin' with a bad lung, well, they's jus' plain dangerous. They needs them lungs for to keep the air flowin' to keep the heat down, yah? An' her gills ain't what they was. Laek as ruptured them both after that mountain. Poor gal, she's got a runaway fire deep in her."

The man pulled on Jawn's arm, moving him farther back. Jawn allowed himself to be led, his indignation and anger turning to agony in an instant. Despite his coarseness, the man cared deeply for the rag.

More water was thrown onto the rag, bursting into steam the moment it hit her scales. The grass around her was now on fire, and the chains and iron pegs pinning her to the ground were glowing a dull red.

Braving the heat, the two axe men stepped forward and began chopping at the marked scale, one on each side. It sounded like steel on rock. They grunted with the effort as the rag shook with each blow. After over a dozen swings, each scale had been hacked away, exposing a roughly one-foot-in-diameter patch of gray, leathery skin.

The large man with the pickaxe came forward, hitting the hole made in the scale at dead center, sinking the wedge-shaped point up to the shaft. The rag roared. Molten, shimmering blood spurted out of the hole as a sulfurous stream of smoke vented skyward, the rag now bellowing a fiery cloud of sparks.

The pickaxe man reefed on the handle, twisting it back and forth in the wound, making it bigger. The steaming blood flow abated as a hissing sound grew. The man withdrew the pickaxe and stepped away as the one with the clay-coated bamboo pipe stepped forward and slid the sharpened end into the wound. It immediately caught fire. Two of the men with sledgehammers began working it deep into the side of the rag.

Jawn tensed, waiting for the explosion. He was no longer trapped in a nightmare, but even now he felt incapable of mustering up enough concentration to perform any kind of thaumic process.

Blood gushed out of the bamboo tube, bursting into flames as it hit the ground. The flow then slowed to a trickle, leaving only the steady hiss of escaping air and frothy bubbles. The waves of heat pouring off the rag lessened. The red glow of the chains began to darken and a grating noise rose as the rag's scales began to slide over one another, tightening back up.

The rag laid her head down on the ground and then did the most amazing thing. She began purring, her breathing far less labored. More men ran up, pushing wheelbarrows filled with a reddish-brown slurry. They tipped their loads in front of the rag's mouth, creating a small pond glittering with metal flecks. The rag lifted her head up and put it back down, burying her muzzle in the muddy mix. Bubbles and steam rose as she began to drink and inhale the slurry.

Jawn stared openmouthed. "What was that?"

The co-driver nodded approvingly at the rag. Tears rolled freely down his cheeks now. "Laek I said, poor thing lost a lung on the way o'er the mountain. Jus' too much strain. You gots to git in there and git it workin' agin, yah? Buts we gots her coolin', so's now she can take on some fire paste and patch the walls."

Jawn nodded though he didn't really understand. He had studied primarily human anatomy at the RAT, but the focus of his instruction had been on better and quicker ways to kill a person, not save one. His knowledge of rags was limited to a few medicinal properties of various body parts.

More steam gushed out of the bamboo tube in the rag's chest, followed by spurts of the metal-impregnated clay slurry. Several of the leather-clad men examined the hot clay, then motioned for more wheelbarrows. Whatever they were doing, they appeared to have it under control.

"Welcome to the Lux!" Rickets said, suddenly appearing at Jawn's side. "It ain't much to look at it, but oh, the smell."

"Did you see that?" Jawn asked, still staring at the rag. What in blazes had he signed up for?

"Ah, I told you she'd get us down," Rickets said. "Old girl really came through. Bit hairy there at the end, but still beats sailing."

I can't deal with this. "I've got to report to the… I've got to report somewhere." Now that the excitement was over, he became aware of his own body again. His head was awash in heat, yet he was shivering. The darkening sky felt like a wet, steaming blanket being draped around his head. If he didn't lie down soon, he'd topple to the ground. "My orders are in my…," Jawn started saying, then trailed off as his fingers brushed against his wet tunic. He knew it was water now, but he feared that if he dared look down he'd see he was still covered in blood.

"That'll keep," Rickets said, taking Jawn by the arm and steering him away from the rag. "I know a little watering hole not far from here where the beer is cold and the whores are hot."

Cold beer sounded amazing, better even than sleep. The desire for sex, however, was currently lost to him. He was done with this crowny. He planted his feet and let Rickets's grip on his elbow slip off. "Thanks for the offer, but I've got to report to the Seventh Phalanx," Jawn said. *Enough of being led around.*

Rickets looked around them again before speaking as he had on the rag, his voice pitched low so only Jawn could hear. "Save yourself the trouble. They'll be moving inland soon. Right now they're on the coast, a good three days' journey by wagon train up and over the mountains we just crossed. Don't get me wrong—it's not a bad place to be out there. Fresh air, all the water you'd ever need for bathing if you're into that sort of thing, and best of all, it's about the safest place to be in this whole damn cesspool. But you'll just be in the way while they're moving, so why bother?"

Jawn didn't appreciate being considered useless, but he had to admit that at the moment he had no idea how he could contribute to the war. Maybe throw up on someone. "Let's say you're right. How do you even know that?"

Rickets smiled. "You work long enough for the Crown, you get to hear things when the high muckety-mucks get into their cups after the day candle has burned out. Maybe read a few things not necessarily meant for your eyes."

Jawn realized his mouth had fallen open. "But… that's spying. You could be hung for that."

"Oh mercy, you are pure silver, you are," Rickets said, his eyes shimmering with mirth. He put a hand on Jawn's shoulder and grasped it firmly, but in a friendly way. "One drink won't kill you. In fact, it might just save your life."

Jawn looked back over the field. He'd dreamed about this moment. He was in a foreign land. He was in a war. It was a moment to remember, to cherish. In the Kingdom's time of need, he'd answered the call as so many brave warriors had done throughout the Kingdom's history. He wasn't a hero, not yet, but this moment was to be the beginning of his journey that would lead him to something... more.

Now, however, he wanted to forget the entire thing. He was standing in a muddy field with nothing but jungle on the horizon. The smell of sulfur and blood mixed with the hot air as he absently ran his fingers through his hair, picking out bits of gore that just a short time ago had been a living, breathing person. Dusk was turning to night, and he had no idea where to go or what to do. This was not how it was supposed to be.

"If we keep standing around here, we're liable to see them feed the rag," Rickets said. "They stuff the ass of a goat with coal and set it on fire. Some folks find it interesting."

Jawn deliberately didn't ask if the goat was alive or dead. He kicked at the mud with the toe of his boot. His guide, for lack of a far more derogatory word, was a foul-mouthed bureaucrat who managed to anger and humble Jawn with frustrating ease, only to turn around and proffer genuine aid while revealing hints of a keen mind that Jawn would be foolish to ignore. Rickets, for all his many annoying qualities, seemed to have a handle on this place and was offering to be an escort.

"Fine," Jawn said, reminding himself that tomorrow was a new day. "One drink."

Rickets bobbed up on his toes in excitement. "Now you're talking! Oh, you'll like this place. They brew a wine that will restore your virginity." He paused and looked Jawn over. "Or lose it."

"Lovely," Jawn said, walking back toward the rag to pick up his two bags from among the pile of luggage hastily tossed from the beast. Rickets followed along like a puppy eager to play.

"You don't know it now, Jawn Rathim, but you just made one of the best decisions of your life."

Jawn didn't bother to answer. He was just as certain that he hadn't.

CHAPTER SEVEN

"WEEL'S GOING TO GET us all killed is what he's going to do," Voof said, pacing around the small clearing the shield had settled into to wait out the night. He covered the distance from one end of their small encampment to the other in just twenty long strides. "Not that he'd care. There ain't no need us being up here. Ain't no rags flying at night. He's just pissed 'cause a few officers got the shit scared out of 'em."

No one could be bothered to echo his gripe. The rest of the shield was bone-tired and flaked out among the vegetation on the mountaintop. They formed a rough circle facing outward, covering every opening in the jungle the slyts might use. Soldiers had finished stringing prick vine, the tough, thin, thorn-covered vine that grew throughout the jungle, around the camp. As an obstacle it wasn't much, but in the dark it might catch an unsuspecting slyt trying to sneak up on them.

The ocean breeze didn't seem inclined to join them at the summit, so they sweltered in the humidity and batted at swarms of bugs. The climb back up had taken most of the daylight with it and the shadows were growing long.

Lead Crossbowman Listowk lifted his head a fraction from where it rested on crossed arms draped over his knees. It was even silver on whether the complaining Vooford would wind himself up into a fury or wear himself down to a mumbling sulk. Normally, Listowk would have bet on the heat sapping the soldier's strength, but Vooford had that rare quality of finding energy in misery and multiplying it until everyone around him suffered.

"Why don't you park your ass, get some food in you, and enjoy the great outdoors?" Listowk asked, mustering just enough energy to point at the trees with his nose. "If you're real nice, Carny might even have a treat for you in one of those haversacks," he finished, turning his head to catch Carny's surprised expression a few feet away. Did Carny think he didn't know what the little cripple had brought him?

"Fuck you, and fuck Carny, too," Voof said, raising his voice even louder. "In fact, fuck you all!" He paused in his pacing to look around. "Just 'cause you got strong-armed into the army don't mean you stop thinking. We're still citizens. We got rights. More than ever. Why should I fight for this king? He ain't even a real king."

"If a slyt doesn't put an arrow in that festering wound you call a mouth, I will," someone grumbled from the other side of their encampment.

"Who said that?" Voof shouted, bringing his crossbow up into a firing position in front of his chest.

Listowk sighed, letting his right hand slide down his leg. His hand came to rest on his own weapon lying on the ground beside him. It was cocked with a bolt resting in the groove. He hooked his thumb under the iron safety latch, gently caressing the smooth metal. A quick flick up and the latch would release, freeing the trigger.

"Now, now, children," Listowk said, looking around the encampment. Tired, dirty, and scared faces looked back him. They really were like children. "Let's all just take a breath and relax. It's hot, we're tired, and we're stuck up here with nothing but dirty thoughts about sweet things. But do keep in mind, this is slyt land. We don't need to be making their job any easier by squabbling among ourselves."

"Since when is thinking for yourself a problem?" Voof said,

still staring in the direction of the hurled insult. "Long past time we woke and did a whole lot more thinking for ourselves."

"Sweet trees a'mighty, Vooford!" Listowk said, his voice rising despite his attempt to remain calm. "I didn't get much book learning as a child, but even I mastered the concept that thinking don't necessarily also mean talking at the same time. It's entirely fine if you do the first without all the latter."

Those bright enough to catch his joke chuckled. It wasn't many.

"Someone's gotta stand up for what's right," Voof said, his voice less strident than before. His crossbow, however, remained in a firing position.

Listowk saw his opening. Vooford had let off his steam and now just needed a way to back down without losing face. "And it's commendable that you take that responsibility on, it truly is. You—"

"*Vooford!*" Sinte bellowed, stepping through the trees and into the middle of their camp. "Sit the fuck down and shut the fuck up! We're surrounded by slyts up here!"

Voof snarled and spun on his heel to face Sinte. An audible gasp went up from the soldiers. The chirping, clicking, screeching insect chorus that greeted every nightfall quieted.

This close to calming the fool down! Listowk tensed his thumb, ready to flip the iron safety latch up. It was all on Sinte now.

"LC Listowk," Sinte said, deliberately angling his body so that he faced Listowk but kept Vooford in sight out of the corner of his eye. "Why the hell are these men idle and gossiping like a gaggle of washerwomen? I don't smell wax. I thought I made it clear that bowstrings were to be waxed daily."

"Ah, Shield Leader, welcome back," Listowk said, nodding. He made it sound like a long-lost brother had just returned. "Really great to see you. I was just about to tell the men to do that very thing." In fact, Listowk had told the shield to do it, but soldiers being boys, they'd focused on other matters like lighting up their pipes and lolling around. He understood and wasn't about to get his lads in trouble with the SL.

Sinte turned to fully face Listowk, exposing his back to Voof. It was a strong statement but also a risky one. "Good, because when I do a weapons check tomorrow morning, I'd better not find a single slack string or the entire shield will be held accountable."

Listowk looked around the encampment, careful not to linger on Voof. Soldiers were hurriedly unhooking the strings from their crossbows. The whipcord they used was strong, especially this new type they'd been issued that had strands of animal sinew woven in, but it still needed waxing to keep from fraying and drying out, or even rotting.

"Let's remember to use our upstairs attic," Listowk said, tapping his helm with the knuckles of his left hand. "Right edge, keep your string on and wax your spare. Left edge, do the opposite. It wouldn't do to have the entire shield stringless at the same time."

Listowk kept an eye on Voof. With only Sinte's back to rail against and seemingly forgotten, Voof grumbled something obscene. Sinte chose to ignore it. Listowk flipped his safety latch off. The bowstring hummed as the main trigger picked up the tension. The entire weapon felt tighter in his hand, like a coiled snake waiting to strike.

"I'm going to get some food," Voof muttered, stomping off to the other end of the clearing.

"Any sign of Black Shield?" Listowk asked Sinte, thumbing the safety latch back down to engage the trigger bar. It took more effort to put it into place than it did to take it off. Stifling a yawn, he eased himself into a standing position.

Sinte walked over until he stood about two feet in front of him. "He's becoming a bigger problem."

Listowk shrugged. "I think of him as the spout on a boiling teapot. The shield needs to let off pressure now and then, and he's the loudest. Lets them all get it out of their systems."

Sinte scowled. "You sound like a damn witch with that folksy wisdom. Vooford is an infection that will spread if we don't stop him."

Listowk didn't like the turn the conversation was taking.

Sinte wasn't blinking. "Any sign of Black Shield?" Listowk asked again.

Sinte didn't answer for a moment, as if weighing whether to continue his original train of thought. "No. I went two hundred yards and couldn't find a thing."

"Shield Leader Trivvos is a cagey rascal," Listowk said. "He's probably got his boys dug in and quiet as Holy Grove mice," he said, making a mental note to ask Trivvos just how the hell he did that.

"Listowk, you look like a damn fool," Sinte said suddenly. "Weel sees you dressed like that, he'll have your balls."

Listowk looked down at his uniform. Without much effort, he'd simply grabbed a leaf here and some fronds there as they marched, weaving them into his leather webbing and aketon. A string or two of vine and some flowers, and he'd pass for just one more part of the jungle. "I do seem to pick up more than my fair share of the shrubbery, don't I? Not exactly parade-ground presentable, but it seems to work out here."

"It's unorthodox," Sinte said.

"I suppose it is at that, but everything has to start out unorthodox at first," Listowk said, refraining from asking Sinte whom he thought the slyts would shoot at first. "And like you said, SL, we're in slyt territory here. They sure as hell blend in. I was planning to take a stroll in a bit and see if I can't locate the Blacks myself. Figured I'd be better off if I blend in, too."

Sinte's left hand brushed at something on his own aketon, perhaps self-consciously, and shook his head. "Forget that. It's too dark. I don't want you wandering around out there getting lost, or worse. We'll sit tight here and make the best of it." Sinte paused for a moment and looked around their camp. "Why, you worried?"

A psaltery being lightly strummed filled the clearing before Listowk answered. Crossbowman Hanjil Sovoad—"the Bard," as the shield called him—carried the thing everywhere. Sinte was surprisingly tolerant of the lad's playing. Maybe the SL had a heart after all.

The Bard sang, his voice a soft flannel.

Dark mountain rising above the sea
Our youth spent upon your velvet thighs
With your head in the clouds
And your heart buried in time.

"Lad needs to learn how to rhyme," Sinte said.

"I'll tell him to stop," Listowk said.

"Not like the slyts don't know we're here," Sinte said. "Let him play for a flicker or two."

Listowk raised an eyebrow but said nothing. Instead, he turned and pointed at Carny. "Divvy up the food, okay? If they sent us any honey oranges, save me a wedge?"

Listowk then waited until the bustle about food and the Bard's singing and strumming had the soldiers preoccupied before answering Sinte. "So, am I worried? We're up here with our asses out of our trousers. Weel chewed out Rhomy, and now we're getting spanked. On a training exercise that'd be fine, but this is different. We have no idea where the other shields are and no way to contact them if we did. Maybe they brought some more carrier pigeons with the newest draft," he said, motioning back down toward the beach, "but that doesn't help us tonight. The slyts are getting bold."

Sinte knocked his knuckles against the iron plates sewn to his aketon. "There are six shields on this little mountain. That's nearly a hundred and twenty trained bows. And there's hundreds more on the beach with more arriving every day. They'll have heavier weapons, too. Catapults, ballistas, trebuchets, the works. You know the slyts—hide, loose off some arrows, then run and hide again."

Listowk didn't take the SL for stupid, but Sinte's faith in the Kingdom's army worried him. "It all sounds good when you say it like that, but that ain't the half of it. We're spread out like six tiny islands. And all those big throwers on the beach are still going to be in pieces. It'll take them a good day or more to put them back together, and probably a couple more after that to string all the sinew and rope and get them tight and aligned. And even when they do, they'll be shooting blind until we rig up a way to talk to them."

Sinte sighed. The man was tired, too, but he'd fall down dead before admitting it. "So what do you suggest? I sure as hell can't march us back down to Weel."

Listowk allowed himself a moment to smile on the inside. You couldn't tell a superior what to do, but you could lead him to ask the right questions. "Odds are the little devils have had eyes on us the whole time. They damn well hear us with the racket these boys make. Wait until it's been dark an eighth of a candle, then we leave this site and slip down the side of the mountain, about two hundred yards, and wait out the night."

Sinte didn't answer right away, which Listowk took as a good sign. "Our orders are to man the summit."

"Hell of an inscription on a grave tree," Listowk said with a measured nonchalance that was almost impossible to take offense to.

"And I suppose you scouted out a place on our way up where we could ride out the night?"

This time Listowk did smile. "We crossed a few ruts that I figure were runoff channels when the rains hit. Remember those? Looked like tiny canyons." Sinte nodded. Listowk couldn't tell if the SL really remembered them or not, but he knew Sinte would never admit it. "I followed one, and just past the bush a few yards, there were some big rocks and a decent-sized dirt bank upslope on the southern side of the path. We could tuck in there. Won't be comfortable, but it's a sight better than sitting in the open out here. If I had to wager a silver coin, I'd bet Trivvos has his shield in a place like that, too."

"I can't leave the summit abandoned," Sinte said. He didn't look at Listowk but instead watched the shield talking and joking as they ate.

It was Listowk's turn to sigh. The chance that Weel would send anyone up to check on them was beyond remote, but if

Trivvos or one of the other shields sent scouts to try to find them, someone had to be there.

"If we all just sit here, we're asking for trouble," Listowk said.

Sinte nodded. "If you were a slyt, and you knew we were here, how would you come at us?"

Listowk had given the idea some thought. "I'd swing around toward the ocean side and come up that way. Not only would it have the element of surprise, but in the dark we could end up shooting at another shield coming up from the beach in support. It'd be a bloodbath."

"So if you were going to put out a small patrol to watch for that… ," Sinte said.

"I'd put it in that little rut I found on the way up," Listowk finished.

"Take three crossbowmen and one long, but not Vooford. I want that bastard where I can see him," Sinte said.

And of course, no thank-you, no nothing. The only way Sinte ever took advice was by believing it was his own.

"Big Hog, Wraith, the Weasel… and Carny," Listowk said, nodding his head in their direction. Sinte looked that way.

On first glance, and even a second, the men didn't inspire. Crossbowman Second Class "Big Hog" Postik, the beefy farm boy with a good, if limited, head on his shoulders, was flat on his back fast asleep. The Weasel, Crossbowman First Class Alminga Meerz, had his aketon off, revealing his scrawny, bug-bitten chest. He was lathering something over the bites, which made his pale skin turn a dirty yellow color.

It took Listowk a moment to spot Wraith. Like Listowk, the backwoods hunter turned longbowman had managed to accumulate leaves on his helm and aketon, making him difficult to see. He'd also acquired a nonregulation bow half the size of his longbow, which was the reason Listowk chose him. Longbowman Nolli Lingletti was the walking embodiment of unorthodox.

"Carnan? You sure?" Sinte asked. The tone of his voice made it sound more like an accusation. "Waste of training, that one. What the fuck good is education if it doesn't make a man strong?"

Listowk studied Carny. Average build, plain face, not particularly adept with the crossbow, did what he was told but rarely any more than that, and little apparent desire than to do his time and get out of the army. And yet, he was bright. He could read words that gave Listowk a headache. He had a view of things bigger than most of the soldiers', even if it was usually pessimistic. But most of all, there was something about the man that Listowk felt was special. Not thaumic special—more like a wild card in a high-stakes game of coppers and silver. Carny looked like a lowly three, but damn if he wouldn't reveal himself to be an ace when it really mattered. At least, that's what Listowk hoped would be the case one day. "There's potential in him, I feel it in my bones. We just haven't found it yet."

Sinte snorted. "He hides it well. Fine. I want you back here at dawn. Make sure you take a couple of signal stars with you. If the slyts do make a move tonight, I want some warning."

"Our screams should handle that nicely."

"Uh-huh. See that they do," Sinte said. "If the bastards do decide to attack, we'll do what we can, but in the dark—"

Listowk cut him off. "We're on our own. I know. Just do me a favor and carry what's left of me down to the ocean. I don't want to rot away in this place."

Sinte didn't smile, didn't even look. "When you're dead, you're dead."

"By your command," Listowk said, lightly tapping his chest with his closed fist. *Ass.*

CHAPTER EIGHT

NIGHTFALL CLOAKED THE MOUNTAIN as the insect chorus grew to a high-pitched whine. It set Carny's teeth on edge. He'd seen enough spiders and other bugs to last a lifetime, and now he was being forced to stay among them all night. In the dark. He started to get up from the ground but forced himself to remain sitting.

He needed something to take the edge off and keep the damn bugs away. *Snow.* He looked over at the soldier nearest him.

"Hey, Wiz, borrow some snow?"

Wizard Orlo Twick looked up from a pile of bowstrings he was untangling. His broad, freckled face and lank red hair draped over his forehead made him look pumpkinlike in the starlight. As the shield had yet to see any battle, Wiz's ministrations to the wounded had consisted of rubbing ointment in cuts and bug bites and applying the odd leech to bleed a soldier's humors back into balance. With little else to do, he'd taken on some extra mundane chores like waxing spare bowstrings.

"You were issued camphor this morning like everyone else," Wiz said, refusing to use the slang term for the white crystalline blocks. He shook his head as he focused on teasing a string from the pile. When he pulled one free, he laid it on a large flat leaf he'd placed on the ground in front of him. "You got a hen's egg worth."

Carny rolled his neck and shoulders, imagining bugs crawling over his skin. "Used it up already. C'mon, be a mate. Just a little?" Watching Wiz separate the mess of bowstrings unsettled Carny. It reminded him of a carrion bird pulling out lengths of intestine from a dead animal. A quick smoke would set him right.

Carny reached into the small canvas bag all soldiers were issued for personal items and pulled out an even smaller, dark green cloth bag with a thin yellow cotton drawstring. He untied the string and upended the contents into his lap. An ebony pipe and pewter tinderbox with flint fell into his lap.

"You mean you used it? All of it?" Wiz asked.

"Every last speck," Carny said. "They don't give us near enough." He tried not to watch Wiz's hands and see them as bird beaks tearing into flesh.

"How could you use it up so fast?"

"I just did," Carny said, frustrated that he was having to explain himself. He put his small pack to the side and flipped open the lid on one of the haversacks Squeak had delivered. He reached in and pulled out a misshapen lump the size of a helm. It was bread, or at least had been at one point in the distant past. He could feel the gouges in the crust where rats had nibbled on it. *Fucking navy*. They were dumping their rotten ship's stores on the beach and the copper-pinching Seventh Phalanx quartermaster was sending the worthless garbage to them.

"You're not eating it, are you?" Wiz asked. "You'll throw your humors out of balance. The human body is very similar to a tree in this regard. Consider the four essential liquids within you like sap. They flow in harmony, each with its purpose."

Carny looked up from the bread. "Could we not talk about my innards? I'm feeling queasy enough as it is."

Wiz shrugged. "I spent half a year studying the body of man. We dissected several corpses. I've seen the damage done by not keeping the humors in balance."

"I get it, I get it," Carny said, regretting that he'd asked Wiz anything. He reached over to his left, where he'd set down his quiver and crossbow, and slipped the small dagger he kept inside the quiver out of its sheath. With the blade in one hand and the bread in the other, he tapped the rock-hard crust gently with the blade until he found the soft spot. He jabbed the point into it and pried. The bread split apart, revealing a hollow center, inside of which were three fist-sized balls of shredded brown leaves.

"Now *that's* right as rain," he said, holding the open loaf up to his nose and taking a deep sniff.

"If Sinte catches you with that, he'll have your guts on a limb," Wiz said, gently twirling a bowstring between his thumb and forefinger. With his other hand, he dipped a finger into a shallow tin of wax and then began daubing it on the string.

Carny looked around to see if anyone else was listening.

"Sinte's too busy polishing anything that doesn't move. Besides, Wild Flower is just a smoother tobacco. Sort of evens out the bumps of the day," Carny said, lowering his voice so that it didn't carry. "We're not in the Kingdom anymore. Live a little. I could trade you a pipe bowl's worth for, say, a half egg of snow."

Wiz stopped waxing his string and looked at Carny. The expression on his face was stern. "I do not smoke or drink. The Leaves of Knowledge and Morality that fell from the Sacred Tree are clear on that. *Consume not any herb or liquid that cloudeth the mind, lest your way on the path to enlightenment be lost.*" He then held his right hand out, palm up, fingers spread, before closing it into a fist and bringing it in to rest over his heart.

"Right, sorry, I forgot you were a practicing Dendro," Carny said, hoping he sounded sincere. While his mother had been devout, her zeal for the Kingdom's dominant faith had not rubbed off on him.

"*Dendrolatrian,*" Wiz said, correcting him, "Order of His Most Illuminated High Druid." He reached under his tunic and pulled out a tiny bronze medallion of a tree and a leather pouch on a string around his neck. There was a bulge inside the pouch about the size of a human eye.

Orthodox, great. "Yes, of course, it was silly of me to suggest it."

"Have you given thought to the afterlife, Carnan? How will your soul rise to the great forest in the sky if you do not plant your roots in the foundation of the one truth?"

"That's a great question, and I'll give it some serious thought. Right now, though, I have a question for you. Would you trade your snow for a hunk of cheese, then? Not a speck of mold." There was more than one way to skin the bark off a tree.

Wiz sighed and put away the pouch and tree medallion. "Goat or cow?"

"I don't know, it's cheese," Carny said. "Look, my fist's worth for a half egg of snow. That's a steal... sorry, great trade."

"That is generous," Wiz said, pausing in his waxing.

"So it's a deal?"

"No, sorry," Wiz said, wiping his fingers against his tunic and restringing his crossbow. "I traded mine earlier with Lingletti for a length of leather thong and some dried fish."

"You're a real pal, you know that?" Carny said.

"Shut the hell up," Shield Leader Sinte hissed, suddenly appearing out of the darkness. "I don't know what you're prattling on about, Carny, but if there's a slyt within ten bowshots, he sure as hell heard it."

Carny stuffed the bread back into the haversack and held up his hands in submission while Wiz focused on his crossbow. Even in the dark, Carny was sure he saw the trace of a smile on Wiz's face.

"Sorry, SL," Carny whispered, doing his best to stare daggers at Wiz. "But the Bard's still strumming and I can't be any louder than him."

"Nice bloody inscription for your grave tree," Sinte said, melting back into the dark.

Something crawled across Carny's right thigh. He tried to stifle his yelp and succeeded in biting the inside of his cheek. It was going to be a long night.

* * *

"IT'S NOT GETTING any darker," Sinte said, looking at Listowk as if expecting him to dispute the natural progression of dusk to nightfall.

"We'll be going then," Listowk said, easing himself into a standing position with the least effort required. It was sticky hot and his armpits were irritated from chafing.

"Keep it tuned and tight," Sinte said, using a bowman's expression and softening his voice so that it didn't come across as an accusation. It surprised Listowk because Sinte normally avoided sounding so… human.

"So it'll fly fast and right," Listowk responded, reaching out a hand.

It met only empty darkness. Sinte was already walking away.

Listowk turned and surveyed the mountaintop. Small orange lights dotted their camp as men settled in with their pipes. He'd let them enjoy one more smoke. The slyts sure as splinters knew they were there.

"Night patrol to me," he said, just loud enough to carry to the nearest soldiers. They would pass it along. Shouting was just so much wasted energy.

"It's suicide, is what it is," Voof muttered.

Listowk sighed. Sinte was right. Vooford *was* an infection.

"It's a stroll among the trees," Listowk said, smiling hard; no one could see it, but he hoped it came through in his words. "And it's for all our benefit, so let's focus on more important things."

That should have been the end of it.

"We shouldn't even be up here," Voof continued.

Listowk looked around for Sinte, expecting to see him charging across the camp with his hewer drawn, but the SL was nowhere in sight.

There was a grumble of agreement from a couple of soldiers standing by Voof. The shield was with him. This was all Listowk needed. Despite the darkness, the air felt even more humid than it had during the day. Moving, even just raising an arm to run it across your forehead, took effort.

Listowk sensed the rising anger and was tempted to let it take its course. Sinte was an ungrateful prick. He could deal with it. See how well he managed. But as sweet as that might have been, letting things spiral out of control helped no one.

"Inside voices, my darlings, the slyts have big ears," he said, walking slowly around the summit and patting each soldier on the arm or shoulder. He did it gently, careful not to irritate sunburned skin and frayed nerves. It was also a sly way of checking to see that no one's skin was dry, which was a clear sign they were suffering from sun vapors and close to passing out. "The SL is looking out for your best interests. I'll be tucked in just a little ways from here, all snug and safe, keeping both eyes open for you. Me and the boys will be fine, and so will you, if you remember your training and keep a level head on your shoulders. Take a good long drink from your water skin every eighth of a candle. You know Weel's edict. Anyone collapsing from vapors will be brought up on charges."

"I drink any more water, I'm going to puke," a soldier said.

"The powder we have to put in the water makes it taste like piss."

"Better than a lashing," Listowk said, spending time on each word so that message got through. Silence, save for the sound of men packing their gear and drinking, reigned. If Vooford said another word, Listowk feared he'd have to shoot the fool.

Silence. Beautiful, peaceful silence... except for the bloody insects. But thankfully Vooford, whether because of the grace of the High Druid or pure luck, was keeping his mouth shut.

The building tension slid away, leaving the night darker yet somehow less threatening than it had been a moment before. Listowk said a silent prayer that Sinte was still nowhere to be seen.

"That's my good boys," Listowk said, making an exaggerated show of lifting up his own water skin, uncorking the spout, and taking a drink. It did taste terrible.

"I wish you weren't going," a soldier said.

Listowk peered into the dark. A pale, frightened-looking boy was staring at him. "You're Omisk, right?"

"Fletcher's Assistant Feern *Ahmist*," the soldier said. He started to come to attention, then thought better of it and ended up adjusting his helm and slinging his crossbow over his left shoulder. "I landed a week ago with the last cohort."

"Already a seasoned veteran then," Listowk said, reaching out and placing his hand on the back of the boy's neck. It was hot and sweaty. He steered Ahmist a couple of yards away from the others. He let his hand drift down the boy's back and along the main spar of his crossbow.

"I went through all the training," Ahmist said, turning his head to see what Listowk was doing. "Even though I'm only an FA, I know how to fire a crossbow."

"Never doubted it for a moment," Listowk said, letting his fingertips trace the bolt sitting in the spar groove. His fingers gently brushed the taut bowstring and came to rest on the iron safety lever. "But in the future, I'd suggest you don't sling a loaded crossbow on your back, especially one with the safety lever off."

Click.

"Oh, no," the boy said, "I—I thought I had, I mean in all the—"

"There's a lot to remember, but making sure your crossbow isn't going to kill you or one of your comrades is one of the more important ones," Listowk said, patting the boy's weapon and then bringing his hand up to rest on his shoulder. "If the SL had seen that… well, I think you can guess what his reaction would have been."

Ahmist's lower lip trembled as he spoke. "It's all so much. All of it. I don't know how the rest of the men are so calm. All we've done is walk up and down the mountain, but I think I see slyts everywhere… so far the only ones I've really seen have been the ladies back at camp."

Listowk shook his head. "Ah, yes, the *ladies*. You heed my warning and stay away from them. They pose a danger greater than any you'll face up here," Listowk said.

"They didn't look that dangerous," Ahmist said, his voice

trailing off as he turned and looked into the dark toward the ocean. "I know the Leaves of Knowledge and Morality say they are evil…."

Listowk kept his smile to himself. He could easily imagine the struggle going on inside the young soldier, his beliefs at war with his loins.

"The LOKAM says many things, but while you're out here, best if you listen to me, all right?"

Ahmist reached under his aketon and tunic, fishing out a small Sacred Tree made of oak on the end of a string necklace.

"I can not abandon my faith, not even in war. To be a Dendrolatrian is to be one with the High Druid, now and forever," Ahmist said, his voice growing stronger.

Listowk paused before responding. True believers usually went one of two ways out here—they lost faith or they became zealots. In either case, the result was often a dead soldier.

"Remember your training and you'll be fine," Listowk finally said. He wanted to say more, but felt the presence of someone standing behind him.

"Ready as we'll ever be," Carny said.

"Then it's off on our little adventure," Listowk said. "Keep an eye on the shield for me while I'm gone, Fletcher's Assistant Feern Ahmist." He winked at the young soldier.

Ahmist stood to attention. "By your command."

Listowk turned to look over his shoulder. His picked men were there. "Stay quiet, no smoking, and safety latches on. Make sure your bolt is securely locked in the groove—it won't do to come across some slyts and there's no bolt when you go to fire. And keep close. Anyone gets lost, the slyts will probably find you before we do. Okay? Let's go."

CHAPTER NINE

L EAD CROSSBOWMAN UGEN LISTOWK led the patrol across the camp and into the jungle on the western side. The rest of the shield watched them go in silence. Sinte didn't bother to see them off, but Listowk was fine with that.

"Psst, LC? Why are we heading west?" Carny asked.

Listowk stopped among some leaves. He nestled himself in, enjoying the rubbery feel of them on his bare arms. He waited for the other four to group around him. Wraith crouched and pivoted while the rest remained standing. "Assume we're being watched. We head west out of the camp, the slyts think we're going west. When we're in the clear, we'll loop around and pick up the path on the ocean side. I'll stay on ST. Wraith, you drift back and cover our tail. If any slyts try to follow us, don't engage, but let me know. Clear?"

Four heads nodded.

"Good, now remember what I taught you. Land on the balls of your feet, grab and hold the branch as you pass, and then put it back, and if you think you see or hear something, don't shout. Two tongue clicks to hold, three for slyts."

Listowk turned and ducked under the palm fronds, easing his way through the jungle. There was just enough starlight coming through gaps in the canopy that he could navigate without tripping. It helped that the undergrowth was soft and pliable. Still, he kept his pace slow, checking regularly to make sure the others were close behind.

It was hot, sticky work moving through the foliage while trying to keep quiet. Sweat trickled into the corners of Listowk's eyes, making them sting. He paused and pulled out a small cotton handkerchief tucked into his belt. Lifting the brim of his helm, he held the liner away from his forehead and stuffed the handkerchief in it so that it covered his forehead. With the extra cloth, the helm felt snug, like the beginnings of a headache, but it would keep the sweat out of his eyes. He'd be better off with no helm at all, but if Sinte saw that, he'd have him up on charges.

Listowk looked around, moving his head slowly while keeping his eyes fixed. He doubted he'd see a slyt, but he might possibly catch some movement. The jungle was a jumble of black and gray shadows. There could be a slyt phalanx standing five feet away and he would never see it. The idea that somewhere out in the dark an arrow was being aimed at his throat, or his crotch, wasn't easy to shake. He realized he'd tucked in his chin and lowered his crossbow to protect himself.

Letting out a long, slow breath, Listowk raised his glance and brought his crossbow back up. He felt naked, his flesh as insubstantial as cobwebs. The jungle humbled him, but he didn't resent it. In exposing his vulnerability, the jungle revealed more of itself to him.

Knowing his eyes could only tell him so much, Listowk focused on his ears. The night sounds of the jungle, chaotic and maddening when he'd first arrived, were giving up their secrets. He'd made a point of leaving the security of their beach encampment—without informing Sinte—and walking into the jungle. He wanted to know this land. What he found amazed him. The "noise" had an order and rhythm that ebbed and flowed throughout the night. In a way he'd never be able to explain, the jungle was talking to itself.

There was a clear difference in the sounds this high up the mountain. The jungle's accent had subtly changed. But what he strained to hear was what wasn't there. Just as the insects had quieted around the patrol, they paused in their chorus as predators neared.

There. A good two hundred yards down the western slope and a hundred to the north, a sliver of silence weaved its way through the jungle. Listowk tilted his head to better track it. Whatever it was moved at a steady, slow pace. It could be slyts—they were wily little bastards—but he suspected it was probably a jaguar or some other big cat. He remained still until the silence faded and he could no longer follow its path.

Realizing the rest of the patrol would be getting antsy, he started walking again, using his left hand to gently push aside leaves and fronds. He could tell by the outline of the leaf whether or not it hid thorns and did his best to steer around those. It had been a quick and painful lesson when they'd first arrived. The plant life in Luitox seemed no more inclined to be hospitable than the damn slyts.

He rested the butt of his crossbow on his right hip and kept the weapon pointing forward as he walked. The safety latch on his weapon was off, but he was walking spear tip. Anything in front of him wasn't going to be friendly. He slid his main finger up and around the stock and gave the bowstring a tap to make sure it was taut. He wasn't about to get caught with a limp string. He cursed himself for not reminding the others, but he had to trust that he'd trained them well enough.

He started to duck under a hanging vine, then stopped and backed up a pace. The vine was really a section of coil from a snake draped over a series of branches. The part of the snake Listowk could see looked as thick as a man's biceps. It was too dark to make out its markings, but judging by its size he figured it for a squeezer. Probably not poisonous, but they still bit hard. He backed up another step and decided now was as good a time as any to begin looping around to the east.

It took close to an eighth of a candle to make the full loop and pick up the main path the shield used going up and down the mountain. After the slow, energy-sapping walk through the jungle, it was tempting to step out onto the path and follow it the rest of the way to their hiding place for the night, but Listowk resisted the urge. They hadn't taken the long way around to suddenly pop out into the open.

"You see something?" Big Hog asked, ambling to a halt beside Listowk.

Listowk looked around the big farmer to see where the rest of the patrol was. He counted two more helms and a tall bush. Wraith. *The boy's a natural.*

"We'll stay off the path and ease our way down to the ruts," he said. "Should be fifty, sixty yards. Keep close and stay quiet."

He waited a beat to see if anyone had anything to say. It was important for the men to feel they were being heard. "All right, follow me." He led them down using trees to control his descent. His thighs ached and his arms stung from dozens of tiny cuts despite his best efforts to avoid the thorns, but he wasn't sorry he'd taken the difficult route. They were all still alive, and the slyts, as far as he could tell, had no idea where they were. The same couldn't be said for the whereabouts of the rest of the shield.

The rut appeared bigger in the dark when he found it. He peered over the edge and couldn't see the bottom. It hadn't been more than five feet in the daylight, which meant it was still five feet in the dark. He thumbed on the safety latch on his crossbow, then pushed some fronds out of the way and sat down on the edge, letting his boots hang over. Keeping his crossbow out from his body, he half-turned to the left, stuck up his hand until he felt Big Hog grab it, then eased himself over the edge.

Big Hog's grip was strong and the back of his hand hairy. It felt like holding on to a bear's paw. Listowk walked his way down the slope, digging the toes of his boots into the dirt. He knew it was only a few feet, but it felt like he was hanging over a fathomless abyss. Gritting his teeth, he swung his right boot out, pointed down with his toes, and finally felt solid ground.

"I'm down," Listowk said, not caring that his whisper sounded elated. He squeezed Big Hog's hand and the soldier let go. Listowk clicked his tongue twice to keep the patrol in place and turned to survey the rut they would call home for the night. He thumbed the safety latch back off and peered down the little gully going away from the path. For as far as he could see, which wasn't too far, there was nothing there. He listened, nodding as the insects chirped and sang a familiar tune.

He followed the rut several yards deeper into the jungle until it branched into several smaller ones. The jungle vegetation was heavy, but mostly leaves and fronds again with no sign of heavy vines to trip a person. If something did happen tonight, this would be their escape route.

He turned and made his way toward the path, crouching low as he did so. The goat path they had trod up and down for weeks appeared through the jungle and he froze in place, because if he could see the path, anything on the path could see him.

After several heartbeats, he sank to his knees and crawled to the edge of the path. The smell of the jungle was more intense down low, rich and fetid. He breathed through his mouth, eased his head out through the leaves, and looked up and down the path. It was completely empty.

Listowk reverse-crawled a yard before standing up slowly, panting as he did so. The air was wet and hot and clung to him like a blanket. He realized he hadn't taken a drink from his water skin since they'd left the mountaintop and chided himself. He grabbed the skin, pulled the cork, and took a quick drink. He grimaced as the warm water went down his throat. Jamming the cork stopper back in, he went back to where the rest of the patrol waited.

"All meadow," he whispered, giving them the all-clear signal. He kept one eye on the path while he guided the rest of the patrol down the slope. Compared to his descent, the rest of the men slid down easily. "Carny, go a yard deep and keep watch on the jungle. Big Hog, grab some sleep, then switch with Carny at midnight."

"How am I supposed to know when that is?" Big Hog asked.

Listowk sighed. "We're right above the main camp down on the beach, and there are ships galore at anchor offshore. You'll hear the bells." The military was as obsessed with telling time as the druids and monks.

"Clever," Wraith said, his helm nodding like a bush in a breeze. He'd definitely picked up more foliage during their walk.

"I have my moments," Listowk said. "You watch the path. It's pretty open there so stay back a bit. Weasel, rest up and relieve him at midnight. I'll sit here in the middle for now and have a nap… then I'm going to do a little scouting. I'd like to know where Black Shield is holed up. Take a long drink of water. No smoking, no talking, and if you hear or see anything, you let me know right away."

"You really think the slyts will try anything?" the Weasel asked. His voice had a manic tone to it that Listowk didn't like.

"I don't know, but we're almost begging them to try. Let's just see if we can't make it to the dawn." Listowk paused for a moment, wondering if he was being prudent or just jumpy. Even if it was nerves, his caution meant he was still alive to feel them. "Look, my children, if the wind hits the branches and there's nothing else for it, follow the rut away from the path, then make your way down to the beach. Don't wait around—just run."

"Shouldn't we try to go back up to the rest of the shield?" Big Hog asked.

Listowk looked toward the top of the mountain before responding. "If the slyts really do make a move, there won't be anything up there to go back to."

CARNY WATCHED THE LC sleeping against the dirt slope. Listowk had removed his aketon and helm and eased himself into the jungle, draping himself around the dirt and vegetation like a wet rag. The LC looked as comfortable as if he were laid out on silk sheets and a down mattress.

The only jarring note was his crossbow cradled across his stomach. Though he looked dead to the world, Carny was certain that at the slightest hint of danger, the LC would spring up ready to fight. Still, seeing the crossbow rise and fall with each breath made Carny nervous. The safety latch had to be secure—it was the LC after all.

Curiosity getting the better of him, Carny inched closer to Listowk to see if the crossbow really was safed but froze when the LC made a noise. It sounded halfway between a growl and a curse. Carny looked up from the weapon. The snarl on Listowk's face was savage. The genial father figure was gone, replaced by something vicious. His eyes remained closed, however, and Carny let out his breath and eased farther back. Whatever the LC was dreaming about, Carny had no interest in it.

"Hey, Big Hog, you awake?" Carny whispered, crawling toward the farmer's position.

"You see something?" Big Hog asked. His voice was strong and clear, even as a whisper. He was definitely wide awake.

"Naw, just checking. I can't sleep. You want to switch watches?"

"Forget that," Big Hog said, shifting slightly in his seated position among some bushes. "I'm here 'til the bells sound, then it's nighty-night."

"Please? I'm going crazy just sitting here."

"Go bother Wraith then—I'm planting crops," Big Hog said. He sounded slightly out of breath in his exasperation.

"What the hell does that mean?" Carny asked. He imagined Big Hog daydreaming about walking a field with a plow pulled by oxen, gouging thick furrows in the soil while a plump Mrs. Big Hog waddled behind him, tossing seeds into the newly turned earth.

"What do you think it means? You need to see my cock to get the idea?"

"That's disgusting," Carny said, moving back away from the soldier. "How can you do that out here?"

"I do it everywhere. Keeps it fit and fine," Big Hog said, the bushes around him rustling lightly in a rhythmic fashion. "As the good leaves say, *'spread thy seed on the wind so that the fruit of your loins may grow in fertile soil.'*"

"For fuck's sake, I held your hand coming down the slope."

The rustling of the leaves stopped. "Fuck, you're a thorn at times," Big Hog said. "Can't concentrate worth a damn with your nattering. I'll have to try again later."

"Fuck you. I'm not the one rubbing his privates every chance he gets."

"You don't know shit. I got four kids back home now and another on the way, and I'm not even twenty years old. And they're all fit and bright. It's 'cause I keep my fluids moving. Just like water. You drink from a fast stream, not a stagnant pond. If you ever want kids, and I don't mean dullards, you should work yours more often."

Carny scooted back more. "Are all farmers like you?"

"The smart ones are," Big Hog said. "See, you need kids on a farm, but damn if they all don't need feeding and clothing, and now you even have to get them some schooling. You believe that? The king himself—well, I guess he's still the king—decreed all children have to learn to read and do maths like you got. Waste of time and silver if you ask me. I didn't learn to read and I turned out fine."

"Really? And what's your plan if a horde of slyts come sneaking up on us? You gonna spread your seed in the wind and hope it gets in their eyes?"

"Think I'd get a medal for that?"

"You're a pig," Carny said.

"Pigs are the smartest animals on a farm," Big Hog said. "Tastiest, too."

"Well, just keep your poker pointed away from me," Carny said, crawling away to let Big Hog get back to his business. He turned to see if Listowk had woken up, but the LC was still flat on his back, eyes closed. The snarl on his face was gone, but Carny didn't stare long in case it came back.

He got up on his feet in a low crouch and moved past Listowk and toward the path. He almost stepped on the Weasel. The soldier was curled up in a ball, snoring softly. Carny started to lift a leg to walk over him, then thought better of it and moved around him instead. Anyone waking up in the jungle at night seeing someone looming over him was not likely to react well. He moved on, reaching the path in a few more steps.

Wraith was gone.

Carny's stomach turned icy. *No, no, no, no!* He reached down and fumbled with the safety latch on his crossbow, finally getting it off.

"Wraith?" he whispered, peering into the jungle for any sign of the longbowman.

Stay calm. Breathe. "C'mon, Wraith, don't fool around."

It was as if the jungle had been plunged into a glacial lake. Carny started shivering. His strength evaporated and he was convinced he'd never move again. He gritted his teeth until he thought he'd break them and forced himself to take one more step forward.

"Lingletti, where the fuck are you?"

"What?" Wraith said, his breath tickling Carny's right ear.

Heat washed over Carny in a tidal wave. His legs spasmed and he tumbled down hard on his ass. Warm piss trickled down his thighs and puddled on the ground.

"Holy fuck, don't do that!" Carny whispered. He was no longer shivering but shaking.

"Me? What about you?" Wraith whispered back. "This ain't the latrine. If you gotta take a piss, go out in the jungle, not beside me."

"I—never fuckin' mind me, where the hell are you?" Carny asked, quickly getting up and moving away from the wet spot on the ground. He reached out a hand toward a bush and grabbed Wraith's upper arm. "You're being harvested!" he hissed. "You're turning into a tree!"

Wraith jerked his arm away and took off his helm, revealing his face. Palm fronds dangled from the helm so that it looked for all the world like one more plant in the jungle. "You chewing Wild Flower out here? Don't go all mystic LOKAM on me. I'm not turning into a tree, I'm just making sure no slyt can see me, same as the LC does. All that shiny metal we wear is just a big flag saying 'Here I am, come kill me.'"

Steadying his breathing, Carny focused his eyes and saw that Wraith was indeed still very much a man. The High Druid was not, in fact, harvesting Wraith's soul and turning him into a tree after all. "Sinte would probably court-martial the entire shield if we did that."

"His book of rules isn't any good out here," Wraith said, turning away from Carny to scan the path. "Aren't you supposed to be sleeping?"

Carny shook his head. "Can't. Too keyed up. Tried talking with Big Hog, but he's planting crops." He pulled a handkerchief out of his trouser pocket and stuffed it into his cotton undergarment to sop up the piss.

Wraith let out a snort. "One of these days, he'll set his cock on fire with all the rubbing he does." He turned again and studied Carny. "If you're going to stay here, then start putting some leaves on your helm and armor."

"I'm not dressing up like a bush," Carny said, pulling his hand out of his trousers and rubbing it on the ground.

"Then get the fuck away from me. I'm not dying out here because of someone like you."

That stung. "Fine, I'll wear some damn leaves if that will make you happy," Carny said, setting his crossbow down and grabbing some ferns and other leaves from around him.

"Not like that," Wraith said, swatting at Carny's hand. "You've got to place the dark side out. It ain't windy, and you only see the underside of leaves when it gets windy."

"There's a wrong way to wear jungle plants?"

"Watch the path; I'll get you sorted," Wraith said, leaning his bow against a swath of fat, drooping leaves. "The slyts have lived here forever. They know this land. If we're going to beat them, we have to think like them... otherwise *we're* going to be leaves in the eternal wind."

"You don't really think the slyts could beat us? We don't lose," Carny said, his chest swelling. "Look at all those ships that just arrived. The slyts don't stand a chance."

"I remember hearing that a year ago, but here we are, and

they keep sending more ships. Why do you think that is?"

Carny had thought about it, but he saw it as a sign of confidence and strength. "What, you honestly believe the slyts are any match for the Kingdom? They shoot a few arrows and scamper. That's all they do. Well, that and there are the whores and beggars outside the main camp." *And the peddlers of greasy meat chunks on bamboo sticks, those copper and tin good-luck trinkets in the shape of tiny palm fronds, and Wild Flower*, he thought to himself.

"All I know is," Wraith said, tucking a handful of long, slender leaves in the cloth pockets of Carny's aketon, "I ain't taking no chances. Out here, it's a lot like hunting. You get one shot. When I hunted, if I missed, I just went hungry. Here, you die."

"If you're going to be all morbid, I'll go back to Big Hog. At least he's focused on living, even if it is disgusting."

"So go," Wraith said, threading a final palm frond with some thin vine and draping it around Carny's helm.

"Fine," Carny said, vowing to take off the jungle crap as soon as he did. He started to turn to leave, then turned back. "Wiz said he traded you for his snow. Can I borrow some?"

The bushes around Wraith rustled for a moment, and then a hand reached out from the dark with a lump of camphor in it. "How about if you promise to not come back the rest of the night, you can have it all?"

Carny tried to think of a comeback but decided he'd rather have the snow, so he grabbed it from Wraith's hand and turned to go. "You're a pal."

"You still here?"

Fuck you, too. Carny got two steps away when he remembered his crossbow and backtracked to pick it up. If Wraith saw, he didn't say anything. Carny flipped the safety latch back on and made his way past the sleeping Weasel. He was going to swing around Listowk when he realized the LC was gone.

He hurried past the empty spot and made his way to Big Hog's position. "Psst, Big Hog, you see the LC? He's not here."

Big Hog turned and looked at him before turning back to

keep watch. "Yeah, said before he was going to stretch his legs and see what he could see." Carny was relieved that the bushes weren't rustling around him.

"I didn't think he was serious. Out there all alone…" The thought made Carny's back shiver.

Big Hog grunted. "He was made for this place, you know? One of those folks that you wouldn't look twice at on the street, but out here… damn, he's more slyt than human. Wraith's like that, too."

"What about me?" Carny asked, rustling his vegetation loud enough to get Big Hog to turn around.

Big Hog glanced at Carny and shook his head. "You? You make more noise than a herd of cattle going to market on a cobblestone street."

"Oh," Carny said. "Well, I'm going to get some sleep, so try to keep it down."

Big Hog didn't bother to respond.

Carny worked his way back to his little nook along the dirt slope and settled in.

I can be just as good as Listowk or Wraith, but why bother? The slyts were peasants, whores, and a few rebels who shot off arrows and then fled. The Kingdom would restore order and before long they'd all be on the next ship home. Learning to live in this jungle would be wasted effort.

The cool feel in the palm of his hand reminded him of the ball of snow there. He brought it up to his nose and drew in a deep, long sniff. His nostrils flared as the icy smell raced through them into his skull, making his eyes water. He started rubbing it over his exposed flesh and sighed as the snow touched his skin. All he needed now was a pipe full of Wild Flower and he'd be set… but there was no way he could risk lighting up.

He settled on mixing a little of the weed with a healthy pinch of snow and sticking it in his left cheek. The whole left side of his face immediately went numb and he smiled, ignoring the drool dripping down his chin.

He reached up and slid his helm up and off his head, letting it roll down his back and off to the side. He laid his crossbow on the ground beside him and leaned his head back against the dirt slope, crushing some earth with the back of his skull, forming a perfectly shaped rest for his head. He closed his eyes, savoring the cool, sharp tang of momentary bliss.

Fuck the Lux, he thought, smiling to himself. *Fuck the Lux.*

CHAPTER TEN

"YOU SURE HE'S STRONG enough for this?" Jawn asked. He held up his small brass-framed oil lantern with its glass panels, marveling that it had survived the trip in his luggage. He trained the light on the wizened creature yoked to the two-wheeled cart that was to be the conveyance into Gremthyn and Rickets's special bar. *So this is a slyt.*

Scrawny only began to describe what Jawn was looking at. He'd seen corpses before at the RAT, including those cut up to reveal the innards and muscle and bone. This slyt reminded him of one of the skeletons. Every joint was knobby and large compared to the limb it was attached to.

"He might look like a bundle of sticks wrapped in parchment, but these slyts are tough," Rickets said.

Jawn was more focused on the appearance of the slyt. The poor thing looked like death in waiting. He stood silently in the yoke, chewing on something and periodically spitting out a dark stream of juice. Jawn stepped forward, bathing the slyt in light.

"His skin…"

"Yeah, disgusting, isn't it?" Rickets said, clearly enjoying Jawn's first encounter with a native. "Look like they never wash, which is probably not far from the truth."

Jawn shuddered. The slyt's skin was mottled. Instead of a

single pigment it was a streaky mess of several shades of brown and green. It was as if someone had painted the slyt.

"Is it a disease?"

"If it is, they all have it. It does vary though. I've seen some that have coloring like tree bark and others that look like their entire body was tattooed with leaves."

"Well, he's still a person," Jawn said.

Gray wisps of hair sprouted from the slyt's wrinkled ears, while his completely bald head both reflected and absorbed the lantern light. The dark spots of his skin made it appear as if the slyt's head had missing pieces. The slyt's eyes were the typical rheumy orbs one saw in the elderly. They didn't twinkle with mirth or flash with menace… more like water and stare aimlessly.

Jawn moved closer to the slyt, doing his best to demonstrate a bond of kinship with the slyt and put Rickets in his place. An odor crept into Jawn's nose and he gagged, halting after a couple of steps. Person though he may have been, the slyt stank. His simple garb of dun-colored short pants and watery-green, sun-bleached vest of thin cotton gave off a pungent mix of aromas that made Jawn's own eyes water.

"It's wrong to use him as a beast of burden," Jawn said, retracing his steps and hoping it looked like he was simply pacing. He did his best to breathe through his mouth. "There must be other transport to take us to this tavern you know."

Undercutting Jawn's advocacy, the slyt spit out a red-tinged stream of juice from some kind of nut he was chewing and gave Jawn a quizzical look. Then he broke wind. He was barely five feet tall, and the smell vastly exceeded his presence.

"Civilization at its zenith," Rickets said, coughing as he climbed into the cart. He settled himself on the tattered canvas-covered board serving as the seat and slouched down against a similarly upholstered backrest. "Unless you want to wait for a team of brorras," Rickets added, "I'd suggest you climb on."

Jawn knew further protest was pointless. He wasn't about to walk a road in a foreign land soon to be shrouded in darkness.

This was a war zone, and he was damn tired.

"What's a brorra?" Jawn asked, tossing his two bags to Rickets one at a time.

Rickets caught the bags and stowed them, then looked to the sky. "Apparently the army doesn't bother teaching officers a damn thing about the land they're invading," Rickets said. He suddenly stood up in the cart and looked around. "How the fuck do they expect us to win a war they don't understand!?"

Jawn stepped back from the cart. This was a new side of Rickets. "I didn't mean to upset you. This is all so new."

Rickets blinked and seemed to realize where he was. He turned to Jawn. His eyes were large and rigidly focused.

"You're right. This is your first day here and I, well, I can sometimes be a bit dramatic," Rickets said. "It was a long flight. Took more out of me than I thought." He sat back down, a smile appearing on his face.

Jawn nodded. "It was a long flight. Still, this is no way to treat the elderly or a slyt," Jawn said, climbing up.

Rickets leaned forward. "Hey!" Rickets shouted, waving at the slyt. *"Viyor dass ghont, haxạn jhi zer phey fwa li?"*

The slyt spit on the ground, flicked his left ear with his finger, and pointed at Rickets. It clearly wasn't a sign of affection. The slyt then turned his back to them, bent down, picked up the two long poles jutting out from the cart, and began walking. The slap of his sandaled feet on the dirt was eerily similar to that of a horse's.

"What did you ask him?"

Rickets leaned back and handed one of Jawn's bags to him. "Would he prefer to ride while *you* pulled the cart. Apparently, he's content to keep the arrangement as is."

The temptation to wipe the satisfied smile off of Rickets's face with a well-placed punch stayed with Jawn for quite a while.

As dusk gave way to dark and the dirt road stretched on without any sign of ending, a sense of unease gripped Jawn. He'd expected to see other carts, and definitely Kingdom soldiers manning checkpoints, but other than the emaciated corpse of a dog a half a mile back, they had had the road to themselves. The countryside offered little in the way of distraction. Jungle lined their route, sporadically thinning out to reveal small fields that appeared to be planted with bushes in brown ponds. The crowny had dozed off, and it was the quietest he'd been since Jawn met him.

"...three cups of oil will make it nice and wet," Rickets murmured, opening his eyes and looking around.

"What?" Jawn asked, too surprised to stay quiet and hope the man would fall back to sleep.

"What, what?" Rickets asked, rubbing his eyes and yawning.

"You were talking about... ," Jawn started to say, then decided he really didn't want to know. "I mean, I was asking you if it's always this hot here," Jawn said, prying himself from the backrest and pulling his sodden tunic away from his body. He felt as if he were smothered in congealing grease.

"Hot? This is nothing," Rickets said, sitting up a little straighter. "Wait until the summer gets here. Keep your eyes open too long, and the heat will boil the jelly in them."

"Sounds divine," Jawn said. He despised the heat. His decision to volunteer was not weathering its first day in Luitox well.

"You get used to it," Rickets said, settling back down on the bench. "It worms its way into you, the heat. Eventually, you just don't notice it. I mean, it's still hot as hell, but you build up a tolerance."

Talking about the warmth here only made it worse. "Where is everyone?" Jawn asked, swinging his arm around to take in the empty roads and fields. "They all go to bed early around here? I haven't seen a soul."

"It's night, and we're not at the city outskirts yet. The farmers stay inside come nightfall. Groups of slyts, either from the Forest Collective or sympathetic to their cause, have been infiltrating the area. Quite brazen, really, but then I did tell you this."

Jawn became more alert. "I thought you were just talking. Is the Forest Collective really this far east? If you had told me that before we left, I never would have agreed to this."

"I surmised that very thing," Rickets said, "hence my not telling you. But not to worry—our driver is no more eager to die than we are, and with you being a thaum, I figure we're as safe as girls in a High Druid monastery."

Jawn sighed and regretted yet again engaging Rickets in conversation. They rode on in silence. Before long, the rutted dirt road—doing its best to jostle Jawn's insides into mulch—abruptly transitioned to a smooth ride. Jawn looked down and made out wide, flat fieldstones laid with some care. While still a far cry from the precision cobble work of the Kingdom's major cities, it was skilled labor and a welcome relief. Their porter, which Jawn had finally decided to call him after rejecting Rickets's more colorful suggestions, seemed to appreciate the change in the road as well, as his pace suddenly accelerated.

"We'll be there in no time now," Rickets said, his voice perking up. "A candle eighth at the most."

Jawn nodded. A hot, wet odor of raw sewage struck him and they couldn't get there fast enough. Small, scurrying black shapes darted across the road as their cart approached. In the dark, it was too difficult to make them out, but Jawn knew they were rats.

"The outskirts of Gremthyn," Rickets said, flourishing his hands in mock pomp and circumstance. "You can smell the civility from here."

Their small cart negotiated a few twists and turns as it descended a low ridge. With each yard, the heat and the smell grew.

A small orange glow winked into existence several yards ahead to the right of the road. Jawn sat up straight; images of flaming arrows were still vivid in his mind. He reached down for the small hunting knife tucked into his left boot.

"Easy there, tiger, it's just a cooking fire," Rickets said.

Jawn noticed that Rickets was nevertheless sitting up as well. Their porter, however, seemed oblivious and kept going at a pace Jawn realized he himself would have had difficulty matching. And the slyt was pulling two full-grown men plus a cart.

As the cart pulled even with the glow, Jawn made out several slyts in similar dress as their own porter. Two tall slyts and three short ones. A family. A hut with bamboo walls and a palm-thatched roof stood a few feet behind them.

The slyts looked up as their cart went by. Jawn tensed, not sure what to expect, but the slyts simply stared at them before returning to whatever domestic chores they were doing. Jawn spotted a sixth slyt, a babe, latched to its mother's breast.

They passed by more cooking fires, and huts that began to look more substantial. The first cross street heralded two houses of gray brick construction, with waist-high stone fences surrounding them.

Over a dozen slyts stood near a small fire at the next intersection. They were dressed similarly to their porter and, oddly, did not appear to be talking but were staring raptly at the fire. It was as if they were in a trance. Each held some kind of farm implement—a shovel or a hoe, a couple with axes. The slyts slowly turned their gaze to the cart as they passed by.

"What's that all about?" Jawn asked.

Rickets waved for him to be quiet.

Jawn looked up the road. The dots of orange flame lining their way took on an ominous tinge. As their porter drew them past each one, Jawn saw that they weren't cooking fires but gathering places for young males. In each case, the slyts stared deep into the fire, their faces eerily lit.

Rickets leaned forward in the cart and spoke to their porter. *"Vust kì parg fera xa?"*

The slyt didn't turn or answer but broke out into a trot.

"Where's the nearest military outpost?" Jawn asked.

"A quarter mile to the right back there at the last intersection," Rickets said, never taking his eyes off the way ahead.

Jawn turned in the cart to look and then quickly spun back around. His heartbeat increased and the sweat drenching his body took on an icy feel. He drew in a long breath and let it out slowly before speaking. "There are slyts behind us. A lot of them."

Rickets nodded. "They look angry?"

This time, Jawn slowly eased his head around until he

97

could see out of the corner of his eye. With each intersection they passed, more slyts joined the crowd following them. Jawn estimated well over two hundred. Despite their youth, their calm demeanor was unsettling. Jawn slowly turned back until he was facing forward. "Some of them are carrying pitchforks and torches."

Rickets started to smile but then stopped when he caught Jawn's expression.

"Keep an eye out for ogres then," Rickets said.

His voice was surprisingly blasé, which was entirely the wrong reaction. This was a time to be concerned. Very concerned.

"What's going on?" Jawn asked.

Rickets looked over his shoulder before replying. "So how much time do you need to, you know, do what you do?"

"Are they going to attack us?!" Jawn's mind raced. He wasn't ready for this. Nothing since the moment he'd landed on Swassi Island was going the way he'd expected.

"You know how many times I've seen the natives gather like this, at night, since I've been over here? And all military-aged slyts to boot? Once, counting now."

"Get our mule to tell them we're on their side!" Jawn blurted.

Rickets's eyes widened and then he smiled. "I think you mean the person acting as our porter."

Even in the heat, Jawn felt his face flush. "I didn't mean... what I meant to say was—"

Rickets held up his hands to forestall Jawn's apology. "Let he who is without sin cut down the first tree."

"I'm not a specist," Jawn said, indignation giving power to his voice. "I believe that all species, no matter—"

"Uh, hold that thought," Rickets said, pointing up ahead. Jawn looked and the heat in his cheeks evaporated.

Slyts poured onto the street from every intersection. There had to be thousands of them. There was no longer any room for the cart to move forward, and their porter slowed and finally stopped. Slyts moved in front of, behind, and beside them. None of them spoke a word. Jawn realized that was the most unnerving thing—he expected angry shouts and gestures, but though they walked with purpose and carried weapons of convenience, the slyts looked... serene.

Jawn balled his fists to stop from screaming. Over a decade of training and study at the RAT had been in preparation for this, but instead of finding his center and solidifying his position in the environment, he felt untethered and adrift. His emotional response overwhelmed the courses in meditation, body control techniques, and agonizing memorization drills, which were critical to creating the necessary harmonics with the environment and the aether beyond. Everything he knew—had known—blurred like a shaken kaleidoscope. It was as if he'd never attended a single lecture.

"Rickets, what do we do?!" There was no way Jawn could defend them both from a horde of this size, even if they were predominantly youngsters. He needed control in order to construct and implement a thaumic process. Manipulating the forces of nature was not advisable for those with shaky dispositions.

For at least the third time that day, he knew he was going to die.

"Stay calm, and look like you're capable of something," Rickets said.

It might have been sincere, but all Jawn heard was disgust. It was his first day in the war and he was falling apart.

I can do this, Jawn told himself, forcing his gaze to unfocus. The difference was that for the first time in his life, it wasn't a matter of choice but of necessity. He pinched his nose between the index finger and thumb of his left hand, closed his mouth, and breathed out through his nostrils. The pressure popped his ears and left his head feeling fuzzy for a moment. When it cleared, he knew what to do.

Fear is a reaction. I am action.

Fear is a tool. Use it.

Jawn drew in a deep breath, plumbing himself until he found his core.

I am pole and ground. Energy flows through me.

He reached out his right hand and laid it on the steel rim of the cartwheel. His skin tingled with the first charge of energy.

My body is—

"Belay that," Rickets said, touching Jawn's shoulder, then quickly drawing his hand back as a thin bolt of lightning arced between them. "Sweet bloody hell, that stings!" He was shaking his hand. "Why aren't you screaming?"

Jawn clenched his jaws and slowly let out his breath. "It's... complicated. And it's... dangerous to interrupt a thaum during a process."

"Noted," Rickets said, blowing on his fingers. "But it was that or knock you cold." He held up a sheathed dagger with a large iron ball for a pommel on the end that looked purpose-built for that very task.

Jawn opened his hand and let go of the cart's wheel. He didn't bother with discharging, as Rickets had conveniently taken care of that.

Jawn finally saw why Rickets had him discontinue the process.

Slyts now streamed past them, their manner unchanged from before. Jawn and Rickets were in no apparent danger. Jawn tried to imagine a similar-sized group of men acting in such a manner and the only thing that came to mind was a funeral.

"What are they doing?" Jawn asked. The slyts moved slowly but with obvious purpose. The humid night air muffled what little noise they made, making their procession all that more eerie. Only the rustle of their clothing and the soft scuffing of their woven grass sandals marked their passage.

"Whatever it is, it's happening just up there," Rickets said, pointing to the next intersection.

Jawn straightened his back and stood up in the cart. He tensed, expecting some kind of reaction from the endless stream of slyts, but they ignored him.

"They're forming a circle, but I can't see what's in the middle of it," Jawn said.

"Just stay calm, and don't make any sudden movements,"

Rickets said, jumping down from the cart and walking forward to their porter.

Jawn wasn't sure if he should stay in the cart or get down but decided he'd rather be on foot if things went bad. He grabbed his two bags and jumped down.

Slyts moved past him with barely a glance. It was as if he were a stone in a river of fish—they simply eased around him as if he'd always been there. He peered closely at the torchlit faces as they passed, looking for signs of possession, madness, disease... anything that would explain this behavior.

Jawn clicked his tongue against his teeth and forced his body to relax. These slyts weren't going to attack them. He rolled his shoulders back and stuck his chin out.

I'm a thaum. They must sense it, just like Rickets did. Jawn placed his hands on his hips. He stood a full head taller than the slyts and probably had a good seventy pounds on them. He was a trained thaum *and* trained military officer in the Kingdom's army. He was in the best physical and mental condition of his life. Now he needed to act like it.

A radical thought popped into Jawn's mind. He stuck out a hand and grabbed a slyt carrying a shovel by the arm. "Excuse me, but what's going on? What are you protesting?"

The slyt stopped and looked down at Jawn's hand in obvious surprise. He didn't yell or swing his shovel at Jawn, but merely tugged his arm, trying to break free.

"I'm not going to hurt you; I just want some answers," Jawn said, keeping a firm grasp on the slyt's arm. It was as thin as a young girl's, but through the light fabric Jawn felt ropey muscle.

"He's an illiterate farmer's son—he doesn't have the foggiest what you're asking him," Rickets said, appearing at Jawn's side. "Best to let him go. They're ignoring us for now, but I can't tell how long that will last."

The dark tone to Rickets's voice worried Jawn. He released the slyt.

"They must be protesting something," Jawn said.

"The government," Rickets said. "They're all sons of farmers, fruit pickers, dosha growers, and the rest of the slyt peasantry. They're always upset about market prices."

"What's dosha?" Jawn asked, wondering if his question would set Rickets off again.

Rickets nodded. "Right, I do keep forgetting you are new here. Dosha is the main staple here. They eat it like we eat potatoes, except it's different. Imagine a potato the size of your eye with a black rind and the inside filled with white slime."

Jawn grimaced. "That sounds horrible."

Rickets smiled. "It is. The trick is you don't chew it. You douse it in spices and swallow globs of it down."

Something Rickets had said just before his description of dosha came back to Jawn. "Wait, you said they were all sons of farmers."

"Firstborn sons to be precise. Sent them into town to agitate."

"Is that normal?"

Rickets continued scanning around them as he talked. "It's a cultural thing. The firstborn male is sent in his father's place. Makes sense. Dear old Dad needs to stay in the orchard or whatnot, and if this turns out to be dangerous, well, Dad's not the one that gets the chop. Meanwhile, the other sons are still safe on the farm."

"What about us?"

Rickets looked up at Jawn with a cat's grin. "If it comes to that, I'm old enough to be your father."

CHAPTER ELEVEN

"D O YOU THINK THIS is connected to the slyts from the Western Wilds?" Jawn asked. Young slyts, all male from what Jawn could see, continued to stream along the road and move toward the intersection. "Maybe you were right about the Forest Collective stirring up trouble."

Rickets nodded. "The Forest Collective aren't just in Western Luitox. They're here, too." He waved his hand at the crowd. "But I don't think this is them. The Fuckin' C's wouldn't congregate like this in the open. They aren't that stupid, especially if there was a chance the Luitoxese army could snatch them up."

Jawn wanted to scream. None of this was how his war was supposed to start. He was vulnerable and all but alone and the air was so hot and wet he found breathing a challenge. He longed for the terrifying moments on the rag's back, if only to feel a breeze.

"Enough of this," Jawn said, pushing his way through the crowd toward the circle. He wasn't going to stand around one flick longer waiting for something to happen. The repeated shouts of his army instructor rang in his head: *Doing something is better than doing nothing.*

"Hoping for that first medal, are we?" Rickets asked, walking just behind Jawn.

"I'm done with following," Jawn said.

"So I see," Rickets said.

"You don't have to come along," Jawn said, not bothering to soften the statement. If Rickets departed right now Jawn wouldn't be upset in the least.

"Oh, I think I'll see this through," Rickets said, not sounding the least bit offended. "You're quite the commodity the Kingdom has invested significant treasure into training. As a crown representative it's my duty to see that investment isn't squandered or otherwise misappropriated."

"You mean killed?"

"That too. At the very least, I should stick around to gather up your parts if things go bloody."

Jawn didn't respond.

The two arrived at the open space in the ring of slyts and stopped. A circle fully ten yards in diameter had been marked out on the pavers with white and red flower petals. A space wide enough for a slyt to walk through interrupted the petals every twelve paces. At each of these openings, additional rows of petals radiated out like sunbeams. Slyts walked past Jawn and Rickets going in the opposite direction, extending the petal rows.

Jawn bent down and reached out to pick up one of the petals but stopped when he sensed he was being watched. He looked up. Every slyt near him was staring at his hand as it hovered over the petals.

"Rickets?"

"I'd say they'd prefer you didn't touch them," Rickets said.

Jawn twitched his fingers, toying with the idea of snatching up a petal, but the part of his brain focused on survival screamed bloody murder and he pulled back his hand and stood up.

An audible sigh rose up from the ranks of slyts.

"That was strange," Jawn finally said.

"Welcome to the Lux."

An elderly slyt with just the faintest wisp of gray hair on his head, wearing a bright green sheet wrapped around his legs, across his chest, over his left shoulder, and down his back, strode into the circle. He calmly directed a dozen young slyts dressed in similar green sheets, who were quietly accepting the farm implements from those present and then placing the tools in neat concentric rows within the circle.

"Do you think they're planning on going back to work tomorrow?" Jawn asked. The slyts continued to ignore them, instead walking around them as they handed over their cudgels, hoes, rakes, shovels, axes, and more. Soon, the rows of tools were stacked three feet high. Spaces had been left to allow the slyts to walk from the edge of the circle toward the center, where the senior slyt continued to oversee the activity with small hand gestures and the occasional nod of his head.

Rickets shrugged. "The government needs food for the army, so they put levies on the farmers' crops. In the last two years, the levies have doubled, and then doubled again. Add in the skimming, the bribes, and the outright theft, and the farmers are close to starvation. You can imagine how much the peasants appreciate it."

Jawn could. He could also see how such tactics would only work to push the slyts away from their own government and into the arms of the Forest Collective rebels. "Then why risk alienating the population?"

"Wars ain't cheap," Rickets said as if that explained it all.

Slyts holding large, shallow wooden bowls two feet across began walking among the crowd. Each bowl was filled with a pyramid of white powder.

"Now what?" Jawn asked.

"That's dosha flour. They use it for all kinds of ceremonies, everything from weddings to funerals."

Each slyt in the crowd received twin stripes of the powder on his forehead. The slyts holding the bowls then took a small portion between their fingers and sprinkled it into the outstretched hands of the slyt before walking on.

A slyt with a bowl stopped in front of Jawn and Rickets. The slyt hesitated, his powder-coated hand hovering over the bowl as he looked at them.

Rickets leaned forward, offering his forehead.

"What are you doing?" Jawn asked. "We still don't know what this is."

A gasp arose from the slyts around them. Jawn tensed. The slyt with the bowl looked back toward the elderly one in the circle, who peered at Rickets and Jawn and then nodded. The slyt turned back to them and smeared powder on Rickets's forehead before sprinkling a small amount in his outstretched hands. Jawn sensed the eyes of the slyts on him again.

"No, thank you," Jawn said to the slyt holding the bowl.

The slyt turned to look at the elderly slyt again, who shrugged. The slyt with the dosha flour moved on.

More slyts began walking among those who had gathered, tossing dosha flour into the air. Jawn coughed as he drew some in, and soon all around them was clouded with the fine particles.

More and more flour flew into the air, making breathing and seeing increasingly difficult.

"If we stay here we're going to suffocate," Jawn said, grabbing Rickets by the arm and hauling him away from the circle.

Rickets coughed. "You'd think the humidity here would keep the dust down, but damn if it doesn't feel dry enough to fry an egg."

Jawn stopped. The air was dry. When had that happened? He wiped his forehead with his fingertips. Not a droplet of sweat. He looked over at Rickets. His balding head no longer glistened. Jawn pounded his fist into his thigh. He'd been so focused on trying to understand the big picture, he'd forgotten to pay attention to the clues right in front of him.

The air was desert dry. He looked around. The dosha flour hung in the air like a thick fog.

"What is it?" Rickets asked.

Jawn turned back toward the circle. The elderly slyt stood in the center of it, his arms outstretched. He held a hoe in one hand and a pitchfork in the other. The tines of the pitchfork pointed to the sky, while the metal of the hoe rested on the ground. His eyes were open, and he was chanting. Jawn couldn't understand the words, but he felt their meaning.

"Oh, fuck..."

"Well now, young man, that kind of language is—" was as far as Rickets got before Jawn yanked his arm and began pushing through the crowd.

"Run, *run*!" Jawn kicked and shoved his way through the kneeling slyts, heedless of where he stepped.

"What is it?" Rickets shouted, finally loosing his arm from Jawn's grasp and leaping over several slyts to take the lead.

The sky above them crackled and the skin on the back of Jawn's neck stood up. He risked looking skyward. The belly of a churning storm cloud was descending over the crowd. Lightning flashed from deep within the cloud's interior, casting a sickly blue light on everything.

"It's thaumic!" Jawn shouted, running faster as the crowd grew thinner farther away from the circle.

Rickets turned as he raced along, losing his footing and crashing to the road. "Thaumic? Are you jesting? You're a damn thaum! How did you not see it?"

"Head for the wall!" Jawn screamed, gripping his leather bags tight to his ribs as he hurdled a kneeling slyt. He reached Rickets and lifted him to his feet without stopping. The crowny snarled at Jawn, but he tore off running and was soon ahead again, slipping between the slyts like a deer through the forest.

The first lightning bolt came down while they were still twenty yards from the wall. It was as if all sound drowned in a sea of white light. Jawn stumbled, falling to the road, his body numbed by the amount of energy. Thaums were trained to safely deal with huge, momentary surges of power—it was the keystone to creating a thaumic process—but only if one was ready for it.

Jawn tasted blood in his mouth and spit. He propped himself up on one elbow and turned to look back at the circle. The slyt was slowly getting back onto his feet. Smoke and sparks flowed from his now-charred green wrap. Even his eyebrows were smoldering. A pair of younger slyts rushed toward him, but he waved them off.

"How is he not dead?" Rickets asked, appearing at Jawn's side and hauling him to his feet. "Or is that something else you don't know?"

Jawn wobbled, unable to get a good feel for the road. He leaned heavily on Rickets and drew in a few breaths to clear his head.

"That supposed to mean something, or are you having a spasm?" Rickets asked.

Jawn looked down and saw that his right hand was shaking. He was pressing his thumb and forefinger together so hard they were turning white.

"There's a saying among thaums," Jawn said, looking back at the slyt. "'The line between glory and smoldering ash is this thick.'"

A chorus of wails rose up from the assembled slyts. Several climbed to their feet in obvious panic, but they didn't run. Instead, they began moving toward the circle. Those slyts still on their knees shuffled forward as well, drawing in tighter. This was not the proper reaction to a near-death experience.

"We need to get out of here." Rickets was already half-dragging, half-carrying him away, making for the wall.

The slyt at the center of the circle spoke in a soothing tone, and the moaning subsided. The slyts threw more flour into the air and dropped back to their knees.

"What's he saying?" Jawn asked.

Rickets didn't bother turning to look back. "Something about ashes and dust."

Above them, the storm cloud churned harder and more lightning flashed within its murky depths.

Jawn kept staring back. He'd never been this close to such a powerful thaumic process. It was frightening, and yet part of him desperately wanted to run the other way to study what the slyt was doing.

Appearing to take strength from the packed crowd, the slyt raised his shaking hands, firmly planting the blade of his hoe on the stones with one while lifting his pitchfork to the sky with the other.

"He's trying again," Jawn said, his reaction a mix of terror and admiration. Jawn doubted he would have survived a failed process using a tenth of that much power.

Rickets scooped Jawn up and ran the last few feet to the wall. Without waiting for Jawn to regain his feet, Rickets heaved and sent Jawn upward, where he landed on his stomach on the top of the wall. Rickets grabbed ahold of Jawn's dangling legs and pulled himself up using Jawn as a ladder. Once on top of the wall, Rickets hauled Jawn up the rest of the way.

Jawn pushed himself into an upright position and readjusted the strap of his leather bag, which was now wrapped around his neck. He turned to look back as the second lightning bolt hit.

A towering column of fire reaching from the ground to the storm cloud occupied the space where the thaum had stood. Chunks of burning debris flew everywhere. The lower half of a leg cartwheeled through the air, trailing flame and smoke. Other body parts too mangled to identify tumbled and fell between the gathered slyts. The flames ignited the floating flour dust, setting the very air on fire.

The gathered slyts did not run. Boiling sheets of orange-red flame washed over them like successive waves crashing on shore. If any of them screamed, Jawn couldn't tell. His ears were filled with a crackling roar that suffocated all other sound. Every slyt in the road was on fire. The smell of burning hair and roasting meat drove its way into his nose and down his throat.

"Sweet fucking High Druid!" Rickets exclaimed.

Some slyts stood, teetering on their feet even as the flames burned hotter. Like wooden marionettes, they jerked and staggered before collapsing back to the ground. Others remained motionless, kneeling in eternal prayer as the conflagration ravaged their bodies and burned them alive.

The air seared Jawn's face. He raised an arm to protect his eyes and saw that his uniform was smoldering. He launched himself backward over the wall and into a cemetery. Rickets jumped after him. They crouched by the wall, saying nothing. Shadows flickered and danced among the headstones as night turned to day. The roar of the flames now took on an eerie whistle. Jawn looked up. The storm cloud was beginning to rotate, slowly gaining speed. The column of flame looked more like a vortex, swirling in a tight spiral.

"What went wrong?" Rickets asked.

Jawn took in a breath to center himself and began coughing. It was like breathing flame itself.

"I don't know, but whatever it was, he fixed it the second time," Jawn said, ripping off a strip of his undershirt and wrapping it around his face to cover his nose and mouth. He knew he was staring, but he couldn't bring himself to blink. The image of what he'd seen wouldn't let him. "He meant to do this."

Rickets stared at him. "This? He's killed everyone, including himself. He's set the damn sky on fire."

Jawn looked up again, but not at the spinning cloud of flame above them. A similar cloud had appeared a mile farther east on the other side of the city.

Ignoring the heat raging down from the cloud above, Rickets stood up. "That's the old part of the city. Mostly government buildings and loyalists." A third column of fire erupted still farther in the distance. "Druid's balls, that's Galmorden." Rickets turned and looked down at Jawn. "Home of the ruling family."

Jawn shook his head, wishing the crackling, spitting sound of burning flesh would get out of his ears.

"Brilliant." Rickets sat down, resting his back against the wall. He quickly moved away from it though. "Hotter than a damn oven."

It took a moment for Rickets's words to register. "Brilliant? They're burning to death! All of them."

Rickets turned and looked at Jawn. The expression on his face made Jawn back away. The man's smile was demonic.

"Absolutely fucking brilliant. You were right. This is deliberate. Don't you see? In one glorious orgy of suicide, they've brought the plight of the peasantry front and center in a way nothing else could."

"They sent their sons to die! To be burned alive!"

Rickets held up his hand, his finger and thumb squeezed together. "This time, the ashes are the glory. If the slyt peasants are prepared to do this, what the hell chance do we have? Look at what one single thaum did," Rickets said, his eyes fixing on Jawn.

Jawn couldn't think. He could barely talk. The heat was cooking him.

"We... we can't stay here," he finally managed to say.

Rickets looked up at the cloud of swirling fire. The wind was gaining speed, howling like a demented beast as it drew up detritus to feed the flames. "So are we dead?"

Jawn tilted his head skyward. He began to mouth the word *yes* when a shadow raced overhead. There was a roar and then more flame erupted in the sky, but this time from outside the fire cloud. Unlike the ragged flames of the vortex, this was thick and solid, like a beam of pure fire, mostly white with just a tinge of red and orange. It punched through the fire cloud like a spear.

Jawn folded over as he sought to bury himself into the ground. The fire cloud burst apart in a rumbling blast. Sheets of flame twisted through the air, growing thinner as they blew apart. Jawn screamed, but he couldn't hear himself over the roar.

After what seemed like an eternity, Jawn lifted his head. At first, he couldn't see anything. He blinked once, then again. Multicolored lights flashed from somewhere deep in his skull.

"Rickets?"

There was the sound of coughing, and then Jawn felt a hand on his shoulder. "I can't see for shit."

"What happened?"

"ASK," Rickets said. "Aero Service of the Kingdom. Must have launched some rags to check out what was going on. Those flyboys earned their pay tonight."

Jawn closed his eyes and focused on his ears. There, off to his left, the sound of heavy wings. After the last day on the back of a rag, Jawn doubted he'd ever forget that sound. "Like the one we flew in on?"

"High Druid's balls, no! That old cow we flew would have coughed her ass through her mouth if she tried breathing a flame like that. No, that was probably a bull… not too old either."

"She did us right," Jawn said, coming to the defense of their recent transport. He could still see the tears in the driver's eyes as he looked at his beast in distress. The man loved that thing, and she, in turn, had delivered them safely. He willfully blocked out the image of a crowny's nearly severed head.

"True enough," Rickets said, though he didn't sound remorseful enough for Jawn's liking.

Jawn shook his head and opened his eyes again. The flashing colors were still there, but he could dimly make out the headstones of the cemetery. "I'm getting my sight back," he said, easing himself up onto his knees.

"Guess mine is coming back, too, because I'm staring at a half-burned scarecrow," Rickets said.

Jawn turned and saw Rickets. His face was filthy with soot and heat shimmered in waves from the top of his head. His pate looked medium-rare. The smile on his face, however, didn't seem to be affected.

"You're missing an eyebrow," Jawn said, reaching up and running a hand through his hair. What he found was a frizzled stubble in place of his once-flowing mane.

"It'll probably grow back," Rickets said.

Jawn didn't know if he meant his eyebrow or Jawn's hair. "Probably." He drew up his right thigh and, placing a hand on his knee, pushed himself up until he was standing. He reached out a hand and offered it to Rickets. The crowny took it and lifted himself up. Jawn started to tip over, but Rickets caught him by the elbow. The two men wobbled back and forth a couple of times before finding equilibrium.

"We should make ourselves scarce. This," Rickets said, waving his hand around, "is going to attract a lot of attention."

"Lead the way," Jawn said, his body and mind long past the point of meaningful action.

Rickets shuffled forward with Jawn's arm firmly draped over his shoulder. They staggered along the wall, avoiding walking through the cemetery proper. It went unspoken between them, but neither wanted to go anywhere near the graves.

Ash began to fall like snow as they traveled, coloring them gray from head to foot. Neither man made an effort to brush the ash away. It damped all sound, giving the night a new kind of silence.

"A fellow could learn to hate this war," Rickets said, his voice barely reaching Jawn's ear though they walked together.

Jawn said nothing.

They came to an opening at the end of the wall and passed through, stopping when they set foot on the road again. The intersection was a hundred yards up the road to the right. Somewhere past that was Rickets's bar.

Jawn started to remove his arm from Rickets's shoulder, but Rickets grabbed his wrist a little tighter and kept it in place. He slowly turned and faced them away from the intersection.

"I know this other bar, not quite as sophisticated, but with its own certain charm," Rickets said as they began to walk again.

Jawn didn't tell him to shut up. Just as Rickets needed to talk, Jawn needed to hear a voice that gave his mind something else to fix on. They trudged on, neither one looking back.

CHAPTER TWELVE

CROSSBOWMAN YUSTACE VOOFORD walked down the path toward the ocean. Visibility was made better by the wall of jungle plants lining both sides of the path. It provided a clear lane, even in the dark. He walked slowly, his head slightly turned to the left. Any moment he expected to hear Sinte yelling at him, asking him what the hell he was doing. He was ready for that. If anyone found him out here, he'd tell them he was going for a piss.

He paused beside the trunk of a large tree after he'd gone ten yards. The farther he walked, the less believable his excuse became. *Am I really going to do this?*

"Fuck the Lux," he said, spitting on the ground. "Fuck Sinte, fuck Red Shield, fuck all of them." He gripped his crossbow hard. Not one of the soldiers in Red Shield had the guts to challenge authority the way he did, even though they all knew he was right. "Stupid fucking sheep is what they are."

He didn't have a plan; he just knew he was done. Done with the Lux, the army, all of it. There were many kinds of ships down th   ll he had to do was sneak onto one and sail away.

lked a few more steps down the path, then stopped
          tree. Who was he kidding? They'd catch him and
          ng up before lunch. Sneering at the dark, he spun
          ury, wanting to scream. Dizzy and exasperated,

he pointed his crossbow into the jungle and squeezed the trigger.

The release of energy as the metal bow sprang forward coupled with the sharp whip of the string sounded terribly loud. The bolt vanished from his sight, but he could hear its progress through the jungle as it ripped through leaves and fronds.

"Shit, shit, shit." Sinte counted bolts—any soldier with less than twenty-four in his quiver had to have a damn good reason for it. Vooford considered walking into the jungle to search for the bolt but gave that up right away. He'd grab one from someone else's quiver. They were cowards anyway for not standing up to Sinte, so let them deal with him and his fucking rules.

With his anger bleeding away, Vooford found the jungle had grown darker. He blinked and realized that no, it wasn't darker, just quieter. He didn't like it. He hated the jungle with all its noise, but there was something worse about hearing it like this. Suddenly, he wanted very much to be back among the protection of the shield.

He bent over and placed his left foot in the metal stirrup at the end of his crossbow while cradling the bow between his knees. He took the end of his belt with its curved metal flange and hooked it under the crossbow string. Grunting, he stood up, taking the strain across his lower back and his thighs as he pulled the bow back to its full draw. When he heard the reassuring click of the trigger cam catching the string, he stopped pulling and bent his knees to unhook his belt and straighten up. Using his foot, he lifted the crossbow up to his hands and grabbed it, cradling it in his left arm while simultaneously reaching around his back to pull a bolt from his quiver.

A shadow appeared out of the jungle and moved onto the path five yards away from where he stood. Vooford froze, his right hand gripping a bolt while his left still held the crossbow. The shadow was between him and the ocean. He could slide the bolt into the firing groove and take the shot, or run back to the shield.

The idea of running back to Sinte infuriated him, but he didn't want to draw attention to himself by reloading, so he remained perfectly still. The shadow hadn't moved since it appeared.

Vooford squinted, trying to make it out, but it was too dark.

Fuck it, he said to himself, whipping his right hand around and slamming the bolt into the groove. He swung the crossbow up to chest height, shouldered the stock in one practiced move, and took aim.

The shadow was gone.

He blinked, dipping his crossbow down so he could scan the path.

He heard the flight of the bolt as a high, thin sound as it sped through the dark. The vibration of the bowstring reached his ears a flick later, but by then the arrow had punched a hole in the iron plate covering his heart. Its metal tip tore flesh, ripped muscle, and shattered a rib before drilling straight through the lower left corner of his heart and on through his chest, tenting his aketon as it came to a halt sticking several inches out his back.

Vooford sank slowly to his knees, the crossbow slipping from his hands. He tried to hold on to it, but his hands no longer worked. His knees dug into the dirt, but if there was pain he couldn't tell. His entire existence now burned with white-hot focus on the shaft in his chest. He swayed, fighting the pull of the ground. If he fell, he'd never get back up.

He tried taking a breath, but though his mouth opened and closed, he couldn't draw in any air. His lungs burned; his mind reeled. A second bolt glanced off his left shoulder and clipped his left ear, lodging itself in his skull.

Shards of pain lanced Vooford's head. He tipped to the right, corrected, and then began to fall to the left. His mouth opened wider, but his scream remained silent as the ground raced up toward him. When his head hit the ground, it would drive the bolt through his—

CARNY WOKE UP slowly, struggling to hold on to a dream already slipping through his fingers. He was back in Timston Falls, the smell of his mother's pottage bubbling away in the large cast-iron pot hung from a steel hook over a bright orange bed of coals. It was the Day of Trees, the day when workers laid down the hoe and the hammer and gloried in the shade of the Sacred Tree, its protection symbolized by the green tablecloth of pressed cotton his mother brought out to cover their battered wooden table once a week.

Even though he knew there would be an hour of reading from the LOKAM that morning, and another at nightfall, he didn't care. Today was a special day. He walked over to the pot slowly, pausing with each step to sniff the aromas rising into the air.

"Opossum?" he asked, hoping it wasn't. He didn't mind the taste, but he hated the look of the animal. It struck him as far too intelligent. He couldn't shake the feeling that when one opossum was killed, the others gathered in the trees plotting their revenge.

"I didn't see any of them whispering in the eaves," his mother said. He'd confessed his concerns about the creatures to her a month ago. Despite their abundance in the village forest, they hadn't had opossum since.

He took a step closer and another sniff. "Porcupine?"

"We don't have enough ink nor paper for the quills we have," she said, bustling about their small one-room cottage.

"Rabbit," he guessed next, stepping right up to the pot. He peered inside, but the brown, bubbling mass gave nothing away.

"That's a jump in the right direction, but you'll have to think bigger."

He leaned over and tried to make out a piece of meat among the vegetable mulch that made up the pottage six days of seven. "Dog?" he said, unable to hide the disappointment in his voice.

His mother stopped her chores long enough to give him a long, hard look. Her face was thin and creased with wrinkles, and her red hair lay flat and dull on her head, but her eyes were bright and her smile warm. "That was a long, cold winter, Carnan, and we did what we had to do to make it to spring. Guess again."

Tiring of the game, he threw out the one animal he knew would never be in their pot. "Deer."

He expected his mother to laugh, or at least cluck her tongue at his foolishness, but she did neither. Instead, she walked over to him, bent down to the pot, and ladled out a portion of the pottage. She pointed at a piece of meat floating on the top. "Try it."

He looked from the ladle to her, and then back at the ladle. Gingerly, he reached forward and plucked the meat from the pottage, quickly popping it into his mouth. He first noticed the tang. Sharp, but with a smooth, rich flavor. It was lean and soft, tearing apart like good, fresh bread. He looked up at his mother in surprise. "Is it *really* deer?"

She smiled and drew him into her embrace with one arm. "You are my love, my light, my tree in the storm."

Carny absently brushed away tears from his eyes as he woke all the way and remembered where he was.

Something was different. It was still dark, his head was fuzzy, and his mouth felt like an old bird nest. He desperately wanted a drink of water, but he kept still. He opened his eyes wider. The jungle offered him nothing new to see.

He looked to the right, hoping to pick out the shape of Big Hog. Even the sight of rustling leaves would be welcome at this point. Fear gripped Carny, sheathing his heart in ice. *What the hell is wrong?*

A twig snapped somewhere off to his left. It echoed in the stillness and Carny understood. The jungle had gone silent.

When they'd first landed in Luitox and made their way past the tree line, Carny was terrified. The sounds were more oppressive than the heat. What made it worse was not knowing the sounds' origins. It took him a month to discover that the source of a high, shrieking cackle belonged not to a deranged monster but to a small bird no bigger than a sparrow back home. Now he longed to hear that maniacal little bastard.

A shadow materialized out of the jungle and came straight at him. Carny reached for his crossbow and scooped it up with his shaking right hand. He pointed it at the shadow as his fingers fumbled for the trigger and squeezed as the shadow reached him.

The crossbow didn't fire.

Fucking safety latch!

LC Listowk reached down and gently pushed the crossbow to the side so that it no longer pointed at his chest.

Every muscle in Carny's body melted and he sank back into the dirt. "Holy—" was all he managed to say before Listowk's other hand covered his mouth and he whispered in Carny's ear.

"Slyts."

Carny froze again. He looked at Listowk's face to see if this was some kind of mad joke, but there wasn't a hint of mirth to be found.

Listowk took his hand away and wiped it on his tunic. He put a finger to his lips, then motioned for Carny to stay put. Carny nodded, thankful he wasn't being asked to do anything.

The LC moved farther down the rut and a few moments later returned with Big Hog in tow. The farmer was wide-eyed. They stopped in front of Carny.

"What's going on?" Carny mouthed.

Before Listowk could answer, the Weasel appeared, shaking. "Slyts, dozens of them," he hissed.

Listowk pointed a finger at the Weasel and mouthed the words *Shut up*.

"Wraith?" Carny mouthed.

Listowk motioned with his thumb over his shoulder and then pointed at his eyes, meaning Wraith remained on watch. He then pointed to the ground and had them all squeeze in tight. Despite the heat, Carny shivered. *Dozens of them!* He was going to die, he just knew it.

"Slyts all over the mountain. Above and below," Listowk said, his voice quiet and tight and hoarse.

Oh, fuck, that's it, Carny thought, shaking his head. *We're completely surrounded.*

Listowk must have figured out what he was thinking, because he reached out and rapped his knuckles on Carny's forehead. "Our way to the beach is cut off. Anyone makes a run for it, and they're dead. Understand?"

Carny nodded. The others did, too.

"Then we go back to the shield," the Weasel said, starting to get up.

Listowk grabbed him by the shoulder and pulled him back down. "They're above us and below us. We try moving now and we'll be skewered."

"How do we warn the shield?" Big Hog asked.

For an answer, Listowk removed the bolt from his crossbow and put it in his quiver, then drew out another bolt and slotted it in place. It was thick and dull white at one end and lacked an iron tip. A signal-star bolt.

"Every slyt will know we're here if you fire that off," Carny said.

Before Listowk could respond a rustle of leaves sounded and Lingletti appeared on the edge of their circle. "They're coming down the ravine."

Listowk got up into a crouch. "Stay low, keep your backs to the embankment, and remember to breathe. Weasel and Big Hog, cover the right flank. Wraith and I will cover the left. Carny, watch the center," Listowk ordered. "And everybody stay as quiet as you can." He stood up, aimed his crossbow into the sky, and squeezed the trigger.

The twang of the metal bow releasing and the hum of the string were drowned out by the hissing sound of the flare bolt as it sped skyward. It punched through a couple of leaves and then soared above the canopy, where it blazed a bright red. The jungle came alive with arcing shadows.

"There!" Listowk shouted.

Carny looked to the left. A cluster of shadowy figures stood ten yards away staring up at the flare. It was difficult to make them out clearly through the leaves, but there was just enough light if he squinted.

He raised his crossbow up and drove the butt into the padding of his aketon at his shoulder. He forgot to control his breathing. He also forgot to brace his stance and didn't come close to getting his eye level with the sight before he jerked the lever and fired. The bolt leaped from the crossbow and immediately disappeared.

Bowstrings hummed and metal arms twanged and creaked as bolts streaked through the jungle. Slyts were screaming and shouting, making Carny's skin crawl. He couldn't understand a single word, but his imagination came up with terrifying possibilities. Leaves shook and branches snapped and cracked as slyts now ran all over the mountainside.

"To the right! To the right!" the LC shouted.

Carny looked but couldn't see a damn thing. He tore his eyes away from the jungle and began reloading his crossbow, totally vulnerable as he bent over and pulled the string back, completely forgetting to use the hook on his belt. His hands were shaking so much that he released the string before the latch caught and the bow arms sprung back down. The bowstring tore out of his fingers, ripping into the flesh of two fingertips. He screamed in pain.

"Carny's hit!" Big Hog shouted.

The LC was over him in a flash. "Where are you hit?"

"Fuck, I'm fine—I just skinned some fingers," he said, his cheeks flushing.

Listowk reached down and quickly patted Carny all over, then pulled away. "Next time you scream like that, you'd better have an arrow sticking out of your skull."

"I got one. Nailed that slyt right in the gut!" the Weasel shouted.

"Shut the fuck up!" Listowk hissed in the Weasel's direction. "You want every slyt on this mountain to know where we are?"

"I think it's too late for that, LC," said Carny.

Screams and shouts mixed with cries all around them. The sound of running feet and thrashing vegetation crisscrossed the mountainside in every direction. Carny gripped his bowstring again and pulled, gritting his teeth at the pain. He felt the latch catch this time and quickly pulled his fingers away.

"Qow nela mranona waw! Qow nela mranona sirn waw!"

"That's a woman," Carny muttered, fumbling for a bolt from his quiver. He was getting blood over everything.

"They can still shoot a bow," Listowk said, turning and training his crossbow on the jungle directly in front of them.

Carny grabbed a bolt and slotted it into his bow. His helm had slid down his forehead and was covering his eyes. He reached up a hand to push it back in place as the leaves of the plants began to shake. Carny heard someone breathing heavily.

A slyt burst through the vegetation and stumbled into the ravine. Carny had no time to aim—he just pointed at the torso and fired.

Listowk's hand slapped his crossbow just as the bolt left. Carny saw the bolt take the slyt in the ribs and then go down.

"Hold your fire! Druid's fucking nuts, *hold your fire*!" LC Listowk shouted.

Carny stared at the fallen slyt lying just three feet away from him. All he could see was a jumble of red-tinged shadows on the ground, but he could tell it was a female. Her long black hair was spread out on the ground around her head like a pool of ink.

"They're not shooting back, LC," Wraith said.

"Damn right!" the Weasel said, his voice high and shaky. "Fuckin' cowards, didn't expect to find us up here, did you? Got what they deserved!"

Listowk didn't answer. He grabbed another signal star from his quiver and violently snapped the tip off across one of his greaves. The signal star burst into light as he held it up like a torch.

At least five slyts lay dead in the immediate area of the ravine. Three were definitely women. A fourth was a boy of maybe seven. A bolt had ripped through his stomach, spilling his innards onto the ground. Must have been the one the Weasel was shouting about.

"Nice shooting, Weasel," Carny said. "You'll get a medal for sure."

The Weasel stood frozen in place, staring down at the boy.

"Stow it," Listowk said. He moved toward the boy and nudged him with the toe of his boot. He'd seen men with their organs hanging out of their bodies still have the strength to shoot a bolt. He checked the other slyts spread around the ravine. None of them moved.

Carny looked at the one he'd shot. His bolt had gone right through her chest and out her back, leaving a hole big enough to put his fist through. The gleam of white bone showed where a rib had splintered. His eyes traveled across her body to where a small burlap sack hung from her shoulder. Small red berries lay spilled on the ground.

"They were gathering fruit?" Carny said, not willing to believe what he saw. "Who the fuck gathers fruit at night?"

The screaming and shouting around them changed into a chorus of anguished wails. The tone and pitch of the cries were now unmistakable. The mountain was filled with slyt women.

"Maybe we should go out and help the wounded," Big Hog said. "I think I shot at least two, maybe more."

"No," Listowk said, grounding the signal star and reloading his crossbow with a regular bolt.

"LC, it's women and children," Big Hog continued. "The LOKAM says—"

Listowk rounded on Big Hog with a clenched fist. "Fuck the LOKAM. You're not in a Holy Grove out here. The only rules that matter are the ones that keep us alive. Wraith!"

"LC," Wraith said.

"You and Carny cover the path. We don't know what else is out there. Don't let any of them near you. You understand me? The shield will have seen and heard this, and if they send a patrol down, I don't want anyone shooting anyone by mistake. Same goes for the beach. Druid knows what Weel will do. Keep your eyes peeled."

Carny started to object, but the look on Listowk's face made him hold his tongue. He took one last look at the slyt he'd shot and then followed after Lingletti back toward the path. He expected to see slyt women screaming and shouting curses at him, but already their cries were fading.

Wraith held up his fist when they got to the end of the ravine. Carny ignored it, stepping around him and onto the path. He looked up toward the shield. Two dark shapes lay in front of them. They could have been logs, or some kind of animal, but he knew. He turned and looked down toward the beach. Three more.

He cocked his head, listening, but the sounds of carnage and its aftermath were little more than echoes. Bells rang down on the beach. Carny imagined Weel would be thrilled, thinking he finally had a battle to sink his teeth into.

"You done being a target?" Wraith whispered.

Carny shrugged and walked back off the path and into the jungle. "Women, Wraith, we were shooting women. And that kid. What the fuck?"

"Better them than me," Wraith said. He sounded bored.

Carny tried to find Wraith's face among the leaves. "You can't believe that. We just slaughtered a bunch of peasants out picking berries."

"Welcome to the Lux," Wraith said.

Carny realized the soldier wasn't even looking at him, but was instead staring up at the trees across the path. Carny started to turn, but Wraith hissed, and Carny froze. Whatever was out there, he had his back to it. The nape of his neck was completely exposed. He'd pried off the chain mail curtain and thrown it away. He tried to look out of the corner of his eye, but without turning his head, he couldn't see where Lingletti was looking.

"Keep talking," Wraith said, "make some more noise." Wraith had his small bow in his hand and an arrow notched.

"What is it?" Carny asked in a whisper.

Wraith drew back his arm in a slow, fluid motion and fired. Carny dove for the ground, curling himself up into a ball. He heard the whine of the string and then the thwack of the arrow hitting something solid. A moment later a branch cracked and something heavy fell through the vegetation and landed on the jungle floor.

"Slyts?" Listowk asked, appearing out of the darkness.

Carny quickly sat up and grabbed his crossbow. "Wraith using me as bloody bait."

Wraith pointed across the path. Listowk moved past Carny

and crept out onto the path. He moved into the jungle on the other side and disappeared from sight. Carny looked down at his crossbow and realized his bolt had come loose and slotted it back in place. When he looked up again, Listowk was stepping back onto the path. He was holding something in his left hand. As he walked across the path, Carny was able to make it out. A sheaf of papers in a leather wrap.

"Left eye?" Wraith asked.

Listowk pointed to the left side of the bridge of his nose just below his eye.

"I thought I pulled it," Wraith said, turning back to keep watch.

"It was a scout, maybe a spy," Listowk said to Carny's unasked question. "Found this on his body." He held out the sheaf of papers.

Carny leaned forward and squinted. What he saw made his stomach knot. "There's Weel's command post. And the shield on the summit. Druid's balls... we only set up there tonight."

"Well, it seems they've been watching us," Listowk said. The admiration in his voice was unmistakable.

"What the hell do we do now?" Carny asked, looking around the jungle with a newfound fear. How many other slyts were aiming arrows at him right now?

Listowk rolled up the papers in their leather sheet and tied the thong before slipping it into his aketon. "We get better. And we do it fast."

Carny spent the rest of the night in a miserable, suffocating sweat. Everything in his bowels turned liquid, but he was terrified to step farther into the jungle to relieve himself. There was no way he was exposing his buttocks with slyts all over. Wraith, however, threatened to cut his throat if he dared do that near him, so in the end Carny crawled a few feet away and took the most terrifying shit of his life.

The morning sun brought salvation. Weel appeared on the path, with what looked like half of the Seventh Phalanx in tow. Carny would have laughed if he could have remembered how.

There was more silver braid and polished bronze and steel gathered than there was at the Royal Mint.

"Report," Commander Weel said, stopping when he reached the ravine. He seemed surprised to see members of Sinte's shield this far down the mountain.

"LC Listowk, outpost commander, sir. We engaged what we believed were slyts infiltrating and massing for an attack against the shield on the mountain. It appears, however, that the majority of them were peasants out picking fruit."

"The majority?" Weel asked. He wasn't yelling, but the disappointment on his face was obvious.

"One of my men shot a slyt scout hiding in a tree. He had this on him," Listowk said, handing over the sheaf of paper.

Weel undid the thong and glanced at the papers, flipping through each one until there were no more. When he looked up again, he was smiling. "How many enemy?"

"Just the one scout that we—"

"Do you know that the other slyts weren't scouting as well?"

Listowk looked confused. "Sir, as far as I can tell they were women and children, I—"

"Morning, Commander! Red Shield leader Sinte reporting!"

Carny turned, startled to see Sinte marching down the path toward them. He was alone. *Fucking lunatic.*

"Congratulations, Shield Leader. You repelled a sizable enemy force last night," Weel said. He leaned forward slightly as he spoke, and Carny caught the implication. They all did.

Sinte nodded. "Yes, sir. I sent out this outpost in anticipation of a slyt attack. Figured the sneaky bastards would have a go and sure enough, they did." He turned to Listowk as if noticing him for the first time. "LC Listowk, how many fatalities?"

Listowk looked from Sinte to Weel and then back to Sinte. "Eleven women, three children, and one enemy scout."

Sinte blinked once. "Then that would be fifteen enemy killed, sir, with only one fatality to report on our side."

Carny shared a look with Listowk. One of theirs?

"What happened?" Weel asked.

Sinte shook his head. "Soldier out taking a piss. Must have stumbled upon the slyts. We found his body this morning."

"Who was it?" Listowk asked.

Sinte pursed his lips, obviously annoyed at the interruption, but he kept his cool. "Vooford."

"Good man, Vooford?" Weel asked, his eyes scanning over the bodies of the slyts laid out on the path.

"He was a soldier, sir, doing his duty. Nothing more," Sinte said.

"Good, good. Well, it's a shame of course, but all in all, fifteen for one are odds I'll take all day. SL, see to it that the bodies are burned up here. No need to drag them down to the beach. But pull out the scout that was carrying this," he said, holding up the papers. "I think it'll be instructive for the new arrivals to see what we're dealing with."

"Very good, sir," Sinte said. "Anything else?"

Weel was already turning away when he paused and turned back. "Actually, yes. I was planning on taking them up to the top myself, but seeing as there's no danger anymore, I'll let you handle it. The mules are here. I want the top of that mountain clear of every tree, branch, and plant by nightfall. Is that understood?"

"It will be done," Sinte said.

"And have them widen this path, too. It's damn confining. I'll have some mules assigned to that detail. No wonder the slyts could sneak around up here." And with that Weel turned and disappeared back down the path, his coterie of staff officers closing ranks behind him.

"Are you fuc—" Carny started to say, but Listowk gave him a fierce glare and Carny shut his mouth.

"This ravine looks as good a place as any," Sinte said, walking down the path until he stood just a yard away from Listowk. "Clear the brush, get a fire going, and get rid of the bodies."

"You mean the women and children?" Listowk asked.

Sinte stepped closer. "All I see are fifteen slyts no longer able to put an arrow through your skull." He stepped back and looked at the rest of the patrol. "After weeks of fucking around up here, you finally did something right. Don't screw it up now."

"So, Vooford," Listowk said, looking down at the ground before raising his gaze.

"He was stupid and didn't listen to orders," Sinte said.

Carny watched the two men closely. There was an entirely separate conversation going on here that he couldn't hear.

"How'd he get it?" Listowk asked.

"Arrows," Sinte said. He turned on his heel and marched back up the path.

Carny watched him go, wondering just what he'd missed. Wraith moved up beside him.

"Not one of them was carrying a bow, LC, not even the scout," Wraith said.

"Then I guess the one that tarped Vooford got away, didn't he?" Listowk said, looking at each of them in turn.

Big Hog scuffed the dirt with the toe of his boot before looking up and giving Listowk a shrug. "Sounds right," he said. "Place is crawling with slyts. Hiding around every damn tree. I'm just looking to earn my rack and get back to the farm."

"Sure, LC, whatever you say," the Weasel said. His eyes were unfocused and seemed to be staring at something no one else could see.

Wraith simply nodded.

Listowk turned his gaze on Carny. *Fuck, fuck, fuck.*

Listowk reached into his haversack and pulled something out. He tossed it to Carny, who caught it and knew immediately what it was: snow.

"That's that," Listowk said, staring at Carny a moment longer before looking away. "You all heard Sinte. Let's get these bodies burned and get the hell out of here."

The sound of heavy thudding on the path turned everyone's head toward the beach.

"Sweet Sacred Tree, finally we got us some mules," Big Hog said.

Carny turned to look. A single officer was slowly climbing up the path with ten of the toughest, burliest mules Carny had ever seen in tow.

"Pioneer Commander Mallowry Tiffanger, Eighteenth Pioneer Support Group," the disheveled, ambling officer said when he finally made it to the ravine. The armpits of his aketon were stained with sweat and his face looked ashen. He tipped back his helm with one hand and dragged an arm of his long-sleeved tunic across his forehead.

"Lead Crossbowman Listowk, Red Shield, Second Javelin," Listowk said, saluting. "I understand you'll be helping us burn a few bodies."

Tiffanger stood up a little straighter. He glanced around and Carny could imagine the man wondering what the hell he'd gotten into.

"Bodies? I thought we were clearing the path," Tiffanger said, looking past Listowk to where the deceased were laid out.

"Yes, sir, but the bodies are first. Sorry to rush you, but we should probably get started. It only gets hotter here," Listowk said.

"Hotter? Well then, I think you're right. Best get at it." He turned and waved a hand at the mules. "C'mon, fellows, up you come. Time to get to work."

Carny leaned out farther on the path to watch as the mules approached. The lead mule stared hard at Carny as it came on, changing its direction just enough that it headed straight at him.

"Welcome to the Lux," Carny said.

"Fuck you and the tree you fell out of," the mule said, lifting a broad, two-headed axe off of one shoulder and casually swinging it around to rest it on the other. "I'm a free dwarf. I don't need you welcoming me anywhere."

Carny couldn't hide his surprise. The dwarf's voice was surprisingly clear and fluid. He'd expected something closer to gravel being ground against steel. Voice aside, he had seen free dwarves before, but not like these. Yes they were stout and broad and low to the ground, which was probably why they were called mules in the first place. They were also heavily bearded, so that little more than their eyes and the tips of their noses gave any indication that there was a face under there.

They wore armor-plated aketons similar to Carny's and carried a mix of axes, shovels, and picks—a very common sight among the mule gangs where he grew up. Really, there was only one thing different.

"Your parents own slaves, did they?" the dwarf asked, stepping closer.

These dwarves weren't afraid. They stood up straight, their huge shoulders pushed back and their chins, or at least their beards, jutting out like rocky piers in a sea of tangled moss. But it was their eyes that truly set them apart. They didn't look down, not one of them. Every dwarf was looking up at Carny and the rest of the patrol. They were free, and nothing, not even death, was going to take that away from them.

"Oh bloody lightning! Master Pioneer Black Pine, we discussed this," Commander Tiffanger said, his shoulders slumping with obvious exasperation. "There is no problem here. Commander Weel assured me his men are civilized and versed in the societal changes that the Kingdom is undergoing. Isn't that right, Mr. Listowk?"

Listowk nodded. "Yes, sir, civilized and versed. We don't have a problem with your—with them." It wasn't a resounding affirmation, but Tiffanger seemed satisfied.

"You see, Black Pine? No problem. You're free, they're free, and we're all in the same army fighting a common enemy. Let's all try to remember that the past is behind us, shall we?"

The mul—*damn*, the dwarves, had only been freed shortly before Carny was born. Dwarves were now considered citizens, to a point. He wasn't sure if they were allowed to own property or not, but they had been granted the privilege of being conscripted into the army.

"Yes, sir, no problem," Black Pine said. The top of his helm barely reached Carny's armpit, but Carny had no illusions about his chances if the dwarf decided there indeed was an issue. His continued glare at Carny guaranteed it.

"Master Pioneer Black Pine, I am your supe... I mean, you know damn well what I mean," Tiffanger said. It was clear he wasn't entirely comfortable with his command, but the man was valiantly doing his best. "That soldier did nothing more than welcome you. If you want to hear slurs in every greeting, you will damn well do it on your own time. Right now, you will get your section to work. That's an... well, that's an order."

Black Pine looked over at Tiffanger, then back at Carny. "Yes, sir. Right away, sir." He stepped forward and Carny moved to the side, allowing him and the rest of the dwarves to pass. As each dwarf marched on by, each one kept his eyes on Carny.

"You sure know how to make friends," Wraith said, coming up behind Carny.

"All I said was hello," Carny said, realizing he was shaking.

"Did your family own slaves?"

Carny looked at Wraith. "We're as poor as squirrels in early spring."

"Well, something about you rubs them the wrong way. I'd watch my step if I were you," Wraith said, patting him on the shoulder.

"But I didn't do anything," Carny said, looking around for support and finding none. He stood there until Listowk threw a stick at him to get his attention.

"Since you're not doing anything, make yourself useful and keep your eyes peeled," he said, motioning with a hand at the jungle around them. "And don't get into that snow and Flower, either. I want you focused."

"Sure, sure," Carny said, cradling his crossbow and scanning the jungle. He yawned, suddenly realizing how damn tired he was. Ignoring the LC's order, he broke off a chunk of snow, mashed it up with some Wild Flower, and popped it between his gum and cheek on the left side of his mouth. The cool sensation of the snow numbed the whole side of his face while the heady sting of the Wild Flower wrapped his mind in light gauze.

Carny smiled, a little drool trickling out of the corner of his mouth. Damn mules. He had no gripe with them. He took a couple of chews and squeezed more of the numbing liquid around his mouth as he inhaled the vapors.

He might be stuck in this shithole of a country, but he didn't have to feel it.

PART TWO

CHAPTER THIRTEEN

VORLY ASTOL LIFTED HIS chin and gloried in the rush of wind cooling the sweat on his neck. The temptation to unbutton the collar of his tunic made his fingers twitch, but he already knew he wouldn't do it. Despite the blazing sun heating up his metal helm so that it was hot to the touch, his uniform would remain intact.

He would rather sweat than burn.

It was that mantra—it sounded better than saying *fear*—that had motivated him to wrap strips of wool cloth soaked in a mixture of wet clay, aloe, and camphor around his legs from ankle to groin before pulling on his heavy canvas trousers and leather boots. The cool, soothing effects of his efforts were the saving grace in what he knew would soon become a pair of stiff woolly casts that he'd have to hack off later with a knife. Still, it was a discomfort he was prepared to endure.

He'd seen men who hadn't taken such precautions. At least, what was left of them.

He snapped the leather straps at the ends of the steel-chain reins in his hands. "Higher, Carduus, higher!"

The rag responded at once, his twenty-yard wingspan gracefully pumping with smooth, heavy strokes. The jungle below lost definition as the rag climbed the sky. Vorly leaned forward in his saddle, squinting as the sulfur-tainted wind blasted his face. This was living.

"Whenever you're ready, sir."

The voice, a bit high and thin to Vorly's ear, sounded appropriately deferential. That only made him resent it more. He turned his head slightly to look at the RAT sitting two feet behind him on Carduus. He caught a smile and helpful nod before turning back. The only good days in the Lux were those when he flew. Now even that was ruined.

"Exactly," Vorly snapped, "when *I'm* ready." He enjoyed his brief victory, knowing damn well that he would eventually carry out what this little prick of a RAT wanted him to do.

The uncomfortable silence didn't last nearly long enough.

"I realize it must come as a bit of shock, sir, but this *is* the future," the thaum said in a voice markedly louder than before. "It's a vast improvement over the old communication system."

There, right there. The wet stain pissing in his ear had as much as said Vorly was old. Vorly snarled but held his tongue, instead focusing his attention on the rectangular sheet of crystal propped up on a short wooden easel, which blocked a sizable chunk of his view to the right. At two feet tall, a foot wide, and over two inches thick, the crystal was a bulky annoyance he could do without. And he didn't trust the copper braid that snaked down from the lower edge of the sheet and back to the RAT behind him, who had a similar contraption. It was all too newfangled.

Despite his initial hope that the… *thing* was far too fragile, the birch frame surrounding the crystal showed no signs of falling apart. Its canvas cover, however, had been blown away in the wind, exposing the sheet. Vorly risked a look into it, ready to slam his fist into the crystal if anything happened that he didn't like. All he saw was refracted sunlight.

"Broken," Vorly said, unable to keep the satisfaction out of his voice. "Looks like your little doohickey isn't up to the task, RAT."

Even in the wind, Vorly heard the sigh.

"It's dormant, sort of like sleeping. It's just waiting for you, sir." Again, deference marked each word, but Vorly listened to the silences in between and heard condescension.

Vorly grunted and eased Carduus out of his climb. Once the rag leveled off, Vorly twisted around to face the thaum. "Let's get one thing straight, *RAT*—you and your contraption are here despite my express wishes that you not be."

The thaum blinked her eyes and dipped her head slightly before raising it again and holding his stare. "Yes, sir, you've made that very clear."

Trees and fucking lightning! They would have to give him a female RAT. Probably hoped he wouldn't punch one.

"Look, it's damn unnatural. I've been doing this going on twenty years without one of these," he said, waving a hand at the crystal sheet device in front of her.

"I know, sir—it's why I asked to be assigned to you," she said, staring at him with green, unblinking eyes. Strands of red hair that had escaped the severe bun she'd put them in swirled about her face in the wind. Even with a spray of freckles rouging her cheeks and a too-thin-looking face that suggested she'd have a hard, severe countenance when she reached crone, she wasn't ugly. Really a wisp of a thing, like a boy without the muscles, though it was hard to say for sure as her canvas pants and tunic were fully two sizes too big on her.

Vorly figured she must be midtwenties, long past the point where she should have been married with a litter of kids tugging at her apron. She sure as hell shouldn't have been *here*.

"Why in the High Druid's green forest would you ask for me?"

"Because choosing you was the easiest path to get what I want."

The boldness of her statement left his mouth agape. He slowly closed it. "Did you just call me stupid?"

Her eyes flared, but her voice remained controlled. "If I convince you of the value of what we're doing, you have the power to convince the others. They listen to you. You are their commander."

The corners of Vorly's mouth twitched as he fought to keep the smile off his face. The little vixen was flattering him. Worse, it was working.

"Fine. What do I do again?"

"Touch the copper braid running down the left leg of the support," she recited, managing to keep any sense of frustration hidden. "That's very important, as it ensures your body is in tune with its surroundings. It aligns the aethereal plane with your cardinal position. Then you simply place the fingertips of your nearest hand on the lower edge of the sheet."

"That's it?" Vorly asked. He'd heard this several times over the last week, but now that it came down to it, he found himself slightly annoyed that there wasn't more here.

"There's actually a lot of thaumic process involved, not to mention the constant need to compensate for any movement. It's one of the reasons we couldn't test the system on the ground. We need to utilize the field energy of the dragon while controlling the flow from the rear position so that—"

"So I touch the copper first," Vorly said, regretting that he'd opened his mouth. The last thing he needed was some snot-nosed RAT lecturing him. "Fine, here goes nothing."

He reached out his right hand and put his fingertips on the copper braid. Nothing happened, which he took as a good sign. He moved his hand up the easel to the crystal sheet. It felt much cooler than the air around them, even with the wind.

"Hold, please," she said.

The vein on the left side of Vorly's forehead began to throb. *If she asks me to start whistling I'm going to—*

"There, I have the pathway!" she shouted, her voice giddy. She coughed and continued. "Okay, sir, the crystal is yours. You can remove your hand."

Something cold brushed the tips of Vorly's fingers, as if he'd left them dangling in a stream as a fish swam underneath them. He quickly plucked his hand away from the sheet. Its surface was now a swirling cloud of black and gray. A different, smaller set of fingertips moved across the sheet with a grace and precision he could only marvel at.

"Those are your fingers," Vorly said, knowing that was the case because he'd been told that's what would happen in several briefings. Still, it was startling to see it.

"Yes, sir. I have aligned your sheet with mine and opened the gate to the first aerius plane. You can begin anytime now."

Vorly continued to stare at the sheet. *This really is happening.* The world he knew was changing before his eyes.

"Sir?"

Vorly closed his eyes, took a deep breath, and opened them again. He leaned over and put his face six inches away from the crystal sheet. The sweat on his cheek turned to frost, sending a shiver down his spine.

"Obsidian Flock, this is Sky Horse Leader! I am conducting a—" was all Vorly got out before a wave of cold needles passed through his body. Carduus must have experienced it as well because he reared and lunged for the sun with a violent pump of his wings.

"You stupid—!" Vorly shouted, struggling to sit up straight on the rag while putting both hands back on the leather straps at the end of the steel-chain reins. The harnesses over his thighs dug in as he tilted backward and his feet flew up in the air.

He swung his boot heels back until the upward-curving iron hook on each stirrup caught the ridge of scale running underneath the rag's collarbone on either side of its neck. Firmly secure, he brought his knees in until each touched the side of Carduus's neck. As he increased the pressure, Carduus got the message and slowed his wing stroke, settling them back into level flight.

"Your damn sheet spooked him!" Vorly shouted. "How in blazes are we going to fly if he does that every time?"

"It was a temporary surge, I have it under control now," the thaum said, sounding out of breath.

Vorly looked behind him past the RAT and saw the rest of Obsidian Flock. He was relieved to see the five other rags with a driver and thaum on each one stretched out in echelon off of his left wing. Despite the sudden move, the flock had stayed tight.

"We'll need to shoot another line to confirm our altitude," the thaum said.

Vorly reached into the front pocket sewn into his tunic and

pulled out his bronze astrolabe. It was a thin, circular disc, a little bigger than his palm, etched with markings, and several smaller discs revolving about a center rivet. He held it up to the sun, squinted, and spun the other discs until he had the altitude of the sun fixed. Doing this on the back of a rag wasn't precise, but it was close enough.

"Eight hundred seventy-five yards, plus or minus fifteen," he said, putting the astrolabe away.

"Which is it?"

Vorly definitely would have punched a male RAT by now. "If I knew that, I would have said it. Now, what the hell am I conducting again?"

"A crystal pathway check, sir, and you don't have to yell when you speak into the crystal. Your voice will carry just fine at a normal tone. In fact, it's better for the crystal."

"Right," Vorly said, turning back to face forward. He unhooked his left boot and gave Carduus a kick on the neck to get his attention. "Scared of your own shadow," he grumbled. Driving the young rag, a three-year-old bull, was like walking on ice in the dark. Carduus could go days without a mishap, responding to every command with quickness and a clear understanding of what Vorly wanted. Then there were the days when Vorly wanted to bash the stupid beast's head in with an iron mallet.

With a wingspan of twenty yards and a length of twenty-five, Carduus was still really a calf. In another ten years, however, he'd be of mammoth proportions, maybe even a breeder. That, however, would depend on whether the rag was right in the head.

And whether he, and Vorly, survived.

"Obsidian Flock, I am conducting a pathway crystal check. Can you hear me?"

A series of jagged lines lanced through the swirling cloud on the sheet like miniature lightning bolts. Vorly was leaning toward the crystal for a closer look when a voice boomed from the sheet. "Vorly! This is wrong. This is against the LOKAM."

Sky Horse Five, Senior Lancer Jaater Potronic, would

complain about the weight if fifty silver coins fell in his lap. Vorly just shook his head. "Jate, for the High Druid's sake, relax. We just made history!"

"It feels wrong, Vorly. It's getting into my head and—"

Whatever Jate was trying to say was lost in a sudden babble of voices coming over the crystal. More sets of fingertips appeared on the sheet.

"Sky Horse Leader! Holy Forest, I can hear you!"

"Mercy's bells and bonnets, it's like you're sitting right beside me!"

"—how close do I need to be to this thing? Are you sure it's working?"

"I think I just pissed my britches! Wait 'til I tell the wife!"

"—unbelievable. I can hear everyone! Oh, it's me, Sky Horse Four." There were so many fingertips tracing lines on the sheet that Vorly couldn't follow who was who.

"I know it's you, Sky Horse Four, I can see you," Vorly said, waving a hand at Lancer Morsis Rimsma riding Caeraegus, less than a hundred yards away. Rimsma looked up from his crystal and waved back. The thaum behind him kept his head down, working on his crystal sheet.

"Excuse me, sir," the RAT said, tapping him lightly on the shoulder. "We really should stick to the procedures we discussed. The enemy could have thaumics in the field as well, which means they might be able to listen in. The chances are very low, we think, but all the same . . ."

Vorly caught her *we think* and found it troubling. Surely the Kingdom's thaums couldn't be worried about a few native witch doctors? "Right, right. Flock, this is Sky Horse Leader. Well what do you know, the RATs got these crystal things to work. Ain't it a crazy world." Vorly realized he was shaking his head and stopped. "I want a pathway check like we learned earlier this week. Sound off."

"Sky Horse Two here."

"Sky Horse Three."

"—so I touch this—" That had to be Rimsma.

"No, don't touch that!" And that, Vorly realized, was Rimsma's RAT.

"All right, all right, grab some shade. Four here, I mean Sky Horse Four."

Vorly rolled his eyes. Rimsma was a hayloft without the hay. The elation of a moment ago settled as the crystals went quiet. Only the flapping of giant wings and the creak of leather, scale, and chain filled the air. After several moments, the crystal sheet emitted a voice.

"Uh, Sky Horse Six is here."

Vorly shrugged his shoulders. "Sky Horse Five, you forget how this works? C'mon, Jate, we're the elders here. You're making us look bad in front of these kids. Sound off." Vorly pulled back on the right rein, easing Carduus out of line. He put his left fist to the side of his head and then pointed at Sky Horse Two, giving him the lead.

"You can use the device to do that now, sir," came the admonition over his shoulder.

Vorly cursed under his breath; he'd forgotten that that was indeed possible now.

"Sky Horse Five, can you hear me, Jate?" Vorly said into the crystal. "Aw, to lightning with this." He turned and watched as Centaurea drew even with Carduus. The two rags held station at fifty yards.

Jate was out of his saddle and turned around waving his arms at the RAT sitting behind him. Vorly couldn't hear what was being said, but it didn't look friendly. Jate finally sat down and faced forward.

"...orse Fi... ind of probl..."

Vorly sighed. He was going to have to have another talk with Jate. Poor bugger just wasn't adapting well to all of this. He turned to look at his RAT. He paused, realizing he was already thinking of her as *his* but couldn't remember her name. "Who's your father again?"

She held up her free hand in a gesture of *Wait a moment*, then looked up from her crystal sheet. "Yaskar Niorsmith, mayor of

Talon Wall. He named me Grunila," she said.

It didn't suit her. Grunilas were beefy farm girls, all thick in the thighs with round asses and plump breasts.

"You must have been a fat baby, then. I'm calling you Breeze instead. Fits your face better, and all that chattering you do. Now tell me, what's going on with Sky Horse Five?"

If the thaum was offended by his callousness, she hid it well. "I'm picking up interference. The crystal on Sky Horse Five is not aligning properly. It's not riding the plane."

Vorly turned back and looked at his sheet. Orange, jagged lines traced the path of one set of fingertips. He reached forward to rap the sheet with his knuckles. *Damn thaumics.*

"Don't touch it!" Breeze shouted, punching him hard in the shoulder. The air sizzled and pins of fire jabbed into his flesh where she hit him.

"You little bitch," he snarled, raising his arm to give her the back of his hand as he turned, but he stopped. The air above Breeze's crystal shimmered like a heat haze.

"All thaums on this plane, slide off now!" Breeze shouted into her crystal. "Sky Horse Five, you are slipping between planes and building up a high charge. Ground out your crystal and slide!"

Vorly turned back to look at his sheet. The air above it was shimmering too, and the crystal was now a blur of fading lines. The jagged orange lines, however, remained, appearing to grow hotter as they took on a red hue.

"This is exactly why—" Vorly started to stay, turning back around to glare at Breeze, but she cut him off.

"Shut up! I'm trying to concentrate!" she shouted. "Sky Horse Five, you are in danger. I say again, Sky Horse Five, you are in danger. Ground and slide, now! You're going to discharge!"

"Jate, it's me, Vorly. What the hell is going on over there? My RAT has lost her bloody mind jabbering all kinds of nonsense."

"—orly! My RAT is trying to put a spell on me!"

Vorly wasn't sure he'd heard him right. "Jate, what the hell are you talking about? Thaums don't do that hocus-pocus

143

shit." Vorly squinted, trying to figure out what was going on. Jate was out of his saddle again and now had his iron gaff in his hand. He spun around and swung it at the thaum, missing the man's head by inches. The thaum leaned back, crossing his arms over his head.

"Fucking lightning, Jate! Stop that!" Vorly shouted, completely forgetting the crystal.

"Bwiter, get back to your crystal!" Breeze shouted. "Sir, move our dragon closer!"

Vorly felt lost. "We're on the blood line now! You can't get rags any closer. Jate, what the hell are you doing? Drop that gaff and sit the fuck down!"

"Dear Druid! He's ripped out the copper braid!" Breeze said. The horror in her voice set Vorly's skin crawling.

"Tell your thaum fellow to put it—"

Thin staccato bursts of light flashed from Vorly's crystal. He blinked, shaking his head. The air around him pulsed with energy, filling his ears until all he could hear was the beating of his heart. The flock scattered. Carduus banked hard to the right and dove away from Centaurea.

Vorly sawed on the reins and tried to swing Carduus back, but the rag again had a mind of his own. Vorly strained until the muscles in his shoulders burned, but Carduus refused to respond. Looking back, Vorly saw why. Bright orange flames tinged with blue shimmered along the back of Centaurea. Jate was now standing on the back of the rag, the gaff still in his hand. The thaum was flailing at his harness, and then he had it free.

He jumped.

"Bwiter!" Breeze shouted. "No!"

Jate's voice suddenly filled the air. "—burning! I'm on fire, I'm on fire! Mother! Help me. Oh Druid, help me!"

Centaurea shuddered, his huge back heaving up and down. The flames raced down his back and were dispersed by his waving tail. Each downward pull of his wings sent the flames higher. And all the while, Jate screamed as he burned.

Vorly reached for his gaff with his right hand. He kept the

twelve-pound iron bar with a pointed chisel tip at one end lashed to a spike drilled into a scale on Carduus's shoulder. He yanked the gaff free and was ready to hammer Carduus into submission when the screaming stopped.

Vorly turned. Centaurea was descending smoothly, the last of the flames going out. There was no sign of the wooden easels and their crystal sheets. All Vorly could see were greasy wisps of black smoke rising from a hunched form bent over the saddle at the rag's shoulders.

Vorly squeezed the pommel of the gaff until his knuckles ached. "Are we safe?" When there was no answer, he slammed the gaff down on Carduus's scales. The rag responded by leveling out.

"*Are we fucking safe?!*" Vorly shouted, raising the gaff and aiming it at the crystal sheet.

"Yes... I don't, I don't know what... ," Breeze said, choking between sobs.

"Is this thing going to kill us, too?" he asked.

"Oh ...no, no it's sa—it's no longer in plane," Breeze said, her voice as tiny as a little girl's. "You can smash it to pieces if you want. You'll just be breaking glass."

He looked at the crystal sheet, aware all the time of Centaurea flying serenely beside them. His arm swung back three times, ready to destroy the abomination, but he stopped himself. Finally, he secured the gaff with a leather thong and looked straight ahead. He put his fist on top of his helm, then lifted his arm straight, taking back the lead.

"Roost, Carduus, roost."

The rag gently banked to the left, slowly descending as he used his innate senses to take them back home.

Vorly spent the rest of the flight staring straight ahead at nothing. Out of the corner of his eye, a bit of charred shadow emitting greasy black smoke followed him all the way. It stayed fifty yards off of Carduus's left wing, never closing, never drifting away. He knew—they all knew—it would never go away.

CHAPTER FOURTEEN

LEGION FLOCK COMMANDER WALF Modelar stood on the highest point in the Jomkier fiefdom fifty miles inland from the Luitoxese coast and shivered. Modelar, perhaps singularly unique in all the Lux, wished the weather were hotter.

"Warm, sunny place my ass," he grumbled. "Give me the Valley of Flame and Damnation when I die. At least I'll be warm."

Based on his life up to this point, he was fairly certain he'd earned the right to roast for eternity.

Pulling the collar of his tunic up a little higher around his neck, he gazed south. While he was only seventy-five feet above the ground, the view was nonetheless expansive as it overlooked the verdant floodplain of the Hols River. From his vantage point, he could take in virtually the entirety of the fiefdom. The sun, fat and white in a gauzy sky, poured its heat on the shimmering green fields; the wide, undulating river as it bisected the fiefdom on a west–east axis before hooking south; and the groves of fruit and nut trees. It was all so… beautiful.

Modelar couldn't have cared less, but he tried.

He was, as he'd just explained again this morning to the joint council of slyt farmers and crown representatives of the Kingdom's Agricultural Mission to Jomkier, not a fucking administrator. Aware that his meaning had become lost in translation—which was particularly frustrating as the crownies in attendance spoke the same language—he emphasized his point by demonstrating the effect of his boot meeting a chair at considerable speed. That a crowny had been occupying said chair was a happy coincidence. Modelar concluded the meeting by shouting at the backs of the fleeing council that if they came back again, he'd feed them to his rags.

"Weather fucking predictions, crop fucking prices, market fucking futures… High Druid give me strength," he said, doubting it would be enough. He started counting down from ten, realizing he was working himself into a "condition," as his wife called it. Ah, Mirina, that sweet old cow. Couldn't cook, couldn't sew, couldn't sing, but damn, the woman could thrust her hips and squeeze her nethers until he thought he'd pass out.

Thinking about Mirina brought with it a sudden attack of guilt. Not for the little slyt whore he'd taken as a "maid," but for all his swearing. Mirs was no fool. She hadn't asked him to stay true or partake not of wines and liquor. No, she'd grabbed him by the balls, looked up at him, and said that if he didn't promise to stop swearing, she'd squeeze until they turned to jelly.

He kicked a clod of dirt, which tumbled down the slope, breaking apart until nothing but a shower of tiny particles splashed into the dosha swamp below. Dosha. Tasted like snot and looked like mulched lice. It wasn't just the dosha though. Jomkier was a veritable farmer's market producing more fu—*bloody* fruits than he'd ever seen in his life on top of tea, cashews, and tons upon tons of dosha. That was bad enough, but this being Jomkier, there was always more, and it was always worse. Slyt fisherman plied the Hols hauling netfuls of perch, carp, yellowfin, whipray, anchovy, sharkminnow, and eel out of the muddy river. They needed open areas to dry their catches and were complaining regularly that the flight paths of the rags were covering the catches in dirt and sulfur. And then sending him a bill! Hand to the High Forest, *a fucking bill*! He wasn't commanding flocks of rags anymore; he was running a damn market!

Modelar snorted and paced along the edge of a massive

crater a half mile across, surrounded on three sides by a thin horseshoe of land no more than two hundred feet at its widest point—all that remained of the original plateau. The heart of the plateau had been progressively hollowed out over centuries of quarrying. The southern end, closest to the Hols, had been collapsed, allowing the huge stone blocks to be carted to the river, where even now barges carried them twenty miles south to the capital, Gremthyn.

"Fuck!" Modelar shouted. A little quarry in the middle of a damn swamp in a faraway country so backward it thought yesterday was next week shouldn't be this vexing.

He blamed the Qreet brothers: Narth, Frol, and Wrol. Modelar had never met them, and never would either, as they'd been murdered along with their families, servants, and even the servants' families over four months ago. Butchered like so many pigs by slyts infiltrating from Western Luitox. Modelar had one of the leaflets left pinned to a body translated. The Forest Collective was avenging all slyts everywhere by attacking predatory landowners and those who supported them.

The bodies had been disposed of after lying out in the sun for two weeks, but Modelar was convinced he could still smell them, especially in the afternoon heat. If only their stench was all that remained, but just his luck, more unpleasantness lingered. Over two hundred and seventy Luitoxese, including children, had been slaughtered, which, while tragic, nonetheless gave him the perfect space for a roost for the flocks. He would have requisitioned the Qreet quarry even if it hadn't been abandoned. It really was ideal.

Then the distant relatives of the Qreets began arriving from all over Luitox, laying claim to the quarry and demanding payment for the Kingdom's use of it. Dozens and dozens of stripey-faced little natives jawing and wailing and making his life miserable.

He fought back another expletive and was feeling proud of himself for that when he caught motion a mile away to the east. A six-rag formation was angling toward the roost at five hundred feet. Modelar squinted up at the sun, then looked down at his shadow. Bit early for Vorly to be bringing Obsidian Flock back. He knew the flock commander wasn't thrilled with the RATs and their new devices, but too bad—this was the latest kit coming out of the RAT and he wanted it. A legion flock commander didn't make army flock commander by playing things safe, not in wartime.

The rags weren't flying the standard V or single-line echelon. He'd give Vorly a hard time about it when he landed. It was good to fire up the troops now and then, keep things tight. He saw smoke coming off of one of the rags and added that to the list. One of the drivers had obviously flown his rag too hard. Didn't look too bad, but clearly Obsidian Flock needed a good tune-up. It would let him get some of this Jomkier frustration out of his system.

As the formation got closer, he could make out the drivers and their RATs. Standing on the rim of the plateau put Modelar at the same height as the rags as they came in. He'd caught more than one driver not wearing his full harness and several other infractions.

Modelar counted the crews this time. He blinked and started his count again. A cold chill radiated out from the pit of his stomach. He stared blankly as Centaurea drew near and descended toward the quarry floor, the wind from his wings buffeting Modelar as he flew past. The smell of the smoke reached his nostrils a moment later.

"…fuck…"

THE FIRST SENSATION that registered was the feeling of the anvil sitting on Jawn's head. He forced open one eye, grimacing as several crud-crusted eyelashes ripped out.

There was no anvil. Just the gallons of alcohol he'd consumed since the night the slyts set themselves on fire. *What was that, three days ago? Five?* He groaned. He was in a simple bamboo hut lying on the floor. It was daytime, but beyond that he really didn't know or care. He closed his eye. No one should be in this much pain and still be alive.

Images of burning bodies flickered behind his eyelids. With them came the charred-flesh smell that still lingered in his nostrils. It was as if the memories were renewing, finding fresh parts of his brain to stain with their horror.

"I'm standing here trying to decide if the reports of your demise are exaggerated," Rickets said, flinging open the linen door of the hut and looking down at Jawn. "Honestly, it's hard to tell. Assuming you are in fact alive, I brought you something to put a little sap back in your leaves," he said, holding out a steaming mug.

Jawn glared up at Rickets from the floor. "You did this to me."

Rickets didn't even have the decency to look mildly remorseful. His crown uniform was freshly laundered and his chubby face was unabashedly aglow. He'd shaved what hair had remained after the fire, and though Jawn wouldn't say it out loud, he actually looked better.

"Oh, it's true, and I feel terrible about it," Rickets said, his demeanor suddenly solemn and repentant. "Pointing that crossbow at your head and making you drink. Ordering you to cavort with those whores. Wantonly, I might add. Aye, I'm a scourge to the chaste and learned, I am."

"You could have stopped me," Jawn said, closing his eyes and laying his head down on the floor. "You should have stopped me."

The rattan floor creaked as Rickets entered the hut. "You needed that bender. I did, too," Rickets said, his voice drifting. "After what we saw, no man has a right to deny another his oblivion. I've been to more shitholes for the Kingdom and never encountered anything like that. I mean, I've done—I've seen things," Rickets said, quickly correcting himself, "and always for the greater fucking good, but nothing like that."

Jawn desperately wanted him to stop talking, but his fascination kept his mouth shut. He carefully opened both eyes.

"The Kingdom asks a lot of a man," Rickets continued, looking into a distance only he could see. "It fills you with ideals and purpose and a sense of duty. It makes you bigger, stronger. Then, with no warning, you're forced to take all those beliefs and run a knife across their throats when diplomacy or merchant interests or whatever else the high and mighty deem important trumps everything we were ever told to believe."

Though his vision was blurry, Jawn was certain Rickets's eyes were misting up. Rickets blinked and a tear rolled down his face. Jawn couldn't handle that right now.

"I'm lucky to be conscious at the moment," Jawn said, trying to lighten the mood. "About the only thing I believe is I will never partake of spirits again."

Rickets turned and looked at Jawn. "Spoken like a survivor." He sat down on the floor, holding out the mug. Jawn pulled himself up to lean against the palm-frond wall. He took the mug with two hands.

Jawn looked down at the mug. "What is this?"

"Tea," Rickets said. "Mostly."

"Mostly?"

"You want to feel better, or do you want to keep asking questions you don't want the answers to?"

Jawn looked down at the mug again. Tea wasn't normally dark red. He raised the mug up to his face and drew in a sniff. His nostrils blew wide open, clearing a path straight to his brain.

"Fire and lightning!" he exclaimed, his eyes watering.

"Probably some of that in there, too," Rickets said.

Jawn closed his eyes and drank. For several moments, he wasn't sitting in a hut in the Lux with a hangover. Where exactly he was, however, he wasn't sure. When he opened his eyes again, he felt close to human. Still tired and with a slight pounding at his temples, but the worst of the hangover was gone.

"Now it's time to get you on your feet and moving. We have work to do."

Jawn shook his head. "I still have time before I have to report."

"About that," Rickets said, pulling out a thin paper scroll from a sleeve and handing it over to Jawn. It was tied with a red string with the dark green wax seal of the Royal Academy of Thaumology.

Jawn popped off the wax seal with the fingernail of his

thumb. Before he could ask, Rickets handed him a small knife, which Jawn took and used to cut through the red string. Only messages of high importance received both the seal and the string. In his life, Jawn had never received one.

Jawn unrolled the scroll and began reading. His mouth dropped open and he looked up. "This can't be right."

"In fact, the RAT has exercised its right to you," Rickets said. "You're about to embark on a new and rewarding career in service of His Royal Whoever."

Jawn went back to reading. "Countryside vitality and productivity research, adjunct to Greater Luitox Agricultural Mission. Effects of battle on crops and livestock? But I'm assigned to the Seventh Phalanx," Jawn said.

Rickets pointed at Jawn. "You're missing the nut and focusing on the bark. This is a promotion. With this, you get a ticket to travel the Lux."

"Why would I want to do that?" Jawn asked. How many more bamboo huts were there to see?

"Chin up, Jawny-boy, your luck's still holding. If you keep reading, you'll see that the mission is tasked with studying the Seventh Phalanx. Well, at least the mess they make. Remember I told you they were sending the Seventh inland? They did. The army is pushing all the way west until they hit the Ultalon River. Should encounter a whole lot of FnCs on the way. So buck up, all is well," Rickets said.

"This doesn't make any sense."

"Of course it doesn't, but therein lies the real truth. As of now you are *officially* part of the group tasked with studying dosha swamps, fig trees, and goat dung as trod on, dug up, eaten, and otherwise defiled by the glorious Seventh Phalanx."

Horror-struck by the notion of studying goat pastures, Jawn almost missed Rickets's emphasis of one word.

"Officially?" Jawn asked. He held the scroll up to the light leaking through the fronds to see if a hidden message would be revealed.

"Officially," Rickets replied, giving nothing away.

Jawn lowered the scroll and looked at Rickets. Hundreds of questions danced in his head, but he realized only one would unlock the rest. "Rickets... who are you?"

Rickets smiled and nodded. "Good, lad. Leo said once you pushed the pudding out of the way, there was a brain in that skull of yours. "

Senior Thaum Leotat Kirsingil had invited Jawn to his office for tea in Jawn's last semester at the academy just after Jawn had made it known he was volunteering for the army. Expecting to be harangued or even threatened if he went through with his plans to leave, Kirsingil had commended Jawn on his decision. What followed was a friendly if intense grilling from midmorning until dinner on Kingdom politics, religion, policy regarding foreign lands, and a myriad of other topics from the inane to the profound. When Jawn had finally been ushered out, exhausted and light-headed, he felt like he'd just sat an exam. What for, however, he'd had no idea.

Until now.

"Do... do you work for the Dark Rangers?" Rumors abounded about the Kingdom's spy service. Jawn had never met anyone in it... or maybe he had in the form of his previous instructor.

"Never heard of them, and even if I had, they don't exist," Rickets said.

"You do, don't you," Jawn said.

Rickets lifted his hands palms up. "I think you're confused. There is, of course, His Majesty's Forest Ranger Service, a noble and vital branch that sees to the welfare of forests in the Kingdom and around the world. As for the Dark Rangers, they have never been officially acknowledged. But even if they were, I'm not one. And as of this moment, neither are you. Not that they exist."

"At this moment, I'm not entirely sure *I* exist," Jawn said.

Rickets winked at him. "Bravo. That's the kind of bewilderment that will fool even the keenest of enemy observers."

"You mean the FnC?" Jawn asked, now developing the habit of ignoring Rickets's insults.

Rickets didn't answer at once. Jawn started to ask again when

Rickets began speaking. "The definition of *enemy* encompasses significantly more than simply the disenchanted natives, but we'll leave that conversation for another day."

It was an unsettling answer, but Jawn didn't have the stomach for a protracted discussion. The heat of the day was quickly raising the temperature inside the hut and Jawn was starting to feel light-headed.

"Assuming I understand this, which I'm fairly certain I don't, what is it I am supposed to do as part of this Cow and Country mission?"

Rickets smiled approvingly. "For cow and country. You're a wit, you are. We'll have to get that embroidered on something."

"I'm really not in the mood. Could you just tell me what I'm supposed to do?"

Rickets held up a finger. "Yes, yes, you do need to be apprised of your new role. There have been... developments since Gremthyn. Do you want the good news or the bad news first?"

"Finding out I've been retasked wasn't the bad news?" Jawn asked.

"Oh, it was, but that was just the appetizer to what is looming on the horizon as one massive shit soufflé."

Jawn's stomach spasmed. "The good news first," he managed to say.

"An optimist. Well, the Lux will beat that out of you before long. Fine. The good news is we're going to be working together. *Officially*, I have been retasked with providing all clerical and other duties as required in support of the mission."

"Together? Us? You and me?"

Rickets nodded enthusiastically. "Two men on an arduous journey through festering swamp and sweltering jungle. They may very well write a book about our adventures one day, just like the famous Ox and Crink." Rickets paused for a moment, then continued. "Ah, well, not entirely like them, I should think."

"I can understand them wanting me, but why you?"

Rickets sighed and looked down at his hands. Jawn followed his gaze. Rickets's hands were strong, the fingers lean and surprisingly agile. For the first time, Jawn noticed a thin lattice of scars on the knuckles. These weren't the hands of a midlevel bureaucrat.

"You keep asking questions you don't want the answers to," Rickets finally said. He said it without any emotion, which made it sound all the more ominous.

Jawn thought back to their rag ride and Rickets's relative calm, despite the harrowing nature of their flight. Who Rickets really was seemed even less clear now. *Could he really be a spy?* The stories about the Dark Rangers were wild and often drenched in blood. He doubted a tenth of what he'd heard about them was true, but even at a tenth…

"Curiosity doesn't just kill cats," one of Jawn's professors, an ancient thaum well into his sixties, used to say right before beginning to teach them a new process. It was an odd motto for a professor, but on the other hand, he did teach mortal thaumics.

"You said good news and bad news. So what's the bad news?" Jawn asked. Rickets's true identity could wait for another day.

"It turns out to be rather fortuitous, as far as that goes," Rickets said. "One of those crystal contraptions your academy dreamed up for talking over long distances stopped working in a very bad way."

"You know about those?" Jawn asked.

Rickets looked Jawn over before responding. "We should talk about the details later. It's all a bit complicated."

"Let's do it now," Jawn said.

Rickets shrugged. "Control was lost. There was a fire. Two dead. Very messy. The RAT, and… other entities, are concerned that there could be a fatal flaw in the system."

Jawn shook his head and squeezed his hands into fists. "That shouldn't have happened. There are safeguards. We established methods to avoid… fires."

"You're not in the RAT anymore. It gets nontheoretical very fast out here."

"I understand that, but what you're missing is that thaumics is neither bad or good. It's simply *power*. That's what all of nature is. Everything around us is power," Jawn said. "Like a boulder on the edge of a cliff. As long as it sits there, it's stable, or at least it appears to be. But with erosion from wind and rain, the cliff beneath wears away until the rock tips over and falls. Now what was once stable is transformed into a massive force of energy."

"So you're the wind and the rain then?"

Jawn nodded. "In a manner of speaking. Thaums don't create the power—we find it, harness it, and redirect it. The RAT is all about pushing the boundaries of what we know and how we can harness more of it."

"Like the slyt thaum," Rickets said.

"Well, yes. If a thaum is willing to die, or wants to, the power he can harness will be huge. We're learning more about the aether and the planes. And the more we learn, the more we discover what we don't know."

Silence reigned in the hut. Jawn's mind flashed to the gathered slyts in the square. It had been horrific, but it had also been controlled and on purpose. That slyt thaum had meant for the slyts to burn. As much as Jawn wanted to forget it, he realized there was a part of him intent on understanding it, dissecting every aspect of the process. He wanted to know how to wield that kind of power.

"In that vein," said Rickets, "we need to look into the use of these crystals and make sure they're functioning as they should be. That goes for the RATs operating them, too. We don't want more accidents."

Jawn's head snapped up and he looked squarely at Rickets. "That's what this is about? You want me to spy on other thaums?"

"We can't have more Gremthyns," Rickets said.

Jawn felt offended. "That was an enemy thaum."

Rickets hung his head as he talked. "It was wrong, not because he killed all those slyts, but because he could. That kind of power... it shouldn't exist."

Jawn realized he wasn't going to get Rickets to see this his way. Thaumics was the future and thaums like Jawn would only become more powerful as they learned to master ever more processes. "Gremthyn was terrible," Jawn said, not knowing what else to say.

Rickets jumped to his feet, startling Jawn.

"Anyway, it's a beautiful morning in the Lux and we have places to be. Let's get you washed up and looking like, well, the opposite of whatever this is." He held out a hand to Jawn.

Seeing nothing else for it, Jawn took Rickets's hand and allowed the man to haul him to his feet. The silk that Jawn had taken for a sheet slid down around his ankles and he realized that it was in fact a woman's dress. Worse, he was wearing a pair of women's unmentionables underneath.

"I probably don't want to know about this, do I?" Jawn said.

Rickets smiled. "Oh, no, I'm going to love telling you about *this*."

CHAPTER FIFTEEN

"WELL, DAMN WELL FIND a way to make it work!" Obsidian Flock leader Vorly Astol stood at attention, his eyes fixed on a three-inch tear in the far canvas wall of Legion Flock Commander Walf Modelar's tent.

Modelar was in full tirade and the air was suffocating. Vorly's head pounded and he thought he might vomit. It took a moment for him to answer.

"Not with those things I won't," Vorly said.

This was the third confrontation Vorly had had with the LFC in as many days since the crystal incident, and they were only getting worse.

Modelar threw a punch at the side of the tent, driving his arm through the canvas up to his elbow. "You think I'm asking you for a fucking favor?" He yanked his arm back in. "I'm telling you what you're going to do, and you are damn well going to do it!"

"But they *aren't safe*."

Modelar punched the canvas again with the same results. When he yanked his arm out this time, it left a foot-long gash revealing the dusty quarry yard of the rag roost. Flockmen walking by the tent sped up their pace and disappeared from view.

"Safe?! Druid fucking trees, Flock Leader! We ride big, stupid dragons that explode! Safe?! What in the—may the High

Druid… safe, he says! You—you…"

Vorly knew Modelar was right, but that didn't change anything. Images of the small, charred lump being pried off of Centaurea's scales lingered in Vorly's mind.

"Are you listening to me?" Modelar asked, standing up on his toes to put his eyes in line with Vorly's. A good three inches shorter than Vorly's less-than-towering five feet six inches, Modelar commanded attention through sheer volume and intensity. With his horseshoe of white hair from ear to ear, large hook nose, heavy brow, and piercing blue eyes, the LFC was known throughout the flocks as Screaming Eagle. Those less charitable, like rag drivers who earned his displeasure, called him Screeching Pigeon, though not to his face, and never without looking over their shoulder first.

Vorly blinked and focused on his commander. "You can court-martial me if you'd like, but I'm not flying with one of those things again."

Modelar's eyes widened and he drew in a breath. His complexion turned from angry rose to throbbing red, but then he pushed down the air in front of him with his hands and let his breath out, hissing like a kettle at full boil. He lowered himself back onto his heels.

"High fuckin' Druid, Vorly. Are you trying to put me in an early grave?" The moment he said it he was waving the thought away. "Bad choice of words. Do you know you are the biggest thorn in my paw? Any other driver and I'd have strung you from the highest tree long ago. Do you even know how lucky you are, you insubordinate shit? A needle in a haystack, Vorly, a needle in Druid-forsaken haystack, but they found the body of that RAT. Luckier still, the crystal sheets, or what was left of them, were still on the rag when it came back. Do you have any idea the kind of nightmare we'd have on our hands if we lost a RAT or some of their precious crystal?"

"We lost Jate, too, not that they seem to care," Vorly said.

Modelar massaged his temples with a pained look on his face. "Vorly, no one is happy about what happened. Jate was a hell of a driver, and he'll be missed. But I got reports from every other driver and RAT on that training flight. Something wasn't right with him. Hell, the aether commander *herself* is involved. This isn't your run-of-the-mill accident. This is *serious*. We need to know what happened, and from everything I've heard, Jate was his own worst enemy."

Vorly gritted his teeth. "Jate said the thaum was casting a spell on him."

"Mmm. What do you think?" Modelar asked.

Vorly looked down at Modelar. He hadn't expected that. "A spell?" Vorly sighed. "It wasn't anything like that. Jate got it into his head that the crystals went against the LOKAM." Vorly knew Jate was a devout Dendrolatrian, but it never seemed to interfere with his ability to fly a rag. Sure, Jate was forever complaining about the drinking and the whoring and taking the High Druid's name in vain, but that was just Jate being Jate. When he started complaining about the crystals, Vorly had chalked it up to one more case of Jate getting on his high branch and preaching. "I should have done something. I had no idea he'd…"

Modelar reached out a hand and grabbed Vorly's right arm at the elbow, giving it a squeeze. The two men had known each other fifteen years and been friends for the last nine. "The world keeps moving faster. Not everyone has a strong enough grip to hold on. It's a damn shame all the way around, what happened to Jate, but it doesn't change shit." Modelar let go of Vorly's arm. He was commander again. "The navy's Third Fleet has been unloading crystals and RATs for the last two weeks and His Majesty Whoever expects us to use them. Every flock in the Lux is going to have RATs and crystals. They're even talking about giving some to the army legions. They think they'll be able to make it so we can talk with the army on the ground while we're flying."

Vorly opened his mouth to protest, but Modelar cut him off. "I don't want to fucking hear it. If you can't handle this, fine, I'm not going to make you. But your gray matter is boiled pudding if you think I'm going to waste my time court-martialing your sorry ass. You would do well to remember that the transport caravans are always looking for seat warmers."

It wasn't an idle threat. More than one rag driver had found himself breathing dust behind a team of oxen. For a high-flying ragger, there wasn't a worse punishment than that.

"He burned, Walf. He screamed and he cried and he burned." Vorly's right eye teared up. *Fucking hell, like meat on a spit.*

Modelar looked away. Vorly brought up a hand and wiped the tear from his eye.

"He's not the first driver that's charked, and he won't be the last," Modelar said, speaking low. "The day you no longer accept that is the day you hang up your spurs." Modelar turned around and fixed Vorly with his eagle stare. "Your flock, including the RATs, is waiting in your tack room. You get them right with this and get your flock ready to fly, or you keep on walking to the caravans. We've got a war to fight."

Vorly knew their meeting was over. He saluted, spun on his heel, and headed toward the pens. Until he got there, he wasn't sure if he was going to stop or keep on walking.

The decision was made for him before he reached the pens. Lancer Rimsma came running along the gravel road, his tunic torn and blood streaming from his nose. When he spotted Vorly, he stumbled to a halt.

"Sir! They're fighting!"

This is all I need. Even though they were from the same litter, rags had separate pens to keep them from having a go at each other. Vorly had learned that most of the aggression they displayed was for show rather than with the intent to injure, but a four-ton rag could still do a hell of a lot of damage to the humans around it.

"Shit." Vorly grabbed Rimsma by his jacket lapels. "Go find the dragonsmith and round up as many flockmen as you can," he ordered, but Rimsma was vigorously shaking his head no.

"It's not the rags, sir. It's the drivers and the RATs."

Vorly immediately took off running, not bothering to see if Rimsma was following him.

He reached his flock's tack room and charged through the door, out of breath and light-headed. Running was a young man's game. The scene that greeted him was chaos. He'd feared the RATs would use their thaumics, but they were throwing conventional fists and boots. That should have put the ivory-tower RATs at a huge disadvantage against his drivers, especially as three of the RATs were women—and Breeze was fighting too?!—but the battle seemed evenly matched.

Vorly sucked in a couple of more breaths while the drivers and RATs traded blows. Realizing he couldn't wait any longer, he stood up straight and roared, *"What the fuck is going on here?!"*

The fight went on unabated. "Son of a witch," he said, wading into the fray. "Stand down! Everyone stop right now!" He grabbed a RAT by her collar and dragged her off one of his drivers. *"Enough!"*

The fighting quickly subsided. The only thing that could be heard was the sound of heavy breathing. The RATs grouped together on the far side of the room while Vorly's drivers clustered near him by the door. He glared around the room—there were enough bloody lips and black eyes for last call at the pub on payday. "Are you all mad?! Are you all *fucking mad*?! We lost two men not four days ago!"

"And we know why," Lancer Frem Sowka said, pointing a finger at the RATs. "Those crystals are dangerous!"

"No more dangerous than fool superstitious drivers who don't follow instructions!" Breeze retorted.

Vorly recognized himself in the insult but let it go. He couldn't afford to be blinded by his emotions. Not now. He noticed that despite Breeze's disheveled hair and one tunic sleeve torn completely off, her face looked unscathed. Her knuckles, however, were a bloody mess.

"Just like a RAT to get all high and mighty," Sowka spat out. "You think because you went to your fancy academy, you know everything about everything. I think you know shit."

"I could learn to fly a rag in a week," Breeze shot back. "You probably can't even spell *academy*."

"Enough!" Vorly shouted, looking at Breeze. "And not another word out of you."

Breeze crossed her arms and glared at him. "You're siding with the drivers. Of course. We figured you would."

Shouting and taunts flew across the room until Vorly picked up a wooden bench and hurled it against the far wall, where it shattered. The noise immediately ceased.

"Anyone else care to comment?" Vorly asked, forcing his anger down.

"I think Sowka's right," Rimsma said. "The crystal sheets are dangerous. But I also think they're important. Imagine the possibilities when we get it all worked out."

Vorly knew his mouth was open and closed it. *Rimsma is the voice of reason?*

"How many more have to die to 'get it all worked out'?" Sowka asked, turning on Rimsma. "You ready to risk your life again to find out?"

"I am," Rimsma said. The other drivers looked stunned. The RATs did, too. They clearly hadn't expected to get support from the other side. "Look, you all know I'm not the brightest star in the sky, but this thaumic stuff isn't going away. Instead of fighting it, we should figure out how to make it work better."

"I think you very much might *be* the brightest one in this room," Breeze said, looking at Rimsma and smiling. When she turned to look at Vorly, the smile was gone. "If you want promises that there will never be another… accident, I can't give them to you, but then, you can't promise us a rag won't explode or try to eat one of us. We're here to do a job—one we're very good at. Let us do it… please."

That caught Vorly off guard. Modelar had made it clear the RATs weren't going anywhere, but maybe these particular RATs had been threatened by their commander with something equally as terrifying as riding a wagon train.

Vorly looked around the room, taking his time to stare down every single driver and RAT. It was childish, but it was also necessary. This was *his* flock. "All of you listen up, because I will *never* say this again. This was your one and only fuckup. You don't get another. If I have to replace every driver and RAT here, I will do it, and don't think for a moment I won't. And that doesn't mean you get transferred to another flock. Oh no. You'll be *done*."

He paused while that sank in. When he saw a few nods he continued. "Something else I want everyone here to get through their heads. *I* am the flock commander. That means every rag, man, and woman in this flock is *my* responsibility. I do not play favorites. No, that's not true—the rags come first, but after that, you're all the same. Driver or RAT, if you do your job and work your ass off, we'll get along fine. Pull shit like this," he said, waving around the room, "and I will *end* you. Is that clear?"

There were more nods and a few ayes.

"No one appears to be choking on their tongue, so let me try that again. Is that *crystal fucking clear*?" he asked, pronouncing his words slowly and clearly.

"Yes, sir!"

"Lovely. Well, now that that's settled, the first order of business is to get this tack room back in order," Vorly said, lowering his shoulders and clasping his hands behind his back. "When that's done, and it *will* be done by the time I get back from lunch, you are all going down to the pens and mucking out the shit. Might help you burn off some of this energy."

He waited, daring one of them to protest. He pointedly looked at Breeze—she stared back, the muscles of her jaw flexing, but she kept her mouth shut.

Vorly turned to leave, then stopped and turned back. "Out of curiosity, who threw the first punch?" All the drivers looked directly at Breeze, while the RATs looked everywhere but at her. To their credit, no one said a thing. Vorly kept the smile to himself, but only just.

"Wipe the blood off your faces, fix this room up, get those stables mucked out by dusk, and do it without killing each other. Remember," he said, turning and walking out the door, "there are a whole lot of slyts out there in the jungle waiting for that chance anyway."

CHAPTER SIXTEEN

THE SUN EMERGED ABOVE the tree line as a shimmering orange ball. The few straggling dosha plants still clinging to life in drought-stricken swamp plots began to wilt as the red loam cracked and lost even more moisture to the relentless heat. Barely an eighth of a candle past dawn, the Luitoxese lowlands were baking.

Stretched out over the plots in a skirmish line forty yards wide and oriented on a north–south axis, the soldiers of several shields in the Second Javelin advanced. They walked west, their shadows stretching out before them like long black fingers.

A low, wide dust cloud another seventy-five yards to the rear marked the position of a caravan of three native brorra-drawn wagons of Deputy Legion Commander Weel's Second Legion Command Group. The lumbering animals were about the size of a cow, but their skin was gray and covered in coarse black hair. It grew thickest in a long strip down their spine from their head to their rump. Their distinguishing feature, however, was the thick, single curving horn three feet long that sprouted from the top ridge of their heads.

A canvas tent roof supported on wooden poles provided shade for Weel's wagon, a luxury the passengers of the other two transports did not enjoy. A half shield known officially as Command Group Guard Detachment—and unofficially as Silver

Shield for their cushy assignment—walked alongside the wagons providing security for Weel and his officers. The mule train, six hundred dwarves and fifty wagons of the Eighteenth Pioneer Support Group, followed one hundred yards farther back.

For added punch, the six twenty-foot-tall field catapults of Bear Battery creaked and clattered across the single dirt road that cut diagonally through the dosha swamps from north to south. The battery was scheduled to reach a collection of three palm trees five hundred yards to the east of Moskoan village by midday. At the moment, Moskoan lay seven hundred yards ahead of the forward skirmish line. Only when Bear Battery was set up, a process that would take one-fourth of a candle, would the catapults be able to offer anything more than moral support to the Seventh Phalanx, Weel's old phalanx, which was leading the attack this morning. If the reports of a large FnC force infiltrating the area were true, that wouldn't suffice.

A soldier riding a pony trotted up to Weel's wagon and slowed to a walk, matching its pace. The pony, a blue roan, might have had a good coat once, but the peaks and valleys of its rib cage marred its sides. A regular-sized man would have driven the pony to the ground, but in this case the rider appeared little larger than a twelve-year-old boy with shockingly thin legs.

Deputy Legion Commander Weel failed to acknowledge the rider even though he glanced up from the map spread out on his lap and looked straight at the messenger. Watching from a few feet away, Subcommander Brobbi Parmik thought Weel was a prick of the first order. *It's because he's tall*, Parmik thought. Tall men were always arrogant. By contrast, at four foot ten, Parmik was stubby and brick shaped, with a sunburned face; small, squinty eyes; and a fiery red beard he kept shorn one inch below his chin. Barely a half foot taller than most dwarves, he was mistaken for one more times than not. Still, the beard stayed. It was a perverse choice on his part, but he couldn't help himself.

Parmik looked around the wagon, curious to see if any of the other officers would draw Weel's attention to the rider. As Bear Battery's liaison with Weel's command group, Parmik was a guest, as Weel himself had put it. Parmik's superior, Commander Newel Joars, had made it clear that Parmik's job was to explain to the army ants what a catapult could and couldn't do, and then keep the ants happy. Parmik looked down at his boots and then back up, deciding to heed Joars's advice.

The rider meanwhile appeared unperturbed by Weel's rudeness, even nodding pleasantly at the other officers. Field Deputy Paet Leieroyo, another tall man, though not nearly as snobbish as Weel, looked around the wagon. Perhaps it was the fact that Leieroyo commanded the Provisions and Fodder Detachment of the Seventh Phalanx that made him more down-to-earth. All he talked about were grains, hays, and the fucking navy and the weevil-infested foodstuffs they kept pawning off on the army. Parmik remembered he still hadn't spoken to Leieroyo about the need to get in touch with the rag commanders in this area so that he could beg, borrow, or steal some of their rock. Catapults worked significantly better when they were hurling stone and not forgetful officers.

Leieroyo glanced at Weel, who was still head-down over the map. Placing a finger to his lips, Leieroyo offered the rider his water skin, even taking the trouble to unstopper it before handing it over. It was a custom job, the outer layer made from a fine, dark brown beaver pelt. In a rare instance when he wasn't talking about food or the navy, Leieroyo had joked that the beaver pelt kept the water wetter.

The rider smiled and took the water skin. He raised it to his lips and took a small sip. He then brought it down and emptied the rest of the water into his other hand. As he did so something shiny tumbled out of the opening and vanished immediately as the rider palmed it and placed it in a small leather pouch strapped to the belt around his waist. When he brought his hand back out, he held several brown folded leaves. In one smooth motion, he placed them in a slit in the fur of the water skin and passed it back. If Parmik hadn't been fascinated by the water skin, he never would have noticed.

Leieroyo quickly placed the water skin in his haversack before buckling it shut. When he looked up and saw Parmik watching him, he started and quickly looked away. Parmik looked over to the rider, who was now staring at Parmik as well. Unlike Leieroyo, the rider looked completely at ease. He even had the audacity to wink at Parmik.

Weel finally looked up from his map and appeared to notice the rider for the first time. The soldier sat up straight and saluted.

"Bristom, where are the catapults?" Weel asked. He didn't return the soldier's salute, instead leaning over the edge of the wagon and holding out the map. The rider identified as Bristom dutifully grabbed the edge of the map and pointed.

"Bear Battery is here," Bristom said, his finger touching near the bottom edge of the map. "They're having a tough time with the road. It's barely wide enough for the catapults. They've had two slide off already."

Parmik silently cursed. *Road? More like goat path.* It was a wonder the catapults had made it this far west as it was.

Weel looked off to the south. Parmik followed his gaze, as did the rest of the officers. A smudge of brown against the distant green of the jungle marked Bear Battery's slow progress. Weel looked back at the map.

"Subcommander Parmik, why aren't your catapults keeping pace?"

Parmik stood up at the back of the wagon, steadying himself on the wooden bench.

"You heard your pony boy—it's the road. Sir." Parmik muscled his way through the six other officers on board until he stood beside Weel. He wasn't going to be intimidated by these men, no matter how tall they were. "Too narrow and rutted, like that old pony's rib cage."

An audible gasp went up from the command group. Weel's cheeks flushed, but he adopted a tight-lipped smile as he faced Parmik.

"Well, Subcommander, that simply won't do," Weel said, each word clipped so sharply it could have cut metal. "I specifically ordered that the six catapults of your battery be in position by noon. The Second Javelin will be assaulting Moskoan inside of a fourth-candle."

"If I could get them there in time, I'd do it... but this doesn't give a true lay of the land," Parmik said, gesturing toward Weel's map. "You see what it's like out here. Distances are way off, what the map says is jungle is now dosha swamp, and what was dosha swamp turns out to be jungle. We've already sent back a dozen messages by rag for royal cartographers to be dispatched, but it's going to take weeks to get better maps."

"I'm not interested in excuses, Subcommander," Weel said. He neatly folded his hands one over the other on his knee and looked at Parmik. Even sitting down he was slightly taller. "I want your catapults at those palm trees and ready by noon."

Parmik turned and looked south again. He lifted his helm from his head and scratched at his thick mat of red hair. He slowly scanned the dosha swamp, noting the progress of the skirmish line. Finally, he looked up at the sun before turning back to Weel.

"I can see you care a lot about your boys, sir," he said, doubting that was true but deciding to give a little. He'd be riding in this wagon for a while. "They deserve all the support they can get. It'll be a right mess, but Commander Joars will move High Forest and earth to get you that support. I'll write a message for the lad to take over to the battery. We can unhook the back three ox teams and then double-team the first three cats. That'll get half the battery to that village by noon. And if I send two additional crews with them, they'll have the cats up and ready to throw within an eighth of a candle."

"And the other three catapults?" Weel asked.

"Not until dusk. The teams will be exhausted," Parmik said. It wasn't perfect, but it was the best to be done on short notice.

A young officer stood up, his face red and his fists clenched. Parmik tried to remember his name. Deswol... Dismawl...

"Subcommander Parmik! The Deputy Legion Commander Weel has given you a direct order," the officer said, his indignation swelling his chest. "Your—"

Weel held up a hand, cutting the officer off. "Thank you, Dehmoll. Subcommander, am I to understand that given the state of the road and the strength of your oxen, you will only be able to get *three* catapults to their assigned position on time?"

Parmik put his helm back on his head. *Here comes the shit storm.* "Yes, Commander, that's exactly what I'm saying."

Weel nodded. "I see. Tell me, Subcommander, would additional oxen help?"

Parmik started to smile, then stopped when he realized Weel was being serious. "Of course, but... look around, Commander. Even if we unhitched these brorras and threw in that little pony, we'd still be nowhere close."

Weel's smiled broadened, but only just. "True, but what about six hundred mules, Subcommander?"

Parmik looked behind them at the column of marching dwarves. *Oh, you fucking bastard.* "They aren't slaves anymore, sir. Harnessing them to pull has been outlawed for thirty years." Parmik had never been comfortable with the way dwarves were treated.

"Of course, Subcommander," Weel said, his voice now light and airy. "They are, however, members of the Royal Army and as such are duty-bound to serve where needed. And right now, *you* need their strength to move *your* catapults to their assigned position by noon."

Parmik barely heard Weel. Childhood taunts echoed once again in his ears: *Bet your mother was raped by a mule! Go back to the quarry with your own kind!* He absently rubbed the bridge of his nose. It had been broken so many times he hadn't breathed through both nostrils at the same time in ten years.

"Even so, convincing them won't be easy," Parmik said, his eyes still on the dwarf column.

"Then it's settled," Weel said, clapping his hands. "Bristom will ride at once to the catapults to inform them that much-needed assistance is on its way. And you, Subcommander, will go tell the mules they have a new task."

Parmik swung around to stare at Weel. "*I* will?"

"You're here to assist me, Subcommander, do not forget that. Besides," Weel said, his voice as smooth as glass, "I think out of the two of us, you're... better suited to speak to them on their level."

Parmik was aware of the grins of the other officers. *If one so much as snickers, I'll fucking murder him.*

"Hurry back, Subcommander," Weel said, turning his back on Parmik and poring over his map. "Battle waits for no man... or dwarf."

CARNY RAISED A hand to shade his eyes and squinted, trying to make out movement in the village up ahead. It was an impossible task. The shield was only to the little stand of palm trees some five hundred yards to the east of Moskoan and the heat haze was making everything blurry.

"Shield... forward!" Sinte shouted, clanging his hewer against his rank shield for emphasis.

Another glorious day in the Lux. Carny swung a boot forward and began walking, using as little effort as possible. Barely turning his head, he looked to the left and right to keep pace with the rest of the shield.

"Anyone see a news crier?" someone asked farther down the skirmish line. "Fackleroy over in Gray Shield said a whole bunch of them came over with the new legions. They're going to watch us fight and tell everyone back home what we did."

Carny snorted. "I'll save them the trouble. We're a sharp group of bright-eyed warriors in sparkling uniforms. We hold our crossbows firm and at the ready as we proudly march across the Lux scattering the enemy before us. Oh, and the sun gleams off our helms all shiny and bright."

"You're a cynic, you know that, Carny?" Wiz said.

"If being a cynic means I tell it like it is, then yes I am," Carny replied.

The heat sapped what little energy the conversation generated and silence resumed. Red Shield plodded on with all the verve of a sick dog. Big Hog, walking on Carny's left, yawned. Carny yawned, too, wishing he was anywhere but here. They'd been roused from sleep a full fourth of a candle before dawn and had been on the move ever since. With each footstep, the coast got farther away as Red Shield moved deeper into the Lux and the unknown.

Carny closed his eyes and let his head slump down until his chin rested on his chest. The next berm was still a hundred yards away and the dosha swamp was as flat as a slate slab. If there were slyts up ahead, someone else would see them and give a shout.

"I don't see why you couldn't grow potatoes here," Big Hog said.

Carny groaned, lifting his head and opening his eyes. *Not this again.*

Big Hog reached down and plucked up a clod of dirt in his hand. He stood back up, holding the dirt to his nose as he walked. The soil was dry and crumbled easily in his hand. Tiny streams of dirt trickled out between his fingers as he sniffed.

"That's disgusting," Carny said, wrinkling up his nose. "You know they use their own shit to fertilize their fields, right?"

Big Hog took an even deeper sniff before upending his hand and letting the rest of the dirt fall to the ground. "Yeah, they really should mix in more pig. Their shit ain't strong enough. It's no wonder everyone over here is skin and bones. How's a person supposed to survive on dosha and greens and fruit? And that stinky fish? When you shit it all out, you don't get enough power out of it to grow strong crops."

Carny groaned again. The sun was barely two fingers above the tree line and it was already stifling. He thought of autumn walks through the woods with his mother and felt his eyes begin to water. Those had been the best days. She'd taught him what mushrooms to pick and which to never touch. As he got older, she let him set the drop traps for squirrels and the snare traps for rabbits. It was one of the reasons he'd thought he'd like being in the army. He knew soldiers spent a lot of time walking—hunting, too.

He stumbled into an unseen rut, jarring his left knee. "Fuck you," he muttered, lifting his left knee high to rub it as he brought it up near his hand for the next few steps. The lowlands were turning out to be the mountains all over again. It was one frustrating patrol after another looking for signs of FnC activity and finding scant fuck-all. The only sign of life other than the shield was a lone brorra a couple hundred yards ahead.

"When we get these slyts sorted over here, first thing we should do is ship in some good Kingdom manure," Big Hog said. "Plow the whole damn place and start over."

"You're mad, Big Hog. No one is going to ship shit," Carny said. The last thing he needed was one more damn speech about manure and potatoes. Since leaving the coast and mountains behind, Big Hog had become fixated on all things farming. Every dosha swamp, stream, orchard, and field they crossed was a new occasion for Big Hog to tell the shield what he'd plant there, what kind of manure was best, or what animal to graze.

"Hey, Wiz, you got something you can give to Carny?" Big Hog shouted, waving to their wizard twenty yards away. "His humors are all out of sorts this morning."

"No," was Wiz's unhelpful reply.

"I'm fine," Carny said, pushing his helm back on his head. "Just quit jawing about farming." *And let me take a bite of snow, or at least a few puffs of Wild Flower.* He felt hollow and on edge. But LC Listowk had made it clear that there would be none of that while on patrol, not with Commander Weel on their heels.

"Eyes forward, my chatty mice," LC Listowk said, walking past them as he moved down the line, checking on the shield. "We'll rest when we reach the village. Lots of shade and cool water." He looked at Carny, his mustache arching up on the left side.

"Promise?" Carny asked.

"Stay alert," the LC said, pointing with his crossbow toward the distant line of trees to the west and avoiding the question. "If those FnC slyts are this far east, you can bet they're looking for trouble."

"They don't stand a chance," Ahmist said from the other side of Big Hog. The young soldier brought his crossbow up to his shoulder as if to fire. "They are inferior creatures. They were born of the root, not the leaf. Their skin shows the color of their souls. It is clear in the LOKAM they are filth. The Birch, in Late Autumn, Fifth Branch: *And so it was that the light from the sun grew thin and the nights long. | And in this darkening time of cold and—*"

"Oh, save the sermon," Listowk said, interrupting Ahmist. Listowk didn't bark like Sinte, but his voice was firm. "It's just too damn early."

Ahmist's lower lip quivered, and he sniffed a couple of times. Carny feared the worst, but he only pouted and lowered his crossbow. Carny mouthed a silent thank-you to Listowk, who winked back.

"Stay on your toes, and don't do anything stupid like getting yourselves hurt," Listowk said, moving off in his slow, weary gait. "I'm going to check on the rest of the lads, but I'll be keeping an eye on you lot."

"It's never too early to sing His praises," Ahmist muttered. Whether Listowk heard him or not, the LC kept walking. Carny gave Ahmist a glare, but the soldier made the sign of the tree and began mouthing the words of the LOKAM to himself.

Fine, as long as it keeps him quiet, Carny thought.

"You know why the Kingdom is the greatest land in the world?" Big Hog asked, picking right back up with their conversation. "Why we have the biggest army and we grow so big and tall? I'll tell you why: potatoes," he said, shifting his crossbow so he cradled it in his left hand. He held up his right and extended a finger. "And beef." Another finger. "And pork, and bread and cheese." He closed his open hand and started again. "And milk, and butter, and beer, oh, and sausage, and…"

Carny held out his left arm as Big Hog prattled on. Bare from the shoulder down in his sleeveless aketon, Carny's skin was sun-browned like a farmhand's. Maybe his muscles did look a bit scrawny, and he knew he'd had to cut two more holes in his belt to keep his trousers from falling down, but he was still bigger than any slyt they'd ever seen.

At some point, Big Hog trailed off and they walked on in a new silence. Carny sped his pace up just enough so that he didn't have to look at anyone else. He reached behind him and tugged his haversack around so that it rode on his right hip. He slipped his hand inside the haversack and felt around. His fingertips landed on the wadded ball of Wild Flower. He flicked at it with a fingernail, desperate to rip off a chunk. Surprising himself, he lifted his hand away. There was just no easy way to hide a big wad of chew and the resulting dark brown drool. Listowk would have his ass if he caught him.

The prospect of a long, excruciating day loomed before Carny. He started to reach for the Wild Flower again when his fingers touched a leaf. He grabbed it between thumb and forefinger and pulled it out of his haversack. It was a dry piece of a banyan leaf that had been folded in half and the edges gummed together to create a thumb-sized envelope. It took him a moment to remember where it had come from. Squeak had included it with his last ball of Wild Flower. Said it was something new. Like snuff, only better.

Carny slowed his pace until the rest of the skirmish line caught up with him. He looked left and right to see if anyone was watching him, but the rest of the shield were looking straight ahead. Cupping the leaf in the palm of his hand, he brought it up to his mouth to bite off an edge.

"LC said no chew," Big Hog said.

Carny started, dropping the leaf to the ground. He bent down and picked it up, scooping up some dirt at the same time. He brought his hand back up to his mouth and tore a corner of the leaf with his teeth. He moved his hand away and peered inside. There was a small amount of white powder between the dried leaves. Shrugging, he placed the opening against his right nostril, pressed the left one closed with his thumb, and took a quick, hard sniff.

His nostril and the back of his throat immediately burned. He lowered his hand, dropping the leaf to the ground with the clod of dirt. The burning faded, to be replaced by a numbness, while his brain felt like it had been dumped in a glacial lake. He smiled, every nerve feeling razor sharp. He looked over at Big Hog.

"Tell me more about shit and potatoes," Carny said, standing up a little straighter and patting his crossbow.

"What the fuck is wrong with you?" Big Hog asked, waving a hand at Carny in obvious disgust.

"Just lovin' the Lux," Carny said, wondering what had been bothering him earlier. It was a beautiful day. He was out for a walk in the sunshine and felt more alive than he could remember ever feeling. He stared into the heat haze and watched the colors dance.

"IT'S AN ENTIRELY reasonable request," Pioneer Commander Mallowry Tiffanger said, addressing himself to Master Pioneer Creavus Black Pine. Tiffanger held his helm in his hands and nervously played with the chain-mail curtain. The column of dwarves of the Eighteenth Pioneer Support Group stood in a tight formation behind him, waiting to hear the result of the confrontation.

Parmik debated stepping in and decided against it. Tiffanger had to make the dwarves understand that their help was crucial to get his cats where they needed to be.

"If it's a request, then the answer is no," Black Pine said. He stood with his thick arms crossed, staring up at Parmik. The sun glinted off the edge of the huge two-headed axe slung on his back.

Tiffanger placed his face in his palm and shook his head. "I phrased that poorly. It is an order, but a reasonable one," he said, looking back up. "The catapults are needed to provide support for the shields. We are in a position to help. It won't take us more than a fourth of a candle."

Black Pine kept staring at Parmik. "Right, because we're just a herd of fuckin' oxen."

Tiffanger looked imploringly at Parmik.

"People used to throw rocks at our house when I was a kid," Parmik said. "Said they should send me back to the quarry and get a real son."

"Oh, poor fuckin' you," Black Pine said, raising his voice so the dwarves nearest them could hear. "He gets a few rocks and catcalls thrown his way. They bury your pa up to his neck and then stone him to death because he asked for more milk and bread for his sick child?"

Parmik shook his head. "No." Damn. He'd wanted to show the dwarf he understood his anger.

Black Pine started breathing heavily. "Anyone hold you down and brand their family crest on your back with a red-hot iron when you turned ten?"

"No," Parmik said, now hating himself.

Master Pioneer Black Pine uncrossed his arms and stepped forward until he was only an inch away from Parmik. His nostrils flared as he spoke. "Then *fuck you*, and *fuck* the Seventh Phalanx, too."

"What's the damn holdup?" a red-bearded dwarf asked, striding up to the front of the column. He wore the same uniform as the other dwarves: sturdy, calf-high leather boots; dark green trousers; a sleeveless light green aketon; and an iron-and-steel helm. He also carried two haversacks, one on each hip, and a small rucksack on his back. He wasn't as bulky as Black Pine and was an inch shorter, but Parmik saw the other dwarves all stiffen as he went past. It took Parmik a moment to realize why he seemed so different. Unlike all the other dwarves, this one didn't carry an axe.

"Ah, Wizard Magnolia," Tiffanger said, the relief in his voice clear. "I was wondering where you'd got to."

Magnolia stood to attention and saluted Tiffanger. "Couple of troopers caught sun vapors or I would have been here sooner," he said, quickly looking at Black Pine and Parmik. "I'm Wizard Ramac Magnolia," he said, turning and saluting Parmik.

"Subcommander Parmik, Bear Battery, Eleventh Field Artillerists," Parmik said, snapping off a quick salute in return.

"What can we do for you, Subcommander?"

"I have cats that need to be moved, and I need your men to help me do it," Parmik said, projecting a gruffness he in no way felt at the moment.

"A reasonable request," Magnolia said, turning and looking at Black Pine.

There was a shuffling of boots as the dwarves reacted to Magnolia's words.

"The fuck it's reasonable!" Black Pine shouted. "He's asking us to be slaves."

Magnolia crossed the ground to Black Pine in a flick and landed a heavy left hook on Black Pine's chin. Black Pine wobbled but didn't fall. A straight right jab from Magnolia followed by another left hook finally sat Black Pine on his ass.

Magnolia panted for breath for several flicks before turning to face the dwarves. "We aren't slaves. We're soldiers. You can follow me, or you can let me explain that concept to you one at a time like I just did with Black Pine."

The dwarves shuffled into a neat column. Parmik risked a quick look at Black Pine. The dwarf's eyes blinked oddly, each one on its own. He stared up at Magnolia, the malevolence unmistakable.

"We don't have time for this," Magnolia said, holding out his hand to Black Pine.

Black Pine ignored Magnolia's hand and got to his feet. "This isn't the end of this," he said through clenched teeth.

Magnolia sighed. "No, I didn't figure it would be."

Black Pine turned and addressed the dwarves.

"Troop! By the left… at double time… march!"

Black Pine set off at a fast trot, not bothering to wait for Parmik or even look behind him. Parmik backed up a few paces as the dwarves rumbled past. He felt a tap on his arm and looked down to see Magnolia pointing after the column. "Probably best we get you up to the front, on account of they don't know where they're going. The mood Black Pine's in, he's liable to march them right through the Western Wilds."

"Yes, right," Parmik said, trying to find words to express what he was feeling and giving up when he realized he didn't know what that was. "Commander, shall we go?"

Tiffanger saluted, then brought his hand down in surprise. "What? Yes, yes, we should go. Their legs are short, but once they get going, it's a bit like a rolling stone down a very steep hill. Oh, no offense, Magnolia."

"Why the fuck would I possibly be offended?" Magnolia said, already a couple of yards away and picking up speed.

CHAPTER SEVENTEEN

"YOU HEAR THAT?" CARNY asked. Red Shield was spread out across a field along with the other shields of the Second Javelin. He stopped walking and cocked his head to one side. They were still several hundred yards from the village and crossing yet another dosha swamp.

"What?" Big Hog asked. He crouched down, raising his crossbow up to his shoulder. The rest of the shield did the same.

"What is it?" Listowk asked, running in a low crouch to kneel between Carny and Big Hog. "Slyts?"

"Singing," Carny said, turning and smiling at the LC. "It's singing."

"I don't hear it," Big Hog said, slowly standing back up.

Listowk stood up, too. He walked over to Carny, grabbed his lower jaw, and pried it open.

Carny batted his hand away. "LC, easy. I kept my promise. No Wild Flower, no snow."

"But you hear singing?" Listowk said. He peered up at Carny like he was examining a suspicious piece of meat in the village market.

Carny nodded. "Yes. Don't you?"

Listowk backed up, staring at Carny, and motioned with his hand for Red Shield to get moving. Soldiers stood up and started walking again.

"Don't be another Vooford," Listowk said. He walked over to Big Hog and whispered something to him, then walked away.

"I'm fine," Carny said after Listowk. He shrugged. *I haven't felt this good in ages.*

A clod of dirt struck his helm, showering the back of his neck with crap. He reached a hand up to wipe it from his neck. "That's big hail," he said. He brought his hand down and looked at it. "Dirty, too. The weather here is terrible."

"Just walk, and keep your mouth shut," Big Hog said, rubbing his right hand on his trousers.

Carny gave Big Hog a thumbs-up. "I can do that," he said. He didn't understand why everyone was in a bad mood. *Everything is so... alive out here.*

The skirmish line walked to the next berm and paused as Wraith crawled over it and looked at the other side. When he stood up the line moved again, walking over the berm and down into the next dosha swamp.

"An enemy beast," Ahmist said, pointing with his free hand.

Carny squinted through the haze. A lone brorra lay with its legs tucked underneath it beside the next berm seventy-five yards in front of them.

"Where'd that come from?" Carny asked. Had it always been there? He looked down at the ground, then back toward where they'd come from. Dust plumes rose into the sky in several places. He heard the singing again, too.

"They're everywhere," Big Hog said. "And they ain't cows," he added.

The brorra raised itself off the ground, first pushing its rear up, then bringing up its front half to stand. It looked at Carny, contentedly chewing its cud.

Movement on Carny's right caught his attention. Ahmist had his crossbow to his shoulder and was aiming at the animal.

"Cut it out, Ahmist," Carny said. "It didn't do anything to you." Carny wriggled his back. It felt itchy. His mouth was dry and the heat was making it worse. He reached into his haversack and fished around for another leaf despite knowing that Bristom had only given him one.

"The creature is in service of the enemy," Ahmist said.

"We could get a good feast off of it," Big Hog said. "Doesn't look too bony."

The brorra turned its head and looked at Carny. The animal chomped contentedly, tufts of thin grass hanging from its mouth. A cloud of black flies rose and fell on its back with each lazy swish of its tail.

"It's not serving anyone right now," Carny said, looking around for support. "It just wants to be left alone. I can tell."

"It serves the enemy," Ahmist said again, dropping down to one knee. He rested his left elbow on his thigh for support and sighted his crossbow on the animal. The skirmish line had frozen again as the shield stopped to watch.

"It's just a—"

The metal arms of Ahmist's crossbow sprung forward with a heavy metal twang as he fired a bolt. The bolt made a shallow arc through the air, striking the brorra at the base of its neck just in front of its shoulder.

The brorra started. Two streams of blood squirted out several feet in the air from either side of the bolt. The animal took two steps forward, then its front legs buckled and its nose struck the ground. Its back legs galloped in an attempt to run, which succeeded in rolling it over its head in a flailing somersault.

Soldiers hooted and cheered. A couple started running forward.

"Hold your position! Keep the skirmish line straight!" SL Sinte shouted.

Ahmist stood up and made the sign of the tree. "The High Druid be praised," he said, looking not to the sky but directly at Carny.

"Keep your positioning, damn it! Keep moving!" Sinte shouted.

Carny walked, not that he could feel his boots hit the ground. He was a dry, crumbling leaf. The force of the entire world spurted out of the brorra's neck and onto the dusty dosha swamp. The animal kicked its back legs and lifted its head, trying to stand, but with less and less energy.

"I know it ain't cow, but that'll make some good steaks," Big Hog said. Carny looked over at him. The farmer had tucked his crossbow under his arm and had his hunting knife out, sharpening the blade with a whetstone.

"We're not stopping so you can dress a brorra," Listowk said, stomping their way again. He stopped when he got to Ahmist. "Who the fuck told you to shoot?"

Ahmist shrugged his shoulders. "It serves the enemy," he said, as if that explained everything.

Listowk's mustache ticked a couple of times before he replied. "Report to Field Deputy Rhomy at the Second Javelin Command Group. They need a runner."

"But—"

Listowk grabbed Ahmist by the arm and flung him out of the skirmish line. "Now!"

Ahmist stood still for a moment, his mouth open in surprise. When Listowk made a motion to walk toward him, Ahmist closed his mouth and started walking back to the rear.

"The rest of you, keep moving. Anyone who stops again without orders will get my boot up their ass."

"Waste of perfectly good meat," Big Hog said hotly, sheathing his hunting knife and putting away his whetstone.

"It's not dead yet," Carny said. Blood still trickled from the wound and the tail made a couple of feeble swishes.

Carny's eyes fixed on the brorra as he approached the next berm. The animal lay just fifteen yards away from him, the tangy smell of blood thick in the air. Carny kept walking, up and over the berm, not bothering to wait for Wraith to scout the other side. No one shouted. He kept walking.

"Still lovin' the Lux?" Big Hog asked.

Carny said nothing. He reached his hand back into the haversack before remembering there were no more leaves. His fingers touched the wad of Wild Flower. He tore off a piece, put it in his mouth, and kept walking.

JUST A MONTH ago, Subcommander Brobbi Parmik had never seen a palm tree and had no idea they existed. *Look more like big weeds than proper trees.* He had a hard time imagining these strange things in the High Druid's eternal forest, but it wasn't his place to judge. What he did know was that he was thrilled to finally be standing under these three particular trees. Bear Battery's six field cats were finally in position and being readied to fire. He looked up at the sun. They'd get a rock in the air before noon. *Fuck you, Weel.*

He'd been tempted to slow things down so they wouldn't have the cats ready on time just to spite him, but all that would have done was deny covering fire to the troops up ahead. He couldn't justify that to himself, and so he trotted at double time with the dwarves all the way to the cats, and even grabbed a rope and did his share to get them in position on time. Now he was anxious to see the dwarves off. Being around this many for this long unsettled him in ways he didn't want to examine.

Heavy oak beams thudded and rumbled as they were swung into place. Sledgehammers rang off of flat-head iron spikes driven into the ground. Stringers of heavy rope were secured to the sides of the cats and attached to the spikes to anchor the cats and keep them steady. The wagon teams carrying the loads of projectiles creaked and rattled as they pulled up to drop off their cargo. Unasked, the dwarves unloaded the wagons and piled the various shot, allowing Parmik's men to focus all their efforts on the cats themselves. "Many thanks for your assistance, Commander Tiffanger," Parmik said, raising his voice above the din.

"It was our pleasure, Subcommander," Tiffanger said with a straight face. "Always happy to help out. Very nice of you, by the way, to offer the lads a drink, too."

Parmik nodded. Everyone present knew there were whole areas of the Kingdom to this day that didn't allow dwarves to eat and drink with humans. Some of the men in the battery would loathe him for this, but that was too damn bad.

"I'll second that," Wizard Magnolia said, walking up to Parmik.

"Really, it was nothing, Wizard." Parmik was feeling self-conscious near Magnolia, being barely half a head taller than the dwarf.

"I'll start getting the boys rounded up," Tiffanger said, nodding at Magnolia and quickly walking off.

Magnolia smiled. "Good fellow. He means well, he really does."

"Yes," Parmik said, wondering how to phrase the question he'd had since encountering Tiffanger and the dwarves. "An interesting choice to command a unit of dwarves."

Magnolia chuckled. "Interesting? That's one way to put it. Fact is, he's our third officer. First one refused the command outright and the second lasted less than a day. Not everyone is ready to embrace the new reality."

"You don't sound angry, Wizard Magnolia," Parmik said.

"You mean like Black Pine?" Magnolia asked. "No, not many dwarves have the level of passion Black Pine does. And please, call me Maggs. All my sharders do."

"Sharders?" Parmik said.

Maggs bowed his head slightly. "Q-talk—ah, quarry talk. So used to it I forget most people don't know it. A sharder is another dwarf. We're all shards from the One Great Mountain."

Parmik knew about the dwarven belief in the Great Mountain. It was their own Sacred Tree.

"But I thought you were a, I mean, you worked in…"

"The *house*?" Maggs asked. "Yes, I was a house dwarf, but I still spent time in the deep. They educated me, you know, the Diefenlanders. I took everything I could learn to the quarry and taught as many as I could. There are some, like Black Pine, who don't think that sort of bargain was worth the price. Who knows, maybe he's right."

"I don't think so," Parmik said. "Education is a tool every man—and dwarf," he added quickly, "should have in his brain box."

Maggs laughed. Unlike Black Pine, his teeth were a dull white. "Clever," Maggs said, tapping his own head. "I look forward to the day when dwarves and men strive as hard to fill their skulls as they do building those," he said, gesturing over at the catapults.

"They're just field cats, pretty small really. You want to see a real cat, you need to check out the Heavies. I hear they're building a battery over here."

"Bigger is always better, isn't that what they say?" Maggs said, no longer laughing.

Parmik knew he'd missed something. "I don't think so, at least not for all things."

"Of course not," Maggs said, looking past him toward the dwarves. "It appears my commander is getting the herd into a semblance of order. Best I go and see it stays that way. A pleasure to meet you, Subcommander," Maggs said, standing to attention and saluting.

Parmik saluted back, trying to figure out where the conversation went off track. *Damn it.* He watched Maggs walk away. He fought the urge to call him back, realizing he had no idea what he wanted to say.

"Cats one and three are ready, sir."

Parmik turned, surprised to see Senior Artillerist Dulsh Osen standing just a few feet away.

"Already?" Parmik asked, still going over the conversation with Maggs in his mind.

"Yes, sir. Those little rock roaches actually did an eighth of a candle of honest work," he said.

Parmik looked up at Osen. Contempt etched his otherwise bland peasant face.

"Glad to hear it," Parmik said, a cool, sustaining anger filling him with purpose. "I was planning on releasing them back to the Seventh Phalanx's control, but your recommendation has made me reconsider."

"Sir?" Osen said. The contempt was gone, replaced with confusion and the first inkling of concern.

"Yes, you've made me see the light. Go find Deputy Legion Commander Weel's caravan and ask him—no, tell him that in order to meet the tasks at hand, Bear Battery will need the services of the Eighteenth Pioneer Support Group for the immediate future."

"Shouldn't you check with Commander Joars first?"

Parmik didn't blink. "I'll handle Joars. On your way."

"But—"

"No need to thank me, Osen," Parmik said, raising his voice to put an end to their conversation. "In fact, I'm going to let the whole battery know it was your idea. I am a true believer in people getting the credit they deserve. Now, off you go," Parmik said. "But do hurry back. We're going to have to make some changes in the battery to accommodate the dwarves. I'll need a good man who understands these things and can explain it to the others, help smooth over the bumps. I can't think of anyone more deserving than you."

Parmik waved Osen on his way. A smile twitched the corners of Parmik's mouth.

"Fuck you, Weel," he said out loud, turning and walking toward the battery with a spring in his step. "I'll show you what being a prick really looks like."

"ACORNS!"

Listowk looked skyward. Several small black dots were sailing into the sky from the east.

"The High Druid's shaking the tree!" Big Hog shouted, pointing at the sky.

The heavy clanking sound of firing catapults reached their ears a moment later.

"Stay down and stay calm," Listowk said, looking up and down the berm to make sure the shield listened.

The black dots rose into the air, seemingly straight up. They shrank in size as they climbed, then began growing as they started on the downward side of their arc. It became harder to track them as they fell back to earth. Each one was a hurtling blur that seemed to be coming straight at Red Shield.

"Here come the acorns!"

"They know we're here, right?" Wraith asked.

Listowk tried to judge the landing spot of the projectiles and became convinced it was right where his head was. "Get ready to run!" he shouted, standing up in a crouch. There were a few shouts and the beginnings of a moan as the catapult shots closed in on them. A whistling windstorm noise grew as the shots came closer.

"They're going to hit us!" someone shouted. Some soldiers started to climb the berm while others ripped off their helms and used them to dig holes in the dirt.

Listowk's entire body broke out in a sweat. There was nowhere to run. He couldn't tell where the damn things would land. "Get down! Lie down and stay down!" he shouted, dropping to his knees and covering his head with his hands.

The whistling wind made by the projectiles grew louder until it was a shriek right over his head as they passed and got quieter. Listowk looked up as the first shot hit the dosha swamp in front of them some fifty yards away. A puff of brown dirt shot into the air. The impact of the shot vibrated the dirt under Listowk. Three more shots fell in quick succession, each one burying itself into the dusty dosha swamp farther away from the shield and closer to the village.

"Good," Listowk said to himself, then realized he'd said it out loud. "Good! They're walking their shots into the village. We'll just sit here and watch the show. Should—"

A whistling shot slammed into the ground two feet behind Listowk, spraying him with dirt. His right hand spasmed and he squeezed the firing lever of his crossbow. Nothing happened. The safety lever remained engaged. The telltale twang of at least two other crossbows told him others did not.

He looked up expecting to see a boulder about to crush him, but the other black dots sailed over his head and struck the edge of the village with shattering force. He turned to watch, telling himself that just like lightning there was no way the artillerists would hit the same exact place twice.

The remains of a bamboo hut spun through the air in a cloud

of shredded palm fronds. Soldiers hollered their delight.

"Pound the fuckers!"

"Did you see that? That was a leg!"

"Glory be to the High Druid!"

Listowk turned, ready to rip Ahmist a new one, but it was Wiz shouting the High Druid's praises. More shots rained down, the rocks shattering on impact and scything through the collection of huts with ease. In a matter of moments, the village ceased to exist. Every hut was either destroyed or severely damaged. Listowk had still to see a single slyt moving about. He started imagining Weel's reaction, then stopped. That was Sinte's problem.

A new sound pierced the air. A shot landed deep in the village with a hollow thud. Instead of sending chunks of rocks flying through the air, this shot gave off a bright yellow smoke that drifted lazily up through the dust cloud over the village.

"Nobody move!" Listowk shouted, spying a couple of soldiers already on their feet and mounting the berm.

"But that's the cease-fire shot," a soldier said.

"Nobody move until I say so," Listowk said, getting up on his knees and quickly looking up and down the berm. After his near miss, Listowk wasn't taking any chances. He turned to look behind him, searching the sky for any more shots in the air. Cocking his head to one side, he listened for the heavy metal and wood clash signaling a catapult had fired.

Nothing.

"All right. We do this smart. Make sure your crossbow is cocked, the bolt is securely in place, and the safety lever is on. Crossbowmen, check your string. Longbowmen, nock. Red Shield, on your feet!"

The shield stood up behind the berm. There was no more hollering. Signs of the Sacred Tree were made while others toggled their aketons closed, choosing to swelter with the protection of the iron plates over their stomachs and chests. "Crossbowmen will go up and over the berm and stop on the other side on my mark. Longbowmen will remain behind and cover. Move!"

The soldiers walked up and over the berm. Listowk turned his body sideways so that he could keep one eye on the village and one on the shield. The dust was already settling in the village. Movement drew Listowk's attention, but it was merely a section of bamboo and palm wall slowly waving back and forth.

Listowk took one last look to the east. The sky was clear. He turned and motioned the shield forward.

CHAPTER EIGHTEEN

J AWN LOOSENED HIS GRIP on the harness chain but did not let go. This rag flight was proving to be a significantly smoother affair than the last one, although memories of the flight across the ocean remained vivid in his mind. Happily for him, no rolly blues were flinging this rag around the sky. It was half the size of the last one, a fact that had initially worried Jawn. The crew, a fine pair of well-spoken men from the capital city, smiled and told him this flight would be FPS. Jawn asked what that stood for, assuming the worst. "Feather-Pillow Soft," was the welcome reply.

"You're a fine beast," Jawn said, taking one hand off the chain and patting the rag's vibrant bluish-green scales. It was also a way of testing how hot the rag was getting, but other than the warming effects of the sun, Jawn detected no dangerous heat building up underneath him. The crew said it was a young male, just past two. Jawn couldn't tell and wasn't interested in confirming it. What he did know is that the animal seemed fit and hearty.

Jawn lifted his head into the wind and drew in a deep breath. He had to really strain to detect the faintest hint of sulfur. Now *this* was flying. Even the beat of this rag's wings was smooth and effortless. There was no frightening noise of grinding shoulder bones. The flight was so smooth Jawn was starting to think he could get used to traveling by rag. Even enjoy it. Best of all, no one's piss and puke were getting in his hair.

There was no blood, either.

"Care for a little nip?" Rickets said, leaning between a pair of dorsal plates and holding out a small pewter flask. "I know, I know, the whole 'balancing your inner liquids' and whatnot, but after the last few days, your innards are probably still pickled."

As they were the only passengers on the rag, there was no polite way for Jawn to avoid Rickets. Jawn doubted there was even an impolite one save braining the man with the driver's iron gaff. On a flight over the Kingdom, Jawn would have enjoyed looking out at the countryside, but he was already bored by what Luitox had to offer. What wasn't jungle was patchworks of dosha swamps, and what weren't swamps were rivers and streams that appeared more mud than water. Seen from two thousand feet in the air, the countryside was one vast green-and-brown mat. The most exciting thing in the last fourth-candle was a stampede of brorras and an agitated flock of bright white storks.

"Sure," Jawn said, certain he'd already seen enough jungle to last him the rest of his life. How the fabled adventurers Ox and Crink stayed sane tramping through miles and miles of the stuff was beyond him. For the first time, Jawn questioned the motives of his heroes. Maybe they were mad. He recalled Rickets's rather cryptic account of meeting those two celebrities. He still hadn't elaborated. Jawn was determined to get the full story out of him, but he had more pressing matters before that.

Jawn took the proffered flask and brought it up to his lips, where he paused. Was it this easy? All the years of training and sacrifice thrown away after just his first encounter with real violence? He was supposed to be better than this. The academy had drilled it into them. They *were* better. But then, why hadn't a professor ever warned him of the horror? No one had talked about the smell of burning flesh and how it lingered in your nostrils long after the body had roasted to ash.

"It's got a kick, but it still won't jump into your throat on its own," Rickets said.

Rickets was one big thorn in Jawn's paw, but damn if the crowny didn't make a lot of sense. It was one little drink after a binge he knew he'd never repeat. He poured a quick shot down his throat before he changed his mind. It burned all the way down, landing in his stomach with a sizzling thud. Jawn gasped. "Oh... don't bother telling me what it is."

"You're a scrappy one, Jawn Rathim," Rickets said, taking back the flask and tucking it away inside his haversack. "Old Leotat told me you'd surprise me."

Jawn managed a weak smile. "Wish he had warned me about *you*."

"Not much to tell," Rickets said, his voice a perfect simulation of sincerity.

If Jawn were meeting Rickets for the first time, he might have believed it. There was still a fourth of a candle to go before they reached Jomkier and Jawn wasn't ready to spend that much time alone with his thoughts. Crackling, burning images of Gremthyn continued to flash through his mind. Talking, even with Rickets, brought welcome relief.

"So... ," Jawn said, stunned that it had come to this. He leaned against a dorsal plate and twisted in his saddle to face Rickets. "Rickets, um..." *Just do it and get it over with!* "So tell me about yourself. You know everything about me, and I know next to nothing about you. If we're going to be working together, I should probably know a little more about my... partner."

For several long, agonizing moments there was only the rhythmic sound of the rag's wings, the dull creaks of chain and leather, and the familiar scratch of scale on scale. Jawn watched Rickets closely, not sure what to expect but fearing an outpouring that would last well beyond their flight.

"If it's all the same to you, I'd rather not discuss my personal life," Rickets said. He didn't smile, he didn't wink, he didn't make a rude gesture of any kind.

Jawn said nothing. There was a punch line coming, there had

to be. He smiled at Rickets, doing his best to show his sincerity. "I'm serious, Rickets. I'm actually curious."

Rickets fidgeted on his saddle. "The last few days took more out of me than I realized. I think I'll catch a little nap. Wake me when we get to Jomkier?"

"Uh… sure," Jawn said, still ready for lightning out of the clear blue. "I'll just stare at the jungle. Lots of trees down there."

"There are indeed," Rickets said, ignoring Jawn's sarcasm completely. He disappeared from view behind the dorsal plates.

Jawn continued staring at the space above the plate, expecting Rickets to pop up at any moment and regale him with a tale so wild that Jawn's eyes would be in danger of rolling right out of their sockets. When Rickets didn't reappear, Jawn peered over the plate. Rickets was curled up against it, eyes closed, his chin tucked into his chest, and his arms wrapped around his body. He appeared to be asleep.

Son of a witch. Jawn pulled back and looked up to the front of the rag. The drivers were too far away to have a conversation with without yelling.

Now what? Jawn turned to rest his back against a plate and stared out at the jungle. A fourth of a candle of green and brown emptiness. He sighed. Nothing to do…

Images of Milouette surfaced for the first time since his flight over. He looked up at the drivers again. They were focused on flying and hadn't looked back at their passengers since they'd reached their cruising height.

Jawn closed his eyes and thought of her. He reached into his trousers and grabbed hold of his member. A fourth of a candle was more than enough time.

"NOT A DAMN thing!" Shield Leader Sinte shouted, sending a piece of broken bamboo flying with a kick of his boot. The soldiers in the path of the bamboo scattered, turning to watch as the debris clattered across the wreckage of Moskoan. The stick punched through a ragged triangle of palm-frond wall that was still standing. The wall teetered, tipping slowly toward the ground. Then it stopped, refusing to fall all the way down.

Carny stared at the section of wall, willing it to fall. His mind still reeled from the drug, although the effects were wearing off. What captivated him now was the fact that something of Moskoan still stood. It was just a few square feet of dusty and torn wall, but it made the destruction seem that much worse. It was a reminder, a grave marker for something that had once bustled and hummed with the daily life of a small farming community. Carny took his eyes off the section of wall and went back to picking through the mangled heap of bamboo, palm, and sharp chunks of rock. There had to be something of value in the wreckage.

He spotted a smooth, curved piece of pottery. He reached down and grabbed it, pulling it free. It was a small orange clay pot with a domed lid that easily fit in the palm of his hand. He pried the lid off the pot with his thumb and, peering inside, saw two teaspoons' worth of a whitish powder. Carny's heart raced.

"What'd you find?" Wraith asked, suddenly standing beside Carny.

"Fuck!" Carny shouted, involuntarily squeezing his hand tight. He crushed the clay pot, spraying the powder and clay fragments into the air. He shook his hand and wiped it clean, looking for cuts. "Look what you made me do."

"You broke it," Wraith said, looking down at the ground. "What was it?"

Carny looked around, aware that other soldiers were looking at them. "Spider," he said. "Almost got me."

"I didn't see a spider," Wraith said, "just that pot with the white powder in it."

"Why don't you go stalk something?" Carny said.

Wraith started to turn away, then stopped. He pulled a palm leaf–wrapped ball out of his haversack and tossed it over to Carny. "Found it over there," he said, motioning to the remains of a nearby hut. "There's more. Go easy on it."

Carny peeled the leaf until he could see what was inside.

Wild Flower! He looked up to thank Wraith, but the soldier was already walking away.

Another chunk of bamboo cartwheeled across the rubble. Carny stuffed the ball into his haversack and tore off a small piece. He brought his fingers to his nose and sniffed. He imagined the High Druid's Forest smelled like this. He stuffed the Wild Flower into his mouth and smiled. *There, that's better.* He began edging toward the spot Wraith had indicated while keeping a wary eye on Sinte.

"We didn't lose anyone," Lead Crossbowman Listowk said, calmly taking the brunt of Sinte's rage. Carny had no idea how Listowk did it. The man had the patience of a... Carny tried to think of something that had a lot of patience. A snail? They were slow, but that wasn't really the same.

"If you'd got here sooner, you might have caught the slyts," Sinte said. Several soldiers looked up from picking through the debris of Moskoan.

Carny stood up. Was Sinte serious? They'd have had to attack Moskoan days ago to find slyts in it, and even then it probably would have been peasants. He looked down at the debris. Not so much as a bowstring or arrowhead that would indicate the FnC had ever been here. They'd destroyed an entire village for nothing.

"We didn't lose anyone," Listowk said.

"We're not here to not lose anyone," Sinte said. "We're here to kill fuckin' slyts." He looked around at the ruined village and then back at Listowk. "The shield look like beggars. I want them cleaned up."

"Of course, Shield Leader," Listowk said, but Sinte was already stomping away.

Carny watched Listowk, waiting to see what he would do.

"Check your string, count your bolts, and try not to fall in a midden," Listowk said, smiling at them. "And for the love of the High Druid, stay out of trouble."

Carny nodded. He turned to walk toward the rest of the stash Wraith had found, then thought better of it.

"Fuck it, I don't need this shit," he said, suddenly strong and clearheaded.

"What?" Big Hog asked, walking toward him over the rubble.

Carny looked up. "I miss the mountain," he said. He bent down and lifted up a long stretch of bamboo and palm wall and jammed the splintered poles into the ground. It wasn't much, but it offered some shade. He sat down and gently eased his back against his makeshift wall. It bowed but held.

He splayed his legs in a wide V and set his crossbow down between them. With one finger, he flipped the flight end of the bolt out of the string to rest it on top, thereby rendering the weapon safe. No one used the safety latches anymore. Fucking things stuck half the time.

He undid the two remaining toggles holding his sleeveless aketon together. It slid open, revealing his stomach, covered in rust stains from the armor plates sewn into the cloth. On quick glance, it looked like he was bleeding.

"I like these fields," Big Hog said, flopping down beside him. He stretched out flat, taking off his helm and using it as a pillow. He'd already lifted his bolt out of the string, so he set his crossbow down on the dirt beside him and pointed it out toward the dosha swamps they'd just humped across.

"They're nothing but dried, dusty shit and dosha. Oh, and there's no dosha."

"You're not seeing their potential," Big Hog said. He pulled out a wooden pipe he kept hanging from a toggle loop on his aketon and stuck it in the side of his mouth closest to Carny. "Light me, will ya?"

Carny fished around in his haversack until he found his tinderbox. He popped the lid and pulled out the flint before closing the lid again. He held the box up against the open bowl of the pipe and flicked the flint across the top of the lid a few times, sending sparks into the wad of tobacco in the bowl. Big Hog drew in a few quick breaths and the tobacco lit.

"You're an oak—don't let no one tell you different," Big Hog said, puffing a few times on the pipe. "You just gotta lay off that crap. It'll rot your brain."

The rest of the shield migrated toward their position, grabbing some shade. It was all about making oneself as comfortable as possible while using the least amount of energy.

Big Hog drew deeply on the pipe, and the leaves inside its chamber glowed bright orange. "You believe those crazy bastards charked themselves?" Big Hog said, taking the pipe out of his mouth and peering at the bowl. Carny looked away from the spot Wraith had pointed to.

"What?" Carny asked.

"Remember I told you I smelled roast beef when we were still on the coast?" Big Hog said.

"When did you say that?" Carny asked, remembering no such thing.

"Ah, who am I talking to? You can't remember shit with all that Wild Flower you chew," Big Hog said, waving away Carny's challenge. "I smelled those bastards burning, I tell you. A farmer's got a sensitive nose when it comes to burning meat."

Carny snorted. "You didn't smell shit. You heard about those slyt farmers charking themselves from Squeak the same way the rest of us did. Hey, you're a farmer, Big Hog. You ain't planning on charking yourself, are you?"

Those who weren't already trying to catch a nap chuckled.

"High Druid's balls, don't joke about that, Carny," Big Hog said. "What a terrible way to go. Can you imagine burning yourself on purpose? Your eyeballs frying right in your head?"

Carny could imagine it and desperately wanted not to. "They had to be crazy. Or maybe under some kind of spell."

"Maybe," Big Hog said.

No one said anything for a while. Out across the dosha swamps they'd just walked, dust clouds marked the movement of the rest of the Seventh Phalanx. Carny hoped they'd take their time. Today was going to be another hot and sticky one.

"Damn shame about that brorra," Big Hog said, no doubt winding up for another speech about all things farming.

"You know, I really miss the mountain," Carny said, his

voice louder than he intended.

"What was so great about the mountain?" a freshly scrubbed crossbowman asked, walking up to stand in front of the shield. He looked like a boy as he scuffed the sole of his boot back and forth across the ground and then peered down to look at where he was going to sit.

He lowered himself to the ground, his clean uniform in stark contrast to the rest of the shield around him. He even had the sleeves still attached to his aketon. *Must be bloody murder like that*, Carny thought, shaking his head.

"Look at what we have here," Big Hog said, eyeing the fawn. "Fresh meat straight from the Vill."

A few soldiers laughed, but most couldn't be bothered to muster the energy.

"The Vill?" the fawn asked.

Carny rolled his eyes.

"Fuckin' High Druid you're new," Big Hog said, his voice taking on a kinder tone. "The Vill, you know, your village back in the Kingdom."

The fawn's eyes lit up. "I'm from Talon Falls, just north of—"

"No one wants your life story, fawn," Big Hog said, cutting him off.

Undeterred, the fawn pressed on. "You guys were talking about the mountains. What was so great about them?"

"Beach, breeze, booze, and whores," Carny and Big Hog said in unison. There were a few chuckles from the rest of the shield spread along the makeshift wall. If they were lucky, they'd be able to stay here all day.

"Really?" the fawn asked. "They let you drink and carouse with women?"

"Shouldn't you be helping your mother bake?" Carny asked.

"I'm fifteen years old," the soldier said, his voice squeaking. "I'll be sixteen this autumn."

"Sorry, an honest mistake," Carny said, deciding to spare the kid. "So what did your parents name you?"

"Teavin Dornawk. My father is the potter in town. He—"

"We still don't care, Knockers," Big Hog said, slapping a nickname on the fawn with impressive speed. "Anyone seen Wiz? I've got a rash on the inside of my thighs redder than a rooster's comb."

"Sounds like a case of friction burn," Carny said. "Maybe if you left your cock alone for a few days, you wouldn't keep aggravating the area."

"You're full of shit, Carny," Big Hog said. "It's the nasty jungy-fungy. I need some snow. That'll fix me up right good. You got any?"

"Not for that," Carny said. "Ask the fawn there."

Big Hog pointed to Dornawk. "Hey, Knockers, you still got your snow ball?"

"My what?"

"Camphor," Big Hog said. "Damn, son, if you were any greener, you'd be sprouting leaves."

Knockers swung his haversack around to his chest and rummaged inside it. A moment later, he pulled out a leather-wrapped ball. He undid it and showed it to Big Hog. "You mean this?"

"There we are! Toss it over here. I'll square up with you tomorrow."

Knockers hesitated, then tossed the ball. Big Hog caught it with one hand and immediately stuffed it down the front of his trousers. "Ah, that'll put things to right. I might not need it all. You want what's left back?"

"No... you can keep it," Knockers said, his eyes wide.

"Mighty oak of you," Big Hog said.

Knockers blinked and pressed on. "Sorry, but... about the mountain... wasn't that where you fought all those slyts?"

The air seemed to chill, despite the heat. Carny looked up to the sky. "Why don't we just rest here quietly?"

"I want to hear all about it," Knockers said, ignoring the hint. "You really showed those slyts."

"Fucking fawns, always looking to shoot something," Big Hog said, his jovial mood melting faster than the snow in his crotch. "Don't have a single point on your rack and you're already looking to triple S and put some heads on your wall."

Knockers's lower lip started to tremble. Carny sighed and not too gently punched Big Hog's upper arm. "He's just cranky because he hasn't planted a crop in a week."

Knockers sniffed and wiped his nose with the back of his hand. Poor bastard, fresh off a ship from the Kingdom less than a week ago.

"I'm not looking for heads. The LOKAM says—"

"Fuck the LOKAM!" came the collective reply from everyone within earshot.

Knockers blushed. "What does *triple S* mean?"

Big Hog snorted. "'Slit some slyt'? See, three S's."

"Slit some slyt," Knockers replied, trying out the phrase as if he were afraid it would bite. "Do you guys do that? I mean, actually slit their throats?"

Carny knew he'd never been as big-eyed a fawn as Knockers.

When no one answered, Knockers pressed on. "I heard about you guys. All about the battle on the mountain. There was that big arrow clash with five hundred slyts one night. Almost overran the command post. All the news criers back home were telling the tale. How you guys killed over a hundred slyts."

The low, contented murmur of the shield at rest vanished. Carny sat up straighter. "That's what they say? We fought off five hundred slyts?" He turned to where Wraith was sitting. The longbowman was watching the distant jungle while slowly sharpening one of his knives against a whetstone balanced on the top of his thigh. He acted as if he hadn't heard.

"The king himself gave your unit a citation for bravery in the field. Commander Weel was personally thanked. They even promoted him for it."

"No shit, Weel?" Big Hog said, lifting up the rim of his helm to stare at Knockers. He swatted Carny in the arm. "Hear that? Weel got a personal mention. Funny, I don't remember him being in that ravine with us, do you?"

"It was dark," Carny said, his happy feeling of a few moments ago bleeding away. "Who the hell knows? Who the fuck cares?"

Knockers was shaking his head. "Oh, no, you're wrong. It was big news back home. A lot of people cared. There's been talk of the war not going well, but when you guys held off those slyts and only lost one guy in return, that shut some people up, I'll tell you."

The sound of Wraith's knife on the whetstone got louder.

"Yeah, one guy," Big Hog said, sitting up straighter. "One guy *that night*."

Knockers looked around, obviously confused. "I'm just telling you what I heard. I was happy when they assigned me to this unit. You guys are heroes."

Wraith was on his feet in a blur. "You use that word around here again and you'll be Kingdom-bound as a handful of ash and bone in an urn."

Knockers raised his hands. "I'm not being sharp, I really mean it!"

"Why don't you try shutting your fuckin' mouth instead?" Big Hog said.

Knockers looked at Carny. The fawn's eyes were pleading for help.

Carny relented. "Look… things ain't always what they say they are, you know? Up ain't always down, black ain't always white, and the war, well… it's not quite the way the news criers are telling you."

"I… I don't understand," Knockers said, looking from one soldier to another. "They talked about your battle for a week. Everyone was so impressed you only had one loss."

"We lost a second man," Wraith said. He spit on the ground near Knockers's boots, then sat back down and looked out at the jungle. He began sharpening his knife again, the blade pressing so hard into the whetstone on his thigh Carny thought he'd break the blade or his leg bone if he kept it up.

"They didn't say anything about that," Knockers said. Sweat beaded on his face.

"He didn't die that night. It happened later, but it was an accident," Carny said.

"What happened?" Knockers asked.

Big Hog flung himself up to a sitting position. "He ate a fucking signal star. Three days after our glorious battle, the Weasel goes and puts his crossbow in his mouth and squeezes the lever."

Carny sat up. "Fuck that. Hog, it was an accident! He tripped."

"Keep telling yourself that if it helps you sleep," Big Hog said.

Silence reigned except for the sound of Wraith's blade on the whetstone. Carny could still see the bits of smoldering skull and brain. "Fuck, Wraith, give it a rest," Carny said, turning and flinging a handful of dirt at the soldier. "Any sharper and you'll be honing air."

Wraith held the blade up and looked at the edge. "I'm going for a walk," he said, getting up and leaving without another word.

"I... I'm sorry, I didn't know," Knockers said, looking around at the shield.

"No way you could," Carny said.

"Carny?" Knockers said quietly, scooting over so he was by his boots. "Why did you call that other soldier Wraith?"

Carny looked at Knockers and lay back down. "That's his Lux name. Just like I'm Carny, he's Big Hog, and you're Knockers."

Knockers seemed to think about that for several flicks. "Why Wraith?"

Carny squinted, trying to spot Wraith and failing. "'Cause he just disappears. We get out in the deep green and you can't find him. It's like he's not even there."

Knockers reached for his chest and Carny knew he had to be clutching a Sacred Tree pendant.

"Is he a thaum, do you think?"

"He's more dangerous than that," Carny said. There were murmurs of agreement.

Carny lay back down and closed his eyes. He was certain he'd only closed them for a flick when he heard his name being called.

"Carny."

Carny looked up to see Listowk sauntering over to the group. It was nearly dusk.

"We found something. I'd like you to take a look."

The tone of Listowk's voice immediately put the hairs on the back of Carny's neck straight up.

"Me?"

"You," Listowk said. "The rest of you, off your arses and keep a lookout. Wraith found a tunnel entrance. There are probably more."

Carny leaped to his feet. There could be a fucking slyt aiming an arrow at him from under the rubble right now.

"Follow me," Listowk said. He got up and moved away.

Carny scrambled to his feet and followed. Listowk moved carefully through the debris until he reached a section of palm-frond wall. Several soldiers of the shield were crouched around it with their crossbows pointed at it. Wraith stood nearby like a cat that had just brought a dead bird home.

Listowk stepped forward and grabbed a corner of the wall. Holding a finger to his lips, he gently lifted up the section of wall. Carny leaned forward and saw the entrance to a tunnel. Carny looked at Listowk.

"I'll bet this is why we never found the little bastards on the mountain," Listowk whispered.

Carny nodded while backing away from the entrance. "Clever."

Listowk lowered the wall and walked a few paces away, motioning for Carny to follow him. "Someone needs to go in there and check it out," Listowk said.

"Sure," Carny said, unable to imagine who would be that stupid.

"Great, thanks for volunteering," Listowk said, handing Carny a small brass lantern.

"What?" Carny looked around. The rest of Red Shield was looking everywhere but at him. "Are you mad?"

"Someone has to go down there. Sinte's been watching you. He thinks you have potential. I do, too. This is the perfect chance for you to show it."

Carny wanted to scream. *Potential to be killed!* "What do I do if I find anything?" Carny asked.

"Hey," Big Hog whispered, "Wraith found another entrance." He was motioning to another pile of debris ten yards away.

Carny hoped that revelation would save him, but Wraith dropped down to his hands and knees and dove into the tunnel without a word.

"You'd best get going," Listowk said.

Whispering a prayer to the High Druid, Carny walked back to the tunnel entrance. The Wiz lifted up the wall and gave Carny a smile and a nod. Carny ignored him and, crouching low, eased his way headfirst into the tunnel. His ass puckered to the point that he doubted he'd ever shit again. Visions of snakes and spiders filled his head as he willed his body all the way in the opening. When nothing immediately presented itself, he pushed the lantern ahead of him with one hand while he held his crossbow in front of him with the other. The arms of the crossbow scraped the sides of each wall. There wasn't room to crouch, either, so he inched his way forward on his belly.

The tunnel walls were surprisingly smooth. The dirt was clearly hand-packed. Carny could only see a few feet ahead with the lantern as the tunnel took a sharp right turn.

The sound of the shield above vanished as he worked his way forward, aware of the gentle downward slope. Within a few yards the feeling of absolute loneliness gripped him and he started to shake. *I'm going to die here!*

He gritted his teeth and forced himself to crawl to where the tunnel turned to the right, vowing to stop there and then back his way out. He counted to five, then eased his head out past the corner and looked down the tunnel. After a yard or so, it was black. Satisfied that nothing and no one was there, he started to pull back his head. A scratching noise made him stop.

Sweat poured down Carny's face, stinging his eyes. He didn't dare move his hands to wipe his forehead, keeping a death grip on the lantern and his crossbow. He strained to see deeper in the darkness, but nothing appeared. *Wraith.* It had to be Wraith making the noise.

A scream ripped through the tunnel. Carny jumped and

squeezed the firing lever on his crossbow. The arms sprang forward, digging into the dirt walls and driving the stock of the crossbow back at Carny. A *thunk* echoed off the walls and the scream changed pitch to a low groan. Despite his mangled shot, he'd still managed to hit something.

Carny scrambled to back up and knocked over the lantern, extinguishing the light. The sound of scrabbling dirt advanced on Carny in the dark and he flailed to get away, but he couldn't get his crossbow unstuck.

"Wraith! Wraith!" Carny shouted, jacking his right arm back along his side and frantically feeling for the small dagger he kept in his boot. He tried bringing his knee up toward his hand, but the walls of the tunnel were too narrow. The end of the dagger handle remained a foot out of reach.

"Grab him!" Wraith shouted. He voice was muffled, but it came from somewhere in front of Carny.

"Grab who?" Carny asked as something touched his left hand.

Carny screamed. He sensed the presence of something directly in front of him and did the only thing he could. He lifted up his head until his helm hit the ceiling, then lunged forward. His helm hit something hard. Whatever it was groaned and something grabbed on to his wrist.

Screaming at the top of his voice, Carny head-butted the thing in front of him over and over until the groaning stopped. He ripped his arm from whatever had grabbed it and again tried to back up. His ears were ringing and his neck throbbed with pain.

"Carny, did you get him?"

The sound of Wraith's voice halted Carny. "Wraith? Holy fucking High Druid, what is it?"

An orange glow filled the tunnel from Wraith's lantern and the unconscious form of a slyt lay on the tunnel floor in front of Carny. Blood pooled beneath his head and Carny's crossbow bolt protruded from the top of his right collarbone.

"I got him. Son of a witch, I got him!"

The slyt moved, his head lolling from side to side. Carny lunged and hit the slyt again in the head with his helm.

"I smell blood. Are you hit?" Wraith asked.

Carny tried to slow his breathing. "No. But I got him good."

"You pull and I'll push," Wraith said, holding up his lantern.

"You want to bring him out?" Carny asked. He grabbed his lantern and unhooked his crossbow from where it had become wedged.

"Sinte'll want to see him."

Fuck. "Fine," Carny said, feeling no such thing. He placed the handle of the lantern in his teeth and reached out with both hands to wiggle his crossbow free. Twisting the weapon at an angle, he placed it on the back of the slyt. Carny then grabbed the tunic of the slyt by its shoulder and pulled. The slyt slid surprisingly easily across the dirt floor of the tunnel.

With much grunting and sweating, Carny crawled backward through the tunnel, tugging and pulling on the slyt. It seemed like it took forever, but suddenly strong hands had ahold of his ankles and he was whisked out of the tunnel and into the relative brightness of the setting sun.

The slyt followed with Wraith right behind him. Carny spit out the lantern handle and rolled over onto his back and gasped for air. Someone put a water skin to his lips and he gulped down a mouthful before choking and having to sit up.

"We thought you'd been stabbed in the balls," Big Hog said, helping Carny to his feet.

Several soldiers stood around the slyt, peering down at him. Instead of the typical peasant garb of green cotton short pants and simple beige tunic, he wore what was clearly a uniform. It was a matching set of reed-green pants and tunic with red stitching on each shoulder in the shape of a crane. A canvas belt, sturdy leather sandals, and a woven bamboo quill with several arrows in it completed his attire. For all of that, he was wisp thin and tiny. He was half Carny's weight at most.

"Is he dead?" Carny asked. His knees refused to lock and only Big Hog's arm around his waist kept him upright.

"He's not long for this world, that's for damn sure," Listowk said, lifting the slyt up into a sitting position. He grabbed the slyt by the hair and pulled up his head. It was like watching a puppeteer at work. Blood poured freely down the slyt's face. Several soldiers gasped.

"He has the pox!"

"It's just their coloring," Listowk said. "They come in several shades. My guess is this lad is from the far west. Never seen color patterns like his before. Maybe they change when they grow up. Doesn't look to be more than thirteen."

Carny was able to clearly see the slyt's face for the first time. Streaks of blood only partially covered the many vertical striations of brown and black shades running down his face. Mixed with the blood, it was a gruesome sight.

"Thirteen?" Carny asked.

"If that," Listowk said. The slyt groaned again and his eyes fluttered.

"So you got one of the bastards," SL Sinte said, striding into the gathering. He walked up to the slyt and kicked him in the thigh. The slyt groaned.

"Back to your posts, all of you," Sinte said, looking around at the group. "Listowk, assign troops to cover these tunnel entrances."

Listowk nodded. "Right away, SL." He motioned to Carny to come over.

Carny did, wobbling before he thankfully sank to his knees beside the slyt. "Keep him propped up," Listowk said, patting Carny on the shoulder. "Good job, Carny. You, too, Wraith."

"What's down there?" Sinte asked, not bothering with praise.

"Tunnels, lots of them," Wraith said. "I passed five offshoots."

"You?" Sinte asked, turning to Carny.

"I was busy with him," Carny said, motioning with his head to the slyt. He cradled the boy's torso in his arms. It felt like holding a fawn, he was so light. "Shot him, but he kept on coming." *He must have been terrified*, Carny realized. Alone in the darkness, two big soldiers from the Kingdom closing in on him, nowhere to run.

"There's blood on your helm," Sinte said, apparently noticing it for the first time.

"Not a lot of room to move down there so I used what

was available," Carny said, suddenly feeling ashamed of his violence. He could have just reached out and grabbed the slyt.

Sinte harrumphed. "Well, make sure you get your helm cleaned." He bent down and slapped the slyt across the face. "How many more of you are around here? Where's your unit?"

The slyt's head jerked and his eyes opened. The irises were a deep green with gold flecks. He opened his mouth, but whatever he tried to say was lost as he spit up blood. Carny grabbed a handful of palm fronds and tried to wipe the blood off the slyt's face, but Sinte knocked his hand away.

"What the fuck are you doing?" Sinte leaned in closer. "Where's your unit?" Sinte asked again.

The slyt blinked and seemed to become aware of his surroundings for the first time. His eyes went wide and he started to struggle in Carny's grasp. Carny had no trouble holding on to him. A flash of steel caught Carny's eye and the slyt held a small dagger in his hand. He was trying to raise it to strike Carny in the face, but he wasn't strong enough to lift his arm, let alone break Carny's grasp.

Sinte snarled, grabbed the bolt in the slyt's collarbone, and shook it back and forth. The slyt dropped the dagger and let out a pitiful scream, his mouth quivering as tears poured down his face.

"Sneaky little fuck!" Sinte shouted.

"He doesn't understand you!" Carny shouted.

"The fuck he doesn't," Sinte said, shaking the bolt again. "These fuckers understand us just fine. Where's your unit? How many are there?"

The slyt started babbling, but it didn't sound like Luitoxese to Carny… more like gibberish.

"We should get Wiz over here to take a look at him," Carny said. "He's hurt bad."

"At this garbage?" Sinte asked. "He's the enemy, Carny, or did you damage your own head as well? He just tried to kill you! This is why we're here. This is what we're fighting."

Carny looked down at the boy in his arms. This wasn't right. He was just a boy.

"Maybe," Carny said, "but right now he needs our help."

"I suppose he does at that," Sinte said. He gripped the bolt in the slyt's collarbone with both hands and plunged it deeper into the slyt's chest. The boy began convulsing. Carny wrapped his arms around him tighter and tried to calm him down, but the convulsions continued as the slyt's eyes rolled back in his head and his mouth fell slack. A moment later his entire body went limp. Carny tried lifting his head back up, but as soon as he let go it flopped forward and didn't move.

Sinte stood up and savagely ripped the bolt out and threw it onto the slyt's crumpled legs. He glared down at the slyt.

"Get me a live one next time," Sinte said, turning and walking away.

Carny sat there, holding the slyt upright, looking from the departing Sinte to the bloody bolt in the slyt's lap. He'd done this. He'd killed him.

"You can let him go," Big Hog said. "C'mon, I'll get you cleaned up."

"He's the enemy," Carny said, "he wanted to kill me."

Big Hog crouched down beside him. "Yeah, ain't that just all kinds of fucked up? You think they're going to be big, scary monsters and then you see them and realize they aren't."

"So this is our enemy?" Carny said, trying and failing to make sense of it.

"Let's get away from here," Big Hog said, pulling Carny to his feet.

The slyt slipped out of Carny's grasp and lay in a heap on the ground. He looked so damn small.

Big Hog gently turned Carny away and started walking. Carny took a couple of steps before a burning rage welled up in his chest and he twisted out of Big Hog's grasp.

"Where's my crossbow? Where's my fucking crossbow?"

Listowk appeared and pinned his arms to his sides.

"Easy, my boy," he said softly while holding Carny in an iron grip.

Carny's entire body shook. "I'll kill Sinte, I'll put a bolt right in his black heart. Did you see what he did?" Carny asked.

Listowk offered him a sad smile but didn't loosen his grip. "It's done. Let it go. The poor bugger would have died one way or the other. Let it go."

Carny tried to wriggle free, but now Big Hog was beside him again with a meaty paw on his shoulder. "The LC's right. It ain't worth it."

"Is any of it?" Carny asked, his rage melting into a despair so deep he gasped. "This is what we're fighting? Destroying villages, killing livestock? Why? How does this make the Kingdom safe? How does any of this matter?"

"The days of knights on horseback are long gone," Listowk said. "Even then though, war wasn't any better. People die. They die for noble reasons and for no damn reason at all. In the end, they're just as dead."

"It's not right," Carny said, knowing it was futile to struggle anymore. He was one man against a world.

Listowk loosened his grip. Carny just stood there. He barely had enough energy to breathe. Listowk let go.

"You go lie down. I don't want to see you on your feet, got that? Big Hog, you make sure," Listowk said.

"I'm not a newborn," Carny said. "You don't have to treat me like one."

"Listowk, what the fuck is going on?" Sinte shouted, striding over to them. He'd had time to polish his helm so that the setting sun made it glow.

Carny's anger came roaring back, but Big Hog clamped a meaty paw on his shoulder and kept him rooted to the spot. Listowk muttered a curse and stepped in front of Carny and faced Sinte.

"Just getting the boys squared away," Listowk said, his voice lacking its normal laconic lilt.

"They'd better be good to go," Sinte said, coming to a stop with his hands on his hips. "We got reports that a group of FnC hard chargers from Western Luitox have set up camp on the outskirts of a village west of here. The Luitoxese Royal Army was going to take the lead, but that's changed. So we're going to go clear out the FnCs."

Carny blinked. "Are you fucking kidding?"

"What did you say?" Sinte shouted.

Listowk held up his hands. "He's just surprised, we all are. How far away?"

"Fifteen miles," Sinte said.

Groans greeted his statement. Carny shook his head. After everything that happened they were now expected to march fifteen miles in the dark?

"Transportation has been arranged," Sinte said, staring past Listowk at Carny.

Carny held his stare.

"What kind?" Listowk asked, shifting his body to block Carny's view.

"Get this rabble in shape—we fly in the morning," Sinte said, moving his head to give Carny one more stare before turning and stomping away.

Carny's right arm was numb. "Big Hog, you can let go, I'm not going after him."

Big Hog kept his hand in place until Listowk turned and nodded.

"He said fly, right?" Carny asked, rubbing feeling back into this arm.

Listowk tried to smile, but couldn't manage it. "Yes, he did."

CHAPTER NINETEEN

OBSIDIAN FLOCK LEADER VORLY Astol squinted through the small aperture of his sextant. "Altitude... one thousand four hundred yards. Scratch that, three hundred and ninety yards," he said, adjusting the frame in relation to the index bar.

"Confirming, one thousand three hundred and ninety," Breeze said, her voice clipped and precise.

As far as the Lux went, it was a beautiful morning. Clear sky, bit of a headwind from the north giving the rags of Obsidian Flock something their wings could grab on to, and best of all, they had a mission. Vorly tucked his sextant back into its pocket on his jacket and buttoned it up. Attention to detail was what kept you alive.

"Give me a crystal pathway check, Breeze," Vorly ordered, not bothering to turn around. He kept his eyes on the horizon, doing his best not to *accidentally* knock the crystal sheet perched on its wood easel by his right thigh.

"By your command, Sky Horse Leader," Breeze said. Ever since that disastrous training flight, Breeze said nothing that wasn't absolutely necessary when they were in the air. It was almost like flying solo again.

Vorly should have been pleased, but he wasn't. As much as he hated to admit it, the crystals were here to stay. That meant the RATs were, too. Gone were the days when a ragger flew alone. Accepting that meant he had to form a relationship with Breeze that worked. He'd said as much to the drivers and RATs after their recent brawl, but it only dawned on him now that he hadn't followed his own orders. He couldn't afford his damn pride up here and Breeze would have to get over her hurt feelings or whatever the hell was wrong with her. If they didn't, they'd wind up dead, like Jate and his RAT. Vorly shook his head to get the image out of his mind. *The fuck if I'm going to be charked.*

"Okay to ground myself in?" Vorly asked, placing both of Carduus's reins in his left hand and raising his right so Breeze could see it before dropping it back down and placing it on his right thigh. It was one of several new measures they had added. A second braided copper cable had also been attached to the crystal sheet. The original still ran back to the RAT's sheet, connecting the two crystals together, while the new cable snaked all the way out onto Carduus's right wing, where it ended in a foot-long iron spike. The cable was held in place by U-shaped copper nails punched through the wing, while the spike had been forged directly into Carduus's metal-rich bones by the flock smithy.

"You are clear to engage, Sky Horse Leader," she said. Flat and lifeless.

"Grounding in," Vorly said, lifting his hand from his thigh and slowly placing it on the first copper braid. When nothing happened, he slid his hand up to the crystal sheet and placed his fingertips on it. Despite the midmorning sun and the heat coming through Carduus, the sheet was cold.

"Our sheets are linked, Sky Horse Leader," Breeze said, her fingertips brushing his through whatever magicks made the thing work.

He looked down at the sheet, still amazed. By sheer force of will, he was making himself come to terms with the things. It helped that he'd seen what happened to Jate. It helped less that Legion Flock Commander Modelar was keen on seeing it done yesterday. Still, they were finding a way.

"Pathway confirmed, we are on the aether," Breeze said.

"On the aether, aye," Vorly confirmed, removing his hand. Since the accident, Vorly had done his best to understand how the sheets worked. It was like trying to scoop water with a fork. No sooner would he get his mind around a concept than it would become hopelessly tangled with the next one. He finally gave up on the thaumics of it and focused instead on what it could do, and most of all, what he could do with it.

"Let me know when the flight is on aether," he said, reaching down with his right hand to stroke Carduus's scales before grabbing the reins.

"Aye, Sky Horse Leader," Breeze said.

It was more error than trial, but they were slowly working the newts out of the cauldron. Vorly half listened as Breeze brought the other RATs onto the aether plane and verified every sheet was fully aligned. She was the youngest RAT assigned to the flock, and even though they all had been given the same rank of aether operator, she was clearly their leader. Based on what he'd now seen and heard, she knew how to throw a punch and how to avoid one. Vorly shook his head. He'd never been as challenged by a woman in his life as he was by her, and certainly not one as young. In a way he didn't understand, he liked it.

"The flight is on the aether and aligned to the plane," Breeze said a moment later.

Vorly looked down at his sheet and saw the now-familiar pattern of fingertips tracing paths. All the lines were blue.

"I have a blue sheet," Vorly said.

"Aye, all blue," Breeze replied.

"Good job, Breeze," Vorly said, his voice gruff lest she make too much of the compliment.

"By your command, Sky Horse Leader," she replied.

Vorly grunted. "High Druid's sake, Breeze, at least use my aether name," he said, his hope that she would snap out of her funk on her own failing.

"Aye... Falcon," she said.

Vorly made a mental note to have a long talk with her when

this mission was over. They'd either come to an understanding or he'd get a new RAT. Maybe the two of them were just too damn stubborn to work well together. Realizing he wasn't going to fix it now, he glanced right, assessing the position of each rag in the flight. Sky Horse Two, Three, and Four off his right wing were holding a clean line with a seventy-five-yard spacing between rags. They were flying at half-wing speed, the rags alternating a wing stroke with a glide. For something so big, rags could be surprisingly gentle, especially in the air. He turned to look to the left and his improving mood did an about-face.

Where the right echelon was smooth and precise, the left wing of their V formation was a witch's hair in a windstorm. Sky Horse Five, Jate's former ride, was now crewed by a driver and RAT fresh off the boat. The RAT, Hyaminth Trecell, didn't seem any more strange than the others, but the new driver, Ormo Brithol, acted as if this were his first rag. Centaurea was all over the sky, refusing to keep position off of Carduus's left wing. The rag drifted out three hundred yards before Brithol brought him back. This put Sky Horse Six in a hopeless situation of trying to stay on Centaurea's wing and make use of the draft created.

"Sky Horse Five, this is Sky Horse Leader," Vorly said, remembering to turn back toward the crystal sheet. They would have to come up with a better system. He had to be able to talk while looking where he needed, not down. "What seems to be the problem?"

"Sorry, Sky Horse Leader, Centaurea just won't calm down. He keeps trying to wheel around. It's like he's looking for something."

Vorly cursed under his breath. Big, terribly destructive, and about as bright as a chunk of coal in a bottle of ink, Centaurea was pining for Jate. Vorly had seen it happen before. Some rags became so attached to a driver that they couldn't be flown again if that driver was killed. If they couldn't get Centaurea under control, the beast would be cut up for parts. A rag heart alone was worth its weight in silver and the fluid in their eyes even more.

"Understood," Vorly said, doing his best to sound positive.

He doubted he'd have better luck on Centaurea than Brithol. "Sky Horse Six, switch positions with Sky Horse Five. Brithol, let Centaurea have his head out to five hundred yards, then drift him back toward the flight. See if he calms down with more space."

"Aye that, Sky Horse Leader," Brithol said.

Vorly turned and watched as Centaurea banked and flew away from the flight. Sky Horse Six slid into position and settled smoothly at seventy-five yards off of Carduus's wing.

"What if—" Breeze started to say, then stopped.

"What?" Vorly asked, actually turning around to look at her. Her head was down, staring at the sheet.

"I was just thinking that we could try cocooning Centaurea in a low plane field."

Vorly didn't even try to pretend he knew what that meant. "What?"

Breeze lifted her head and started when she saw Vorly looking at her. "Think of it like a big, warm blanket wrapped around Centaurea. Except it will be the residual energy from the pathway being generated by Hyaminth. Right now, we're simply letting it flow away with the second cable we added, but if she directed even a tenth of it, it might work."

"Is this anything like what happened to Jate and his RAT— damn, I mean Bwiter?" Vorly asked.

Breeze shook her head. "No, completely different. This would be totally safe."

Vorly looked at her. She blinked, but she didn't look away. *Good.* He took a deep breath. "Fine, try it with Carduus first."

Breeze's eyes opened wide. "Sir?"

"You said it was safe, so give it a try. We're a team, Breeze, the three of us. Up here, we're all we've got. If we can't trust each other, it isn't going to work." He made a point of looking down at her hands and her bruised and swollen knuckles. "The next fight we get into won't be driver against RAT." Vorly turned around and faced forward. "Whenever you're ready." He debated breaking formation and taking Carduus down to treetop level but decided against it. He wanted Breeze to know she had his full confidence.

"Sir, it's just that—"

"Either do it or don't, but don't waste my time with hemming and hawing," Vorly said, letting her hear his annoyance. "Maybe a male RAT would be better to do this."

"The inside of your skull is going to vibrate. Don't panic," she said, her voice steely.

"Inside my... oh," Vorly said, his focus blurring as something completely foreign gripped him from inside. His entire body was vibrating with a slow, heavy pulse. Carduus snapped his jaws and shook his head. It felt wrong. Vorly gritted his teeth, ready to yell at Breeze to stop, but then it smoothed out. It was as if three different rhythms had blended into one.

It felt... good. Carduus must have liked it too because he started to purr, sending an entirely new vibration up through the seat of Vorly's pants.

"How do you feel, sir?" Breeze asked. She sounded out of breath but defiant.

"I'm fine... in fact, I feel better than I did before you started. What did you do?"

Pride gave Breeze's voice strength. "I used the residual energy to combine our three heartbeats into one."

Vorly instinctively raised a hand and placed it against his chest. "You mean like one of those musical recitals where they play different instruments but get them to all sound good together?"

"Why yes, that's a perfect way to describe it," she said. "I've created a three-part harmony that ties us together—you, me, and Carduus. We are a team, after all."

Vorly smiled but didn't turn around to let Breeze see it. "Can Haymint over there do it?"

"*Hyaminth* is very capable. She'll have no trouble with this."

Vorly nodded. "Right." He tapped his crystal. "Sky Horse Five, this is Sky Horse Leader. Hyaminth is going to set up a harmony for you. Should sort Centaurea out. Stay calm. It smooths out after the first jolt. Breeze will explain."

Breeze ran through the procedure twice with Hyaminth, who was immediately receptive to it. Brithol, however, was not as eager.

"You sure about this, Sky Horse Leader? Sounds a little risky. I, um, heard about what happened to the last driver of this rag."

Vorly didn't blame the lad, but he didn't have time to coddle him. He needed all six rags and crew flying sharp and tight. "I had my RAT do it first. I'm in harmony right now and feel great," Vorly said.

There was a long pause before Brithol came back on. "Aye that, Sky Horse Leader. Will give it a try."

Vorly turned his head slightly so that he could keep Sky Horse Five in view out of the corner of his eye.

At first, Centaurea continued his erratic behavior, flying toward the flight and then wheeling away again. He was on his way back toward them when he shook his head and snapped his jaws at the empty air. Vorly gripped the reins tight, wondering if he'd just made an incredibly foolish decision.

Centaurea continued to snap his jaws long after Carduus had stopped. Vorly was about to shout into the crystal for Hyaminth to stop when Centaurea closed his jaws and didn't open them again. Vorly waited. Centaurea continued to fly straight and true toward the flight. He reached the point where he normally wheeled away and kept on coming. He settled in at around one hundred yards off of Sky Horse Six's left wing. It wasn't perfect, but it was good enough.

"Breeze?"

"Yes, sir?"

"This might be the harmony talking, but that was a damn fine bit of thaumics. That's a compliment, and you will accept it."

Carduus's wings beat several times before Breeze answered.

"By your command, Sky Horse Leader," she said.

Vorly huffed, wondering how in blazes you got through to a woman, when he felt her hand on his back.

"Thank you, sir," she said. Her hand lifted and was gone.

Vorly focused his eyes on the horizon, a three-part harmony

pulsing steadily in his chest. As mornings went in the Lux, this was turning out to be a pretty damn good one.

LC LISTOWK LED the shield out of Moskoan and toward the west side of the dosha swamps. He kept the pace slow. It wasn't that he was afraid of the coming battle, but as long as they were walking there was much less chance for the boys to get into trouble. Walking kept them occupied. They could yap, smoke, grab a drink and something to eat, and burn off a little nervous energy. The slower he walked, the better. He was especially concerned about Carny. He seemed to have gotten over the worst of the tunnel, but it had marked him.

Listowk hefted his crossbow from the crook of his right arm to the crook of his left. It wasn't required, but he'd learned to shoot equally well from either hand. He drifted his fingers over the bow, checking the tautness of the string, the position of the bolt and the safety lever. His eyes never left the tree line. He judged the jungle to be four hundred yards away. It was tempting to get a measurement to see how accurate his estimate was, but they didn't have time.

The dirt was dry under his boots, far different from the damp muck they'd encountered on the mountain. He looked down and watched dust swirl up with each step. Damn hard to farm when it was this dry. He raised his eyes and resumed scanning the edge of the jungle. It'd be wetter in there. It always was.

He reached the two-foot-high dirt berm that marked the close edge of the dosha swamp and stepped on top of it. Taking a breath, he turned his back to the jungle and motioned for the soldiers behind to turn and walk beside the berm. He smiled as they passed. They were a sun-kissed, filthy, shuffling mob, and he loved them dearly.

"LC," Ropit said as he walked past. Listowk nodded. Good soldier—never needed to be told anything twice. A few more walked past, nodding or ignoring him altogether.

Carny walked past without a word.

Listowk watched him go by, taking the opportunity to check him over. He wasn't looking for infractions; hell, even Sinte had calmed down about spit and polish. The soldier was hitting the Wild Flower heavy. But he wasn't going to call him on it, not today.

The new soldier, Knockers, followed after Carny.

"Seen much of the squirrel this morning, Knockers?" Listowk asked, using an ancient phrase about getting up early in the forest.

"Just his nuts, LC, and I think they're cracked," Knockers replied. The soldiers in earshot chuckled.

Listowk smiled. It was important to integrate a new soldier as quickly as possible.

"Need rain," Big Hog said, walking up to the edge of the berm and pausing to stand by Listowk. He used his crossbow to point at the dosha swamps. "Gonna lose the crop if it doesn't come soon."

Listowk looked out over the fields, but his eyes kept locking back on the jungle.

"We're lucky it's dry, or we'd be up to our asses in water out here," Listowk said, turning back to watch the rest of the shield walk past. "I don't even know if rags float."

"Need rain," Big Hog repeated, shouldering his crossbow and walking on.

Listowk waited until Sinte arrived but turned and started moving across the berm before the SL could say something. He reached the far end of the shield and crouched down on top of the berm, pivoting on the soles of his boots so that he could keep one eye on the far tree line and the other on the shield.

SL Sinte stepped up onto the berm where Listowk had. He barely glanced at the jungle before he started walking down the berm. "When the rags arrive you will not run! You will not scream! You will not point and shout and act like bloody little children." Listowk groaned. Sinte couldn't relax even if he were ordered to do so. "You are soldiers in the Army of the Kingdom. You aren't a peasant rabble, despite the deplorable condition of your uniforms. You will not fuck this up. Is that clear?"

"Clear as beer, SL!" roared the shield in response. Listowk nodded. He couldn't recall when the refrain had become popular, but there wasn't a truer thing said. The beer they were issued in the Lux tasted like water that had pissed itself.

"You will stay in formation and only move when given an order to do so. And no smoking!"

The groans rolled up and down the line.

Carny made a noise.

Sinte strode over to where Carny was sitting. "I don't want to see a pipe or a smoke or anything. They're attracted to fire. You light up a pipe and they're just as likely to think you're giving them a signal to mate."

Several soldiers started to laugh.

"That is not a joke! These are monsters! You understand? *Monsters!*" Spittle flecked both corners of Sinte's mouth and his eyes were bulging.

Shit, the bastard's scared to death, Listowk thought. He stood up and walked across the berm toward Sinte. "You heard the SL. No smoking. Sorry about that, SL, I'll keep the boys in line."

Sinte turned to focus on Listowk. The SL was breathing heavily and sweat beaded his face. *High Druid's balls, he's losing it.*

"If I smell even one whiff of smoke…"

Listowk raised his hands in a placating gesture. "They know better, but I'll stay on top of them."

Sinte looked over the troops and then back at Listowk. "We could have marched it no problem. Weel's coddling them," he said, lowering his voice so only Listowk could hear.

Fifteen miles in half a day and then assault a slyt force? "It is hot, and that's a long way to go to fight a battle," Listowk said, unable to sympathize with his leader.

Sinte sneered. "You're getting soft. Mark my words, this kind of luxury has a price," he said. He turned and strode away, kicking up a miniature dust storm in his wake.

Listowk waited until Sinte was long out of earshot before letting out a sigh. As if he didn't have enough on his plate, now the SL was showing signs of strain.

"Here they come!"

Listowk turned toward the jungle, then realized his mistake. He raised a hand to shield his eyes and looked skyward. A heavy flapping sound reached his ears. He turned his head to the side to better pinpoint the location, then looked back. There, to the south, maybe two miles out, six dark smudges in the sky.

"Stay where you are," he said, raising his voice just enough to make sure it got through. They'd all been briefed very carefully about what to do around rags. The most important thing was don't get in front of their maws, especially when they're landing. Listowk thought that pretty damn obvious and wondered who in the world hadn't thought so.

"What say we review procedures one more time," Listowk said, balancing his crossbow on his shoulder and placing his hands on his hips. As soon as he did, he decided that looked too much like Sinte, so he let his hands fall to his sides. "Rags are not horses. They will eat you if given half a chance."

All eyes were on him. The shield had already been given two hurried briefings on mounting and dismounting rags without becoming something caught in their teeth, but Listowk suspected this was the first time most of them were paying attention. The sound of beating wings growing louder was clearly aiding their focus.

"Number one. You do not move until you're given the order to move. A rag's wing is big enough and heavy enough to break your spine if it hits you.

"Number two. Do not approach the head or the tail. One will eat you, the other will crush you.

"Number three. Take the bolt out of your crossbow now and secure it in your quiver. And I don't mean flipping the bolt out of the notch. I want it right out.

"Number four. Make sure everything on you is tied, buckled, and otherwise secure. Once we get in the air, it gets windy.

"Number five. When, and only when, the order has been given to mount the rags will you get up from where you are now.

You will fall in single file per demi-shield and approach the rag.

"Number six. The drivers will hold the rags' wings on an upstroke in what they call a double sail. This will give us easy access to the side of the rag. Should the wings come back down for any reason during boarding, do not stay against the side of the rag. The safest place to be is flat on the ground.

"Number seven. On boarding, you will find a chain running down each side of the rag's spine between the… damn, whatever they call those tall plate things that stick up."

"Dorsal plates!" Carny shouted.

"Right, dorsal plates. There will be small leather saddles with straps attached to the chains. You will sit on the saddle and strap in your thighs and your waist. I repeat, *you will strap in your thighs and across your waist*. Keep your weapons slung at all times. Do not set anything down on the back of the rag.

"Number eight. When you are securely tied in, you will look behind and in front to ensure those men are tied in as well.

"Number nine. Leaving the ground can be rough, so hold on tight. You will remain strapped in for the duration of the flight. Do not adjust your straps for any reason. If you have to piss, piss where you are, but don't try to hang over the side.

"Lastly, when we land, you will stay strapped in until the order is given to release. The drivers will hold the rags' wings in a double sail again and you will get off the same way you got on. Once you hit the ground, do not stand around. Run, don't walk, away from the rag until you have cleared its wing. Then and only then will you reload your crossbow."

"What if the slyts are shooting at us?"

Listowk had wondered the same thing. They could be cut down like wheat before they had a chance to load.

"The rags will no doubt scare them off, so we shouldn't have anything to worry about," he said, repeating what he had been told and believing it as much as the troops did. "Look, you're smart lads. If it looks to be hairy when we land, I'm sure you'll figure it out. I know I won't be running around without a loaded bow." There, that was as close to disobeying a direct order as he could go. "Wraith, launch the smoker!"

Wraith already had a smoke arrow notched. With its distinctive series of small holes running the length of the much heavier shaft, there was no way to mistake it for a regular arrow or a signal star. He aimed into the sky, drew, and released. The smoker wobbled airborne. At five feet, the force of acceleration drove a thin glass tube in the arrow into a metal pin, which broke the glass. By fifty feet in the air, the acid inside came in contact with the walls of the shaft and a thick purple smoke began pouring out of the arrow.

Something primal rose up in Listowk as the rags neared. It was the urge to run far, run fast, and keep going until his lungs gave out. Logic seemed pointless in the face of such terrible power. He suddenly found himself feeling sympathy for Sinte.

"They're going to eat us!" Knockers shouted.

Listowk spun around, forcing himself to have his back to the incoming rags.

"Hold your position! No one move!" Listowk shouted, taking a few steps toward the troops. Knockers stood up, his eyes wide. "Big Hog, grab Knockers and keep him down!"

Big Hog swept an arm and knocked Knockers to his ass. The young soldier tried to get back up, but Big Hog simply leaned on top of him, pinning him to the ground.

The steady *whup whup* sound of the rags' wings suddenly changed into a vicious, roaring gale kicking up dust and dirt. Listowk turned, immediately getting a face full of dirt.

The rags were at a hundred feet from the ground and falling fast. Listowk estimated they were coming in at an angle of thirty degrees, steeper than the mountain they'd climbed for weeks. Their huge wings suddenly tucked in partway toward their bodies and began beating faster in short, sharp strokes.

Listowk shook his head in amazement. He'd never seen anything so big and terrifying up close.

At ten feet above the ground, the rags' tails swung down until the bottom half of the vertical plate on the tail touched the earth. It immediately dug in, gouging a furrow into the dosha swamp a foot deep as the rag kept coming. As soon as the tails hit, their wings shot out straight and flared like two massive sails catching the wind. The rags' bodies tilted up like ducks landing in water before slamming down on the ground.

The lead rag opened its maw, a red-throated, black-toothed doorway into a fiery hell, and let out a high-pitched shriek mixed with a deep, rumbling roar.

"Fucking hell!" Listowk shouted, thanking the High Druid he hadn't eaten anything that morning or else he'd have shit his trousers. He slammed his hands to his ears, but it did little to deaden the sound, his rib cage vibrating with the noise.

A dust cloud rolled across the dosha swamp like smoke. Listowk choked and covered his mouth.

Soldiers shouted and swore, and at least two cried for their mothers. Not one, however, had broken ranks. *Good lads*.

Listowk smiled, showing them all it was no big deal. When he was satisfied the shield was in good shape, he turned to look at the rags now on the ground. They were still frightening but no longer instilled the bowel-churning fear they had while in the air. On the ground, they were enormous lizards. Sinte was right, they were monsters, but they were also under control. He was shocked to see women numbered among some of the crew on the rags. *When the hell did that happen?*

"They don't look so bad," a soldier said.

Listowk didn't bother to turn around. "That's the spirit! Keep telling yourself that." That elicited a few more laughs. *Good, this is working.* The shield was full of nervous energy, but it was channeling it toward humor, not panic. Listowk knew it could easily go the other way in a heartbeat. It only took one fearful soldier to poison an entire shield.

"Hey, LC, there's something wrong with one of them."

Listowk scanned the six rags now settled in the dosha swamp, their wings spread wide and slowly pulsing. *What's right about them?* Listowk wanted to say, but then saw that one of them had its wing flat out and its driver was walking along it looking down.

"Probably just a routine check," Listowk said, aware that

none of the other drivers were checking the wings of their rags. "They know they're carrying valuable cargo today."

The shield laughed, but there was a subtle edge to it. *This is how the panic begins.*

"Right, while the sky jockeys get ready for us, I want a weapons, water, and food check. We could be out there for a few days."

Groans filled the air, but the troops diligently began going over their kits one more time. It was busywork and wouldn't keep them occupied for long. Listowk hoped it would be enough.

"SKY HORSE FOUR to Sky Horse Leader."

"Go ahead, Red Hawk," Vorly said, turning to look behind him. He couldn't see past the other dragons. He had to admit, there were some benefits to having the crystal sheets.

"Cytisus caught his left wing on landing. I walked it and he didn't break anything, but there's a tear in the membrane between the fourth and fifth bones. Two feet long and a bit ragged, but contained. Still a good three feet from the trailing edge."

Vorly cursed under his breath. "Aye that, Red Hawk. Is he keening?"

"Negative, Falcon, but he is a bit owly. I really should burn the edges to stop the bleeding and stitch it before we take off again. The tear could rip right through and then we would have a problem."

Vorly instinctively reached down and patted Carduus. For all their fangs and fire, rags were still fragile in a few areas, especially the wings. The husbandry of rags had come a long way since Vorly first joined the army, but there was still a ways to go.

"How bad's the bleeding?"

"Slow right now, but it'll pump pretty good once we get back in the air and he heats up."

Vorly looked up at the sun. "We don't have the time for a full repair, Red Hawk. Throw some pitch on the bleeders and paste on a lead patch. We'll look at it after we drop off the ants."

"Aye that," Red Hawk said.

"Is it serious?" Breeze asked.

Vorly turned around in his saddle to look at her. It was no longer a shock to him every time he remembered she was there. "Normally, no. We'd start a fire and burn all the bleeders, then stitch up the wound with copper strips, put on the pitch, and anneal some copper sheeting over it. That would hold until we could get a dragonsmith to do a more extensive repair. Damn!"

Breeze sat back. "Gorlan's as competent as Hyaminth. He could do the harmony procedure, but in a situation like this, I think it would do more harm than good."

Vorly realized he was staring over her head trying to see Cytisus and refocused on her. "No, I was just realizing how much of an ass I am."

Breeze, to her credit, held her tongue.

"Modelar has the entire roost in an uproar with our impending move and couldn't spare any of the dragonsmiths for us on this mission. They know better than anyone how to keep a rag flying. I should have insisted."

Breeze gave him a small smile. "The legion flock commander seems rather… *firm* in his convictions when he's set his mind to them."

"Remind you of anyone?" Vorly asked, looking over her head again.

"Actually, Falcon, I've found you to be quite open to change, once you understand its benefits."

Vorly tilted his head and squinted at her. "Why is it I have a hell of a time figuring out if you're complimenting me or insulting me?"

"In this case, it's neither," Breeze said, neatly sidestepping the question. "I've come to realize that it's incumbent on me to present my ideas in a clear and practical way. That allows you to assess them for their tactical value and how best to implement them."

Vorly shook his head. "Do they teach you to talk like that at the RAT, or do you go into it already sort of—"

"Weird?" Breeze said, finishing his thought.

"I was going to say *bloody odd*," he said, "but *weird* covers it."

"I don't think I need to ask if that was a compliment or an insult," Breeze said. "As it happens, I've always been bloody odd. I learned to read when I was two and a half."

Vorly looked closely at her. "Growing up, the druid in my village said teaching girls to read makes 'em hard to control. Agitates their brains. Gives them funny ideas."

Breeze looked down at her crystal sheet. "Breeze here, sliding off plane." She took her time, her hand movements very precise. When she was done, she neatly folded her hands in her lap and stared at Vorly.

The part of Vorly's brain that told him something was wrong was screaming. He chose to ignore it. "I think he was onto something. All you girl RATs are odd. Course, so are the lads, come to think of it."

"What would be less odd?" Breeze asked.

Vorly shrugged. "Just about anything. Cooking, cleaning, sewing, having babies. All good jobs for women."

Breeze nodded. Her neck and her cheeks were red. "I see. And if I and the other women RATs had chosen the path of domesticity instead of pursuing higher thaumics, where do you think you'd be right now? Would you have a working system of communication opening up a world of possibilities?" Her voice grew higher as her enunciation sharpened.

"Ah, I see the problem," Vorly said, hoping to mollify her. "Look, you and the rest of the RATs are odder than a three-headed goat, no question. But turns out, that's not a bad thing. I don't think you'd be suited to a life of domes… domisty… cooking and cleaning and whatnot. Probably put the baby in the pot and the roast in the crib. The point I'm making is that it's good there's some odd ducks like you in the world. I couldn't come up with all this," he said, pointing at her crystal sheet, "if I lived to be seventy."

Breeze brought her hands to her face and lowered her head. Her body began shaking as her breath grew ragged.

This is all I need! Vorly looked around to see if anyone else

229

could see what was happening, but the soldiers were too far away and the rest of the drivers and RATs were busy.

"Look, I—"

Breeze lifted her head and wiped the tears from her eyes. Her laughter, however, continued.

Vorly raised an eyebrow. "What?"

Breeze gasped for breath, her laughs high and melodic, reminding Vorly of a wandering minstrel show that had visited his village. "I don't think anyone has ever traveled so far over such a tortuous path in order to give me a compliment."

"Is that what I did?"

Breeze smiled. "Yes, sir, actually it is. Now, I should go back on plane. And I believe the soldier down there would like to have a word with you."

Vorly turned. An infantry soldier stood ten feet away in front of Carduus's right shoulder. That put him just a few feet from Carduus's head, but if the soldier was scared, he didn't show it.

"The men are ready to board, sir," the soldier said. He used his crossbow to point back toward the shield. Vorly noted with satisfaction that it wasn't loaded. He didn't want any of these army ants panicking their first time and putting an arrow in one of his rags, or worse, him.

Vorly turned his head slightly toward Breeze.

"Sky Horse Four reports the repair is made and Cytisus is sky-worthy," she said.

Vorly turned back to the soldier. "Ready to board. Once the wings go up, you'll have about the time it takes to hard-boil an egg, so get them moving."

The soldier saluted and ran back toward the waiting shield.

"All right, Carduus, time to get back to work." Vorly picked up the iron gaff and gave the rag a good rap on the top of his neck. Carduus responded by lowering his long neck and resting his head on the ground. Vorly kicked back with his heels twice against the shoulder joints. He snarled in conjunction with Carduus as the beast's muscles tightened around the shoulders.

Scales slid over one another with a grating sound. It was music to Vorly's ears.

"Wings high, Carduus, wings high!"

"DON'T DO ANYTHING stupid!" LC Listowk shouted, waving his crossbow and pointing toward the waiting rags. Carny took his eyes off the LC and stared ahead, preparing to move. First one, then the rest of the rags lifted their wings until they were nearly vertical in the air. It was a stunning sight.

"Go, go, go!"

Carny led off, followed by Ahmist, Knockers, and Wraith bringing up the rear. LC Listowk led the other team with Big Hog last. Carny fast-walked toward the rear, his eyes fixed on the massive wing towering above him. If it came down on him, he'd be crushed like an insect. He forced himself to ignore it and focused on not tripping in the dirt.

He'd expected the rags to smell like death, or at least like a filthy brorra or pig, but the scent that filled his nose was an acrid mix of sulfur and metal. It reminded him of walking past a blacksmith's shop. He picked up his pace, aware that other teams were closing on their rags.

He came to the side of the rag and stopped. A ladder made of heavy leather straps with wooden dowels tied in at one-foot intervals hung down its side. Carny reached for the ladder and grabbed it. The strap was warm from resting against the rag's scales, but not uncomfortably so. He stepped up with his left leg, reached to grab a rung with his right hand, and hoisted himself up. In four short steps, he was up on the rag's back. If the rag noticed his presence, it didn't seem to care. Carny figured he was about as significant as a gnat: annoying, but easily dealt with if necessary.

True to their briefing, a long, heavy chain with leather and wood saddles attached to it ran down each side of the rag's dorsal plates. Carny paused. The plates closest to him had to be four feet tall and three feet wide.

"Move your fuckin' ass, Carny!"

Carny waved a hand and took a couple of steps along the rag's back until he came to the chain. The links were as thick as his thumb. He kicked the chain to see how secure it was. It barely budged. He looked closer—the chain was secured in several places by iron spikes driven into the rag's scales. No wonder the rag didn't react when he climbed on board.

The LC was now up on the rag at the front of the wing five yards away. Carny realized he'd been gawking and quickly squeezed through a pair of the vertical plates lining the rag's back, emerging on the far side. He began moving forward, following an identical chain. When he got to the final saddle attached to the chain, he sat down and immediately began strapping himself in.

It wasn't complicated and Carny quickly had the straps secure. He took a moment to look behind him and was relieved to see the rest of the team was on board and getting ready, even Knockers. LC Listowk began calling out the checklist and Carny spent the next few moments securing his straps, his gear, and his crossbow, and then verifying it all again when Ahmist leaned forward to check it for him.

With the procedures complete and his racing heart slowing back down, Carny took in a breath and sat up straight. That's when he noticed the woman sitting farther ahead directly behind the driver. The plates up here were smaller, maybe a foot tall at the most. Carny looked across the plate at Big Hog.

"See that? A woman. I didn't know they drove rags," Carny said.

Big Hog shrugged. "Women do just about everything a man does on the farm."

"That's helpful," Carny said, not bothering to pursue it. The whole experience was too amazing and after the tunnel he wanted to absorb it. He, Carny, was on the back of a giant rag halfway around the world. In his wildest dreams as a child, he never could have imagined this was where he'd be. He thought of his mother and how proud she would have been.

The other driver, a man, stood up and turned around to face them. He wore a uniform of heavy brown leather, the front of which was stained charcoal black.

"You are now on board the finest rag in the Kingdom. Do anything to hurt Carduus and I will feed you to him."

Hurt him? Is he kidding?

"I'm Falcon, and my AO is called Breeze." The woman shrugged her shoulders and never bothered to turn around.

"As this is your first time on a rag, I'll give you the long briefing," he said. He pointed behind him. "Head." He pointed forward. "Tail." He used both hands to point to the sides. "Wings."

There was no laughter. Someone farther back on the rag stifled a moan.

"Falcon, you're scaring them," the woman said.

"Damn right I am," Falcon replied out of the corner of his mouth. "I don't want these army ants messing up Carduus."

Carny was having a hard time believing the man was worried about the rag. It was huge—the entire shield couldn't so much as dent a scale.

"There are any number of ways to die on or near a rag," Falcon continued. "Carduus has big paws and sharp claws. I know they're sharp because the smithy files them once a week. Do not stand directly in front of them when you get off. The straps on your saddle should be cinched tight for the duration of our flight. Loosen them too soon and you will fall off and die. Accidentally shoot my rag, my RAT, or myself with one of your crossbows and you will absolutely die, because I will personally break your neck and feed you to Carduus. Should you feel the urge to shit your pants or puke up your last meal, you might as well have a piss, too, and wash it off. Thus ends the briefing. Questions?"

Carny would have smiled if he wasn't sitting on the back of a fifty-foot-long beast about to launch itself into the sky. He shook his head, knowing the driver expected no one to take him up on his offer.

"Is this really safe?"

Knockers!

"Safe?" Falcon said. A big grin appeared on his face. "I haven't lost a soldier yet. Of course, I've never had one actually ask me a question before when I give my briefing. But to put your mind at ease, should you at any time feel the flight is unsafe and you wish to get off, the exits are… everywhere."

Carny said a silent prayer that Wraith would throttle Knockers if he tried to ask another question.

"Very well, gentlemen, we are about to leave the earth. Screaming is permitted. Enjoy the flight." Falcon was still grinning as he turned around and sat back down. The woman shook her head.

Bastard, Carny thought. He turned to look over at Big Hog. "Almost as bad as—" was as far as he got. The wings suddenly dropped down as the rag's head came up. The rag lurched forward, rocking Carny backward in his saddle. If not for the straps, he would have been flung off the rag for sure. The rag's wings began to move up and down, creating a windstorm on either side of his head. He dove forward and grabbed on to the chain, burying his head between his arms. The entire rag was bouncing as it started lumbering forward. Scales creaked and clattered and the world around him became a rumbling nightmare.

"High Druid full of grace! Protect this traveler through the dark forest of—fuuuuuuuck!"

A giant invisible hand slammed Carny's body into the back of the rag, squeezing the air out of his lungs. His ears popped. His stomach heaved and he was about to throw up when the pressure pushing him down lessened and the jarring and rattling stopped. The violent storm of takeoff was instantly replaced with smooth, rhythmic motions. Carny lifted his head and was greeted with a warm and sulfurous-smelling wind on his face. He sat up, gripping the chain tighter as he leaned a little to the side. The dosha swamp was already a hundred yards below him. He forced himself to keep looking. With each wing flap the earth widened out below him.

"We're flying!" he shouted, realizing and not caring how obvious that was.

He turned to look at Big Hog. The farmer's face was a mask of absolute panic. His lower lip quivered and his skin had turned ashen gray.

"Hey, it's all right!" Carny shouted. "Can you believe this? We're really flying!"

The rag rolled to the right, tilting its body so that Big Hog loomed over Carny for a moment. Carny pulled himself tight to the heavy chain and leaned with all his might to push the rag back the other way. There were a couple of screams and at least one maniacal laugh before the rag righted itself.

Carny shivered and sat back up, smiling with nervous energy. He looked over at Big Hog to see how he fared. The soldier wasn't there! Carny leaned up against the plates separating them and peered over. Big Hog was bent over his legs with his head against the rag's back.

"Hog? You can get up. Just a little rolling. You've been on ships at sea that did more than this," Carny said.

Big Hog remained facedown on the rag. Carny looked at the soldier behind Big Hog. "Wiz, work your magicks, I think he passed out."

"You'd rather he was flailing and screaming?" Wiz asked.

"At least make sure he's breathing."

"Fine," Wiz said. He reached forward and slapped Big Hog on the back. Big Hog didn't react. Wiz tried again, harder. This time Big Hog groaned but continued to lie flat out.

"He lives," Wiz said, staring hard at Carny as if daring him to ask anything else.

"You'll make a great wizard in civilian life," Carny said.

"If you ever pass out I'll happily kick you back to life," Wiz said.

"Not really a morning person, are you," Carny said, taking one last look at Big Hog before turning away. Clearly, flying wasn't for everyone.

The rag made a gentle turn and this time Carny didn't try to fight it. He even let go of the chain and held out his arms. Feeling silly but not caring, he closed his eyes. The wind whistled in his ears and though it was hot and laced with sulfur, he loved it. The horror of the tunnel and its aftermath were fading.

His grin still in place, Carny opened his eyes and lowered his arms. He glanced forward and what he saw put a lump in his throat. The world stretched out before him like a giant quilt of dull brown squares surrounded by fuzzy green wool. Sunlight flashed off of standing pools of water here and there where the drought hadn't completely dried up the ground. He realized a large group of black dots crowding around the edge of a river was a herd of brorras.

As the rag's wing lowered on a downstroke he caught movement out of the corner of his eye off to his right. One of the other rags had flown close, maybe a hundred yards away and about ten yards higher in the sky.

"Sweet High Druid," Carny said, his mouth agape. It was a wondrous sight. He couldn't help marveling at its beauty. A soldier on the other rag waved. Carny waved back. Other soldiers waved, too. Carny smiled like an idiot and waved harder.

The soldier who'd first waved at Carny cupped his mouth and shouted. Carny tilted his head, trying to make out the words.

"—time to triple S!"

Carny turned away, his joy evaporating. *Fuck.* There was still a damn war to fight.

He spent the rest of the flight in silence.

CHAPTER TWENTY

VORLY TOOK THE FLIGHT up to twenty-seven hundred feet and leveled out. He used to judge the distance by timing, counting Carduus's wing beats as they climbed. Then the Aero service introduced sextants shortly after the first rag touched down in Luitox and flying heights became much more precise, if you bothered to use the device. Vorly rarely had. He was a seat-of-the-pants flyer, *was* being a very sad word. He sighed. There was a time in the not-too-distant past when you just took your rag up until you found your spot. But it wasn't just your spot; it was the rag's, too. Compromise was required. Carduus was young and eager to test his strength. He had a tendency to drift up into the colder air if Vorly didn't give him a rap with his gaff.

"Twenty-eight hundred feet, Sky Horse Leader," Breeze said.

And now it was her spot, as well, and of the three of them, Breeze was the most exacting. She'd tried explaining the importance of knowing their physical height in relation to aligning the aethereal plane, but it went in one ear, drilled through his brain, and flew right out the other.

Vorly grunted. He punched Carduus once. "Ease up. We want to give the poor bastards a smooth ride," he said, having decided he'd scared them enough with his briefing.

He nudged Carduus with his knees into a couple of slow,

wide S-turns so that he could check out the flock. He had done that a lot when the flock first formed but over time had phased it out. His drivers were good, damn good, because he trained them to be that way. Still, with troops on board and a new driver on Centaurea he was erring on the side of caution.

He nodded at what he saw. The flock was keeping good formation, and their passengers appeared to be in check. No screamers and no straps flapping in the wind suggesting they'd lost anyone. A few of the soldiers were either passed out or praying, but that was fine. They were a lot less trouble that way.

"Sky Horse Four to Sky Horse Leader."

Vorly glanced down at the sheet and tapped the screen. He was learning to pick out the different tracings and identify who was who. Breeze's finger made a quick circle around a pulsing blue line that grew brighter. *Got it right.* He now knew that when she did that she was able to focus the plane to increase the power between Sky Horse Four's crystals and theirs. It made it sound as if the other driver was sitting right beside him.

"Go ahead, Hawk."

"Repair is holding, but Cytisus is having trouble keeping pace. Looks like the number four wing bone is cracked. Must have fractured on landing and let go up here. I'm seeing some vibration in the wing on the downstroke."

Vorly turned around to look back at the formation. Cytisus had been holding station but was starting to slip back. He looked to be trailing by six hundred yards and definitely favoring his left wing.

"We're still four miles out from Gyth. Can you make it or do you need to turn back?"

For several moments, only the sound of the wind, the odd rattle of the chains, and Carduus's wings could be heard.

"We'll make it, but we'll probably be an eighth of a candle behind you. I'm going to let him go at his own pace so he doesn't rip the wing any more."

"Aye that, Sky Horse Four. If the wing gets worse let me know."

"Aye, Sky Horse Leader. Sky Horse Four, out."

"I don't suppose you have any other thaumic tricks up your sleeves that could deal with this?" Vorly asked.

"No, sorry," Breeze said. "I wouldn't even try the harmony with eight additional hearts on board."

"Right, hadn't thought of that," Vorly said. He was still amazed she was able to do it with three. "Remind me when we get back to kidnap a dragonsmith," Vorly said, not kidding. "From now on we don't fly anywhere without one on board."

"Aye that, Falcon," Breeze said. She began talking softly, no doubt to one of the other RATs.

The crystal flashed. He looked down and saw a stray white line moving in a constant spiral unattached to a fingertip.

"What's that?" Vorly asked. Anything new with the crystal was cause for concern. "Is everything okay?"

"Sorry, Falcon, I should have warned you," Breeze said. "Yes, it's fine. That's just a reminder about the dragonsmith."

Vorly leaned down to look closer at the screen. He touched the white spiral.

"D-smith... flts." It was faint, like he was hearing the echo of a voice. Still, Breeze's voice was clear enough, as was the meaning.

Vorly sat up straight and pointed at the sheet. "What the hell? How did you do that?" The cold edge of a knife ran down his spine. Now there were voices floating around on their own.

"It's a thaumic process. I could explain it to you, but..."

"I don't want to know," Vorly said, finishing her sentence. *I really don't want to know.* Morsis Rimsma's speech about the possibilities of the crystal sheets came back to him. That boy wasn't nearly as dim as he appeared. Then he remembered how Rimsma and Breeze had looked at each other after the big fight. The crystal sheets weren't going to be the only new thing he had to deal with.

"Joth Ri River dead ahead," Breeze said.

"Got it," Vorly said, bringing his attention back to the here and now. He tapped the sheet. "Obsidian Flock, this is Sky Horse Leader. The Joth Ri River is ten degrees to port off our nose. The village is six hundred yards north of the big U-shaped bend. We'll come in over the river and set down in the dosha swamps between the bend and the village. If the slyts are there they should run like rabbits when they see us, but stay alert. I don't want any flames unless you are in imminent danger. I repeat, keep your rag under control."

"Are you worried about starting a fire in the village?" Breeze asked.

"Shouldn't you be polishing the crystal or something?" Vorly shot back. His focus was on locating the landing area. Putting a rag down in unfamiliar terrain was always dicey.

Breeze didn't back down. "We're a team. If you don't want the dragons spitting flame I should know why."

Vorly sighed. *Damn it, she's right.* "How much do you actually know about rags?"

"Not nearly enough," Breeze said.

Vorly didn't offer a rejoinder. As frustrating as she was, the woman was a straight shooter.

"I've spent every waking flick working on the crystal," Breeze said. "Mucking out the pens was the most time I've spent around them other than when we fly."

Vorly smiled. "Glad I could help with your education. Fine, here's a crash course on rags. Breathing fire takes a lot out of a rag. The bigger they are, the more it tires them out. We get them to fly as far as they do by beating the urge to breathe fire *out* of them. That way, all that heat gets used to power their flying."

"But I've heard of dragons that breathe fire all the time," Breeze said. "The Aero Service has whole flocks that do that."

"Those are a different species of rag. Sparkers. Squirrely little bastards. They're about a third of the size of Carduus here but burn twice as hot. Too small to be much good as transports. About the only thing they do well is spit fire, so we use them up flaming anything that moves. Shortens their life spans by a good twenty years, but at least they're useful."

"How terribly cruel," Breeze said.

"You won't think that when one of them charks a group of slyts firing crossbows at us," Vorly said, snapping Carduus's reins. "Let the ants know we're about a sixteenth of a candle out and we're dropping down now," Vorly said, spurring Carduus into a descent.

"Aye, sir," Breeze said.

Vorly focused on the bend in the river and the dosha swamp beyond. He gauged the closest chunk of jungle to be five hundred yards from where he planned to put down. That would give the troops some room to get organized before they had to take on the slyts.

Carduus turned his head and stared at the tree line to the east as they came in. Vorly tugged on the reins twice before Carduus brought his head back. Vorly looked over at the jungle but couldn't see anything out of the ordinary. Maybe Carduus smelled some brorras.

The wind buffeted Vorly's face. He turned his head slightly from side to side, listening to the wind as he watched Carduus's wings. *Twenty knots, twenty-one tops*. He did a quick calculation and decided to flare Carduus at fifty yards and let the beast float seventy-five before touching down. The poor ants on board deserved a soft landing if nothing else.

LISTOWK SHIFTED HIS crossbow so that it hung from its strap across his chest. He ran his hands over the weapon while keeping his eyes on the view ahead so he knew where they were at all times. It was like caressing a lover in the dark. He didn't need to look to know every curve, every line and joint. Unlike a lover, however, he wasn't seeking pleasure, or to please. He was searching for flaws: a small burr on a metal flange, the beginnings of a crack in the polished wood, or a loose fitting that threatened to throw his aim off.

Finding nothing amiss, he looked down at the weapon, now studying it only with his eyes. It made him nervous to take his eyes off their path. Flying on a rag ate up the miles, but it was easy to become disoriented if you didn't pay attention. Still, checking that his main weapon would function trumped even that concern, and so he took his time to ensure that his fingers hadn't lied.

Finally satisfied that the crossbow was in perfect working order, he let it rest against his chest and resumed watching the Luitoxese countryside race by underneath him. He'd ridden on rags before and while he wasn't thrilled by the experience, especially as the buggers got hotter the longer they were in the air, he could tolerate it. Ships held far more terror for him. Sweat beaded on his forehead and a pain grew in his chest at the thought of drowning.

"Prepare for landing!"

Listowk raised his fist so that the co-driver or whatever she was saw that they'd heard her at the back. The fact that they were starting to fall probably made his gesture moot, but she waved back anyway.

"I didn't know women could be thaums," Knockers said. "Is that allowed?"

"It isn't right," Ahmist said, managing to sound offended and terrified at the same time. The lad was gripping the main chain so tightly his arms were shaking. "Nor is riding these beasts. They are fell creatures, their blood a sulfurous poison. They were created below in lakes of fire."

"Easy, Ahmist, we're all on the same side up here." Listowk wondered if there'd ever come a time when shepherding a shield didn't feel like watching over a brood of toddlers.

"I don't really mind the dragon," Knockers said, reaching down and patting a scale. "But women thaums, that's... unnatural. I heard that doing thaumics was only for men. If women do it they can't have babies. Or if they do, the babies are monsters. A cousin of mine knew a girl who..."

Listowk dove into his own thoughts, ignoring Knockers's prattling. She could very well be a RAT, not that you could tell. Listowk had heard that they were putting thaums on all the rags now, though he couldn't see why. Rags were terrifying weapons in their own right. The army, that's where they needed more thaums. Damn handy to have a thaum chucking lightning and

242

whatnot when you're charging a hill. What were they good for up here? Staying out of harm's way, that's what.

The rag's wings slowed and Listowk's stomach fluttered. They were falling out of the sky toward the ground. He'd been through this before, and it never felt good. It was falling to your death with a last-flicker reprieve. He looked forward and noted with satisfaction the bend in the river. At least they were going to set down in the right place.

Listowk sat up high in his saddle and did a quick head count. *Good, all still there.* On his four previous rag flights he'd always chosen the rear so he could keep an eye on the troops in front of him. He also had a theory that in case the rag crashed, the front half of the animal would absorb the shock and those sitting at the back would survive. He kept the theory to himself, suspecting it wouldn't hold up to scrutiny, but nonetheless still sat at the back. *Hope to the Great Green Forest I never find out.*

The rag tilted to the left, corrected, and leveled back toward the right. Listowk concentrated on his breathing, forcing himself to remain calm. Motion ahead of him drew his attention to Carny. The soldier was leaning over the dorsal plates to steady Big Hog. The farmer looked like he'd been out all night drinking. Listowk didn't think any less of him for not reacting well to flying. All that mattered was that he did his job once his feet were back on solid ground.

The smell of the jungle reached Listowk's nose. It was a hot, wet odor layered with the fetid and the fresh. When he first arrived in the Lux he'd thought of the jungle as a place where things lived. Now he understood the jungle itself was a living thing.

He scanned the area ahead, looking for signs of the FnC forces reported to be here, but unsurprisingly they weren't out sunning themselves. *If they really are here the rags will put the run on them.* He knew it was wishful thinking, but sometimes wishes came true. He'd settle for a glimpse of their erstwhile allies, the Luitoxese Orange Heron Phalanx, tasked with supporting them. If the LooTees were in the area, however, they were equally well hidden.

He bent his head down toward his chest as the rag's wings went into the familiar rapid beating just before landing. Sunlight flashed off the surface of the river as they crossed the bend and then they were over the dosha swamp. When the wing stroke changed again to what looked like a wide embrace he closed his eyes. The rag tipped up into its flare. Listowk held his breath, ready for the dust storm. What he got was a muddy spray. Soldiers coughed and cursed, Listowk along with them. He opened his eyes. Unlike the abandoned fields they'd walked across that morning, these were clearly in use.

The rag shuddered as its tail dropped down with a massive splash and began to furrow the dirt. Listowk quickly flicked off the restraining straps of his saddle. It was against protocol, but too damn bad. He'd heard of a rag catching a wing and flipping over on landing, crushing every poor bastard strapped in. The horror of being trapped like that while pinned underwater was more than he could bear. They could bust him down to assistant fletcher, but he wasn't going to drown.

The rag tipped forward and jolted as its rear legs hit the ground and began running. Filthy water geysered twenty feet into the air. It smelled like shit. Listowk lifted his head and breathed through his teeth. He gripped the chain with one hand and slid a bolt out of his quiver with the other. He'd be ready to fight the moment his feet hit the earth.

"Remember the drill!" he shouted, getting the attention of the men while the rag was still moving. "First two men get off in front of the wing, last two men get off behind the wing! When you hit the ground, run twenty yards and kneel down. Do not stand under the wing!"

The rag shuddered and bumped like a wagon cart going over a rutted road and then slid a few feet before coming to a halt. Its shoulder joints creaked as it flexed its wings to their full span. Listowk found it unsettling, like he was looking at a great ship that had tipped over, its massive sail spread out on the waves. And then the wings folded upward until they stood almost vertical above the rag.

"Unstrap and get off!" Listowk shouted, already out of his saddle and sliding across the rag's back to the rear of the wing joint. He ignored the ladder, said a silent prayer to the High Druid, and pushed himself off. The six-foot fall sank him up to his knees in the swamp. The water smelled even worse this close to it. He struggled to get his boots out of the muck and then took off running for the twenty-yard mark.

Running in muddy, stinking water wasn't the easiest thing in the world, especially when you were keeping one eye on the distant tree line looking for slyt arrows arcing into the sky. It was when he'd run ten yards that he remembered that there were five other rags coming in to land behind this one. He turned his head, half-expecting to see the maw of a rag about to swallow him whole, but luckily, none of the massive creatures were bearing down. He cursed his own stupidity for not checking before he ran. All it took was one damn mistake to get yourself or your men killed.

At twenty yards Listowk kneeled down in the muck and turned to wave in the other three men from his side of the rag. He counted four running toward him. *Shit, what happened?*

Wraith reached him first. "Big Hog was having trouble getting out of his saddle and no one could get by."

Listowk looked past him toward the rag, but with the spray and the rag's huge wings still held high he couldn't make out if anyone was left on the rag or not. He hoped the driver wouldn't leave without kicking everyone off.

"Anyone seen the SL?"

Listowk looked up. "He isn't here?"

Wraith raised his eyebrows in response before smoothly notching an arrow in his bow.

Listowk looked around the dosha swamp. Five rags were down and soldiers were in the act of climbing and jumping off of them. It dawned on him then that a rag was missing. "Anyone see what happened to one of the rags? I only count five." He looked up at the sky, but there was no sign of the missing beast with its load of eight troops.

The rags lifted their heads and roared as one. Listowk ducked. Men screamed. Someone shouted the Faery Crud were going to kill them all. A crossbow fired, the bolt sailing aimlessly into the sky. The roar lasted several moments. When it ended silence fell on the dosha swamp.

"What the fuck was that?" Carny asked.

"I think they're calling to the missing rag," Listowk said.

Without warning, the wings of the rags collapsed downward and then began pumping as the rags lifted themselves out of the muck and began their takeoff run. Unlike earlier, the rags launched themselves skyward in just two bounds. The violence of the takeoff blew a shower of water and mud over the soldiers.

"They're in a hurry."

Listowk wiped the filth from his face. "Everyone stay calm. Clean your string and all working parts." He cursed under his breath. There was nothing more destructive to a crossbow than water and mud.

As the heavy clap of the rags' wings died away, the dosha swamp grew quiet again. Soldiers began to move toward Listowk's group. He saw what was happening and waved them away. They were nervous, and Sinte wasn't there yelling at them and telling them what to do.

Listowk stood up, making himself a target, but he had to get the shield under control. "Shield. Form a skirmish line and stay in your positions," he said. He felt very vulnerable but willed himself to stay upright until he saw all the troops were following his order. When they had he crouched back down.

"We're exposed out here," Wraith said. "No movement in the village so far."

Listowk nodded. Sinte's rag was missing. They couldn't sit in this dosha swamp hoping he'd show up. If slyts were in the village the rags had probably scared the living shit out of them, but that wouldn't last. He had to move the shield now.

"Anyone see the LooTees?" Listowk asked. He had little faith in the Luitoxese soldiers, but all the same, he'd rather they were there than not. The silence and blank stares that greeted his question were exactly the answer he feared and expected. Red Shield was on its own.

"All right," Listowk said, speaking slowly. They'd get through this. "Nothing's changed, my little rabbits. We move forward and secure the village. Keep an eye out for tunnel entrances. We don't want a surprise like last time."

Soldiers nodded, staring at Listowk like frightened children, which truth be told was the case for most of them.

"I don't like the feel of this," someone said, echoing the general mind-set of the shield.

"Don't let the Faery Crud get into your brain," Listowk said, using the shouted phrase of a few flicks ago. He liked it. Made the Fuckin' C's sound less threatening.

A few soldiers grinned at the phrase. *Good.*

Listowk whistled and caught the attention of the soldiers to the far left. "When we get to the berm at the far side of the dosha swamp, set up there and cover us."

Listowk looked up in the sky toward the south, hoping Sinte's rag would appear. The sky remained empty. He allowed his head to turn slightly to scan the jungle off to the west, prepared to eat his words if the Orange Herons marched into the sunlight prepared to do battle. They did not. He turned, pushed the rim of his helm higher on his forehead, and started walking. His boots squelched in the muck with each step. He didn't bother giving the order to move out. He knew the boys would follow.

Sweat trickled down his back, but it wasn't from the heat. Water, even in a dosha swamp, could be lethal. A man could drown in a puddle. *I'm not going to drown, I'm not going to drown.* He took a quick glance to either flank. The tree lines to either side of them were well out of bowshot. As long as the slyts didn't have anything bigger than a longbow in there they'd have time enough to react. No, the real danger, if there was any, lay dead ahead.

Four bamboo-walled huts with palm-frond roofs clustered around a fifth, larger hut that Listowk took for either the village chieftain's or perhaps a communal meeting hall. It was easily big enough to hold fifty slyts in it, although no commander would cram that many troops into one structure.

Listowk scanned the village, noting the position of the corral to the left and the well over on the right. No animals. No smoke curling up from cooking fires. It appeared vacant, but the fields had been recently worked and the village wasn't in disrepair. The villagers had been here until very recently.

He reached the berm that marked the edge of the dosha swamp. The village was now only twenty-five yards away. Well within bowshot.

"Wraith." He kept his voice low. There was no need to shout. Every soldier was straining to hear a bowstring being drawn.

Wraith eased himself over the berm and moved onto the hard-packed dirt of the village area. He no longer carried his longbow and had his short bow in his hands. Wraith moved slowly but deliberately, crouched over to about two-thirds his full height. His footsteps were smooth and soft, his body seemingly floating across the dirt as if it weighed nothing at all.

"I see something," Knockers whispered, although he might as well have shouted he was so loud.

Listowk tensed and pulled the stock of his crossbow hard against his shoulder, ready to fire. He looked over at Knockers and placed a finger to his lips with his other hand. Wraith sank down to one knee.

Knockers pointed to the far edge of the water well. Something moved behind the small wooden box over the well hole. It reappeared a moment later on the other side.

"It's a chicken."

Listowk eased his crossbow down and worked a kink out of his neck.

Wraith got back up into his crouch and moved toward the closest hut. He approached it slowly, his bow held in tight to his chest. He was vulnerable out in the open, but Listowk knew Wraith was a quick draw with keen eyes. Another LC might have sent a fawn like Knockers, figuring that if he caught an arrow it wouldn't be that great of a loss. There was a cold logic to that, but Listowk refused to consider it.

Wraith peered between the bamboo rods and into the hut. He raised an arm and gave a quick thumbs-up. Staying close to the wall, he moved along it until he came to the western edge. He paused, then crouched down until he was squatting and looked around the corner. When he ducked back he turned and faced Listowk and gave the clear signal again.

Listowk vaulted up and over the berm. He was relieved to be out of the damn water. He covered the ground to Wraith in a few bounds, then crouched down beside him at the edge of the hut. He put his back to the bamboo wall and watched the rest of the shield minus the team left at the berm to cover them move across the open space until they reached the hut. Their equipment clattered and a few of them were huffing hard as they scurried across the open ground.

"Villagers were here this morning. Left in a hurry," Wraith said.

Listowk stood up and turned around. He pulled his hewer from its scabbard on his hip and used it to pry apart the bamboo stalks. Peering into the hut, he saw overturned bowls with fruit spilled on the grass-matted floor. Flies buzzed on the food. He stuck his nose into the gap and sniffed. Nothing had spoiled yet. He crouched back down and ran through his options. Their orders were to take the village and link up with the Orange Herons. As the village appeared to be abandoned their first task was essentially accomplished. The only thing left for them to do was sit tight and wait. Someone, friend or foe, would eventually find them.

"Where are the slyts?" Carny asked, peeking around the hut. "The rags scare them off?"

Listowk motioned for him to keep his voice low. "The villagers were gone before we got here. No sign of any FnCs either." He looked over at Wraith, who gave him a small shrug.

"So what do we do?" Big Hog asked. Puke covered the front of his aketon, but he appeared to be steady enough.

"We hold this village until someone comes along and tells us to do different," Listowk said.

"We're down eight men, including the SL," Carny said. "And our LooTee support seems to have vanished like the rest of the slyts around here."

"Doesn't change anything," Listowk said, looking around at the troops clustered by the hut. "For all we know, the LooTees are just a few hundred yards away. Same goes for the SL. I don't want him to find us sitting around with our thumbs up our asses. We're going to clear this village, set up a perimeter, and then sit tight."

Listowk turned and pointed at Wraith. "Take half of the men and work your way around the west side of the village. I'll take the east, and we'll meet on the other side."

Wraith nodded, pointed at his men, and set off, working his way toward the next hut. Listowk pointed at Carny to take spear tip and then let the rest of the soldiers follow behind him. It wasn't cowardice that held Listowk back; it was intelligence. With the SL out of the picture, he was the one in charge.

Listowk kept his eyes moving, checking the tree line, then coming back to study the huts. Everything looked peaceful and normal except for the fact that the village was deserted. Carny darted into a hut through the doorway and emerged a few moments later shaking his head. They approached the large communal hut last, but Wraith stepped out of it giving the all-clear sign.

Listowk clucked his tongue against the roof of his mouth. The village was empty. Something had obviously gotten the villagers out of there in a hurry. Maybe they'd been tipped off they were coming. He cast his eyes on the jungle again.

"LC?" Carny was looking at him under the brim of his helm.

"Carny, get the cover team in here and start setting up a perimeter. I don't want to be too obvious so set two-man teams on the four corners of the village. The rest we'll split up into the five huts. If we're still here after dark we'll reset."

"What about the Orange Herons? They're supposed to be around here somewhere, maybe just the other side of the river,"

Carny said, moving a wad of chew from one side of his mouth to the other as he talked. His eyes were clear so Listowk let it slide.

"You volunteering to go and find them?"

Carny smiled as a little reddish-brown drool dripped onto his chin. Listowk suppressed the urge to reach out and wipe it off. "Hell no, just asking," Carny said.

Listowk sighed. "Just go do what I asked you to do."

"On it, LC," Carny said, wiping the drool from his face.

Listowk felt a presence off to his left. "Carny's right," Listowk said, addressing Wraith. No one else could sneak up on him like that. "The Orange Herons could be just the other side of the river."

"Or the FnC force," Wraith said.

Listowk turned to face him. "Who do you want to take with you?" As before, Wraith was the best choice.

Wraith looked down at the dirt, then out toward the jungle. "Better off by myself." He unslung his haversack and sat it on the ground, removing his helm next and placing it on top.

"Maybe," Listowk said, "but that ain't going to happen. Take two men who know how to keep their mouths shut and their eyes open. Make sure you're back by dusk."

Wraith turned his head and looked Listowk in the eye. It was unnerving how the soldier could stare at you without blinking, without really showing any kind of emotion at all. Wraith's olive-colored eyes looked peaceful, calm, and you had the feeling they would still look that way even as he was gutting you.

"Dusk," Wraith said. He pointed toward two of the longbowmen nearby. "Panke, Mothrin. You're with me. Leave your haversacks and helms."

Listowk agreed with his picks. They were solid men. "No helm?"

Wraith was wrapping a piece of dyed-green linen around his head. "Strains my neck and branches make too much sound when they hit it."

"Don't get shot in the head then," Listowk said, offering Wraith a brief smile.

"I won't," Wraith said, giving no indication he saw the humor.

"If you're late, don't just walk in. Challenge will be 'Chipmunk.' Reply will be 'Fuzzy Nuts.'"

Wraith raised an eyebrow but said nothing. Panke and Mothrin walked toward him, their bows slung over their shoulders. They, too, now carried shorter bows far more suited to the Lux. Wraith led them away, walking nonchalantly toward the river and the bamboo footbridge. There was no way to tell if they were being watched. Listowk knew Wraith would assume they were and act as if he hadn't a care in the world until he reached the tree line. Once in the jungle, however, he'd start hunting.

Listowk kept an eye on the three-man patrol as they crossed the bridge and walked toward the jungle. He tensed. Wraith reached the end of the dosha swamp and walked straight into the jungle, disappearing from view. Panke and Mothrin followed him in. Listowk waited, listening for shouts, screams, but all remained as before.

"All right," Listowk said, turning back to the village. Soldiers were already sitting down in the shade. "No rest yet, my ducks. I want this village fortified." He ignored the groans. "Those not assigned to the corners I want tearing down the corral. Use the wood to create shooting barriers. If there's time, make some stakes, too. Knockers, find every bucket and bowl in this place and fill it with water from the well. Make sure everyone has a full water skin, too. Ahmist, scrounge whatever food is here and put it in the big hut.

"Hop to it, lads, hop to it. Night is coming and we're a long way from home." As the troops grumbled their way toward their tasks, Listowk walked toward the dosha swamp and looked up into the sky.

Sinte, you prick, where the hell are you?

CHAPTER TWENTY-ONE

"ANYTHING, BREEZE?" VORLY ASKED, kicking Carduus harder than he needed to, putting the rag into a sweeping turn to starboard. Carduus let out a deep rumbling sound that vibrated up through Vorly's saddle. He reached down and patted the beast in apology.

"He's either off plane or out of range. I'm running through phase shifts looking for a weak pulse… I'm checking everything," she said, thankfully boiling it down to something Vorly could understand.

"Could this be another case of the crystal—"

"No!" Breeze shouted. "I mean, no, I don't think so," she continued, lowering her voice. "I saw no indication of anything like what happened before. There was no building charge. And he said his driver was sound. Sorry," she added. "Maybe they just turned around and headed back to the roost."

Jate's screams echoed in Vorly's ears, but only for a moment. "It was that damn wing." He gripped Carduus's reins hard between his hands, squeezing until his knuckles turned white. *Should have insisted on a dragonsmith.*

"Sky Horse Leader, this is Sky Horse Two. No sign of Sky Horse Four anywhere, and my RAT isn't picking up a signal."

The other drivers reported in with the same result. Vorly had them scattered over a five-mile area as they flew south, crisscrossing the path they'd followed to the village. *How in the hell did a rag just disappear?*

"Aye that, Sky Horse Two. Obsidian Flight, return to our start point. We still have more troops to ferry. Hopefully when you get back you'll find Sky Horse Four there. I'll stay out here and keep looking."

"What if Sky Horse Four was attacked?" Sky Horse Two asked.

Vorly doubted it. Nothing he'd seen or heard since they landed in Luitox suggested the slyts had anything in the air. Rags didn't live in this part of the world, and he couldn't blame them.

"Just keep your eyes peeled," Vorly said. "Tell Legion Flock Commander Modelar what I'm doing. If he has a problem with it he can come out here and tell me about it in person. And he can bring a damn dragonsmith with him!"

"Aye that, Sky Horse Leader. Good luck."

Vorly turned his head and spit. "Breeze, any luck extending the range on these sheets?"

"I'm trying, Falcon," Breeze said. "It's a mathaumical formula based on the size of the sheet, the energy of the plane, and variables such as weather. I think I can push it out to around six miles if I really concentrate, but I won't be able to hold it for long."

"Push," Vorly said.

Vorly spent the next three-quarters of a candle berating himself as he flew Carduus back and forth over their original flight path. Losing Jate and Bwiter had been bad enough, but to lose a second rag and crew with eight troops on board was more than he was willing to accept. He didn't give a damn about his career—this was about something far more meaningful. Every rag, man, and woman who flew in Obsidian Flight or worked in the stables was his responsibility. Losing any of them meant the flock was weaker, and that wasn't acceptable.

Carduus let out a small growl. Vorly looked to the horizon but already knew the source of the rag's discontent. The sun was setting, which meant feeding time. Vorly gave Carduus a thump with the flat of his fist. "I know, but you're just going to have to wait."

Whether Carduus understood or not, he continued flying smoothly, obeying Vorly's commands without a fuss. Having voiced his concern, the rag now seemed content to fly on. Vorly, however, was growing increasingly agitated. "Breeze! Anything?"

"I'm working on it, sir, but there's still no sign of them."

"That isn't good enough, damn it. They have to be here somewhere. Find them."

"I'm doing the best I can," she said.

Vorly bit off his next retort and nodded a few times. He turned his head to talk to Breeze. "I know, I know. Damn it, I can't lose another crew, Breeze, but we have to turn back. If I don't, it'll be too dark to see."

"Can't we just keep flying? I know rags can fly in the dark."

Vorly shook his head. "I've only flown Carduus a handful of times at night. It takes time for a rag to get comfortable flying then; most of them only travel in daylight. There's maybe three or four breeds that are true night flyers. The rest have to be trained to do it."

Breeze wasn't about to be deterred. "But I've heard of rags finding their way back to their roost in snowstorms, and in the dark."

"I know, but those rags had been at those roosts a long time. It takes rags months to adapt to a new roost. And having relocated them over an entire ocean has only made it that much more difficult. I don't know if they're homesick, confused, or just moody, but they get lost in two shakes of a witch's tit over here. Fuck, sorry," Vorly said. "It's one of the reasons we stick to daylight flights. We need to be able to see where we're going and so do they. We have no choice—we have to turn back."

"No, we can't," Breeze said, her voice surprisingly firm.

Vorly wondered if he was as vexing to Modelar as Breeze was to him. It was a strange feeling to admire a person and want to beat her with an iron gaff at the same time. "Breeze, your determination is... exceptional, but this is out of both of our hands. We're cutting it close as it is."

"But, sir—"

"Damn it, Breeze, we'd have no way of finding our way

back," Vorly said, wondering where in the hell she got the energy. "And even if we could, how in the hell are we going to find them in the dark? And then if we do manage that, how do we land? Carduus would bolt if I tried to make him."

"But if they lit a fire—"

"Breeze, look around. There's cooking fires all over the place already."

Only the sound of Carduus's wings filled the air. Vorly thought he'd finally put an end to it and was starting to relax.

"Sir," Breeze said, "you're not going to like what I'm about to tell you, but please hear me out."

Vorly couldn't muster up the energy to yell. "You've got the time it takes Carduus to make this last sweep. Once we're over the river again I'm turning for home."

"You know we have orders not to let ourselves or the crystals fall into enemy hands," she said.

A sudden chill worked its way up Vorly's back. "Yes."

"And you know that we are instructed to destroy the sheets and cleanse our minds if capture is imminent."

"Yes," he said. "You do some kind of thaumic thing that affects your memory."

"That's correct. But there's more to that order that you were never told," she said.

The chill reached his heart. "What wasn't I told?"

Breeze didn't say anything for several moments. Vorly was about to shout when she started talking. "In the event that a thaum and her driver are downed and facing capture, the thaum is to destroy the crystals and anyone with knowledge of them before cleansing her memories."

Her voice was calm and so matter-of-fact that it took Vorly a moment to realize the import of what she was saying. "Destroy? You mean kill?"

"If Gorlan believes they are in danger, he will kill Rosker."

Vorly twisted around so that he was facing Breeze. "What? Why wouldn't he just do the memory thing on him?"

"It's only something we can do to ourselves. It's called a

cleanse, but in reality we are able to bury our abilities deep in our minds."

"Would you kill me if you thought we were going to be captured?"

Breeze didn't hesitate. "Yes, sir, I would."

"Damn... ," Vorly said, turning to face forward. He stared straight ahead, forgetting to search the ground.

"I'm sorry, sir, but those are our orders. The Royal Academy determined that the thaumic properties within the crystals and our knowledge of them makes it too great a risk for any of us to fall into enemy hands."

"Cold-hearted bastards," Vorly said.

"Yes, sir, but they're still right."

Vorly blinked and looked down at the ground again. "There's eight troopers on Cytisus. Would he kill them too?"

"No, I mean, I don't think so," Breeze said, her statement far from confident. "They have no real knowledge of what the sheets are, but if he is injured, scared, and tries to conduct a thaumic process, his proficiency could be jeopardized."

"Does Modelar know about this? About your kill-and-cleanse order?" Vorly asked.

"I believe he does, yes," Breeze said. "I should have told you before, but I was sworn to secrecy. We're all highly trained thaums. Any one of us can call on more than enough power to kill a group their size... including the rag."

Vorly spun around again. "The poor beast doesn't know a damn thing!"

Breeze held her hands in front of her. "It's not that. Everything within the vicinity of an unstable thaum conducting a process is in danger."

Vorly stared at her. "I can't lose another crew," he said, turning back around.

"I never thought we'd have to deal with this," Breeze said.

Vorly slapped the palm of his right hand against his knee. The fire-wall paste that impregnated his trousers was almost rock hard and his legs were starting to itch. "We won't, not as long as I have breath in me. We know they landed somewhere around here, and this is friendly territory. There's no reason for Gorlan to fear capture."

Breeze didn't answer.

"I said, we're in friendly territory!" Vorly shouted.

"We were sent out to deliver troops to battle an FnC force. We were told before we came here that nowhere in Luitox is truly safe."

Vorly hung his head. "He wouldn't kill him tonight, would he?" Vorly finally asked, the thought of losing another driver knotting his stomach.

"No, not unless the FnC found them."

"Would he know the difference between the LooTees and the FnC slyts?"

Breeze's silence said it all. Vorly found his anger again and cursed until he was short of breath. When he finally regained his composure he looked to the horizon and the setting sun.

"We have to go."

Breeze didn't answer. Vorly took that as her acceptance. He tightened up on the reins. He took one last look down as they flew over the jungle, but it was now dark enough that he could see little more than the tops of the trees. As he looked up his eye caught a strange movement on the crystal sheet. He stared at it but missed what it was. Disgusted at himself for getting his hopes up, he turned away from the crystal. As he did he caught the faintest of traces on the sheet out of the corner of his eye.

"Breeze, do you see that?"

"What?" she asked.

Vorly hesitated, not wanting to sound like a desperate fool. *Aw, hell*, he thought, realizing it was too late for that. "I saw something on the sheet. If I look straight at it I don't see anything, but when I turn my head I see a thin line."

"What quadrant?" Breeze asked.

"Upper left," Vorly said, turning his head and trying to keep the faint line in sight.

"I'm not sure—yes! I see it. It's very weak. It could be what we call a ghost on the plane. Random energy. Or possibly an enemy thaum. I can't tell."

Vorly turned around, ignoring the twinge in his neck. They had to come up with a better system or he'd cripple himself. "But it could be Sky Horse Four. Can you talk to it?"

Breeze kept her head down, staring at her crystal. "It's too weak to sustain a connection."

Vorly's hope crashed. "No way at all?"

"Even if it is them it would be impossible to hold a conversation."

"Then that's it," Vorly said, accepting that they'd run out of options.

"Perhaps not," Breeze said, looking up to acknowledge him before returning her focus to the sheet. Her hands glided across the sheet as she talked. "The crystals were crafted to allow communication. Because the communication has to begin from a point in aether and time that means it's theoretically possible to locate the position of the other talker." She looked up again. "But no one has done it. Not really."

"Good enough," Vorly said. "Do it."

"If I try and fail—"

"You won't chark us. You're too damn smart to make that kind of mistake, you have too much pride to fail, and I'm stable... more or less."

Breeze stared at him for a long time. "There are risks," she finally said.

Vorly shrugged, looking around them. "Risky is where we start every morning. Breeze, you can do this. You can locate that signal."

"All right. Stay calm and just keep flying. Whatever happens, stay calm."

Vorly nodded.

Breeze closed her eyes and began whispering to herself. When she opened her eyes again, Vorly was shuddering.

"I didn't mean to scare you," she said.

"Your eyes are blood-red! All red. What happened?"

"It's normal," Breeze said, blinking. A bloody tear traced a red smear down her cheek.

"What in blazes is not normal? Wait, forget I asked."

"I'm not a monster," Breeze said.

Vorly was learning to recognize quicksand when he stepped in it. "High Druid preserve me! I know you're not a monster. Now, Carduus here, he's a monster. Full-grown men see him and shit their britches. First time I rode a rag, I nearly passed out. No one can say that about you."

"True," Breeze said, "but then none have ridden me."

Vorly's entire body broke out into a sweat. He was certain his cheeks were on fire. "That's not—I mean... what I meant to say—"

Breeze smiled at him. It looked forced, but he was glad of it all the same. If she'd started crying he would have been lost. "Please fly Carduus in as perfect a circle as possible. Keep him level and flying at a constant speed."

"Height?"

"This is fine."

Vorly turned around. "So what happens now?" he asked.

"A few moments of silence I hope," Breeze said, her voice deepening as she spoke.

Vorly glanced down at the sheet. A bright blue line shaped like the toothed edge of a saw blade crawled outward from the center of the sheet in an ever-widening spiral. Vorly looked away and focused on flying. He could tolerate thaumics as part of flying, grudgingly, but looking at Breeze's process prickled his skin.

"Nice and smooth, Carduus, FPS all the way," he whispered to the beast.

They flew on in silence. Vorly thanked the Druid that it was a clear night with a half-moon. Even then he could barely make out the horizon. At this point their only safe option was to stay aloft all night until the dawn returned. Landing in this darkness would be little different than flying straight into a mountain.

A single point of light flickered from the sheet. Vorly ignored it. The light continued pulsing. He turned his head to the left to put the sheet out of eyesight. After a few moments he looked forward again. The flickering light was still there.

Vorly bent over the sheet, peering intently at the light. A drop of blood landed on the sheet with a crack, disintegrating into minute bits that were instantly carried away by the wind. He reached up to his face and put a finger to his eye. When he pulled it away, he saw blood glistening on his glove.

"Breeze?"

"Wait."

Vorly shivered. A bitter cold pumped out from the sheet. His breath misted in front of him despite the day's heat still hanging thick in the air.

"High Druid preserve me," he muttered. Vorly turned to see how Breeze was doing. She was struggling to stay upright.

"Are you all right?"

She lifted her head and smiled at him. He didn't wince when he looked into her bloody eyes, and her smile grew bigger. "I'm good," she said. She made an effort to sit up straight and pushed her shoulders back. "I should tell you… your eyes…"

Vorly pointed to his eyes and shrugged. "It's normal. I'm not a monster, you know."

Breeze held up a hand. "I have something to the north!"

Vorly snapped the reins. Carduus's wing tempo increased as the rushing wind whistled in Vorly's ears. "Find my crew, Breeze!"

"Aye, sir!" Breeze shouted back.

"Sky Horse Four, this is Sky Horse Leader. You there, Hawk?" Vorly stared at the crystal, willing it to come alive. He reached out and tapped it a few times.

"Please don't do that, sir," Breeze said, her fingertips dancing across the sheet.

Vorly grunted and tapped the screen again. The invisible needles continued to drill into his flesh, but his emotions, especially his hope coupled with a pulsing anger, numbed the sensation.

This time something hard hit him square between the shoulder blades. Vorly turned. Breeze held her helmet in her left hand and was readying to hit him again.

"Fine, damn it, I just thought I could help," he said, rolling and stretching his back. "That little light got really bright before it disappeared. That means they're here, right?"

"I think so, but it's difficult to tell," Breeze said. "The thaumic processes for the sheets were designed for communication. They weren't designed to find someone. I'm winging this."

Vorly pulled hard on the left rein, banking Carduus into a steep turn. As the world slid underneath them Vorly stared down at the jungle, trying to see something, anything, that would indicate Sky Horse Four was down there.

The sound of gagging was followed a moment later by Breeze vomiting. Vorly eased Carduus back to level flight. They'd been flying since dawn. His legs ached, his eyes stung, and the kink in his neck was threatening to freeze his head in place. "Sorry. Damn it, I should have warned you. You all right?"

"I'm fine," Breeze said. "The turn caught me off guard."

Remembering he was no longer alone up here wasn't coming easily to Vorly. It wouldn't do him any good to make his RAT so ill she couldn't work her crystal. Whenever he turned around she always had her head down, deep in concentration as she manipulated the lines on the crystal sheet. As a result, every turn caught her by surprise. Vorly started to ask her to make a voice note about seeing if there was a way to address that but decided instead he'd remember that himself.

"I'll try to give you some warning, but it won't always be possible," he said. "I'm just not used—"

"There! It's them!" Breeze said, cutting him off.

A bright flash on the sheet appeared at the same moment. Vorly looked down to the jungle below. All he could see was a thick black mat. "Where?"

"I... we just flew over them. Turn around, now!"

Vorly began easing Carduus into the turn. With just a half-moon he had little reference point on the ground to focus on.

"No, hard, damn it! I need to be on the exact same path," Breeze said. "I can't do this for much longer . . ."

"Hang on!" Vorly shouted, pulling back on the right rein and spurring Carduus into a steeper turn. The rag growled but complied. Vorly leaned against the turn, his back nearly touching Carduus's as the rag wheeled around until he was flying on his side parallel to the ground. It wasn't the smartest maneuver at only three hundred yards above the jungle. Vorly trusted in Carduus's youth and power to bring them around, knowing that every candle flicker they flew on their side they lost precious height.

Vorly grunted as the familiar heaviness blanketed his limbs. It felt like soft iron sheets being wrapped around his body. The edges of his vision blurred. Recognizing the danger signs, he eased Carduus out of the banking turn, trusting that they'd swung around and were now flying back along the same track as before.

"Well?" Vorly asked when he'd cleared his head.

"A moment... ," Breeze said, her voice straining with effort.

He looked down at his sheet. The faint blue line had returned. Breeze appeared to be chasing it, attempting to box it in with the tracings left by her fingertips. Unlike before, her lines were shaky and having a difficult time encircling the light.

Vorly picked up the iron gaff and gave Carduus a double tap. "Call, Carduus, call to Cytisus."

Carduus ignored him. Vorly knew the rag was tired, hungry, annoyed, and maybe even a little scared as they continued flying in the dark, but that was too damn bad. Vorly raised the gaff and tapped Carduus again, harder. "Call your brother, Carduus."

Carduus twisted his head to the right and fixed Vorly with his eye. He arched the side of his muzzle to reveal the interlocking rows of his teeth.

"Don't you give me that look," Vorly said, thumping Carduus once more with the gaff. "Call, damn you, call!" Vorly shouted, slamming the gaff with all his remaining strength against Carduus's scales.

A high-pitched whistling erupted from either side of Carduus's massive chest as his entire body began to vibrate. An eerie red light spread out from either side of him just forward of his wing joints, illuminating the undersides of his wings.

"What's that?" Breeze screamed.

"Thunder and fucking lightning!" Vorly shouted, realizing his mistake and knowing it was too late to do anything about it. Carduus was angry, and Vorly had given him permission to vent. "Dumb bastard opened his air gills! Cover your head and hold your breath!"

"What's happening?" Breeze shouted.

"Get down, girl! He's going to fire!" Vorly dove forward and curled himself up as best he could, remembering at the last moment to pull the collar of his jacket up to cover the back of his neck.

Carduus's wings gained speed with each beat. Every upstroke was followed by an increase in the howling shriek emanating from his open air gills. The thrum of the air racing inside the rag set up a rumbling vibration as the air funneled into his chest and the raging furnace that burned there.

"He's heating up!" Breeze shouted.

"Just hang on!" Vorly shouted back, doing his best to shield his face with his arms from the blistering heat rising up from Carduus.

"The crystal sheets!"

Vorly lifted his head. The ends of the birch stand where they rested on Carduus were smoldering and the copper braid was changing color. A few months ago he would have been ecstatic to see the crystals destroyed. Now he prayed for their survival.

"Forget them! Cover up and stay down!" Vorly shouted over his shoulder before ducking his head again.

He gritted his teeth as the heat from Carduus continued to rise. Like a fool he hadn't bothered with the insulating blankets with their wet clay protection before their flight this morning. They were a massive chore to strap on and then take off again, especially when there was no expectation your rag would fire.

"Damn, damn, damn, damn, da—"

Carduus opened his maw. The added influx of air rushing down the rag's throat shook Vorly's saddle like a leaf in a storm.

The red glow around Carduus brightened, turning cherry and then pink. Vorly counted it as a blessing that Carduus wasn't yet a mature bull capable of generating white heat. Still, heat was heat, and Vorly gave voice to one long obscenity as the plume of fire roared up Carduus's throat and painted the sky fiery orange. Even with his eyes closed and his arms over his head, flashes of light danced in front of Vorly's eyes. The burning wind seared the tops of his ears and his curse turned into a racking cough as an acrid metallic and sulfur fume engulfed him.

Breeze screamed behind him. Tongues of flame whipped past Vorly, blown back by the wind as Carduus continued flying. Vorly sucked in a lungful of hot air and started choking. Each swallow ignited an ember of fiery pain. Tears welled up in his eyes. Even though his voice was now little more than a rasp, he kept trying to shout.

"—fucking stupid idiot! —awn of the Druidless fucking—"

Vorly continued cursing several flicks after Carduus had stopped firing. Vorly gingerly lifted his head and pushed himself into a sitting position. The heat hurt his hands through the palms of his gloves. Flames danced along the birch frame of the crystal sheet. He quickly reached out to pat out the flames. Then stopped. The copper braid had partially melted. Throwing caution to the wind, he swatted at the small fire. The sheet looked intact, but it was dark.

He turned around to see how Breeze had fared.

The frame of her crystal sheet was smoldering and charred, but the copper braid looked in much better shape than his. She was still curled up with her hands covering her ears. Wisps of smoke trailed from her clothing and he saw Jate again. Pushing that horror down, he twisted around in his saddle as far as he could and reached back, putting his hand on her head.

"Breeze," he wheezed, trying to get his voice above a whisper. "It's all right, you can get up now."

She lifted her head, her hands reaching to grab on to his. Tears streamed down her cheeks and she was gasping like a fish out of water. She looked at him, staring with an intensity he found difficult to hold, and it had nothing to do with her bloody eyes.

"My fault," Vorly said, shaking his head. "My own damn fault. I told him to call and should have realized he'd be in a foul mood," he said. "I'm a fool. That took weeks off his life, and we could have been charked."

Breeze continued to hold his hand in hers as she looked at him. "Will he do it again? Breathe fire?"

Vorly shook his head. "Not tonight, and never again without us being ready for it. That I can promise you. I'm… I'm sorry."

She squeezed his hand and let it go. She turned and immediately began to trace patterns on her sheet. After several moments she looked up at him again. "I have the plane, but I am not picking up your crystal. I think it's too badly damaged."

Vorly nodded, turning around to face forward. He fumbled around and pulled on the strap of his water skin until he had it up to his lips. There were many foolish things he was angry at himself for, but at least he hadn't secured the skin to Carduus's scales. You only poured yourself a scalding mouthful of water once before you learned. He pulled out the cork stopper with his teeth and sucked on the spout. The water was hot, but it helped his throat. After a few more gulps, he put the cork stopper back in the spout and let the water skin fall to his side. He gathered up Carduus's reins in his hands. Maybe he was getting too old for this. Maybe it was time—

"Sir, look!"

Vorly looked down at the jungle below. Three flaming arrows climbed into the sky from one location. Vorly traced the arrows back to their source and saw bonfires erupt on the jungle floor, revealing a clearing. Cytisus sat surrounded by broken and felled trees. Men stood on the rag's back, waving and shouting.

Vorly reached down and patted Carduus's scales, ignoring the heat.

"You magnificent fucking bastard," he said, speaking as much to Carduus as himself.

"I have Gorlan on plane," Breeze said. "It's weak. His crystal must be damaged. Gorlan, this is Breeze. How are you?"

"…reat to hear your voice, Br—" Gorlan said. It sounded as if he were speaking from the other side of a waterfall. "…ve two walking wounded …litter case with a broken leg."

"Ask him about Cytisus," Vorly growled.

"Uh, that's great to hear, Gorlan. Sky Horse Leader would like to know how Cytisus is doing."

There was silence for several moments. "Sky Horse ...ader, this is ...orse Four. Hell of a light show ...ere. Great to ...We thought we heard you fly over a ...couldn't see... My RAT's been workin... the crystal working again. Pretty... I can..."

"Cytisus!" Vorly shouted, immediately regretting it as his throat burned with the effort.

"...stopped the bleeding. Damn rough landing, but our big problem now—"

Vorly turned to look at Breeze. "What happened?"

She looked up from the crystal. "I lost them. Their signal was weak and they were barely on plane. I'll try to get them back."

Vorly spun around on his saddle, his neck giving him more trouble than his throat. He put Carduus into a slow circle above the clearing, bringing him down to one hundred yards. The bonfires had grown, allowing him to see the general outline of the clearing.

A long scar of broken and bent branches marked where Cytisus had skimmed across the jungle canopy before dropping into the little clearing, dragging a tangle of trees and foliage in his wake. Vorly started to whistle and then gave it up. If Sky Horse Four had misjudged it by even five yards they would have wrecked.

"Breeze, I think I see the problem," Vorly said. "Get ready to send them this message."

"I'm sorry, sir, but I don't think I'm going to be able to bring Gorlan back on plane."

Vorly started to turn around, the pain in his neck flaring. He saw stars and took a moment to catch his breath. "Old-fashioned way," he said. "Charcoal and paper."

"Right, of course," Breeze said. "Just a moment, sir, I have my writing kit in my bag..."

"Hold on to the paper or it will blow away," he said.

"Yes, sir, thank you. The old ways are new to me," she said.

Vorly smiled. Not that long ago he would have heard that as an insult. Now he took it as more an admission that perhaps she had some things to learn, too.

"Here's the message," he said, speaking deliberately so as not to strain his voice. *"Sit tight. Everything is fine. Help will arrive at dawn."*

"That's it?" Breeze asked.

Vorly thought for a moment. *"P.S. Gorlan, don't kill driver. Or Cytisus. Or anyone else."*

"Do you really want me to include that?" Breeze asked.

"Do you think there's a possibility he might kill them before we get back here?" Vorly asked.

There was a pause before Breeze answered. "I'll include it."

"When you're done, roll it up and secure it in this," he said, taking off his helm and handing it back to her. "When I say *now*, you toss it over the side."

"Yes, sir."

"Banking!" Vorly shouted, rolling Carduus so that he was perpendicular to the ground. Vorly grunted as Carduus wheeled in the sky, the weight of the turn growing with each passing moment.

"Now!" Vorly shouted. He caught a glimpse of his helm flying through the air and quickly righted Carduus and spurred him to pick up speed as he leveled him out and turned him back south.

"What now?" Breeze asked.

"Now I have another message for you to write."

CHAPTER TWENTY-TWO

"THE HIGH DRUID LOVES the natural world and all things in it, even rags," Wiz said, staring up at the night sky. He stood a few feet away from Carny beside one of the huts in the village. Carny didn't mind the Wiz's prattling. Listening to him talk kept Carny's mind from wandering too far down the tunnel in Moskoan.

"He gathered the nuts and seeds from the Eternal Forest and scattered them on the earth. All creatures great and small began in that glorious spring, including they that breathe fire and fly through the air above."

Carny looked at Wiz and then up at the sky again. He'd sat in a Holy Grove listening to much of the same about the High Druid and the creation of all things. It had always seemed too complicated for him, like a puzzle with missing pieces. There was just so much you had to take on faith.

Wiz sighed. "I felt close to the High Druid today. When we were flying. It was as if I could just reach out and touch him." He turned and looked at Carny. "For a moment, I knew that if I just undid my straps and jumped I would soar to the Eternal Forest."

The smile on his face remained, but Carny no longer felt it drawing him in.

"You know that wouldn't happen, right?" Carny said, making a dropping motion with his hand to illustrate his point. "You take off those straps and the only soaring you'd do is straight down into the dirt."

Wiz placed the flat of his palm on Carny's chest. "You know your problem, Carny? You lack faith, in here." He kept his hand there for several moments, staring deeply into Carny's eyes. Then he removed his hand and wandered off, occasionally stopping to look up.

Carny stuffed a huge wad of snow and Wild Flower into his mouth and looked up into the night. He saw nothing.

LISTOWK LOOKED ACROSS the dosha swamp toward the tree line. There were no distinct shapes, only a dark, shadowy wall. He knew it watched him. Every horror he could imagine and more that he couldn't lurked just beyond the blackness. And he desperately wanted to be in there. He was alive in the jungle in ways he never was back in the Vill, and every moment he wasn't in the jungle he became more detached from it. Out here, in *civilization*, he grew weak. But there, in the heart of that darkness, he was born anew. There, where shadow bled into shadow, the darkness inside him found a home. He could let it run free.

A new sound drifted to his ears, but it wasn't from the jungle. He looked up. A rag appeared ten yards above him, its nostrils glowing dull red. Listowk threw himself to the ground as the beast barreled overhead. Grass-thatched roofs blew apart and the walls of one hut collapsed in its wake. Men cursed and shouted. Something fell from the sky and smashed through the roof of the big hut, bounced off of the hard-packed floor, and then tumbled through the open doorway.

Soldiers stumbled out of the huts half-naked, some clutching their crossbows, others simply staring skyward. The smell of burning sulfur filled the air. Listowk jumped to his feet and began running his fingers over his crossbow, searching for any damage.

"What the hell was that?" Carny said, running up to Listowk. He looked stunned. His mouth hung open and his eyes blinked rapidly. He was barefoot and wearing only his trousers. Instead of his crossbow he held a piece of bamboo in his hand.

"I'm not sure," Listowk said, turning to follow the bouncing path of the object that had fallen from the rag. He spotted it as it rolled to a stop by the water well. "Check that everyone is okay and get dressed. Get them all dressed. No one goes back to sleep."

"What do—"

"Just do it!" Listowk said, turning away and walking toward the well. He slowed as he got to the well, then stopped when he saw it was a helm resting on its side with the top facing him. It was one of the special padded ones with the pull-down visor the rag drivers wore. Was there a head inside? He crouched down and gently spun the helm around using one of the bow arms of his crossbow. The helm was empty save for a rolled-up piece of paper tucked into the leather banding inside.

"Where's the candle keeper?" he asked, scooping up the helm as he stood up. He walked back toward the huts.

Longbowman Koel Trunket ran up with the time candle in its sturdy glass and brass cylindrical case. Barely five feet tall, Trunk was the shortest longbowman in the shield and probably the entire Seventh Phalanx. What he lacked in height, however, he made up for in muscles. From his calves to his neck it appeared that every part of his body was swollen. With his dark brown skin and flat, open face he'd been called a mud ape more than once, but never by the same person twice. It was exceedingly difficult to insult someone when your jaw was in pieces.

"It's a quarter before dawn," Trunket said, showing Listowk the candle and the remainder of the time scale inked down its length. The flame at the top of the candle burned an unnatural green color just as the candle itself gave off a fuzzy green glow. Listowk had never liked the candles. They were too damn strange. He'd been told that there was nothing more to the odd green flame and glow than a couple of chemicals added to the wax and wick to ensure all time candles burned at the same rate, but he remained suspicious. Thaums had to be involved, and that meant messing with forces that were better left alone.

"Hold it steady," Listowk said, tucking the helm underneath his arm and unrolling the piece of paper. The writing was a ragged scrawl.

"What's it say?" Big Hog said.

Listowk peered closer, working to decipher the words. He read the paper three times before rolling it back up and looking around at the shield.

"They found Sinte and the rest of the boys. Sounds like they got a little lost and landed some miles to the north of us," Listowk said, pointing in that direction.

Soldiers nodded and a couple patted each other on the back. The fear that eight men in their shield had been killed had been weighing on all of them.

"Does it say when they're coming back?" Knockers asked.

Listowk shook his head. "Their rag is stuck in a jungle clearing and can't take off again until some trees are felled to clear a path. So we're going to catch a ride on the rag that flew over when it comes back this way at dawn."

"What about Wraith and Panke and Mothrin?" Trunk asked. "We can't just leave them out there. That's three-quarters of our longbows."

Listowk gave himself a moment to take a swig from his water skin. It was near empty, but for once they had the luxury of a well nearby. He looked around at the men. They were hot, tired, sweaty, and confused. He would have ordered them back to sleep save for those on watch, but that was no longer an option. "We aren't all going. Eight men will board the rag and fly to the SL's position while the rest will stay here."

The men grew quiet. It was Carny who finally spoke up. "But that'll mean defending the village with less than a full shield."

"I know," Listowk said, "but it can't be helped. There's still a slyt force out there. If they get to Sinte and the boys before we do, they're done. We have to get those trees cut and get out as quickly as possible."

He saw the nervousness and fear. They were so very far from

home and in the dark. *My poor, sweet lads.*

"Wraith's patrol will be back in the morning, and hopefully with the Orange Herons in tow," Listowk said. "And once the sun comes up there will be rags galore flying about. The slyts won't try anything, but if they do, they'll regret it."

"So who's going, and who's staying?" Big Hog asked. "I'm good either way."

Listowk smiled at the soldier. Big Hog *was* good either way. Solid and dependable. Listowk looked at Carny and realized he wasn't sure he could say the same about him. The boy looked like he hadn't eaten in a week. Whenever he was chewing it was more likely to be snow and Wild Flower than food. Still, the boy had brains. Listowk was determined to make the soldier use them.

"I have to stay here at the village with the shield," he said, knowing it was the responsible decision and hating it. "Carny, you up for leading the patrol to Sinte?"

To his credit, Carny nodded and smiled. "Ready now," Carny said.

"Any volunteers to go with him?"

Hands shot up, but not all of them. Listowk wasn't sure who was braver, those willing to go or those prepared to stay behind. Both choices held unknown risks.

"Big Hog, Knockers, Trunk, Wiz, Porchek, Glest, and..."— he saw Ahmist waving his hand but looked past him—"...and Razchuts. Make sure you've got your gear stowed and your weapon secure. Fill up your water skins, too. In fact, fill up extras. Do it now, don't wait until first light. The rest of us will hold down the fort."

The shield dispersed. Listowk saw Ahmist walking toward him and tried to turn away, but the young soldier sped up and got in front of him.

"I want to go, LC. Why didn't you pick me?"

Listowk sighed. "What'd you do, before you were conscripted?"

Ahmist stood up a little straighter. "I worked in my father's apothecary. I made deliveries for the most part, but I was starting

273

to learn how to grind and mix some of the ingredients."

"Sounds like you should have been a wizard," Listowk said. "You probably know more about potions and ointments than our own Wiz does."

Ahmist shook his head. "The army tried to enroll me in the wizard course, but I turned it down. I want to fight, not pick splinters out of fingers and make poultices."

"Let me see your hands," Listowk said, reaching out and grabbing Ahmist by the wrists before he could respond. He turned the boy's hands over so they were palm up. "Smooth, nary a callus or scar. You ever swing an axe in your life?"

Ahmist tugged his hands back. "No, but I'm not afraid to kill."

Listowk remembered the brorra all too clearly. "There's more to being a soldier than that," Listowk said. "The lads that are going in the morning are from farms and little villages. They're used to working in the fields and forests. There's going to be trees that need cutting. That's why Big Hog goes and you stay here. Besides, for all we know, the action is going to be *here*. Our arrival in this village wasn't exactly quiet, and our special delivery from that last rag let anyone in a five-mile radius know that we're *still* here."

Ahmist didn't look convinced, but he nodded. "Yes, LC."

"Good lad," Listowk said. "Now go round up your gear and make sure your water skin is full. This heat bleeds the vitality out of a man. Off you go."

Ahmist turned and walked away, his stride the sulking slouch of a disappointed boy. *Too damn bad, my lad.* Listowk made another slow tour of the village, checking that his instructions were being carried out. The soldiers weren't thrilled, but they weren't yowling to the treetops either. He thought about Vooford and how things would have been if the soldier were here. A shame, really, but Sinte had been right; the man had been dangerous.

Listowk stopped when he found himself once again facing the tree line where Wraith's patrol had entered the jungle. The bustle of the troops behind him faded away.

The darkness called to him. It urged him to enter the blackened jungle, to sink into it until nothing that he was remained. He could be free in there.

Listowk stared at the wall of shadows, no longer aware of time or place. He didn't move until the first hint of dawn began to color the sky.

CHAPTER TWENTY-THREE

"I'VE GOT SILLSEN BACK at the roost on plane," Breeze said. "And, oh…"

"What?" Vorly asked. They were three hundred yards above the ground and Carduus was flying a good twenty beats faster per one-twelfth of a candle than his normal cruising speed. The rag was hot, damn hot, but it couldn't be helped. Vorly had taken off his flight jacket and shirt and placed them underneath his saddle to shield him from some of the heat. The wind on his bare chest felt wonderful even as his ass roasted.

The night around them was a dull red, illuminated by the glow of Carduus's molten blood. Vorly's first time on a rag that went hot scared the hell out of him. He was certain he was going to burn alive right then and there. It wasn't so much the heat as the eerie glowing of the vein network inside the rag, especially in its wings, where the outer sheathing was much thinner.

"There's some interference with the plane, hold on," Breeze said.

Vorly didn't turn around to see. Partly because his neck and back wouldn't let him, and mostly because Breeze had taken off her jacket and shirt as well and sat half-naked just two feet behind him.

They continued to fly on a heading that Vorly hoped was taking them back to the roost at Jomkier. Truth be told, he was relying on Carduus. Navigating at night was a fool's game, especially with cloud cover rolling in from the coast. He checked on the winding progress of the Hols River as an occasional glint off its brown surface flashed from below. If it was indeed the Hols then they were almost home. It was Carduus's desire to get back to his litter that would get them there safely.

Rags born from the same litter had a bond that stayed true even when they were separated at birth and placed with rags from different broods. Trying to create flocks out of different litters proved frustratingly difficult, so in the end it was just easier to keep them together and form the flocks that way.

"Legion Flock Commander Modelar is with Sillsen," Breeze said. "On plane," she added.

Of course he is. Vorly hung his head. He didn't have the energy to spar with the legion flock commander.

"Tell him to light some fires so we can see to land," Vorly said. "We should be close, maybe a sixteenth of a candle out. Then tell him about Cytisus."

Modelar's voice boomed out from Breeze's crystal. *"Vorly, can you hear me?"*

Vorly jerked, inadvertently pulling the reins. Carduus growled and shook his head but continued flying south.

"Legion Flock Commander, this is Aether Operator Breeze on board Carduus. We are inbound in one-sixteenth and request fires for landing. We are coming in true from the northwest following the Hols River."

Vorly smiled. With everything going on Breeze still had the sense to look over the side and pick out the river herself. He might have—no—he would have been pissed when they first started flying together if she had done that, believing she was checking up on him. Now he welcomed the extra set of eyes, no matter how bloody.

"Aye that," Modelar said, his voice still louder than necessary. *"Did you find the missing rag?"*

"Aye that," Breeze responded. "Please have the flock ready to launch. We're going to go get them."

"I've had to threaten to nail their boots to the ground to keep them from launching," Modelar replied, unmistakable pride in his voice. *"We're ready."*

"Sir, there!" Breeze said, pointing forward.

Vorly turned. A dagger of white-blue flame shot skyward two thousand yards away off to starboard. He knew that marked the edge of the quarry plateau. The tricky part now would be convincing Carduus.

"Let's get down in one piece, all right?" Vorly said, thumping Carduus's scales with the heel of his fist. The rag growled. He moved his head from side to side, studying the flame. He'd seen it at dawn and dusk, but this was his first time seeing it in full night. Vorly eased Carduus into a slow turn to port, angling away from the beacon. Carduus immediately began to pull back to starboard.

"Not yet, Carduus," Vorly commanded, pulling harder on the port rein. Carduus continued to resist. He knew the beacon was home and wanted to get there the quickest way possible.

Vorly reached for the iron gaff, a part of him instinctively ready to pound Carduus into submission… but then he changed his mind. He leaned forward, stretching out so that his body lay flat against the rag's neck. Closing his eyes against the heat, he stroked Carduus's neck with the gaff. "Trust me, boy. We're almost home."

Carduus responded with a rumbling purr and allowed his head to be pulled to port. Vorly eased himself back up, opening his eyes and blinking. They were now curving around the beacon to come at it straight on heading north. That would put them safely through the southern gap where the quarry had been hollowed out.

More flames appeared as they rounded the beacon. A strip of ground looking barely an inch wide marked the landing strip inside the quarry.

"Do you need me to do anything?" Breeze asked.

"Get off plane and hold on tight," Vorly said, crouching forward as he aligned his head with Carduus's. Vorly knew the rocky shoulders of the entrance to the quarry offered a good twenty yards off of either wing tip. That, however, was when one could see them. Now, as they flew straight toward the quarry, they were lost in darkness. As long as they flew dead center toward the strip they'd clear both sides.

Carduus's purring ceased, replaced by a growl Vorly rarely heard from the rag. "Easy, boy, you're doing great," Vorly said, hoping his assurances would keep Carduus calm. "Just keep going at those fires and we'll be fine."

Sudden pressure under Vorly's rear told him Carduus was starting to climb. "No... no, damn it. Down, Carduus, down."

The pressure eased, but Carduus's wing beats sped up. He was four tons of claw, fang, and molten fury, but he was also a three-year-old pup in a foreign land flying at night without his flock.

"Breeze, can you do the harmony thing?" Vorly asked. "Carduus is jumpy." Vorly couldn't bring himself to say the poor bugger was scared. For all their size and violent tendencies, rags were surprisingly sensitive.

"I'll try," Breeze said.

"Anything will help," Vorly said, staring hard at the twin row of fires. They were less than a thousand yards away and no more than one hundred fifty yards off the ground. So close.

A subtle buzz rippled through Vorly's body. He recognized it as Breeze's thaumics. *Damn, it's weak.* If Carduus felt it he didn't let on, continuing to fight Vorly's commands to go lower as they closed in on the roost.

He peered forward. The quarry floor was a flickering mess of shadows and light. To Carduus it must have looked like waves on the ocean. No wonder he was nervous. Vorly hoped he'd have the chance to come up with a better system than this.

Carduus picked up his wing beats again. They were four hundred yards away and closing fast. Vorly was kneeing Carduus with all the force he could muster, but if the rag didn't want to land, nothing short of cutting his head off would make him.

"I know it's asking a lot, Breeze, but we need to land now. If we circle until dawn we'll lose a lot of candle."

"I... I think—" was as far as Breeze got when a powerful thrum set Vorly's teeth on edge.

Lights flashed behind his eyes. His heart beat faster, then slowed as it came into harmony with Carduus and Breeze... and another? Vorly gripped the reins and blinked, focusing on the landing. He was beyond tired.

"Keep it up, Breeze, you're doing great!" Vorly shouted.

Carduus slowed his wings, finally letting himself float down toward the quarry floor. The blue-white beacon flashed off of Carduus's port wing. Towering rock faces rushed past on either side and then they were in the heart of the quarry, gliding toward the marker fires burning in stone cairns.

At the last flicker, Vorly pulled back on the reins and put Carduus into a flare. Carduus's head shot skyward and his wings stretched out wide as he turned them full on to the wind. The sudden deceleration drove Vorly down into his saddle. A flicker later Carduus's massive hind legs touched down with a satisfying crunch and shower of sparks.

"Good boy, Carduus, good boy!" Vorly shouted, unable to hide his smile as Carduus lumbered to a halt and dropped down on all fours. Flockmen ran into view from every angle. Buckets of water flew and burst into steam as they hit Carduus's overheated scales. More flockmen arrived pushing wheelbarrows full of metallic clay slurry, which they poured into a growing puddle right in front of Carduus's snout. The rag didn't need to be asked twice; he plunged his muzzle into the slurry and began blowing bubbles through his nose as he drank it up.

Motion below Vorly made him turn. "Hello, Walf," he said, addressing the legion flock commander. "Nice night for a flight."

Modelar shook his head, his smile fading as he looked at Vorly.

"You look like absolute shit. And your eyes..."

"It's normal," Vorly said, unclipping his harness and easing himself out of his saddle. His muscles screamed in protest. Spots danced in front of his eyes. He took a few breaths to steady himself, realizing it was the first time he'd stood in almost a day. "I am off plane and glad to be back."

"Damn glad to have you back," Modelar said, his smile returning as he reached up and shook Vorly's hand. "That was a landing for the scrolls. Touched down smooth as fucking silk."

"You can thank my RAT, Breeze, for that," Vorly said, motioning with his head toward her. He immediately regretted it as pain lit up his neck and shoulders.

"Well done, Breeze," Modelar said, turning from Vorly and holding out his hand. Breeze remained bent over her crystal. "She's half-naked," Walf said.

"We're half-cooked," Vorly said. "Breeze, the legion flock commander is paying you a compliment."

Breeze didn't move. Before Vorly could get to her the RAT Hyaminth climbed up beside her. "She's off plane, and she's out cold."

Vorly recognized suppressed rage when he saw it. The RAT looked ready to hurl a lightning bolt straight through Vorly.

"She pulled a big harmony out of her hat right as we landed," Vorly said. "Calmed Carduus down. Wouldn't have been able to land if she hadn't."

"Lucky you," Hyaminth said, easing Breeze away from the crystal. Modelar gasped as the RAT tipped her back. Blood covered Breeze's face and neck and had flowed down her chest. Vorly knew to expect it, but it still made him shiver.

"Get her to the sick tent at once!" Modelar shouted, motioning for more help. "Him, too," he said, pointing at Vorly.

Vorly shook his head. "No way, sir. We've got to get prepped to fly back out there and get Cytisus."

Modelar waved for him to calm down. "Vorly, I'm not grounding you. I just want you checked out. I'll see to it that Carduus and the rest of the flock are ready to fly. Grab a drink, wash up, and get a little shut-eye. We'll launch in a twelfth at predawn." With that, Modelar jumped down from Carduus and marched away shouting orders and generally adding to the chaos.

Vorly turned away and watched Hyaminth as she gently

passed Breeze down to the waiting arms of flockmen, who quickly carried her off. Numb with exhaustion and relief, Vorly slid down Carduus's right shoulder and landed on the ground. The soles of his feet stung when he hit and he stumbled before righting himself. It took him two tries to get his knees to lock. Modelar was right. He needed a quick nap to get himself ready for the next flight.

"Finest flying I've ever seen, sir," Rimsma said, coming up and grabbing Vorly by the elbow to steady him.

Vorly looked down at the man's hand, then at him. "You planning on proposing?"

Rimsma quickly withdrew his hand. "No, sir, sorry. I... your eyes."

Vorly held the stone face of command for one more flicker before finally granting the young driver a smile. "Just a bit of overexertion," he said, hoping that was the case.

"Breeze looked bad, what happened?" Rimsma asked.

Vorly didn't answer at first, instead walking the length of Carduus's neck until he got to the rag's head. Carduus was purring contentedly, his muzzle deep in his pool of slurry. The dull red glow under his scales was gone and the familiar sound of clicking and pinging filled the quarry. Flockmen surrounded Carduus, tending to him like he was a small child, which, in terms of rag years, he was. Five flockmen carrying lanterns pored over each wing looking for tears and stress marks. Anything found was circled with a red clay-copper stick for the dragonsmith to examine.

"Deep mountain heart! What the thundering fuck have you been up to with my dragon?"

Vorly turned and looked down into the glaring stare of Dragonsmith Pagath Rose. Dressed from head to toe in black leathers, the dwarf looked like a demon straight from the Valley of Fire and Damnation.

"Carduus is fine, Pagath," Vorly said.

"So he didn't fire?"

Vorly sighed. "It was a short burst. It couldn't be helped."

Pagath's stare suggested otherwise. Vorly leaned down and opened his eyes wide. *Go ahead, stare into these eyes, you short bastard.*

"Did you get hit in the head then?" Pagath asked, holding Vorly's stare.

Vorly blinked a couple of times, slowly. "Why do you ask?"

Pagath leaned forward until their noses almost touched. "Because the pudding you call a brain is leaking out through your eyes."

"I'm fine, thanks for asking," Vorly said, groaning as he stood up.

"Of course you are—it's Cytisus I'm worried about," Pagath said, pulling a small flask from underneath his leather apron and handing it to Vorly.

"We're going to get him back, I promise," Vorly said, putting the flask to his lips and taking a draw. The gin burned all the way down. Vorly handed the flask back. "That takes care of dinner."

Pagath grunted. "Go. Get yourself cleaned up. I'll make sure Carduus is ready," he said, turning and climbing up onto Carduus's back. "Poor lamb must have been scared half out of his tiny little mind flying all alone in the dark like that."

Vorly shook his head. He gently rolled his shoulders. The pain from the base of his skull to his ass was still there, but not as fierce as before. The gin was doing its job. Another drink would dull the pain even more, but he knew that to be the trap it was. He'd settle for a wash, a change of clothes, and a nap.

Remembering Modelar's order and wanting to check in on Breeze, Vorly walked across the quarry floor toward the sick tent. He normally avoided the place at all costs. Like the crystal sheets, everything that went on in that tent was unnatural. He liked enemies you could see. All that gibberish about humors and such unsettled him. How was a man supposed to fight that?

Lanterns lit the tent in a blinding glow as Vorly walked through the open flap and stopped. The canvas, whitewashed with lime slake, made the tent unbearably bright. He squinted, waiting for his eyes to adjust. He realized he was holding his breath and let it out. The tent didn't smell like sulfur, which he found slightly distressing. Instead, the tent smelled like mint and camphor and even flowers, but no sulfur. Everything in a roost took on the smell of rags. It was natural. Just like a sty smelled of pigs and a bakery of bread. The sick tent was part of the roost and so it should damn well have smelled like the rest of the roost. That it didn't was one of the reasons he avoided the tent, but it wasn't the main one.

A roost was a man's world—at least, that was what Vorly had always believed. As unsettling as the arrival of women RATs had been, a shock he was still trying to deal with, the sick tent had been a thorn in his worldview much, much longer. Unlike every other facet of a military roost, the sick tent was run by women. Witches, to be precise.

He blinked, finally able to make out the interior of the tent. He was perturbed by its level of cleanliness and order. Leave it to women to clean up this much. A roost was supposed to be covered in layers of grime, crunchy strata of rock dust, sulfur, carbon, and even a little dried blood. The very existence of the sick tent suggested that his view of the roost was under siege.

Instead of plain canvas or palm fronds covering the ground, they had constructed a wooden floor from bamboo, which, in incomprehensible fashion, they had whitewashed as well. Water buckets were placed by every lantern in case of fire. There were even canvas lids placed over the buckets. Eight cots, four along each side wall, were neatly arranged. In the center of the tent a bubbling cauldron released steam that swirled its way skyward through a mesh opening in the top of the tent. A pair of junior-grade wizards in white skullcaps and white full-length aprons over their standard military uniforms bent over the cauldron. One stirred its contents with a large wooden ladle while the other sprinkled in a powder that turned the steam bright green. A witch, similarly garbed and with her brown hair tied up in a bun underneath her skullcap, watched them carefully.

Vorly started to say hello, then realized he couldn't remember any of their names. He looked past them to where another witch stood by a cot at the far end of the tent with two men wearing thin white robes over their uniforms. Master Witch Elmitia Bogston, purveyor of more High Druid–forsaken potions and elixirs than a pushcart peddler, looked up and frowned when she saw him. Vorly ignored her, focusing his attention on the pair of strangers. *Who the fuck are these two?*

"Ah, Flock Commander, I see you're still covered in filth," Bogston said. "There are robes to your right. Please put one on over what's left of your uniform."

Vorly looked down at his bare chest and realized he hadn't put his shirt or jacket back on. He turned, wincing as he did so. A pile of neatly stacked robes sat on top of a small wooden dresser by the tent flap. "You recruiting?" he asked.

"Hardly," Bogston said. She spoke with a clipped precision that dug into Vorly's brain like the point of a needle. "Unlike the squalid conditions you choose to live in, this is a place of healing. As such, it will remain clean. Balancing the humors is hard enough without bringing in extraneous dirt and foul humors."

Vorly grabbed a robe and slipped it on. Bogston, better known as the Bitch Witch around the roost, was more thorn than flower. A spinster in her late thirties, she'd devoted her life to the healing arts with an all-encompassing ferocity that left no room for a husband or family. It was a shame, Vorly thought. For all her prickly ways, she was plump where it counted.

Vorly walked past the cauldron, giving it as wide a berth as possible without seeming to do so. The trio around it never looked up as he passed.

"You smell," Bogston said when Vorly reached her.

"So do you," Vorly responded, biting off a curse. *Damn her!*

"You know, Flock Commander, even dogs lick themselves clean from time to time," Bogston said, her mouth a tight crease on her face.

Vorly moved around to the side of Breeze's cot. She smiled up at him. Her face and hair had been washed and her eyes, though still bloody, looked good to him.

"How are you feeling?" Vorly asked.

"Ready to fly," Breeze said, propping herself up on her elbows. She looked like she had all the strength of thin gruel, but he knew he'd have to beat her off Carduus with his iron gaff before she'd stay behind.

"Glad to hear it. We launch at predawn," he said. "Nap while you can, it's going to be another busy day." Breeze's fierce smile told him he was right.

"Flock Commander, I—" Bogston managed before Vorly cut her off.

"Is she dead?" Vorly asked.

Bogston drew in a breath, which expanded her already expansive bosom. "I don't know what you two were up to on that rag, but—"

Vorly cut her off again. "You're right, you don't. In here, you're queen witch. But outside this little whitewashed dungeon, I rule. When we launch, Breeze will be sitting on Carduus, even if I have to poke his head inside this tent to get her. Is that clear?"

Bogston's blue eyes stared unblinkingly at Vorly as the skin of her neck turned fiery red. "As always, Flock Commander, you make your point with all the tact of one of your infernal beasts."

"Thank you," Vorly said, realizing his cock was getting hard and feeling his own cheeks blush. He coughed and looked up at the ceiling. "LFC wanted me checked out, too. What do you think? Will I make it?"

"It appears we won't be graced with your absence for some time yet," Bogston said, regaining her composure and sighing. "However," she continued, a wry smile forming on her lips, "as the legion flock commander himself has ordered you here I would be derelict in my duty if I didn't conduct a proper... examination."

The emphasis she placed on the last word sent chills up Vorly's back. He could have sworn Breeze chuckled, but when he looked down at her she had her eyes closed and appeared to be sleeping.

"Look, I—"

"You'll take the cot beside Breeze. You'll be given water and food to begin to bring your humors back in balance. You'll bathe, or you will be bathed. I'll conduct your examination to determine your condition, especially your eyes, and then you'll rest until you are called back to duty."

Bathe or be bathed... fucking High Druid, she's got me by the balls. The thought was... stimulating. "Who will conduct my examination?" Vorly asked.

Bogston jutted out her chin. "I am master witch here, Flock Commander," she said. She fussed with the lapel of her white robe, then looked up and past Vorly. The sound of a ladle stirring in the cauldron sped up appreciably. "I am in charge and the most experienced healer in this tent, in this roost, and, I daresay, in this land."

Smile and accept your fate, Vorly heard in his head, imagining Breeze whispering in his ear.

Vorly nodded and offered Bogston the barest hint of a smile.

"Ah, lovely," Bogston said, looking him up and down as if he were a skinned hare hanging in a butcher's shop. "This should prove enlightening."

Vorly watched her turn and walk away. Even under the voluminous robe the sway of her hips was obvious. A small cough turned his head.

The two strangers stood quietly on the other side of the cot. Vorly didn't like them. The tall one stood straight with his chest out and chin up, but it was the short, chubby one who tickled Vorly's warning sense.

"Who are you?" Vorly asked.

The tall one opened his mouth, but the crowny started talking first. "Flock Commander, a pleasure to meet you," he said, holding out his hand across Breeze's cot. Vorly stared at it for a moment before finally reaching out and grabbing it. The man had a strong grip, not at all what Vorly expected. He noticed the young one didn't offer his hand.

"I'm Field Inspector Rande Ketts, Commerce and Taxation, and this strapping example of manhood beside me is Junior Officer Jawn Rathim, Seventh Phalanx Command Group. We're part of a little survey being conducted by the Greater Luitox Agricultural Mission and have been assigned to your flock."

Silence reigned in the tent. Vorly looked from Ketts to Rathim and then down at Breeze who continued to feign sleep.

Vorly couldn't muster the energy to shout, or even growl. "Well, that's so much bullshit," he said, sitting down on his cot and looking up at the two men. "I'm about to pass out, so either tell me the real story or get the fuck out."

Rathim looked to Ketts, who smiled widely. "Your legion flock commander was equally as direct, and astute. The survey *is* real, and I would be most appreciative if you would keep up the fiction while we're here. Our actual mission, however, regards the crystals."

"Killed two men," Vorly said.

"Now, wait one—" was as far as Rathim got before Ketts's elbow to his ribs silenced him.

"A tragedy to be sure. It's why we're here," Ketts said.

Vorly studied the two men. Ketts was obviously in charge, although Rathim outranked him. Vorly noted that Rathim clearly didn't think the crystals were at fault and cleverly sidestepped the issue. Vorly turned to Breeze. "Well?"

Breeze opened her eyes, no longer pretending. "He helped us," she said, pointing at Rathim. "He initiated a process that allowed me to use some of his strength as we came in to land. That's why the harmony had four parts."

"So, another RAT," Vorly said, looking Rathim up and down. *Fucking great.* Vorly leaned forward for a better look at the thaum. "How come *your* eyes aren't bleeding?"

"It's complicated," Rathim said. He stood up straighter. Whatever that meant, it was clearly something he was proud of.

"It always is with you RATs," Vorly said. He turned his attention to Ketts. "Whatever you really are, you're no RAT, at least not like these two."

Ketts nodded his head. "I like you, Flock Commander. No buggering the sheep in the long grass with you."

Vorly snorted. "I'm taking my nap. If you haven't been eaten by a rag by the time I wake up we'll talk more."

Ketts's smile never wavered. "Pleasant dreams then, Flock Commander."

CHAPTER TWENTY-FOUR

I T WAS HARD TO imagine any sane person choosing to be near a flock of rags. It was even harder to comprehend why one would stand among military-grade rags preparing to launch from within the confines of a quarry roost in the dark of night. Jawn Rathim tried, but his imagination was no match for the surreal spectacle before him. The quarry floor was the LOKAM's Valley of Fire and Damnation brought to life.

The noise, the heat, and the sheer overwhelming violence of the launch operation assaulted Jawn in waves. Nothing had prepared him to be this close to such massive and intense force. After witnessing the mass deaths at Gremthyn, he truly thought he had seen it all, but this was something wholly different again.

Jawn pressed his back against a granite boulder, ignoring the pain as the sharp rock dug into his flesh. *This is insane.* Men and women ran about between behemoths, risking decapitation, crushing, burning, and disemboweling, with little apparent care. Jawn ducked as a huge, twelve-foot-long tail ridged with bony plates swung over his head. Claws fully as long as he was tall dug into the stony ground, flinging chunks of rock easily twenty pounds through the air. Wings taller than the largest sails of the Royal Navy's warships pumped and flexed, kicking up blinding whirlwinds of dust and debris. Any one of these things could have ended Jawn in a heartbeat, and the beast that did it wouldn't even feel a thing.

"There you are!" Rickets said, ambling casually through the chaos toward Jawn. "I was getting worried one of the rags gobbled you up. Can't imagine what ingesting one of you lot would do to the poor creature's humors." The crowny's smile suggested he found the madness around them to his liking.

"I have no intention of finding out," Jawn said when Rickets reached him. Every day in the Lux was one more lesson in fear that Jawn had to overcome. He'd survived his flight into the country, an unanticipated victory in and of itself. The horror of Gremthyn was mercifully receding into memories that he could, with extreme effort, push to the side. And less than a twelfth of a candle ago he'd conducted his first thaumic process in the country to aid another thaum in the landing of a rag. It felt amazing to finally use his powers over here. For the first time since he'd arrived, he was in control. The pride that welled up inside him lasted for the time it took to face the next challenge the Lux threw his way—this roost floor before launch.

"Not to worry, my lad, these rags are well fed and well trained. You'd have to crawl into their maw and tickle their throat to get one to eat you," Rickets said, his irritating smile growing bigger.

"You have far more faith in their training than I do," Jawn said, suddenly wondering if his distrust of rags was at all like the distrust some people felt for thaums.

"You're looking at the forest and not seeing the trees," Rickets said, waving a hand to encompass the quarry floor of the roost. "First time in a flock roost is shocking, no doubt about it. The key is focus. It looks like a painting of the Valley of Fire and Damnation, but look closer and there's a poetry of movement. Patterns, if you will."

Patterns. The RAT curriculum was all about patterns. How to find them, how to make them, how to know when to avoid them. But those years of learning had been in a nurturing, safe environment. Even his training in the army, while far more coarse, had exposed him to violence in a controlled fashion.

"I can't see one," Jawn said. The Lux was nothing like he'd

read about and nothing he'd expected it to be. His experience with fear had been fixed on not making mistakes, on using his mind to focus the energies of the thaumic process. Here, in the Lux, he was face-to-face with fears wholly beyond his control.

"Start with colors," Flock Commander Vorly Astol said, striding into view. Like Rickets, he seemed utterly unconcerned with the prospect of death by one of the massive beasts.

"Colors?" Jawn asked.

"He's right," Rickets said. Astol stared at Rickets without blinking.

"Modelar wants to see you," Astol said.

"Ah, then I shan't keep him waiting," Rickets said, bowing slightly to Astol before turning and giving Jawn a wink. "Patterns, my boy, patterns. Listen and learn." With that he was off, swallowed up by the chaos.

"Interesting fellow," Astol said, watching Rickets disappear.

"He excels at being interesting," Jawn said, suddenly wishing Rickets were still there. "Overly so at times."

"I don't like interesting," Astol said, turning to train his bloody eyes on Jawn.

The process the other thaum must have used awed Jawn. You didn't get bloody eyes unless you went deep and hard into the aether. Too deep, too hard, and you didn't come back.

"Ah," Jawn said, not sure what else to say.

"I find interesting people to be more trouble than they're worth," Astol said, taking a step so that he stood just inches from Jawn. "And here you are, part of a so-called survey team with *him*."

Cold shivers crawled up Jawn's back. "Do you know Rickets? I mean Crown Representative Ketts?"

Astol shook his head. "No, but I damn sure know what he isn't. And that makes me wonder just who in High Druid's fire you really are." Astol wobbled, then righted himself. "Come with me," he said, setting off across the quarry floor.

Despite the master witch's orders, Jawn doubted the man had rested at all. He had managed to wash up and change his flying uniform to one relatively free of soot and blood, but his voice was still hoarse and his eyes bloody from the aftereffects of the other thaum's process.

Jawn hurried after him. Flock Commander Astol marched through the assembled rags as if he were strolling among horses in a stable. The remarkable thing was, the rags clearly recognized him as he walked past. Each rag lowered its head and allowed the man to pat it, which really was more like a few solid thumps on the skull between the eyes with a closed fist. The rags seemed to like it.

"That's amazing," Jawn said, doing his best to keep Astol between him and the rag's jaws. "How do you know one won't decide to kill you?"

Astol stopped between a pair of rags and looked at Jawn. "I don't, not really. But then, that's like asking how do you know *I* won't kill you?"

Jawn started to smile but stopped when he saw Astol wasn't. "We're on the same side." He felt the focus of the rag behind him and did his best to ignore it.

"And what side is that?"

"I realize this survey is odd, but we're not looking to cause any trouble, I assure you," Jawn said, realizing that was a promise he had no power to keep. "The crystals are powerful, but they are controllable. We just want to make sure that everything is functioning properly."

"You mean 'everyone,' don't you?" Astol asked.

Hot, sulfurous breath wafted over Jawn. He froze where he was. The muzzle of a rag was directly behind him. The collar of Jawn's tunic fluttered with every breath. *High Druid, did Astol walk me out here to be eaten?*

"The crystals are hunks of glass without a thaum, so yes, they want us to make sure everyone is fine," Jawn said, wondering if he would have time to jump if the rag lunged.

"That seems sensible," Astol said. He flicked his right hand at the rag behind Jawn and the rag withdrew its head. "By the way, I never thanked you for helping us land."

"All I did was amplify a process channeling power to your thaum," Jawn said. "She conducted the harmony."

"So you didn't help that much then after all," Astol said, setting off again across the quarry floor and forcing Jawn to catch up.

"You mentioned something about colors," Jawn said, hoping he might turn the conversation into something slightly more cordial.

"Your Rickets fellow was right. The pattern is in the colors. See these flockmen?" Astol said, pointing to a group of three mules shoveling coal and charred hunks of meat onto a bonfire in front of one of the rags. The rag strained its neck trying to reach the fire, but it was a good yard out of its reach. "The sashes around their waists are red. They're feeders."

"Feeders," Jawn repeated, wanting to understand.

"The blue ones are wing and scale. They repair any surface damage and if they can't, or if it's more serious, they report it to the dragonsmith."

"It's all quite amazing," Jawn said, choosing a word that barely expressed his mix of terror and awe.

The flock commander looked at him, his bloody eyes unwavering in their stare.

"I've known this litter since they were pups," he said. "That's over three years now. They could have killed me or anyone here a hundred times over, but they haven't. Can you say the same about your lot?"

Jawn paused before answering. A glib response would not serve him here. "Truthfully, no. Thaumics is not without risk. That's why I'm here. I believe in it; I believe that the study and practice of thaumics aids far more than it hurts."

FC Astol seemed to think about that. When he spoke again, his tone had lost some of its edge.

"So what do I do with you?"

Jawn hadn't expected that, but he was past the point of being a leaf blown on the wind. Between Rickets, the fiery slaughter of innocents at Gremthyn, and now this cloak-and-shadow mission, he'd let himself be pulled deeper into things he didn't understand.

"You don't do anything," Jawn said, standing up straight and meeting the man's stare. "As my subordinate said, we're here to conduct research on the use and effectiveness of the crystals. Continue as if we weren't here."

Astol stood stock still, holding Jawn's stare. Finally, he grinned and leaned forward, clamping a hand down on Jawn's shoulder and drawing him close until their noses almost touched.

"I don't begrudge a young man his swagger," Astol said, his grip firm and unyielding. "You're a RAT fresh from the Kingdom on his first adventure. I remember that feeling—not all that thaumic shit, mind you, but needing to prove myself. My RAT says you ain't half-bad, and I've come to trust her judgment, so that's in your favor. I'm going to cut you and that viper you're with some slack."

Jawn held his ground, a mix of pride and fear rooting him to the spot.

"Fuck up, just once, however," Astol continued, "and put any of my rags and crews in danger, and the last thing you will ever see will be the bowels of a rag. Are we crystal fucking clear?"

"We are," Jawn said. He recalled his once-heroic if silly dream when he first entered the Royal Academy of becoming a legendary thaum and going out in a blaze of glory. That dream was now irrevocably shattered. He'd never considered that his wish could very well be fulfilled passing through the fiery ass of a dragon.

LEGION FLOCK COMMANDER Walf Modelar walked up the granite steps carved out of the starboard side of the quarry. He took them slowly, one at a time, enjoying the scrape of his boots on the roughhewn stone. The quarry was silent—well, as silent as one could ever be. All eyes were on him, and he wouldn't lie—he loved it.

A rag dragged a claw along the ground, sending a shower

of sparks into the air. He paused in his ascent a good thirty feet above the roost floor. Centaurea was still a bit squirrely after losing his crew. Modelar didn't blame the creature—the whole thing had been a fucking mess.

He continued climbing, feeling the stares of every flockman, driver, thaum, and mule on him. He wished Mirina could see him now. This was when he was in his element, not at one of those insufferable balls she made him attend. Good for his career or not, the things smelled like an abattoir soaked in perfume. He didn't see the point in wasting an evening talking with half-witted officers and smug crownies when he could be here, in a roost where he belonged.

Modelar reached the small balcony the mule stonemasons had set in place fifty feet above the floor. He examined it while he bent over and took a flick to catch his breath. He pretended to admire the railing they'd fashioned from iron bar and chain. Solid, just like the mules who built it.

He straightened up and looked at the quarry wall behind him. Carved in the stone were a set of mule runes. He'd never bothered to learn their language—no good reason to—but he'd memorized these particular runes by heart. They spelled out the name of Modelar's Eyrie. The short buggers knew who put honey in their mead.

Confident his lungs were up to the task, he turned and strode to the edge of the balcony, gripping the chain railing in both hands. He looked down and admired his kingdom. Five three-year-old rags stood ready in their pens, surrounded by their attending flockmen, dragonsmiths, and crew. A twinge of unease crept into his heart as he surveyed the sixth pen. Cytisus was out there, and he wanted that rag back. After almost losing Centaurea he was bloody well not going to lose another.

"Until now," Modelar began, "we have seen little of the enemy in this war. Where is the vaunted Forest Collective we keep hearing about?" He paused, allowing for the echo that was ever present in a quarry roost. It amplified his voice, making him seem larger than he was. He jutted out his chin and continued.

"The only conclusion is that the little fuckers fear us!"

Cheers rose up from the quarry floor.

"Sly little Faery Cruds, aren't they?" Modelar said, invoking the flockmen's unflattering moniker for their enemy.

The cheers grew louder.

"They hide in their jungle and among the peasants, fighting only when they can quickly sneak away, never standing firm and meeting us man-to-man!"

The quarry shook with the flock's roar of approval. A rag added its voice, which only egged the men on more.

Modelar smiled. He knew his men, and he knew the frustration they felt. This damn war—fuck, you could barely call it a war— was in serious danger of becoming one shit-filled midden with nothing to hit except flies. They'd trained to support the army in large battles. Instead, they spent their days flying endless sorties searching for any little sign of the enemy slyts and having fuck-all to show for it except the occasional arrow shot up at them as they flew past.

I could order them into the heart of the Western Wilds and they'd run there, Modelar realized. He stood on the balls of his feet and leaned out over the railing.

"It's time we brought the fight to them! It's time these little *people*," he shouted, putting as much sneer into *people* as he could, "learned their place!" It occurred to him a flick later that the mules present were often called little people, and not fondly. *Well, they know what I mean.*

"We're going to go get our rag and its crew back, and woe be to the slyts who get in our way!"

The noise in the quarry rolled in waves. The stone balcony beneath Modelar shook under his boots. He was glad he was up this high. He'd be embarrassed if his men could see the tears in his eyes.

"So I say to you," he shouted, deliberately slowing his cadence to make them hang on every word. "I say to you, you defenders of civilization, you fighters for freedom, you warriors of the greatest kingdom in the world… light 'em up!"

The High Druid can hear this, Modelar thought, looking up into the sky and smiling.

It was possible men had cheered longer and louder, but Modelar doubted it. The walls of the quarry vibrated as the flock roared with the power of storm-tossed breakers. Dust powdered the air and glowed orange as mule-operated bellows blew air into the chark pits, fanning the charcoal and carcasses into blossoming flame.

Modelar nodded at the flockmen as he made it to the roost floor. For the vast majority of them, this was as close as they would ever get to the fight. Slyts would no more attack an active roost than they would stand and fight in traditional battle. He knew many of the men had volunteered to ride on the rags in any capacity they could. He admired that.

Modelar stopped and took it all in, drawing in a deep breath and gritting his teeth as the familiar sting of sulfur and rock dust bit into his lungs. By the High Druid, he loved this.

Those slyts were going to get a war if Modelar had to burn every fucking acre of jungle to the ground.

"HE'S GOT A future in politics, that one," Rickets said, appearing at Vorly's side.

Vorly snorted, but he agreed with the crowny. Modelar had always had his eyes on the next rung on the ladder. Vorly thought his wife played a part in that, but Modelar couldn't have minded too much.

"The king's still the king as far as I'm concerned," Vorly said, turning and walking the fire line. Feeders were shoveling chark into the open maws of the rags. It was hot, foul, and dangerous work, but the mules were all volunteers. From what little Vorly knew of dwarf life, working the fire line beat working in the mines.

"A traditionalist—I like that," Rickets said. He sounded like he meant it, but that only made Vorly distrust him more.

"What little we hear over here, it sounds like the Kingdom

is in a bigger mess than Luitox," Vorly said. "They should have left well enough alone. The Kingdom was working fine."

"For some, definitely," Rickets said, agreeing pleasantly with him.

Vorly stopped and looked at the man. "You think riots and strikes are better? I heard women were actually in the street burning brooms. Can you believe that? Burning their brooms! What's the world coming to?"

"Believe it or not, Commander, I think we agree far more than we disagree."

Vorly didn't but held his tongue. He had more important things to do.

"Are you coming along?" Vorly asked, picking up his pace.

"Wouldn't miss it," Rickets said, matching him stride for stride.

"Fucking great," Vorly said, forgetting to hold his tongue.

LISTOWK WAS SO intent on the incoming flock of rags that he didn't notice the presence behind him until he felt breath on the back of his neck.

Fucking Wraith!

"The Orange Herons?" Listowk asked, not bothering to turn around.

"They'd set up camp three miles west of here. Left in a hurry," he said.

"Guess they knew the slyts weren't here," Listowk said, knowing damn well the more likely explanation was that the LooTees had fled.

"We going somewhere?" Wraith asked.

The rags skimmed along the treetops, their wing tips thrashing the jungle foliage with each downstroke. Geysers of shredded leaves filled the air behind them, tinting the horizon green. It was unsettling to watch, and made all the worse because the sound of their wings lagged behind their motion, making the rags' impending arrival that much more jarring.

"Another day, another adventure," Listowk said. "They found the missing rag and Sinte."

"I got back just in time," Wraith said, moving away.

If any other soldier had said that, Listowk would have taken it as sarcasm, but he knew Wraith meant it.

Listowk focused again on the rags. Their wings glowed a dull orange, while their sides were brick red. He didn't like the looks of it. He'd seen metal turn that color in a forge.

"Secure your gear!" Listowk shouted. "And find a place to get low. These rag drivers have got the whips out!" The sharp, concussive flaps of their wings began hitting the village. Each stroke hit him in the chest with a heavy thud.

Listowk did a quick mental calculation of the length of the dosha swamp and started backing up. He seriously doubted the rags would be able to slow down and land without plowing right through the village at the speed they were going.

"Move!" Listowk shouted, turning and running back toward the village. He'd gone ten steps when a wall of hot air slammed him in the back, flinging him to the ground.

The wind roared across the dosha swamps and into the village. The bamboo huts rocked and shook. One gave under the strain and flew apart in a spray of bamboo splinters and whirling fronds. Listowk rolled onto his side and squinted into the storm.

Twenty yards away the five rags fell through the air, their wings spread straight out to their sides catching wind so that the skin billowed. Their hind legs were fully stretched as their taloned claws reached for the earth. They plunged their talons into the dirt and grabbed hold. Their forward momentum ceased as if they'd flown into a mountainside. The beasts' huge chests tipped forward and they slammed down on their front claws. The muzzle of the nearest rag bounced off the ground only two yards from Listowk. Sparks flew from the rag's mouth as its teeth grated against each other. The rag opened its jaws wide and for a heart-stopping moment Listowk saw deep into the raging orange fire of the beast. He threw his hands across his face as the heat washed over him.

"Carduus! Shut your damn mouth!"

Listowk recognized the sound of the man's voice. It was the rag driver from yesterday, although his voice was hoarse, a far cry from the booming instrument Listowk remembered.

The heat cooking Listowk vanished with a loud crack. He lowered his hands and sat up. The rag's head was now several feet in the air.

The flock commander stood up from his saddle, wobbling with the effort. He wore no helm and squinted in the morning sun. *Druid preserve me!* His eyes were filled with blood.

"You!" the flock commander shouted, pointing at Listowk. "You in command?"

The rag, Carduus, tilted its head to the side and stared down at Listowk. Of the two, Listowk chose to stare into the bloody eyes of the flock commander.

"Yes, sir," Listowk said, gingerly rising to his feet. "Lead Crossbowman Listowk. We got your message last—"

The flock commander waved away the rest of Listowk's sentence. "Forget that. The Fuckin' C's are moving in on my rag and crew. Your men, too. If we don't get there fast they're all dead."

"But—"

"Get all your men on board now, Lead Crossbowman!"

"Your eyes," Listowk said, unable to accept the sight before him.

"It's normal," the flock commander said, pointing a thumb over his shoulder. Listowk looked and shuddered. His co-driver, a wisp of a woman with a witch's broom of red hair, was looking at him from her station on the rag's back. She had equally bloody eyes.

"That's normal?" Listowk asked.

"So I've been told," the flock commander said. He sounded less than convinced. "Now get your men on board!"

Listowk started shaking his head when a gaping wound in the side of the rag's chest opened up, revealing more of the boiling orange fire burning deep inside the beast. Heat flooded out.

"It's wounded!"

"What! Where?" The flock commander leaned over and looked to where Listowk was pointing, then stood back up. "That's his fucking air gills! That's normal, too!"

"Did you wound my poor Carduus, then?" The head of an angry mule popped up from behind a dorsal plate halfway along Carduus's back. What at first sight looked like two black snakes clamped onto his jaw turned out to be the braided halves of his beard, each a foot long. The mule's face was a dark mahogany and glistened with sweat.

"High fuckin' Druid, Pagath," the flock commander said, turning and addressing the mule. "Carduus is fine!"

"I'll be the judge of that," Pagath said. Spry as a spring rabbit, Pagath hopped over the plates and jogged forward. Clad in black leathers from neck to boots with a soot-stained helm pushed back on his head, the mule huffed as he made it up to Carduus's wing joint.

"Where?" he asked, looking straight at Listowk.

Listowk motioned to the gaping wound in the rag's side with his crossbow.

"That's his fucking air gill," Pagath said, looking to the ground and smashing his clenched fists together in a prayer that no doubt sought to save him from fools like Listowk.

"That's what I just said!" the flock commander shouted.

"I thought it was wounded," Listowk said. He'd spent little time among mules, and never in his life had one looked down on him as this one did now. The shock of it combined with bloody eyes and fiery wounds that weren't left his mind wandering without an anchor.

"Look," the flock commander said, running a hand through his hair. "You can ride on top, or we can pick your shield up in their claws. You've got the time it takes me to sit back down and strap in!"

Listowk tore his eyes away and located the rest of the shield. Soldiers milled around in various states of agitation. Several were pointing their weapons at the rags. "I need to go over the—"

The flock commander shook his head. "We don't have time. I need you on now!"

Listowk took a breath, choking on the fumes and the heat roiling off the rag. His gut told him to run. *Fuck it.*

"Carny, Wraith, get everyone on! No one stays behind."

The shield didn't move.

Listowk dug deep and found the voice of authority. "That wasn't a fucking suggestion! The FnCs are bearing down on Sinte and the boys. If we don't go now they won't stand a chance!"

The shield scrambled toward the rags. Men clambered up wherever they could, ignoring every safety precaution they'd learned the day before. Curses rang out as bare hands touched hot scales, but they continued climbing onto the rags. Listowk double-timed it to the rag in front of him. With the beast's long neck laid flat against the ground Listowk could just reach the flock commander's outstretched hand. He grabbed it and jumped up beside him.

"Don't they teach you army ants anything?" Pagath said, staring up at Listowk. The dwarf's eyes were brown with flecks of gold and not a hint of blood, but looking into them was barely an improvement.

"They train us to fight," Listowk said, finding a rudder now that things were happening. They were going to fight. That he understood. He gripped his crossbow a little tighter and leaned toward the mule. "They trained us well."

"That's comforting," Pagath said.

"Get the ants tied in, Pagath," the flock commander said.

"By your command, FC," Pagath said, turning and stomping off along Carduus's back.

Listowk struggled with the desire to put a bolt in the mule. The little fuck reminded him of Vooford.

"Here, sit your ass between me and Breeze," the flock commander said, pointing at a patch of quilted gray blanket tacked into the scales with iron nails. Listowk looked around and saw more of the quilts tacked in place. Copper braid ran between two charred easels with crystal sheets mounted on

303

them. Listowk steered clear of them.

"There's no saddle," Listowk said. He looked down Carduus's back and realized all the saddles were gone. All that remained of the original furniture were the two central chains running down either side of the dorsal plates. In place of the saddles were pairs of sturdy leather thongs hung from the chains every couple of feet. Each set featured a thong one foot long and another that was three feet long. Both had knotted loops at their ends. More of the gray quilts had been tacked into place, each corresponding with a pair of thongs.

"Had to take the saddles off," the flock commander said, handing a leather thong to Listowk. "They add weight. Rags might look indestructible, but they have their limits. This way we can carry more troops and supplies."

Listowk had never considered that a monster might get tired. Maybe that's what had happened to the rag Sinte had been on. *Lovely.*

"Use the cocking hooks on your belts to lock you in place. Put an arm in the short loop and a foot in the long one," Pagath shouted at the shield, chivvying the soldiers into place. "The blankets will keep you from cooking, so don't rip them!"

"This is madness. We'll fall off!" Knockers shouted.

Pagath placed his hands on his hips and looked down at the shield. "There ain't a spike or a hook as strong as your desire to live. Any one of you does fall off, well, you're probably better off without him."

"How dare a mule speak to us like that!" someone yelled. It sounded like Ahmist.

As quickly as Listowk had wanted to hurt Pagath, now he sprung to his defense. "Do as you're fucking told or I'll personally feed you to the rag!" It wasn't from a sudden desire to befriend the mule, it was simply a matter of keeping order.

Any more expressions of distaste died on the vine. Soldiers went back to wrapping arms and legs in the thongs. A few even wedged themselves between dorsal plates and grabbed on to the man across from them. Pagath didn't seem to mind as he simply walked over them toward the tail. Listowk looked over at the other rags and saw the rest of the shield was following suit. He noticed large bundles wrapped in tarps secured above those rags' hindquarters.

"It's a short flight," the flock commander said, his voice lowering to something almost kind. "I might have been a bit of an ass yesterday, but I promise you this—I'll get you and your lads there in one piece. As for the landing, that'll depend on what we find."

Listowk looked at the woman sitting a foot away from him in front of a wooden easel with a piece of glass on it. She smiled at him, her blood-red eyes twinkling in the morning sun, then bowed her head and focused on her easel.

"One piece sounds good," Listowk said, sitting down on the quilt. It was damp and heavy. He put a hand down to feel it and wet clay mixed with palm fibers oozed out of a small tear. Clever. He adjusted his crossbow so that it was slung across his back before wrapping his arm in the thong.

"Hold on tight," the flock commander said, turning and sitting back down in his saddle. "Breeze, Pagath, we fly in three flicks!"

Listowk cupped his left hand around his mouth and shouted at the shield behind him. "Grab on and don't let go!"

The rag crouched, dropping its chest and stomach to the ground in a cloud of dust.

"Is it—"

The rag pushed up using its legs, its tail, and the length of its neck for force. Listowk's head tried to impale itself on his spine as they hurtled straight up on a hurricane of thunderous wing flaps. No one screamed, or if they did, Listowk couldn't hear them. His ears popped as his ass was driven downward so hard that he was sure he would break through the rag's scales to be consumed by the fire within. A moment later, the oppressive weight crushing him was replaced by the sickening feeling of floating. He gripped the leather thong tight with shaking hands.

Unlike yesterday's flight, the rags didn't continue climbing for height. All their power went into forward speed. With

305

booming wing beats they raced above the treetops. The jungle melted into a blur of green. It reminded Listowk of the one time he'd looked over the side of the ship sailing them to the Lux, only this was much, much faster.

Dosha swamps appeared and disappeared in a flash. A bird with red, blue, and green feathers rose up from the treetops as the rags approached. It flew directly into Carduus's path and vanished in an explosion of feathers and pink mist.

"Damn parrots!" the flock commander said, turning. His face, filthy with soot, now glinted with fine red droplets of blood. "I swear to the High Druid they try to mate with the rags in flight!"

Listowk stared at his grinning face with its blood-red eyes and black-and-red-smeared skin. The man was a demon. A scream clawed deep in Listowk's throat, wanting desperately to be set free, but he gritted his teeth until his temples throbbed and the urge subsided.

"Don't think I didn't see that!" Pagath shouted from somewhere near the back of Carduus. The flock commander rolled his eyes, a bloody tear trickling down his cheek, and turned back to the job of flying.

Give me the jungle at night! Listowk eased himself around, doing his best to shield his face from the buffeting winds. He gripped the leather thong so hard he worried he would tear it from the chain. The shield clung to the side of Carduus for dear life. All were hunched over against the wind. The mule, on the other hand, was walking the left-side saddle chain checking on the leather thongs with apparently no regard for his own safety. The two braids of his beard whipped about his face like dancing snakes.

The rag's wings rose and fell like walls constantly being constructed and torn down in the blink of an eye. The violence of the act left Listowk breathless. *Such incredible force!* How man ever tamed such power was beyond him.

The girl—Breeze, he remembered—looked up from her easel. He couldn't explain it, but her bloody eyes disturbed him far more than the flock commander's.

"We'll be there soon!" she said, offering him a smile that should have reassured him but didn't.

Remember your damn job, Listowk thought, chiding himself, allowing his hands to lessen their grip ever so slightly. Sinte could be dead. If he was, then Listowk really would be in charge. He couldn't be mewling like a kitten whenever they flew. The shield needed a leader they could follow.

"Nice day for a flight," Listowk said out loud. He hoped some of the shield heard it.

"It always is," the flock commander said over his shoulder. "It's the fucking landings that are a bitch."

Hopefully, Listowk thought, increasing his grip again, *they didn't hear that.*

CHAPTER TWENTY-FIVE

CARNY MISSED THE WOOD-AND-LEATHER saddle contraptions that had been on the rag for their previous flight. He had felt secure enough in one to enjoy being in the air. Now, with only one arm through a leather strap and one foot in a stirrup and the other resting on a spike hammered into one of the rag's scales, he prayed for the flight to be over.

Safely.

Carny lifted his head off the quilt padding covering the rag's scales and studied the land. The jungle looked dark and gray, the sun barely a slim crescent on the horizon. He thought of Sinte and the lost members of the shield. They'd had to spend the night completely alone and cut off. Were they even still alive? His thoughts drifted back to the mountain. What if the slyts picking berries had been soldiers instead? Would *he* still be alive?

The need to reach into his haversack for a pinch of Flower gnawed at him, but he wanted his wits about him while they were flying and so he told himself his haversack was empty. The temptation to check to make sure the lie was in fact only that stoked the fire of his need.

A scratching sound from the other side of the dorsal plate diverted his attention. He pushed himself up from his crouched position and peered between the plates. Ahmist had a small dagger in his hand and was carving something into the plate.

"What are you doing?" Carny asked.

"As it seems we are to continue to use these foul beasts," Ahmist said, not bothering to look up from his work, "I will consecrate each one with the Psalm of Necessity in Righteous Battle. Thus the High Druid commands, and the righteous obey."

Carny looked up and down his side of the rag, curious if any other soldiers had decided to do any carving. From the huddled shapes it seemed only Ahmist was so inclined.

"Isn't that psalm like two leaves long?" Carny asked.

Ahmist paused in his carving. "I am carving the psalm using the sacred runes as the High Druid himself did."

Carny still didn't see the point. "So why didn't you consecrate the brorra? You could have carved the runes on his horn."

Ahmist finally looked up. His eyes were clear and bright, as if illuminated by an inner light. Carny eased himself back, putting a little more distance between himself and the dagger Ahmist held in his hand.

"Though it be born of the filth and refuse of the underworld, this beast serves a greater purpose in delivering us to the enemy so that we might smite them down," Ahmist said, his voice carrying surprisingly well in the wind.

Carny was all too familiar with this way of thinking. True believers like Ahmist thought anything deeper in the ground than an oak tree's roots was poison, both physically and spiritually. The LOKAM made it clear that dwarves and rags came from the depths where evil had once been banished from the world. Slyts, on the other hand, weren't from the depths but were also evil. Carny didn't understand, but as the local druid back home told the congregation, you needed only believe.

"I'd keep your voice down," Carny said, motioning with his head toward the back of the rag, where the dwarf dragonsmith was sitting.

Ahmist leaned closer, pressing his face between the two plates. "I do not fear him," he said, though his voice was lower now, causing Carny to lean in to hear him. "His time, so mirrored by his height, is short."

"They're free men now—well, free dwarves," Carny said, wishing he'd left well enough alone.

"They are abominations," Ahmist said. "It is bad enough that we ride on a creature not of His making, but do you think it happenstance that it should be tended to by two more unclean ones?"

"There's only one dwarf, Ahmist."

Ahmist looked forward. Carny followed his gaze.

"The girl?"

Ahmist turned back to Carny. "She is a thaum, an interloper into His most glorious realm. Only the Great High Druid should wield the power of the cosmos. All thaumics mar His perfection, none more so than that wielded by a lowly woman. The female form is meant to carry children and prepare daily meals. They are weak of mind and body and—"

"You shut the fuck up!" Carny said. He released his grip on the leather strap and threw himself against the dorsal plate. He reached across and grabbed Ahmist by the collar of his aketon. "You don't know anything about women!"

Ahmist struggled to break free. "Let go of me!"

Carny pulled hard, slamming Ahmist's head against the dorsal plate. Ahmist's helm rang like a bell as it hit the plate. Carny pulled again, slamming Ahmist's head even harder. The dagger in Ahmist's hand fell and went flying off.

Tears streamed down Carny's face. "You don't know, you fuck! You don't know!" he shouted, pulling Ahmist forward again, bouncing his head for a third time against the plate. Blood poured down Ahmist's face from a long horizontal gash on his forehead.

"Carny, what the hell are you doing?" Knockers shouted, reaching forward and grabbing Carny by the arm. "Let him go."

Carny's entire body shook. He sobbed, his vision blurring as tears flowed uncontrollably. "He doesn't fucking know."

A heavy hit on the top of his helm stunned Carny. He lost his grip on Ahmist, who slipped out of sight on the other side of the dorsal plates. The dragonsmith stood over Carny, a large steel hammer held in his hand. The braids of his beard whipped and curled around his neck in the wind. The dwarf, however, seemed totally unaffected by the wind and the fact that they were on the back of a flying dragon.

"Are you fuckin' mad, the lot of you?! Save your fighting for the slyts, you stupid asses!"

"The LOKAM foretold this evil!" Ahmist shouted, pushing himself into a kneeling position. His eyes were wide in a mix of anger and fear.

No one responded with *Fuck the LOKAM*.

"Pagath, shut him the fuck up!" the driver shouted. "Don't make me come back there!"

"Carny, get him under control!" LC Listowk shouted.

Carny waved at them while he tried to regain his balance. He turned to face Ahmist. The soldier's face was a mask of red from the cut on his forehead. "Ahmist, don't ever speak to me again about your fucking High Druid. Not a word."

Knockers gasped. Carny didn't give a fuck. The High and Mighty Fuckin' Druid could kiss his ass.

"You dare blaspheme—" Ahmist started to say, but Carny cut him off.

"You're fucking right I dare," Carny said, a brittle calm gripping him. His mother's smile flashed in his mind and he felt her hand on his shoulder. "I dare with every bone and muscle in my body. Don't ever tell me again what you believe. And don't tell me about women."

The rushing wind seemed to blow the heat away from the rag. Everything around Carny grew cold. He felt impossibly light, no more substantial than a dandelion in a storm. He was aware of the stares. He saw Listowk out of the corner of his eye. The LC was in a half crouch, as if debating whether to come back and intervene.

"I will not be silenced!" Ahmist said, grabbing ahold of a dorsal plate and reaching over his back for his crossbow. "The LOKAM is the highest order by which we live! Not even the Kingdom or the military may exercise dominion over it. I—"

The dwarf's hammer swung through the air and came down with a clang on the top of Ahmist's helm. Ahmist disappeared for the second time behind the dorsal plates. The dragonsmith looked at Carny. "Never been much of a fan of the High Druid either."

Carny glanced in Listowk's direction. The LC had unslung his crossbow and was cradling it in one arm. *Fuck.* "Thanks."

The dwarf hefted his hammer a couple of times before turning his head and spitting. "Fine, but if he does anything like that again I'll finish him and then come looking for you."

Why the fuck does every dwarf want to kill me? "Understood," Carny said. "Is he still breathing?"

Pagath didn't even look down. "Don't know. Don't care." He turned and walked back along the rag's spine, his hammer held firmly in his left hand.

"Check him!" Listowk shouted.

Carny sighed. "Bard! Is he breathing?"

Directly behind Ahmist, the Bard lifted his head from his crossed arms and looked up in surprise. "Is who breathing?"

"Ahmist! Didn't you see what happened?"

Bard shook his head. "I ain't no hero, Carny. Hey," he said, finally noticing the slumped form of Ahmist, "what happened to Ahmy?"

Carny was beginning to understand the looks of frustration that crossed Listowk's face. "Bard, is he breathing?"

Bard reached forward, grabbed the butt of Ahmist's crossbow, and pulled on it. He managed to twist Ahmist around so that his back was against the dorsal plates and his face pointed skyward. A large, round divot marred Ahmist's helm near the top. "He's breathing, but he's sound asleep or passed out. Nasty cut on his head, too."

Carny looked forward at Listowk and gave him a thumbs-up. The steel plate of their helms was a good eighth of an inch thick and fire hardened. In addition, between the steel and quilted linen skullcap there was usually a wad of horsehair padding for extra cushioning. Hopefully, Ahmist had left his in and the worst he'd have was a splitting headache. Carny certainly had one.

The rag lurched, side-slipping fifteen yards to the left and thirty feet down. Carny's stomach heaved. Men groaned. Several others retched. The rag began beating its wings faster. They were climbing again.

A thin blur passed by the rag to the right, going nearly vertical. Another one followed after it a moment later. A third punched a neat, round hole one inch in diameter in the rag's right wing near the wingtip.

"We're under attack!" the thaum shouted. She reached into a pocket of her leather flying jacket and flung something into the air. A small, dark shape arced above the rag and then burst into a bright red flash.

Arrows whistled into the sky, some trailing smoke and flame.

Everyone ducked. Carny closed his eyes, but the red light easily penetrated his eyelids like the sun through lace curtains.

"Hang on!" the driver shouted. Carny opened his eyes as the red light was left behind, still burning furiously as it floated toward the ground.

The rag roared and made a sharp turn to the left. Carny's body lifted up off the rag and was flung into thin air. He tried and failed to grab the leather thong as he fell backward. A jarring pain in his left ankle halted his flight as the stirrup arrested his descent. His trajectory changed to that of a pendulum and he swung down and slammed back against the side of the rag, hanging upside down. The contents of his rucksack went flying.

"Carny!" Knockers shouted, reaching forward and grabbing Carny's other foot.

The formation of rags broke apart, their lighter-colored bellies flashing as they banked and caught the rays of the sun.

His crossbow dangled below his head, the sling riding up until it was wrapped around his neck. Carny's head grew heavy and he flailed with his arms to grab something to hold on to.

The trailing edge of the rag's massive wing swung past Carny's face and his breath was sucked out of his lungs. He didn't even try to scream. More hands grabbed his legs. His ears filled with a roaring that wasn't the rag's. He felt a tug on his belt and he was suddenly perpendicular to the rag.

"Are you trying to piss me off?" the dwarf asked, leaning out from the side of the rag. One square block of a hand had ahold of Knockers's trouser leg while the other hand gripped Carny's belt. Knockers, for his part, was bent over double with both hands on Carny's right calf. The dwarf gritted his teeth, his cheeks turning bright red, and heaved. Carny flew upright and then slammed down onto the heat blanket.

"Thanks," Carny said, grabbing the leather thong and holding it with as much strength as he could muster.

The dwarf let go of Carny's belt and fixed him with a glare. "I didn't do it for you. You almost hit poor Carduus's wing, you wool-headed ass."

"My mistake," Carny said, but the dwarf had already hopped through a gap between dorsal plates and was gone.

More arrows laced the sky. It looked to Carny like they were flying through a swarm of long, thin insects. The heat coming through the clay blanket increased, as did the glow of the rag's wings.

"Carny, get your ass up here now!" Listowk shouted.

Carny looked past Listowk to the jungle ahead. Thick green vegetation covered most of the surrounding land save for a large, rough pie section carved out of the jungle with the point nearest them. Large stands of bamboo were interspersed between swathes of tall elephant grass. Here and there huts dotted the edges of the clearing. Small shapes ran across the clearing heading for the jungle.

A smaller clearing, if it could be called that, lay a few hundred yards to the east of the larger one. A trail of broken trees pointed to it like an arrow. The missing rag sat in the middle of that clearing looking skyward.

Motion at the left edge of the larger clearing drew Carny's attention. Another blur leaped into the sky heading straight at them.

"They've got ballistas!" Carny shouted, pressing his body against the rag as it tilted to the left and away from the incoming spear. Carny knew the chances of being hit by a ballista, really just huge crossbows mounted on pedestals, were close to none. Carny judged the one that flew past to be around four feet long. He thought—hoped—the rag's scales would defeat the spear, but unlike its body, its wings weren't armored, and those were what was keeping them in the air.

Soldiers started wrestling with their crossbows, trying to unsling them while still keeping themselves secured in the leather strapping.

"Keep your weapons safe! No one fire!" Listowk shouted, standing in a half crouch and facing back to address the soldiers. "You couldn't hit a castle with a cow from this distance. Carny, get up here!"

"How in bloody lightning am I supposed to do that?" Carny asked. He judged the distance between him and Listowk to be no more than fifteen feet, but it was the distance between the rag and the ground that kept Carny rooted to his spot.

"Like nursemaiding a herd of lambs," the dragonsmith said, reappearing on the other side of the dorsal plate nearest Carny. "Carduus just took an arrow through the wing, but do you hear him moaning? I'll walk you up, but don't think it means I'm courting you."

Carny looked up at the dwarf peering over the dorsal plate. *He's serious!*

"I'll die!"

"It happens," the dwarf said.

"Carny! Now!"

"Fuck, fine!" Carny shouted, reaching up with his left hand and grabbing the dwarf's. It felt like gripping roughhewn stone. Carny felt a tug and was lifted onto the back of the rag in one smooth motion.

"Stay low, always keep one hand on a plate, and whatever you do, don't—"

Carny lost the last part as Carduus roared and banked to the right. Carny dropped to his knees and clutched a dorsal plate with both hands.

"What?" Carny shouted.

"Follow me!" the dwarf said, walking up the rag's spine toward its head.

Carny forced himself to stand, his legs shaking. As he stood, he saw Ahmist strapped down to the side of the rag. The sight of the soldier gave Carny a new strength.

Gingerly, fully expecting each step to be his last, Carny made his way forward. The swarm of arrows and spears no longer dotted the sky and Carny risked looking up from his handholds. They'd climbed again and were circling back around toward the clearing.

He made it as far as the thaum's position when his knees gave out and he slid down the side of a plate, hooking his left leg under the big chain.

Listowk leaned toward him. "Look, this could get pretty rough. I need to know you've got your head on straight if something happens."

Carny looked over at the thaum, who was busy tracing patterns on the sheet of crystal in front of her. He had no idea what she was doing or why, but he could have watched it all day. Her hands moved like they were in water, all slow and smooth with sudden quick surges. He turned back to Listowk.

"I haven't taken anything!" Carny shouted, then lowered his voice. "I sure as fuck want to, but I haven't."

Listowk nodded. "Good. Keep it that way. If I go down, you're in charge."

Carny shook his head. "Why me? Wraith is the better soldier."

"He is," Listowk said, agreeing far faster than Carny thought necessary, "but he's not the better leader. Wraith works best on his own. If I catch it, you take over."

"But Sinte's down there," Carny said. It was an odd feeling to be happy about the presence of Sinte.

"Maybe," Listowk said. "And maybe the slyts have already tarped him."

Carny could tell by the look on Listowk's face that there was no arguing with him, but he didn't care. *I'm not ready to lead! I don't want to fuckin' lead!* He had just opened his mouth to say that when the rag nosed over and began picking up speed.

"Prepare for landing!" the driver shouted, half turning in his saddle and waving his arm in the air.

Carny looked over the side and then looked away.

"Landing or falling?" he said to himself, bracing himself as best he could. He tucked his head as far into his shoulders as possible and searched for a memory of his mother that would make him feel better.

"You heard him, hold on tight!" Listowk shouted. "Bard, make sure Ahmist is secure. FnCs are everywhere. The moment we land, unstrap him and drag him off. The rest of you, run from the rag and stay low. The moment he takes off get out of the clearing. Head for the tree line to the east and hold there!"

"Which way is east?" someone shouted. Sounded like Knockers.

"Just follow everyone else!" Listowk shouted back.

Carny looked over at the thaum. Despite the rushing wind and the steep downward angle of the rag, she continued tracing on her sheet of crystal like she was sitting at a table at home.

"Should we load our crossbows?" Knockers shouted.

"No," Listowk shouted back. "Just get off the rag as fast as you can and run. If a slyt pops up in front of you kick it, hit it with your crossbow, slash it with your hewer. Just keep running until you get to the tree line."

"We're coming in hard and fast. Press your tongue against the roof of your mouth and bite down on some leather!" the driver shouted.

Carny didn't bother to ask why. He turned his head, grabbed some of the cloth of his aketon between his teeth, and bit down. As he did, the flashing green of the jungle canopy gave way to open space. The rag's wings flared and the beast tipped up until Carny was certain it was going to flip over backward.

For the briefest of moments, the rag hung in the air. Arrows and ballista bolts fired at its anticipated place in the sky went wide.

And then the rag leaned forward, dropped its tail low, and fell from the sky like a rock.

CHAPTER TWENTY-SIX

CARDUUS HIT THE CLEARING hard, crashing through stands of bamboo and six-foot-tall saw grass. He bounced back up a good twenty feet in the air accompanied by the screams and wails of the soldiers on his back. He landed again fifteen yards farther away. His tail slammed down, its fins stabbing into the ground and digging a deep furrow to break his momentum. Dirt and vegetation flew everywhere, immediately enveloping Carduus in a cloud of debris as his wings drew the fouled air up and forward with each rapid beat. He tensed his rear legs and splayed the talons of his rear paws. They plunged into the dirt and dug in. Carduus pitched forward and his forelegs hit the ground a moment later, his entire body jolting. Neck muscles stronger than the mainmast of a warship were not enough to keep his head from slamming into the ground. He skidded to a stop ten yards later, his snout plowing a furrow through the grass.

Vorly groaned, the straps of his harness biting into his thighs. That wasn't the landing he'd hoped for.

Arrows zipped overhead, crisscrossing their landing zone. The sound of shouting, from both men and slyts, rose around him. Carduus lifted his head and roared, spewing a geyser of dirt and vegetation twenty yards into the air.

Vorly tapped Carduus four times with the gaff, two hard

and two medium hits. Carduus rolled his wing shoulder joints and stretched his wings out parallel to the ground. With all the arrows and ballistas flying it helped present a smaller target.

"Get your troops off my rag!" Vorly shouted, turning around in the saddle and thumping the lead crossbow on the shoulder. "And go under his wings, not over them!"

The soldier glared at him but quickly unbuckled his strap, stood up, and faced his troops. "Go, go, go!" The soldiers scrambled off the sides of Carduus and disappeared in the tall grass.

An arrow flew between Vorly and the soldier. The soldier either didn't see it or didn't care. A huge shadow raced over Vorly and he looked up to see the belly of a rag twenty feet above him as it came in to land.

"I'm picking up cross-currents on plane," Breeze said. "This... this is incredible."

Vorly looked at her. She was as oblivious to the arrows as the soldier. "And that means what?"

"There's a thaum at work," she said.

"Every rag has a thaum, and we've got that special RAT along, too," Vorly said, wondering how he ever got involved in this much thaumics.

Breeze looked up from her crystal. Her all-red eyes were wide and her mouth formed a perfect O. "No. An enemy thaum. I never thought I would encounter one."

"Here?" Vorly asked, looking past her as two of the soldiers pulled another one off of Carduus. Pagath ran up Carduus's spine, checking the chains and heat blankets as he went.

"Close," Breeze said. "Somewhere right around here."

"What's he up to?" Vorly asked, inching away from the crystal sheet beside him.

"It's a she, and I don't know. Whatever it is, it won't be helpful," Breeze said.

Pagath arrived and took a knee beside Vorly.

"Whatever it takes, get Cytisus flying," Vorly said, imagining ballistas being cranked around to aim straight for his neck... guided by an enemy thaum. *Fuck!*

"Keep the slyts at bay and I will," Pagath said.

Vorly leaned forward and punched the dwarf in the chest above his heart. "Don't do anything stupid like getting yourself killed."

Pagath nodded and returned the ancient dwarf salutation. Vorly grunted. *Little bastard always has to hit harder.*

"You too." Pagath grinned, flashing his gold teeth. He turned and slid down Carduus's side and vanished in the tall grass.

Vorly watched the rustling grass for a moment. "Other way, Pagath!"

A steel hammer rose from the grass, waved, and then disappeared.

"I think I can find her," Breeze said.

"What?"

"The enemy thaum. I'm using the same process I used to find Gorlan," Breeze said.

Vorly turned around in his saddle. "Our eyes already look ghoulish and the last time just about wore you down to nothing." *Not to mention me.*

"She's a lot closer than Gorlan was and I have a better understanding of the process this time. If I can pinpoint her location—"

"Got it," Vorly said, turning around to check the clearing. The other four rags of the flock were all safely down and shedding their troops. "Hang on."

Vorly snapped the reins. "Sky, Carduus, sky!"

The rag needed no extra coaxing and immediately pushed himself into the air. Vorly braced as the momentary heavy feeling drove him downward. He was convinced that years of flying had shortened him by a good inch and a half.

Vorly kicked Carduus into a series of quick turns as they climbed. It made for an unpleasant ascent, but it kept any keen-eyed slyt down below from getting a good bead on them.

"Level out at one thousand yards," Breeze said. "Swing Carduus around the compass north to west and make each circuit wider than the last. Start at two hundred yards and widen by another two hundred on subsequent circuits. I'm going to bring Rathim on plane and use his power."

Vorly snorted. Girl was getting a bit big for her britches.

Breeze looked up from her crystal. "Watch out for Caedu," she said, looking past him.

Vorly turned and grabbed the rein back. Caedu was spiraling up in front of Carduus one hundred yards away. "Aw, fuck," Vorly said, kicking Carduus into a hard bank to starboard. Unlike birds, rags didn't fly in flocks naturally. While they did roost together in the wild, they flew as individuals or in largely spaced groups. They liked their room in the air and got increasingly skittish the closer they flew to one another.

Vorly eased back on Carduus's turn and kept his eyes forward, scanning the sky for the rest of the flock. This turning around to talk was getting old fast.

"A thousand yards, if you please, sir," Breeze said.

Vorly sighed, looked down at his crystal, and got a bearing on their position.

"A thousand yards, aye."

"YOU COULD HAVE got off when we landed," Jawn said, not bothering to glance at Rickets. Jawn was too busy working his tracing on the crystal. The thaum on board had bowed to Jawn's seniority and vacated the sheet. He now sat a few feet behind Jawn. The look on his face was neutral enough, but he had to be pissed. Jawn would apologize later, maybe.

"What, and miss you in action? Not a chance," Rickets said.

"Fine, but keep quiet and whatever you do, don't touch me while I'm on plane."

"I'll be as quiet as a squirrel on the Day of Trees," Rickets said.

"Hang on!" their driver, Rimsma, shouted. The rag shot skyward, then rolled to its left in a wide, sweeping move. The power of the beast was startling, but Jawn didn't panic as he had on the decrepit cow they'd flown in on. This dragon was raw, youthful power. It plied the air with impossible grace.

Admittedly, takeoff and landing weren't nearly as smooth, but even then Jawn trusted in this animal. A desire to harness the rag's power welled in his chest, but he ignored it. Tapping into a dragon's deep inner being was an invitation to insanity and death, not that thaums hadn't tried it in the past. Assisting Breeze in the harmony process with Carduus had been heady enough, and that was barely scratching the surface.

The rag leveled out and its wings took on a rhythmic beat.

"I'm going in an opposite turn to Carduus, a hundred yards farther out," the driver said. "I'll maintain this course, speed, and height until you say otherwise."

"Perfect," Jawn said, not bothering to correct the man. Breeze was calling the shots up here. Yes, he had more power, but she was far more experienced with the crystal and doing things with it he'd never seen before. It was intoxicating. The urge to plunge deep into the plane infused his body like wine. Arrows and spears streaked the sky with thin, black blurs and somewhere below an enemy thaum was at work, but for all that he was happier than he had been since arriving in the Lux. Now he had to concentrate on echoing Breeze's movements on the crystal and augmenting her patterns.

"Pick up your pace, Black Star, you're creating a gap," Breeze said, her voice coming over the crystal sheet with a slight background hiss.

"Sorry, Breeze, I'm on it," Jawn said, increasing the speed of his tracing to keep up with hers.

"Black Star?" Rickets asked.

Jawn grinned but kept his attention on the crystal. "Breeze said my help stood out on the crystal like the flame of a black star."

The rag lurched to the left, then quickly corrected.

"Sorry!" Rimsma shouted.

"A little warning next time," Jawn said, unkinking his neck.

"Ballistas don't give you a lot of time."

Jawn didn't bother to respond. Breeze's fingers were now circling an area on the crystal sheet. He felt the intensity of her focus through his fingers and channeled his process through the plane.

"I think we have her," Jawn said.

"Let's hope she doesn't pull something like the one in Gremthyn," Rickets said, his voice noticeably farther away than before.

The stink of charred flesh filled Jawn's nostrils. He shook his head, chasing the nightmare away. If he had anything to say about it, and he did, this thaum would die before she got the chance.

CARNY PLODDED THROUGH the tall grass, dragging a stumbling and only half-alert Ahmist behind him. The blades of saw grass sliced his exposed skin and the bamboo slapped his body and rattled off his helm. He ducked every time, thinking it was an arrow.

He slashed at the grass and bamboo with his hewer with his free hand, but it had little effect. The blade either stuck in the bamboo or slid off the grass.

Fuck the Lux.

"I'm lost!"

Carny paused in midswing. That sounded like Wiz. "Wiz! Move toward the jungle!" Carny shouted.

"I can't see it!" Wiz shouted back.

"Turn the fuck around!" Big Hog shouted. "It's the big green thing."

"It all looks the same."

"Head for the sun!" Carny shouted, noting it was still low on the horizon.

"Got it!"

Carny went back to hacking with one hand while dragging Ahmist along with the other. He was already sweating, tired, and feeling dizzy. He needed some Flower. Or some of that white powder. That shit had lightning in it.

The grass flattened and Carny was blown off his feet a moment later as a rag took off, the rush of air from the downward force of its wings like invisible hands pressing him to the ground.

He curled into a ball as bamboo swayed back and forth with vicious force.

"Keep moving! Head for the jungle edge!" Listowk shouted from somewhere among the grass and bamboo.

Carny climbed back to his feet and then hauled Ahmist up by the collar of his aketon.

"I'm fine," Ahmist said, shrugging away Carny's grasp. His lower lip stuck out as if he were going to cry. At some point he'd tried to wipe the blood off his face, which now made it look as if huge claws had gouged him.

"Great, you lead," Carny said, pointing the way forward.

Ahmist pushed past him and stomped his way through the vegetation. Carny followed close behind. The swish of the grass and the crunch of bamboo as the shield moved might as well have been the sound of a herd of brorra, not that the slyts didn't know they were there. Still, Carny felt increasingly exposed despite his inability to see more than a few feet in any direction. It was a relief when he parted the last of the grass and made it to the jungle's edge. He looked down at his bare arms and winced. He was bleeding from a dozen cuts and bruised all over.

"What took you?" Big Hog asked. He was crouched down a few feet away to Carny's left. He'd already cocked his crossbow and was chewing on a piece of saw grass as if it were soft bread. How he didn't cut his mouth to pieces, Carny had no clue.

More soldiers crashed through the bamboo and arrived near Carny. He spotted Bard, Trunk, Knockers, and the Weasel. He looked again. *Fuck, that's Razchuts. Weasel's dead.* He reached back to tug his rucksack around and grab some Flower, then remembered everything had spilled out on the rag.

"Fuck." He looked for Listowk to start getting them in order.

"I see movement in the trees!"

Carny squinted, trying to make out shapes. A crossbow fired. Several more followed, the metallic twang of their bow arms loud in the morning air.

There was no return fire.

Carny pressed himself closer to the ground. "LC?"

No answer.

"I heard him a flicker a go," Big Hog said, pointing over his shoulder toward the clearing.

"LC? Where are you?" Carny shouted again, spinning around to try to catch a glimpse of Listowk.

"Easy, Carny, I'm here," Listowk said, stepping out of the clearing with the Wiz in tow. Listowk had already festooned his uniform with leaves and saw grass.

Carny smiled in relief. "Thank the Druid."

Listowk waved away the thought. "Don't thank Him yet," Listowk said, looking around. "Red Shield on me!" he shouted, raising his crossbow in the air and waving it.

"Carny, cock your crossbow," Big Hog said, motioning at Carny's weapon.

"Fuck," Carny said, sheathing his hewer and unslinging his crossbow. "I completely forgot."

"All that damn weed you chew," Big Hog said, chomping happily on his stalk of saw grass. "Rots your brain."

Carny ignored him and cocked his weapon while keeping an eye on the jungle.

Knockers came up and crouched down beside him. "Carny, where'd the slyts go? Did we scare them off?"

"How the fuck should I know?" Carny said, looking up into the treetops.

"It's just that I—"

"Get down!"

Something large crashed through the canopy of trees twenty yards in front of Carny and blew apart with an ear-piercing crack. There was no smoke or fire, but a moment later a rain of shredded leaves and branches tumbled to the ground.

"What was that? Was that a rag?" the Bard shouted.

"Stay down!" Listowk shouted back. "It wasn't no rag. I think—"

Two more objects plowed into the jungle canopy and disintegrated with the same loud crack. A third one flew over the canopy and struck thirty yards behind the shield in the clearing.

Wooden splinters flew into the air, scything down swathes of grass and bamboo.

"High fucking Druid, it's thaumics," Big Hog said.

"It ain't thaumics!" Listowk said, crawling forward and picking up one of the splinters. Carny did the same. The splinter was warm and smeared with something like pitch, but it hadn't been on fire. It was a good three inches long and sharp at both ends as well as along its length. He grabbed a few more. They were all about the same size.

"Some kind of catapult shot maybe, or a ballista bolt that flies apart when it hits something," Carny said.

Wraith appeared at his side and leaned in to peer at the splinters in Carny's hand. "I wonder if they're poisoned."

Carny flung the splinters away and wiped his hand on his thigh.

"Let's go," Listowk said, standing up and pointing at the jungle. "Wraith, take spear tip. Bard, you back him up. Carny, take Knockers and Ahmist and cover our rear. We'll push through to the rag and set up a perimeter. If we run across any slyts, fire, reload, and keep moving."

Wraith set off into the jungle, easing through the vegetation like water. Carny kept an eye on the shield as they transitioned from the clearing to the jungle, every few flicks scanning the clearing. He cradled his crossbow in the crook of his right arm, his finger resting just to the side of the firing lever. A shadow flitted overhead and he ducked, tensing for the loud crack, but none came. He looked up. The rags were circling the area, their wings flapping slowly and easily. From this distance they looked peaceful, gentle even.

"Just us left," Knockers said, patting Carny on the arm.

Carny turned and motioned with his left hand toward the jungle. "Knockers, then Ahmist. I'll take the rear."

Knockers nodded, following in the trail of the shield. Ahmist stood still, his crossbow clutched tightly in his hands.

"Ahmist, move," Carny said, easing himself a couple of feet to the right of the soldier so he could see his face. Ahmist's eyes were closed and his lips were moving. The fucker was praying.

Carny stepped forward and kicked Ahmist in the thigh, propelling him forward. Ahmist turned, his eyes flashing open. Carny glared back.

"Keep it to yourself. Now move, or I swear I will kick your ass all the way."

Ahmist held Carny's glare a few more flicks, then said something under his breath and turned and headed after Knockers.

Carny let him get five steps before following after him. The moment he stepped through the trees and into the jungle it got darker and hotter. It was as if he'd put a wet, hot blanket over his head. He patted his uniform with his left hand while holding his crossbow in his right, hoping to find a small wad of Flower tucked away.

A loud snap up ahead froze him in place. Ahmist dropped to one knee. Carny followed suit, straining to see through the thick foliage. He could barely make out Knockers in front of Ahmist, and he was only ten yards ahead. A rag roared somewhere above them, followed by cursing.

After what felt like a lifetime, Knockers vanished into the bush. Ahmist rose to his feet and began walking after him. Carny stood up, slowly swinging his crossbow in an arc. Slyts could be anywhere. He reached up and eased his helm backward on his head, then thought better of it and pushed it back down. He'd suddenly pictured a slyt archer aiming straight at the point between his eyebrows.

A whirring noise grew on the air. It was somewhere above the trees and falling toward the ground.

Carny pictured a rag cartwheeling through the sky, its wing shattered, its furnace of a body glowing bright red as it plunged toward the earth.

The noise got louder, grinding into his ears until it reached his brain. Ahmist ran, crashing through the trees like a frightened deer. Carny wanted to run, but his legs wouldn't let him.

The rag—Carny was sure that was what it was—hit the top of the trees sixty feet above. Wood splintered and shrieked as bone and scale ripped through the foliage. Carny tried to move his legs, but all he succeeded in doing was stumbling to the ground. Chunks of wood fell around him. He curled up in a ball and closed his eyes tight, hoping he'd be crushed before he was burned.

Trees shattered and debris rained down as the entire world shook. Carny opened his mouth to scream, but the noise of the falling rag made it impossible for him to tell if his voice made any sound at all.

Carny pissed himself as the very heavens collapsed on top of him. He drew in one last breath, only now thinking to call for his mother, when the destruction above him ground to a chattering halt.

Bits of jungle continued to fall on Carny, burying him in a thick mat of humid vegetation. He spit a leaf out of his mouth and pried open his eyes. At first, all he saw was black. Trembling, he forced his hands to push away the debris until sunlight broke through. He squinted. How could it be so bright?

"Carny?"

That was Big Hog.

Carny pushed himself up, shedding the pile of leaves and chunks of wood on top of him. Big Hog stood at the edge of a clearing eight feet away. It took Carny's mind several flicks before he understood what he was seeing. A rough circle twelve feet across had been carved into the jungle. Every tree and bush had been sheared to no more than a couple feet off the ground. All except one spindly trunk dead center of the clearing.

"Thought you were dead!" Big Hog said, a huge grin stretched across his face.

"Where's the rag?" Carny asked, reaching for a leaf and cleaning himself as best he could before standing up. The air was filled with shredded bits of jungle. It looked like green snow.

"Wasn't no rag," Big Hog said, stepping over mounds of splintered logs. "It was *that*."

Carny looked at where he was pointing. A single log lay stretched across the clearing, skewered in the middle by the one standing trunk, except now Carny saw it wasn't a trunk at all, but a long bamboo pole. He took a closer look at the log. It had been honed to a blade shape on each side, although the edge was chewed and cracked now.

"I don't—"

"Damn clever," Big Hog said, stopping when he reached Carny. "It's a giant scythe spun like a child's top. Gets launched through the air, spins up something wild, then falls to earth. That pole sticks into the ground and the log there spins around chewing everything to shit. Another foot and it would have got you."

Carny looked around the clearing. "But that's not fair," he finally said.

Big Hog clapped him on the shoulder. "Maybe, but you know, it gives me some ideas about taking in the hay. A contraption like this would mow my large field before lunch. Course, if thaumics is involved that'll complicate things, but I think it's just a whole lot of mechanicals, you know? Fiddly bits working together."

Carny turned from the destruction to look at Big Hog. "What?"

"I'll tell you later, we have to move. Listowk told me to bring your ass back dead or alive. Seeing as you're alive, I don't have to carry you." He wrinkled his nose but refrained from commenting on the odor. "Follow me," Big Hog said, turning and stepping back over the debris.

Carny looked skyward through the gaping hole that had been cut through the jungle all the way to just above him.

A tree on the edge of the clearing cracked and began falling. Carny grabbed his crossbow and ran after Big Hog.

CHAPTER TWENTY-SEVEN

"HOLD HIM STEADY!" BREEZE shouted.

Vorly kept Carduus in a tight, banking turn as a spinning scythe whirled up from the jungle. The weapon was graceful and terrifying at the same time. It was big enough and spinning fast enough that it would cleave Carduus in two if it hit him. The spinning blade reached the top of its arc another two hundred feet above them, then tipped over and spun down, crashing into the jungle in a spray of green mulch.

"If you'd take your face out of that unholy sheet for a flicker you might notice we're getting shot at!"

"My job is to hunt the thaum. Yours is to fly Carduus and keep him steady," Breeze said.

"Well I can't very well keep him steady when every fucking slyt in the Lux is chucking something up at us!" Vorly said, turning in his saddle to look at her.

Breeze looked up from her crystal. Her windblown red hair formed a briar patch sprouting out from beneath her helm. "Then send the other rags down to attack the slyts," she said.

Vorly growled. "That's a great way to lose more rags. These rags aren't nimble enough for that kind of play. We need sparkers," he said. "Get Modelar on plane and ask him where the hell that flock got to."

Breeze muttered something in a language he couldn't

understand, but he knew a curse when he heard it. He was equally pissed, but for a reason he didn't want to admit to her. The damn sparker flock should have crystal sheets and thaums on them. If they did he'd know exactly where in the fucking Lux they were.

"I can't track the thaum and call Modelar at the same time," she said. "That would be straddling two planes covering a great distance. I—"

"Sky Horse Leader, this is Sky Horse Three. We've got company coming in from the east," Gruupher said, his voice booming from the crystal sheet.

Vorly turned and looked over his left shoulder. Several black dots were approaching their position just above the jungle ceiling.

"About damn time," Vorly said. "Breeze, keep on that thaum. The sparkers will deal with the slyts."

"I will once you get Carduus back on a stable track," she said.

"This is why I never got married," Vorly said. "Okay, boy, let's get back in our turn so Breeze can find the slyt thaum," he said, nudging Carduus with his left boot heel.

Carduus responded, swinging his tail hard to bring them back onto their previous course.

"Better?" Vorly asked, peering down at the jungle to look for more chunks of wood hurtling skyward. He had yet to spot a single slyt in the open. If this was the way it was going to be, High Command had better come up with some new ideas on defeating the slyts, and fast.

"Ten yards up, increase speed two beats," Breeze said in answer.

"Fucking right I'm never getting married," Vorly said, adjusting Carduus's height and speed per Breeze's wishes. "Got all the nagging I need right here."

SINTE DIDN'T SMILE when Listowk stepped out of the jungle and trotted across the clearing. Several soldiers hooted, happy to see their missing comrades, but Listowk waved them silent. *Bastard's in a mood.*

"I want a skirmish line twenty yards in from the tree line from there to there," he said, motioning with his left hand. He slowed down to a walk, not wanting to get to Sinte before he'd positioned the shield. Carny and Big Hog emerged from the jungle. Big Hog was smiling like he'd just fathered another child. Carny was covered in leaves and staring up at the sky.

"Carny. Carny! Anchor the left side. Big Hog, I want you all the way to the right. Wraith, set up with your bowmen another twenty yards back and cover the line."

The shadow of a rag flitted across the clearing and a ballista shot into the air, but it was nowhere near the rag.

"Five hundred yards into the jungle at least," Wraith said, tracking the flight of the spear.

"You stay put. I'm not losing the shield in there," Listowk said, hoping Sinte didn't countermand his order. This rescue had all the makings of a disaster. The sooner they got out of here, the better.

Listowk watched to make sure his orders were being carried out, then turned and faced Sinte.

"Red Shield reporting, SL," Listowk said, looking past Sinte at the downed rag. The mule dragonsmiths were already crawling all over it, making whatever repairs were needed to get the beast in the air again. He turned his focus to Sinte and blinked. The man looked like shit.

"Casualties?" Sinte asked, looking off into the jungle and removing his helm.

His face was pale and his eyes red rimmed, like he hadn't slept at all. Most shocking, black stubble marred his normally smooth skull. Listowk couldn't remember a time when the SL hadn't found a moment to shave at least once. *Guess falling out of the sky loosens even the tightest asses.*

"None, nothing major anyway," Listowk said. He was damn proud of that, too. No need to bore Sinte with Ahmist and Carny. Listowk would sort them out. The boys had just tackled their first hot landing and survived. Now they had to survive this battle. That meant getting that rag back in the air as quickly as possible.

"We need to deploy the shield," Sinte said, his voice trailing off as if he were preoccupied.

"Already under way," Listowk said, looking closer at Sinte. His aketon was unbuttoned and one of his greaves was covered in mud. This wasn't the shield leader he knew. He'd seen Sinte in combat and even then he'd kept his Kingdom-issued ramrod firmly stuck up his ass.

"Good… good," Sinte said.

"SL, we've got slyts in the trees!"

Listowk turned. The shield was spread out across the clearing, the men either crouched down or already on their knees. Crossbows twanged as bolt after bolt ripped into the foliage. He couldn't see a damn thing but counted at least five arrows flying out from the jungle.

"This could all go in the midden in a hurry," Listowk said.

Sinte blinked and stood up straighter. He fixed his gaze on Listowk and sneered. "Pull yourself together, LC, you sound like a whining beggar on Merser Street."

"SL, we're out on a pretty long limb here. If—"

"Stow that shit. Our orders are clear," Sinte said, putting his helm back on his head and buttoning up his aketon. "You see to that infernal beast. I'll take care of *my* shield."

"By your command," Listowk said, turning away before he said something he'd regret. "Dragonsmith!" Listowk shouted, running toward the downed rag. "How long until you get your beastie in the air?"

The mule, Pagath, stood up from the far side of the rag's spine plates. "An eighth of a candle, and that's a high hope."

"We've got slyts coming in on us," Listowk said, looking back to the jungle. The shield was now firing in a more disciplined manner. He needed to be there. Sinte was back to being the same fucking hard-ass, but something was missing.

A whirring noise passed overhead. Listowk looked up. Another one of those sinister spinning blades went sailing past before plunging into the jungle. Leaves and wood geysered into the air a moment later, followed by a cracking, grinding noise.

"I am aware," Pagath said, waving at the air. "Look, I'm no more keen to be here than you are, but it's going to take time to stitch Cytisus's wing back into flying shape. You can hold them off, can't you?"

A salvo of ballista spears arced through the air and fell into the clearing, marching their way toward Listowk and the downed rag. The last one hit less than twenty yards from where Listowk stood. He looked back at the shield. Sinte continued striding across the clearing like he did on the parade square. He never changed his pace or direction. How the hell the spears missed him Listowk didn't know.

"We're taking a lot of fire," Listowk said, turning back to Pagath. "A lot more than some scout force. Ballistas aren't small, and they need a herd of brorra to haul them around, not to mention those whirlers. We might need to get out of here sooner than we figured."

"I'm not leaving Cytisus behind," Pagath said, grabbing the rag's dorsal plate and holding on.

Listowk shook his head. "I get that. But can't you just make a patch so he can fly a mile or so? Then you can do more repairs."

Pagath started cursing in mule and stomping along Cytisus's back. He stopped when he got to the rag's hindquarters. "All right, a sixteenth of a candle, and that's against my better judgment!"

Listowk was ready to tell the mule to fuck his better judgment when a pair of whirlers sliced into the edges of the jungle to either side of the rag. The bloody things had come in almost horizontally. Whole trees flew through the air.

"That'll speed the bastard up," Listowk said, turning and running toward the shield. Movement in the tree line slowed his steps. A volley of arrows burst through the jungle a few feet above head height. They sailed over the crouching shield, over the marching Sinte, and came straight at Listowk. He dove for the ground, crashing into the stump of a tree barely wider than he was. Arrows thunked into the stump and into the ground around him. He drew his knees up to his chest and wrapped his arms around his helm, tensing for the arrow that would puncture his spine.

A horn blew three sharp notes in rapid succession. High-pitched screams filled the air. Listowk uncurled and looked up over the stump as slyts poured out of the jungle, running toward the shield. Listowk counted forty, maybe fifty. They wore the same peasant garb as every slyt farmer he'd ever seen. Most held simple spears or swords in their hands. A few wore breastplates of bamboo stalks stitched together with palm frond. None wore a helm.

The distance from the tree line to the shield was barely seventy-five yards, but it was strewn with downed trees and shattered bamboo. Crossbows chattered as the shield fired. Bolts easily covered the short distance in a couple of flicks and sent the lead slyts tumbling to the ground. The bamboo armor proved no match for the bolts.

The lighter twang of bows now sang out as Wraith and his bowmen covered the shield while the crossbowmen frantically reloaded. More slyts fell, this time from arrows, often to the head. The charge faltered as the slyts farther behind began to step over the bodies of their comrades. Sinte continued his march, drawing his hewer as he did so.

Listowk jumped to his feet and began picking his way through the small forest of arrows around his position. He looked up as the horn sounded again, this time blowing two long notes. The slyts turned and began running back to the tree line. The bowmen took several more, dropping the slyts with studied precision.

A rumbling in the air sent a chill down Listowk's back. A voice roared from somewhere above him. "Get your heads down!"

He looked up as a pair of rags flying abreast flew overhead. They were no more than a hundred feet off the ground and still descending as they passed. It dawned on Listowk that they weren't yelling at him, but at the shield in front of him.

The sides of the rags glowed bright red and the air around them shimmered like water. Their heat washed over Listowk a moment later and he choked on the sulfur. Listowk crouched lower and continued running.

"Get down! Get down!" Listowk shouted, waving his left arm in the air as he charged after the rags. Sinte was now among the shield, but if he heard Listowk's cries or that of the driver of the rags, he gave no indication. He continued walking at a steady pace through the shield and several yards in front of them, straight toward the tree line.

Just when he thought Sinte would walk right into the jungle after the retreating slyts, Sinte stopped, half turned, and waved at the shield to follow him. *Holy fucking Druid! He's going to lead a charge!*

"NO, NO, NO, no, no!" Jawn shouted, fighting Breeze's tracings. They'd pinpointed the slyt thaum to an area of jungle no larger than six hundred yards square. It was a stunning accomplishment. They had located a thaum through the aethereal plane, but now that success threatened to kill them both.

"We …ve her, Black Star, what… you doing?" Breeze asked, her voice scratchy through the crystal. "She's trapped in plane. I'll keep her pinned while you develop a process."

"We have to disengage and slide off!" Jawn said. He kept trying to untrace Breeze's patterns and allow the slyt thaum an escape, but Breeze was far more adept on plane than he was and closed every avenue as fast as he made it. He looked over his right shoulder, then back at the crystal. The sparker rags were approaching at almost treetop level, their sides glowing cherry red.

"Courage, Jawn, you can do this," Rickets said.

"You should listen to her—she knows what she's about," Rimsma added.

Jawn ignored both of them. "Breeze, listen to me. They're going to burn the jungle. Those other rags are going to breathe fire. If we're still engaged on plane with her, she could use that energy to channel a process."

"Like Gremthyn?" Rickets asked.

"Worse," Jawn said. "That thaum was working off of the

base energy around him and look what he did. Those rags are going to provide a hundredfold more energy. Breeze, we have to slide!"

"I understa... Black Star, but we're deep in the plane. I can't..."

"Say again, Breeze. We need to slide now!"

Bright orange light erupted in the jungle below. Jawn tore his gaze from the crystal sheet in time to see the rags' fire plunge into the tree line.

"They just fired!" Breeze shouted.

Jawn knew there was no more time. He drew in a deep breath and focused all his thought on the aethereal plane he and Breeze were navigating. He found the weak spot he was looking for. Grunting with the effort, he plunged his mind through that plane and into the next one, binding them together in a surge of power. This would work, or he'd have his terminal blaze of glory.

The deep cold of the aethereal abyss latched on to Jawn's fingertips, driving unseen needles of black ice into his hands. Jawn's ass puckered as every vein was shot through with ice water. Bands of searing pain spread from his temples to the back of his skull. He gasped. The agony was exquisite.

He heard his name being called, but it was somewhere distant. He was in the aether now.

Black Star, what have you done?

That was Breeze. Her thoughts moved seamlessly into his mind. The other thaums on plane grew to a chorus of thoughts screaming in his head.

Jawn worked the rift, leaving the thaums' cries far behind. All his concentration was needed to maintain the connection between the two planes. If he lost focus and drifted between planes, his mind would be lost forever in the aether. The academy drilled them over and over on the dangers of cross-planing, but where there was danger, there was also reward. Straddling two planes gave a thaum access to two sources of power. Thaumic processes conducted in two planes were that much more powerful. And he needed that power now to kill the slyt thaum and disengage Breeze and himself before the rags found her.

Jawn tapped the energy, letting it flow through him. His body began shaking as its force coursed through him. It was too much, too fast. He couldn't control a process this powerful. He let go, tumbling between the planes without anything to latch on to.

Black Star, use me. Find me in the aether.

Jawn focused on Breeze, searching for her among the vastness. Slowly, he found his balance and brought the planes back into focus. He realized he was shivering, but that was his body. His mind was clear.

The force of a punch hit Jawn in the chest. The pain radiated into his back and down his left arm. He gasped, breathing in but finding no relief.

I'm suffocating.

Another mind entered his. It was saying gibberish, but he realized it had to be the enemy thaum. She had attacked him first.

Jawn dug deep into his training, directing everything that he was into a single point. He'd always pictured the very peak of a mountain, and on it, the very highest crystal of ice. That was his clarity, and he found his focus again. His body was faltering. He had time to find the slyt thaum and kill her and return to the world, but he had to do it fast.

A numbing pain crept into Jawn, but he ignored it. The thaum had revealed herself in attacking him. Because she hadn't killed him, she was now vulnerable, but only if Jawn got to her before she tapped the fire.

Jawn reestablished his connection with the two planes, driving himself into the energy and channeling all of it through the single shimmering point of light that he was. The surge was beyond measure. For a flicker he saw everything—the enemy thaum, Breeze, the rags, Rickets... *Wait, something about Rick*— The crystal point fractured. Energy flew into the aether. Jawn marshaled his strength and directed what he could at the thaum.

There was light, a searing pain, and then the roaring sound of wind in his ears. The image of the slyt thaum disintegrated, her presence on plane ruptured beyond repair. He'd done it. He'd killed her.

"Fuck!" Jawn shouted, folding in on himself.

Hands grabbed him and pulled him backward, laying him out on his back. The world around him was movement and pain and noise. He was off plane.

"Easy, Jawn, easy. I've got you," Rickets said from somewhere above him.

Jawn tried to open his eyes, but a wet cloth was placed over his head. He struggled to remove it, but his left arm wouldn't respond, and his right was pinned.

He grunted, searching his body for parts that moved, but he may as well have still been on plane. Nothing worked.

"I got her, Rickets, I got her," Jawn said. He needed to say it out loud. It wasn't pride; it wasn't even duty. It was survival. He'd done what had to be done, what no one else could do.

"You got her," Rickets said. "Now lie still and try not to move."

The sound of beating wings vibrated in his chest. He took comfort in that. He realized his heart no longer felt like it was being crushed, and his breathing was improving.

Warm, coppery liquid trickled into his mouth. He spit, but more came in. In a rush of senses his entire body jerked and he felt pain over and through every inch of it.

"Ohhh, fuck. Druid fucking fire!"

"Easy, Jawn, you're going to be fine. Just drink some of this."

A small glass bottle was placed against his lips and the contents poured into his mouth. The liquid was ice-cold and stung, but wherever it touched the pain receded. He swallowed, tasting more of the coppery liquid as he did.

He realized he was flexing the fingers on his right hand and brought his hand up to his face. He had to get that damn cloth off his eyes.

"Just leave it there," Rickets said, placing his hand on Jawn's.

Jawn pushed it aside and pulled the cloth off. It was soaking wet. He reached up to his eyes. More wet, but now he knew.

"Blood," Jawn said, feeling it covering his face.

"You'll be all right," Rickets said. "That Breeze girl and the flock commander look like ghouls, but otherwise they're hale and healthy. You will be too."

Jawn blinked and turned his face toward the sun. He felt its heat on his cheeks, but his vision remained pitch-black.

"No, Rickets," Jawn said, his world shattering around him. "I won't."

LISTOWK DIDN'T UNDERSTAND time. It was a witchcraft all its own. It was even different from thaumics. Changing time was something almost anyone could do, though how remained a mystery. It wasn't like you could alter it in a big way, but enough so you noticed. He himself had felt it speed up, often on the very occasions when he wished it would slow down. Now, when he desperately wanted it to slow so that he could reach Sinte and the shield, it did, but it was already too late.

Sinte was still half turned, his left arm high in the air. He was bathed in a shimmering orange light, his helm a gleaming beacon against the dark green of the tree line. It reminded Listowk of the stained glass he'd seen in a Holy Grove depicting the High Druid ascending the Sacred Tree to the Eternal Forest of Salvation. Except that light had been soft and yellow, almost white.

The tree line wilted, its outline fading in the intensity of the light. Sinte's shape wavered, its edges softening, even as the gleam of his helm grew. Listowk squinted, trying to keep him in focus.

Flame chased the light, pouring out of the rags in a torrent. The tree line swayed and buckled. Gouts of fire bounced off trunks like waves crashing against the rocks. The gleam from Sinte's helm surged, then flew apart, leaving nothing for Listowk to focus on.

A wave of heat rolled over Listowk, driving him to his knees to cover his face. A roaring, rushing noise like a waterfall descended around him. He stayed down, keeping his eyes closed, but the sound told him everything. The roar was gone, replaced by a crackling, spitting noise as everything in the jungle succumbed to the flame.

Something hit Listowk in the shoulder. He pushed himself up and opened his eyes.

"Move!" Wraith shouted, pointing back toward the jungle.

A wall of fire eighty feet tall engulfed the tree line. Heavy brown smoke blotted out the sky to the west. The shield was running toward him, some still holding their crossbows, others without their weapon or helm. Behind them, small pillars of fire dotted the clearing where the slyts burned.

"We need to back up," Wraith said, an uncharacteristic restating of his point.

Listowk looked at him. The foliage he'd so painstakingly arranged on his uniform was little more than ash. Wisps of smoke curled lazily from the flights of his arrows, the feather edges wilted and frayed. Wraith was breathing heavily, something else Listowk had rarely seen the soldier do, even after hiking up the mountain on the coast.

Listowk heard Sinte's voice in his head, complete with sneer. *Soldiers of the Kingdom don't retreat.*

"We need to regroup," Listowk said, saying it loud enough that it carried. The running soldiers slowed to a walk.

Wraith shrugged. Listowk knew none of the military bullshit mattered to Wraith. He was out here to hunt. It made him a first-class killer but a less-than-ideal leader.

"The slyts?" Listowk asked, realizing he could answer that himself. No one in that chunk of jungle was alive.

"Charked," Wraith said.

Listowk got to his feet, taking Wraith's offered hand. The man's skin was desert dry and warm enough to bake bread on.

"Drink some water," Listowk said.

"Lost my water skin," Wraith said.

Listowk reached for his own water skin and handed it to Wraith. Wraith took it and drank three gulps before handing it back.

"More slyts are bound to show up," Listowk said, surveying

341

the shield as they made their way toward him. As if to prove his point, a new salvo of ballista spears shot into the air as one of the rags they'd flown in on passed by overhead. Listowk watched their trajectory long enough to see they were well behind the beast.

"That's going to be a problem," Wraith said, holding up his bow.

"Your string broke," Listowk said.

"Everyone's did. The heat snapped them like twigs," Wraith said. "Stressed the wood, too."

"Another glorious day in the Lux," Listowk said, slowly moving back from the wall of fire that was now spreading into the clearing. For such wet, green wood the jungle burned bright and wild.

"You wouldn't think it would burn that well," Wraith said, as if reading Listowk's thoughts.

"Is everyone accounted for?" Listowk asked.

Wraith stopped walking. "Sinte's... missing."

Sinte's disintegrating outline remained etched in front of Listowk's eyes. He tried to feel something but couldn't. "Anyone else?"

Wraith shook his head.

A whistling in the air cut their conversation. The flight of sparker rags dove again, this time coming in from the north and torching the jungle several hundred yards farther west. Orange light bloomed through the haze and smoke of the first fire as they unleashed another spray. A flick later the manic roar of their fire reached his ears. Listowk thought he heard screams.

Most of the shield now stood around them. Listowk became aware of their silence. Eyes stared at the fire, some with tears streaming down soot-blackened cheeks, others blinking as if that would change the image. Time, so agonizingly slow when the rags first attacked, now sped at him like a volley of arrows. The shield had met the enemy and killed many, but they had lost their leader and their weapons were currently useless.

Wraith began uncurling a backup bowstring. He looked at Listowk but said nothing. Listowk heard him all the same. *Get your fucking shit right and start leading.*

"Everyone drink some water," Listowk said, holding up his own water skin as if demonstrating something to a child. "Break out new strings and start restringing. If you dropped something, find it. Crossbows and bolts first, everything else after that. Big Hog, take half the shield and set up on the left side of the rag. Carny, you take the other half and set up on the right. Wraith, put your bowmen at the edge of the clearing and keep an eye out for slyts trying to flank the fire."

"What about the SL?" Knockers asked.

Listowk felt the shield hesitate. This was the first time they'd lost someone in battle, and in a horrifying manner. It wasn't like the Weasel, or even Vooford. They had all seen Sinte die. Now they needed direction, purpose. If they thought any more about what had just happened he could lose them.

"He's dead," Listowk said, more harshly than Knockers deserved, but this was for the whole shield. "That happens to soldiers. I'm in charge now, and Carny is acting lead crossbowman."

"But don't we do something when someone dies?" Knockers asked, looking around for support. Tears cleaned streaks of dirt from his cheeks as they fell.

"We regroup, restring, and get back in the fucking fight," Listowk said, turning to Carny and pointing. "Get your men on the flank and do it now! Big Hog, you too. All of you, move!"

The shield shuffled back and then began moving to their tasks. Carny waved his crossbow around like a madman while shouting, which would have worried Listowk more, but like everyone else, he had no string.

The rag behind him roared. Listowk turned in time to see it raise both its wings high into the air and flap them a few times. There were shouts from the mules. Sounded good. Dragonsmith Pagath walked down the length of the rag's tail and hopped into the clearing, heading toward Listowk.

"Sorry about your man," Pagath said, walking up to stand beside Listowk. "Charking's a bad way to go, but he wouldn'ta felt a thing."

Listowk stared at the fire where Sinte had disappeared. He

imagined he saw him among the flames, still walking, still sneering.

"Nothing?" Listowk asked.

Pagath coughed. "Maybe for a flicker or two. A rag's flame is straight from the Valley of Fire and Damnation," Pagath said. "Oh, and Cytisus is airworthy."

"Good," Listowk said, ignoring the rag and staring deep into the fire.

PART THREE

CHAPTER TWENTY-EIGHT

"DO YOU THINK HE felt anything?" Knockers asked, nervously shifting his crossbow in his hands.

"Fuck, Knockers, enough," Carny said, squinting up at him from his seat on a fallen tree trunk. The sun was a frayed orange ball behind Knockers, casting him in a glowing shadow. Carny's head pounded, his eyes itched from lack of sleep, and it was too hot and sticky for this shit again.

"But it was so hot," Knockers said, ignoring Carny's anger. "I've burnt my hands a few times over the cook fire when I was young and it hurt. A lot. He must have felt something."

A month gone and two hundred miles north from where Sinte charked, and Knockers still couldn't let it go. Truth be told, Carny hadn't forgotten it either. He doubted anyone in Red Shield had, but holy fuck you didn't keep talking about it.

"High bloody Druid, Knockers, let it go, please. He vanished in a flick. You saw it, I saw it, the whole fucking shield saw it. He couldn't have felt a thing," Carny said, trying hard to believe that.

Carny stood up abruptly, brushing ash from his trousers, and looked around. Red Shield was perched on a fire-charred hill surrounded by jungle in the middle of, fuck, it wasn't even the middle of nowhere. Nowhere was somewhere compared to this. Soldiers were either standing guard or stringing more prick vine around their perimeter while Big Hog whistled as he hacked bamboo stalks into crude stakes to be set into the ground facing outward. The Bard kept tune with his psaltery, sort of, the instrument's notes vibrating in increasingly odd and jarring ways as he explored "the dark, mystical soul of the Lux" as he put it.

Poor bastard's going deep in the green, Carny figured, knowing he probably was, too. The jungle still scared Carny, but he'd come to terms with his fear. He'd never be Wraith or Listowk when it came to embracing the black, fetid depths of the jungle at night, but he'd learned how to walk without making noise, keep his crossbow from snagging on a vine, and where to drop his trousers to take a shit without a swarm of army ants trying to crawl up his ass.

Knockers opened his mouth to ask another question, then thought better of it and slowly walked away from Carny. Any sympathy Carny had had for Knockers was long gone. Carny was Lead Crossbow now and that was already more than he needed to deal with. Soldiers that used to bitch and moan to Listowk now came to him. And Listowk expected him to deal with that shit.

Carny sat down and fished into his trouser pockets for a folded leaf with a pinch of Sliver in it. He didn't find one. There hadn't been a rag flight to their hill in four days, which meant no supplies, which meant Squeak couldn't slip some of his special provisions in with the rest of the cargo. Carny was down to a smidge of Wild Flower. He'd used the last of his camphor two days ago and no one else had any left, or so they said.

The distinctive *whup-whup-whup* of rag wings carried on the air. Carny stood up again, not bothering to brush off his trousers this time. Praise the High Druid, fresh supplies at last!

The hill buzzed as Red Shield scurried to make ready for the rag's arrival. Listowk shouted orders in a humbler volume than Sinte, and the soldiers listened and obeyed, policing up their gear and clearing the very top of the hill. Between the whirlwind kicked up by the rag's wings and its tail swishing around like a spinning scythe, anything not firmly tied or weighted down would be blown hundreds of yards into the jungle, never to be seen again.

"Secure your quivers," Carny said, doing his part to get Red Shield ready without much enthusiasm. Any soldier who didn't keep his shit tight deserved whatever he got out here.

The rag approached from the west, coming in at a thousand yards above the jungle. Black smoke trailed it, and Carny knew that wasn't a good sign. The driver had put the gaff to the rag, which meant speed, and they only did that when something was up.

"He's going too fast to land," the Bard said, coming to stand beside Carny.

Only a few thousand yards out, the rag continued flying at the same speed and height.

"Maybe he's new," Carny said, willing the rag to descend.

At two hundred yards out, a small bundle fell from the rag and landed on the far side of the hill as the beast flew overhead and kept on flying, no doubt heading for the other shields dotted over the hills for miles around.

"Tell me that's a message saying a flock of rags is heading our way with gallons of mead, fresh bread, and real meat," Carny said, pointing at Listowk as a soldier handed him the satchel dropped from the rag.

Listowk slowly opened the flap and pulled out a single piece of paper and read it. When he was done, he put the paper back in the satchel and closed the flap. His mustache rolled up and down under his nose as he seemed to ponder what to say.

"Fuck, SL, what?" Carny said, speaking for all of them.

Listowk shrugged. "No supplies, but tomorrow morning they're flying in to take us off this little hill of ours."

There were smiles and even a few cheers, but mostly from the newer soldiers.

"What's the catch?" Carny asked.

Listowk looked to the sky before answering.

"Instead of another hill, they've found us a valley."

* * *

"YOU'RE PRETTY, LIKE ONE of those oil paintings, only your skin is smoother."

League of Worldly Fellowship crier Miska Hounowger massaged her temples. She sat near the front of a young bull dragon named Carduus, just behind the female thaum, Breeze. Miska had tried to talk to her, but Breeze made it clear that she was not to be disturbed while in flight. Doing so would result in a "kick where you split." Miska had never heard a woman, let alone one who was a thaum, speak so crudely. Miska found Breeze that much more fascinating.

"Real pretty," Wiz said, beaming a smile at her.

The driver, Flock Commander Astol, yelled something at Carduus, who bellowed in response. The vibration went up through her saddle, shaking her entire innards. She took the opportunity to look away and out at the land passing below them.

Luitox was carpeted in a verdant, startling, vast jungle. She had never seen anything like it. It was made all the more overwhelming by the occasional rows of palm trees and fruit orchards and the square and rectangular dosha swamps of shimmering brown that offered the eye a contrast. And through it all there seemed to always be at least one thick, fat brown river snaking its way toward the coast.

It was harvest season back in the Kingdom, but this land obviously didn't know it. Miska knew that foreign lands experienced the seasons differently, but it was still surprising. The sun beat down on the jungle with wave after wave of shimmering heat, which served to propel the towering trees ever higher into the sky. The leaves, far from turning and falling, grew fatter and greener. She wondered if they ever stopped growing.

Miska smiled and shook her head. She was letting Luitox get to her. She took pride in the fact that she was a "woman of character," the term favored by traditionalists for renegades who didn't conform, especially women who were educated. Miska always thought that unfair. Yes, she was educated, but she could also cook, understood the basic principles of cleaning even if she didn't practice them, and believed that had she met a man of equal character she would have had a family. As for knowing her place, well, she was still figuring that out and happy to do so on her own.

The wind picked up, which meant the rag had gained speed. She watched its massive wings go up and down. It was mesmerizing. So much power and grace contained in an animal of unimaginable fury. She saw a little of herself in the dragon. She was more than people saw, more even than they wanted her to be.

"Nice day," the Wizard said, trying again.

Unlike the other soldiers—unsurprisingly, Miska conceded—the shield's wizard looked less like a soldier and more like a traveling beggar, although to be fair they all looked exceedingly scruffy. Wiz, as he'd been introduced to her, took that scruffiness to a new level. Three different canvas satchels bulging with various weeds, strips of bark, mushrooms, and small glass vials were slung over his shoulders. More curious, he'd clearly removed several of the protective iron plates sewn into his aketon and stuffed the empty pockets with all manner of flowers and herbs.

"Do you really use all that?" she asked, motioning to his miniature garden.

The Wiz looked down at his chest then back at her. "Depends. If someone's got the Lux Pox real bad, then I try a bit of everything."

"Lux Pox?"

"It's like a rash, only nastier," the Wiz said, leaning forward.

Miska smelled bright green scents, a tangy one she couldn't place, and just a touch of cinnamon.

"Is it contagious?"

The Wiz smiled brightly. "Only if you rub your privates against someone else's. It usually settles in the crotch area. Burns like hot embers. Gets all pus-y, too, but that's actually a good sign. It's when you get the boils that—"

Miska held up her hand. She would not be relaying these

interesting facts back to the people of the Kingdom.

"So, you're with the Bleeding Hearts society, are you?" the Wiz asked.

Miska shifted in her saddle and wondered if she'd made a mistake coming to Luixtox. The battle for the future of the Kingdom was taking place back home, not out here. And yet, she'd heard enough stories at the pubs from soldiers who had returned that made her think more was going on in Luitox than the people were being told.

The closer she got to Luitox, however, the more she doubted everything she thought she knew. The rag she'd been flying on had stopped at Swassi Island. A rambling sanitarium covered a third of the island, but was divided in two. Men were housed in the north in crude but solid-enough huts while sick and wounded dwarves were housed to the south under little more than canvas tarps over a mat of palm fronds. The more things changed...

Miska sighed and turned to face the soldiers of Red Shield riding on the rag with her. More than one stared at her like a lovelorn puppy. She'd found this male attention flattering, once, when she was a girl. Now, long into spinsterhood at thirty-one, it was a briar patch of pricks she would just as soon burn to ash.

"League of Worldly Fellowship," Miska said, not rising to the bait. "We believe that all the lands and all the races should live together in peace and harmony and that no one is better than anyone else."

"You haven't met the slyts yet then," someone said, eliciting laughter.

Slyts. It was an ugly, ugly word. Why men had to be so crude and so cruel she didn't understand.

"If I may, I was hoping to talk to you some more about the murder of King Wynnthorpe," she said, adopting a stern look. "It must be very unwelcome news to you."

"They say he wasn't the real king anyway, so what does it matter?" the soldier named Big Hog said, lifting his head from his arms long enough to chime in. The big fellow didn't seem that keen on flying. There was a pale green tinge about him.

Miska would have to get his real name later. All the soldiers had been introduced to her by nicknames. It was the oddest thing to rename everyone, but she'd found it prevalent throughout the army. Even the thaums were going by monikers, like Breeze.

"Legitimate or not, he was assassinated," she said, surprised she was struggling to impart the significance of this. "An arrow shot from over a hundred yards away went in his left eye and out the back of his skull while he was riding in his carriage."

"What was the wind?"

Miska jumped, unaware a soldier had settled in behind her. *How had he done that?* She turned and saw the one they called Wraith. He was a thin, serious-looking man with dark eyes and a gaunt face that suggested less a soldier and more a... predator.

"The wind?"

"A head shot from a hundred yards into a moving carriage. Tail wind?"

Miska shook her head. "I have no idea, but that's really not the point. There hasn't been a royal assassination in over one hundred years. The Kingdom is in turmoil. No one cares about the wind."

"The assassin did," Wraith said, standing up and nonchalantly walking along the back of the rag toward its tail.

News of the king's assassination had reached the Lux inside of a day, and that was over a week ago, but this was the first time these troops were hearing details from someone in the know. Still, most of them seemed far more fascinated by her breasts— or the wind of all things—than by the world-shaking news she had to convey.

"The Druid Council should assume command," Ahmy said, staring at Miska with something that felt a lot like hate. The skin on his boyish face was taut over his cheekbones, as if he were in a perpetual state of trying to control his rage. "The Kingdom needs the saving grace of the High Druid now more than ever."

"Fuck your council, Ahmy," Lead Crossbowman Carny said. Actually, it was more a mumble, as his left cheek was filled with some kind of chaw. A dark brown liquid dribbled out of the corner of his mouth; he wiped it away with the back of his hand. His eyes were slightly glazed, as if he hadn't slept well. "It don't mean shit out here. We march, we fly, we fight, and then we do it all again. King, queen, druid… won't make a damn bit of difference to us."

Most of the soldiers on the rag nodded. Miska had heard rumors of discontent among the legions in Luitox from the returning veterans, but she'd put that down to a few bad apples. It appeared there was far more to it after all.

"How long have you been over here?" she asked.

"Six months for most of us," Big Hog said. The other soldiers appeared comfortable with his speaking for the group. "Knockers there came in a couple of months ago with the big sail," he said, referring to the influx of nine additional legions that was supposed to end the war.

"I ain't the new guy," Knockers said, taking his pipe out of his mouth to talk. It wasn't lit, and hadn't been since Miska arrived, but the soldier puffed on it as if it were. None of the other soldiers seemed to notice anything was amiss, so she said nothing. "Frogleg's the new guy. Came over two weeks ago, fuckin' fawn."

"I don't think I met him," Miska said, wondering what in the world had led to that name.

"He's riding on Cytisus," Knockers said, using his pipe to point at one of the other dragons flying in formation with Carduus.

Miska looked. Stretched out behind Carduus like a flock of geese, the other five dragons in Obsidian Flock flew in single echelon to the right—starboard—of Carduus, each one a healthy two hundred yards behind the one in front. It was a truly awe-inspiring sight.

Carduus coughed, and a cloud of black smoke and sulfur engulfed her. She gagged, but truth be told, it was a nice change from the gamey odor given off by the soldiers, all save Wiz. She looked at them a little more closely once the smoke cleared and tried to come up with something more than *scruffy* to describe them. Were they to show up on the streets of the capital today they'd be mistaken for brigands instead of the bright-eyed warriors of civilization that had marched onto ships to set sail for Luitox.

Their helms weren't polished. In fact, most were deliberately covered in mud and vegetation. When she first saw them she thought they had chunks of sod on their heads. Few, if any, wore greaves, while their sleeveless aketons might as well have been dishrags stitched together by blind beggars. Only their weapons were well maintained. The heavy, mean-looking crossbows; the elegantly curved hunting bows; and the array of daggers, knives, hewers, and even axes bristling from their belts and pockets and the tops of their boots looked every bit as lethal as they had the day they were made.

They were a contradiction she didn't yet understand, but then that's why she was here. Her official orders, like those of all the criers sent to Luitox, were to tell the troops that everything back in the Kingdom was fine. Yes, she could admit that the king's death was very unfortunate, but she was to tell them that they should rest assured a proper succession was in place and all would be well.

Carny's right, it don't mean shit out here.

"Carny—excuse me, Lead Crossbowman, I'd very much like to understand what is going on out here in the… Lux," she said, deliberately hesitating before using their term.

Soldiers smiled; a couple even winked. Carny stared at her for several flicks, then turned and spit before turning back. She took that as a good sign.

"You want to know what's really going on out here in the Lux?"

"I do," she said, leaning forward. The wind whipped the top of her tunic and she felt the warm sun flash on exposed bosom and made no attempt to cover herself. You used what you had. "And I owe it to you, all of you, to tell the people back home what's really going on out here."

This time Carny nodded. The dull look in his eyes cleared and he sat up a little straighter.

"First off, you hear anyone say that the slyts out here are nothing but cowards with all the fight of a dandelion on a windy day, you don't believe him. Ol' Faery Crud is about the cunningest, meanest little fucker you ever want to tangle with, and that's no lie."

"Fucking right about that," Big Hog said, not bothering to lift his head. Even Ahmy nodded.

"Faery Crud?"

"Fuckin' C's, Forest Collective... Faery Crud."

They were creating a whole new language out here. Miska widened her eyes and allowed the hint of a smile to brighten her face. There was a future in relaying events from one land to another, she just knew it. The royal criers would tell the populace that all was well even as the walls crumbled around them. She had a chance to tell the people what was really going on. That was more than a future—that was power.

"I had no idea," she said, genuinely intrigued. "This is all so fascinating. Please, tell me more."

"SKY HORSE LEADER, this is Blue Charger. I am coming in on your port side. Let your army ants know we're friendly, clear?"

Vorly glanced in the polished piece of tin Pagath had attached to the top of his crystal sheet. Vorly had been fed up with having a sore neck from turning around to talk to Breeze, so Pagath had come up with the brilliant and simple solution of the mirror. Not only could Vorly see Breeze without turning around, he could view the double row of troops on Carduus's back, the crier woman, and a fair chunk of the sky behind him filled with the rest of Obsidian Flock. They were flying at three-quarter normal cruise as Cytisus was still not back to form. It'd been two months since his wound and while he was healing, it was a slow process.

A series of three blue lines etched their way onto his sheet, all moving along the same path as that of Obsidian Flock. Vorly reached out and tilted the mirror to scan more sky. It was just midmorning, the sky a light fuzzy blue with barely a skiff of clouds. It wasn't as hot as Vorly had expected, but he wasn't disappointed about that unless it meant a storm was blowing in. He'd put the question to the RATs, but to a woman and man they said they couldn't predict the weather more than a day or so out. Vorly's left elbow did better than that.

Vorly lowered his chin to use the speaking tube buttoned to the front of his tunic. Pagath was a wonder. He'd fashioned a length of flexible tube using the sticky sap from some trees that when cooked turned into a semihard substance. He'd then wrapped it in linen and attached copper cones to either end. You could speak in one end and your voice, though a bit muffled, came out the other.

"You see them, Breeze?" Vorly asked, looking away from the mirror to scan the rest of the sky. He couldn't find Blue Charger and his flock.

"Definitely strong on plane and in our vicinity," she said, the dots of her fingertips skillfully racing across Vorly's sheet. "They should be right there."

Vorly hung his head. "I'm getting stupid in my old age. Rolling port." He lifted his chin, popped a whistle made from a bamboo shoot into his mouth, and gave it a sharp blast. It let the troops riding on Carduus know a turn was about to happen. It was just one more element in an ever-growing manual of procedures that a driver had to know to fly these days. It also reduced the puke, piss, and shit cleanup after a flight, which, Pagath had indicated while waving his hammer about, was a good thing.

Carduus was already banking when Vorly tugged on the rein, tilting him until he was perpendicular to the ground. *Bugger learns fast*. Vorly was using far less rein and gaff these days on Carduus. Not only did he respond to the whistle, he responded faster.

"Welcome to the party, Blue Charger," Vorly said, waving at the flight of three rags a thousand yards below them and coming up fast. Vorly blew his whistle again, not bothering to snap the reins at all.

Carduus resumed level flight, a low growl rumbling from deep in his throat.

"Easy, boy, they're friendly," Vorly said, patting Carduus.

Blue Charger's rag rose up beside Carduus two hundred yards to port and dead abreast. The rest of his flock popped up and took position in port echelon with each rag another hundred feet above the one in front. Each rag was puffing hard, leaving trails of black smoke behind them.

Sparkers. Mean little bastards. Barely enough room for the driver and thaum. Looked cramped, especially with the extra layers of clay insulation packed around the two crew members. The walls of their protective cocoon were now two feet high. The joke was the sparker crews were gradually building a house on their rags and when the war was over they'd fly it back home.

"Your rags feeling the cold?" Vorly asked, noticing that each rag's belly and sides were adorned with steel plates. *That's new.* The plates just aft of the rags' rib cages glowed the brightest, although all the plates were cherry.

"I wish. I'm roasting my fucking balls," Blue Charger said. "Faery Crud's been shooting a new kind of arrow. Some kind of crystal tip that'll punch a hole through scale. One even scratched a talon on Filix."

Vorly whistled. Talon was the toughest part of a rag. "High fucking Druid. That plate enough to stop them?"

"Flock Command seems to think so," Blue Charger said, perhaps being circumspect because they were on an open plane. "All I know is it's slowed our rags down and made them cranky. Still, when they're cranky, they fire up extra hot. You oughtta see those little slyts burn when—"

"Getting a line from the roost, clear plane," Vorly said, cutting off Blue Charger. Vorly didn't need the image of burning slyts in his head today.

"Why didn't command order plates on our flock?" Breeze asked.

Vorly smiled. At some point in the last few months, Obsidian Flock had become her flock, and she and her thaums every bit a part of it. If only that poor fool Jate could have seen the future. Vorly's smile drained away. Probably wouldn't have changed a thing.

"We don't skim treetops trying to fry slyts on a rag that could ball if it sneezes too hard," he said, using the euphemism for *fireball*.

"We do get shot at enough, though," Breeze said. "I counted thirty-seven patches on Carduus this morning before we launched. That's six more since last week. Pagath was spitting spikes."

Vorly had only counted thirty-five. He hadn't realized Breeze looked over Carduus as well. "I'll talk to him about it," he said. Right now he was lead rag in a ten-flock formation of some fifty rags stretching out over four miles of what was very unfriendly jungle. They were three hundred and fifty miles inland and heading deeper west toward some Druid-forsaken valley command decided it wanted. They called it a choke point for most of the western slyts pouring east into Luitox. Stop it up and you end the war. Naturally, Obsidian Flock was delivering the cork.

"Better you than me," Breeze said.

"Hear any more about that thaum?" Vorly asked, changing the subject.

There was a long pause before Breeze responded. "He's still blind."

Vorly didn't doubt it. It was a wonder the boy had lived at all. "They think he'll see again?"

"They don't know. He went deep, on two planes. Thaums don't usually come back from that."

"Awarded him the Medal of Courageous Thaumics. Highest medal in your service. That's something," Vorly said, wondering now why he'd brought the subject up.

"He'd rather have his sight," Breeze said.

It wasn't a rebuke, but Vorly felt the sting all the same. She was right. They could keep all their damn medals. He wanted out of this war with all his parts still attached and working.

"Poor bastard. He deserves better."

"He says he saw a flash of light this morning. He's not sure now, but if he did, it might be coming back."

Vorly felt a little better, then realized what was wrong with that statement.

"We launched predawn, Breeze. How could you know what he saw this morning?"

There was another long pause. Vorly turned around in his saddle to look at Breeze.

"We communicate on plane," she said, looking up to meet Vorly's gaze.

Vorly tilted his head. "On plane? But didn't they send him to that invalid island, Swassi?" Vorly shuddered. He'd only landed on the island once, and that was more than enough. He'd picked up the smell of the crematorium while still ten miles out. Spooked Carduus, too. "That's nearly eight hundred miles from here."

Breeze looked back down. "Yes, but Jawn has become adept at extending the range of the crystal. He flies the aether the way Carduus flies the air. It's... it's amazing." She looked back up, her eyes misty.

"He almost died. You could have died, too. How in—"

"It's as safe as anything else we do," Breeze said, her eyes hardening. "I am safer on plane with him than I am up here with... I mean, it's safe."

Vorly turned back to face forward. *Fuck her.*

"Commander, I'm sorry. I didn't mean that. I just meant—"

"Forget it," Vorly said, staring straight ahead. "What we do ain't no walk in the meadow."

The smooth, even beating of Carduus's wings was the only sound for the next ten miles. Vorly wanted to work up a rage, but it wasn't in him. Breeze was right; what they did was dangerous. Incredibly so. So why did it bother him so much about the thaum?

"We're a team up here, but on the ground I guess I need to get used to the idea of sharing you," Vorly said, cringing as the words came out.

"It's only ever the three of us up here," Breeze said.

Vorly smiled, then quickly frowned lest Breeze hear his joy in his voice.

"Sooooo, what's this I hear about you and Rimsma?" Vorly asked.

"None of your concern," she said, the gentleness in her voice turning to ice.

"Now, now," Vorly clucked, "it's my job to know what my flock is up to. That includes you, too, Breeze."

"So what, you want to know if he's fucking me?"

Vorly swallowed a bug and started coughing. "What? Bloody hell, woman, were you raised by wolves? No! I mean, I just, well…"

"He's a gentleman," Breeze said, her voice softening. "And you're easy to rattle."

Vorly looked in the mirror. Breeze was staring at him, a huge smile on her face.

"You little—"

Breeze held up her left hand. "Line coming in." She lowered her hand and began tracing on the High Plane crystal sheet while her right hand held station on the Low Plane sheet. Vorly had strenuously resisted having a second crystal added to his position and to his amazement he'd been successful, though he doubted it would last.

"It's a White Three," Breeze said.

Vorly looked skyward. Anything white was command. A triple line meant the communication on plane was being masked to avoid detection by slyt thaums. It took a significant thaumic process to run a three line. They only did it when something was serious.

"Let me know when," Vorly said, running his right hand along the braided copper up to the crystal sheet.

"You are good to plane," Breeze said.

Vorly moved his fingertips onto the crystal sheet. He shuddered. The energy on plane was growing colder week by week. Breeze said it had something to do with the increasing number of thaums and a lot of other stuff that got caught in

Vorly's earwax and never made it to his brain.

"I'm on plane," Vorly said, watching his sheet. The three line appeared a moment later, seeming to rise up from the depths. Vorly suppressed another shudder and duly circled the three line before touching it in order to access the message.

"Vorly, it's Walf," the disembodied voice of Legion Flock Commander Walf Modelar said.

Fuck, he's using our first names. This can't be good.

"Plans have changed. Obsidian Flock is staying at Frontier Castle Iron Fist until relieved. I know your flock was due some downtime, but there's nothing for it. I need you there. Report when you land. Clear."

Vorly stared at the crystal sheet. "That son of a bitch. He waited until I was in the air to tell me," Vorly said.

"You're still on plane," Breeze reminded him.

Vorly cursed under his breath and slid off plane. He'd promised Master Witch Matilda he'd take her to a fair in Gremthyn when he got back.

"When will you tell them?" Breeze asked.

Vorly pushed the speaking tube away before opening his mouth and screaming every obscenity he knew into the sky. Carduus lifted his head and cast an eye back at Vorly.

Vorly cursed Carduus, Modelar, the Lux, the war, and life in general until his voice gave out.

"I think that will do fine," Breeze said.

CHAPTER TWENTY-NINE

"WELCOME TO THE VALLEY of Bawnnd Ondor," Flock Commander Astol said. He blew on his bamboo whistle and Carduus dipped his head momentarily. Carduus drove his wings hard on the downstroke, creating a rumbling whoosh. The invisible weight of rapid climbing pushed down on Carny, but he kept on polishing his crossbow. He only worried now when his ass started floating away.

"What did he say?" Wiz asked.

Carny shook his head. Wiz had taken to Flower faster than Carny did. The man smiled like he was being paid in silver. His memory was shit, but he could stitch a cut and whip up a potion with his eyes closed, so Carny said nothing.

"Sounded like 'Valley of Bone and Thunder,'" Knockers said.

Carny opened his mouth to correct him but thought better of it. Valley of Bone and Thunder... beat the hell out of the slyt name, which probably meant Valley of Runny Shit and Stomach Cramps anyway.

Carny wiped his chin with the back of his hand and finished polishing his crossbow before tucking the cloth into a pocket. When he looked up, Miska was bouncing her big tits in excitement as they flew into the valley. Most of the men on board were looking at her instead of the land below. Carny was onto her—at least, he thought he was. She considered them just a bunch of dumb peasants from villages so backward they thought ice was dead water.

Well, she could think what she wanted. Sure, less than half of them could write more than their name and they looked like beggars and thieves, but they still had pride. Most important, they had each other. Carny sat up and nodded to himself. It was a hell of a revelation to realize that the most important people in the world to him were sitting on the back of this rag. He trusted them, and they trusted him. Ahmy… he wasn't so sure about. It was hard to trust a man who believed in worlds you couldn't see. What Carny did trust, however, was that Ahmy's crossbow was in perfect working order, just like the rest of the shield, and when the arrows started flying, that's what mattered.

"How's it look for farming?" Carny asked, standing up and grabbing a plate to support himself.

"I'll tell you when we land," Big Hog said, keeping his head between his knees.

Carny knew he would. He rolled his head on his neck a couple of times and looked out at the valley. Their last briefing was fresh in his mind and he wanted to put detail to the crudely drawn map he'd looked at.

Running on a north–south axis, the valley stretched three miles along its length, divided down the middle by the Formaske River, a gray-brown streak that flooded twice a year but was currently at half its normal height as this part of Luitox was hit hard by the drought. Barely a mile across at its widest point, the valley floor was a tattered collection of dried-up dosha swamps, fields of ten-foot-tall saw grass, and scattered stands of trees and bamboo.

Forming the valley wall to the west was a series of jungle-covered mountains, the highest peak a thousand feet below them. The mountains to the east were similar, although a single peak near the north end looked to be right at five thousand feet with them.

It was, as their briefings had said it was, a valley in the middle of nowhere. Looking at the mountains, Carny felt no joy despite their similarity to the ones back on the coast. There was no beach, no navy bringing in fresh food, and sure as fuck no slyt whores waiting to ease his pain every night. He'd spoken to Squeak about his biggest concern, but the little cripple had smiled and said to trust him. He could get Flower and the much more powerful white powder called Sliver anywhere, even in a hole like this.

"We'll see," Carny said under his breath, turning his head and spitting.

"I don't know why the Forest Collective would want this place," Knockers said.

"I'll pay the slyts to keep it," someone said. No one laughed.

"Iron Fist up ahead!"

They were halfway up the valley, which looked to be its widest point. From the air, Frontier Castle Iron Fist appeared as a brown stain on top of a nondescript hill. The name didn't mean shit though. It was a castle the way Carny was a bright, shining warrior of civilization. Under construction for a month, Iron Fist was in reality a large camp covering forty acres. It was surrounded by a six-foot-tall earthen wall, a meager two-foot moat, and four heavy wooden gates, one facing each cardinal direction.

Troop barracks had been built using surplus navy sailcloth stitched together to form one-hundred-fifty-foot-long roofs hung over a frame of bamboo and sunk into the dirt. The walls were dried mud piled three feet high and smoothed by trowel. The only structures made of more substantial material were eleven stone watchtowers dotted around the perimeter set just back from the wall and the keep in the center of the camp.

Carny looked closer at the keep as they passed overhead. It was larger than he'd expected. He guessed it to be two hundred yards by three hundred yards. It was difficult to tell how tall it was, but he could definitely see the thickness of the walls. There was an outer row of blocks, a space that appeared to be filled with debris, then an inner row of blocks. Maybe someone was planning on building a castle.

"Guess we're staying after all," Carny said, looking up and finding Miska looking at him.

She beamed. "I know. With the Kingdom this far west and establishing a permanent presence, the Forest Collective must be all but finished," she said, completely missing his sarcasm.

"What's that?" Knockers asked, pointing to a large area being excavated near Iron Fist.

"Guess that's the roost for the rags," Carny said. He'd never seen an actual roost, but as there were already several rags penned in part of the depression, it was a good bet.

"I see other castles, too," Knockers said, pointing to the west.

Carny couldn't get mad at Knockers, but the boy was forever grinding on him with his constant curiosity and general amazement at every fucking thing they saw.

"Those aren't castles—too small," the Bard said. He'd kept his head down and worked on lyrics almost the entire flight. As one of the few literate soldiers in the shield, possibly the entire javelin, the Bard held a special position. For taking a few flicks to sit and listen to one of the songs he was working on, he'd pen a missive home for you to your wife or family.

Carny looked. "The Bard's right. Those are small forts. Looks like they're putting one up on every hill taller than the grass."

"What are those wooden towers for then?" Miska asked.

Carny squinted. "For scaring slyts. Those are cats."

Miska shrugged.

"Catapults." He counted at least fifteen of them spread around in the different fortress positions. Looked like two per fortress, although he saw a couple with only one each. Those cats looked significantly bigger than the others. "High Command is really going all out."

"The Forest Collective is on the run!" Ahmy said, reiterating his beliefs in case anyone within shouting distance wasn't already perfectly clear about them. "We will overcome. You will see."

"You could be right, Ahmy," Carny said.

The devout Dendro looked surprised. Carny didn't have the

energy to have yet another deep discussion with Ahmy about the High Druid and the meaning of life. Agreeing with him actually worked to shut him up… sometimes.

"Say, LC," Knockers said, pulling himself up to a kneeling position. "They've gone and put forts on all the hills, but how come they haven't put any on the tops of the mountains?"

Men laughed. Carny thought about that.

"Well, it's a long way to climb up there, for starters. We half wore our legs off going up and down the mountain on the coast, and we weren't trying to haul anything bigger than Big Hog's carcass."

Those who had been on the mountain laughed. Big Hog held up a hand and made an appropriate rude gesture.

"Even if you did, not much you could do from up there anyway. If the slyts attack they'll have to come into the valley and by the looks of it, if they do that, they'll wish they hadn't."

Knockers nodded, but he didn't look convinced. Carny decided to indulge him.

"You doubt our fearless leaders?"

Knockers's eyes widened. "No. No, it's just that they taught us in training that having the high ground was always the best."

The shield grew quiet. Knockers was right, and that was troubling enough without looking at the ramifications of what that meant for them.

The normally son-of-a-prick flock commander came to the rescue. He turned in his saddle and addressed them. "Lads, you see those nasty little rags that have been flying with us? Well, even if every slyt in the FnC were to haul bony ass up to those mountain peaks, those sparkers would make sure they were R-and-T'd before the slyts had a chance to boil a pot of water."

Laughter broke out as the tension evaporated. "Fucking right!"

Carny caught the flock commander's eye. The man wasn't grinning. He nodded at Carny and turned away.

Miska called to Carny, asking what *R-and-T'd* meant.

"'Roasted and toasted,'" Carny said, enjoying her obvious

discomfort at the image. "You ain't seen nothing until you see a charred slyt. They curl up like a caterpillar. Skin and muscles shrink so much the bones often snap. And the smell…"

Miska turned her head and heaved, trying to cover her mouth. Wiz shot Carny a glare and leaned over to help her. Carny shrugged and sat back down, ignoring the eyes of the men looking at him. He'd gone too far. *Fuck her.* She wanted to know what it was really like out here. Let her go and walk through a pile of charred slyts, hear the fat crackle as they burned. Maybe then she'd drop the bullshit.

The bamboo whistle sounded.

"You heard the man," Carny said, strapping himself back in and taking stock of his equipment. "Strap up, cinch up, and bolt up," he said, cocking his crossbow and sliding a bolt into the firing groove. "Looks peaceful down there, but that's just the way Faery Crud likes it."

Carduus slowed his wings, then held them out perpendicular to his body. The sudden silence was always unnerving, but Carny had grown to appreciate the feel of the wind. If he closed his eyes, he could imagine he was flying by himself.

Then the angle of the rag changed, and what was a glorious sensation of flight became one of accelerating fall. Carduus hit some rolly blues as they descended below the mountain peaks. His massive body shook and bucked like a canoe in rapids. Carny looked up and down the rag making sure everyone was in place. He caught Miska's eye. She looked miserable. Her bosom was bouncing, but no one was enjoying the show now. He grinned and waved at her.

"Welcome to the Valley of Bone and Thunder!"

SHIELD LEADER LISTOWK reached up and took his pipe out of the linen band he'd wrapped around his helm. Until the Lux he'd never smoked, but it calmed his nerves, which seemed more on edge these days. He sat on the northern wall of the castle and watched the valley as dusk gave way to night. It had been a long day in the air and he was glad to have dirt under his boots again.

He'd asked the sentries in the watchtower nearest him if slyts were in the area, but they'd laughed and told him to take all the wall he wanted.

"I have to say," the senior sentry had said, leaning out over the parapet of his tower, "we haven't seen a slyt since we got here, and that was three weeks ago. Little bastards must have turned tail and run when they heard us coming."

Listowk didn't bother to reveal his rank and climbed the wall with thanks. He walked along it until he found a spot just far enough away from the tower that chatting would be discouraged, but not so far that they couldn't see him. It was night, and this was slyt country.

He glanced to the right and made out the light of the small oil lamp they had in their watch post. Nodding, he turned back to the valley. The saw grass, so named for its serrated edges, stood silent watch. It covered the hill all along the north and west sides, giving way to dosha swamps when it reached the bottom. An occasional rustle in the grass was most likely a rat or some other varmint.

A heron, or maybe it was a crane, slowly flew past Listowk's vantage point heading south. He never could remember which was which. He watched it until it vanished into the darkness.

A boy like Ahmist probably would have seen an omen in that. Listowk didn't, but all the same, he would have preferred it had headed north. He turned and looked that way. The valley narrowed as it went north, hemmed in to the east by the tall mountain the troops were already calling the Codpiece for its roughly similar outline. Listowk didn't see it, but he hadn't had anything to drink yet, either.

Behind him, the din of hundreds of soldiers, flockmen, rags, and mules ebbed and flowed. He did his best to ignore it, but every so often a voice would pierce the night and he would catch a sliver of conversation, part of a joke, the tail end of a threat. That was one of the reasons he was out here and not back there. The boys needed a night to get settled. They'd already found three distilleries set up for business by the first shields to arrive. Best thing for Listowk was to stay out of the way and let them enjoy.

Something crawled on his right arm and he swatted it with his left hand, not bothering to see what it was. Rubbing away the carcass, he reached down and placed his hand on his crossbow. He knew the weapon was still there—he felt its weight on his thighs—but he liked to feel it with his fingertips. Reassured, he went about filling his pipe, taking his time to tap the tobacco down deep into the bowl.

Knockers had taken to carving pipes out of a black-brown wood he'd found that was nearly as hard as iron. Took the poor lad a week to make one pipe, but he went at it like his life depended on it. Knockers had insisted on giving the first one to him. He'd tried to refuse, but Knockers looked like he might cry, so Listowk accepted the pipe.

Satisfied with his tamping job, Listowk put the stem of the pipe in his mouth and began patting down his aketon looking for his flint striker. He realized it had gotten so dark he could barely see the tops of his boots. *Maybe left this a little late*, he thought, but kept patting for the striker anyway.

"Found it," he said, pulling it out of a pocket. He slipped the C-shaped steel striker over the knuckles of his right hand and took the piece of flint in his left. Positioning the flint over the bowl of the pipe, he raised the striker and then brought it down, sending a shower of sparks into the bowl. On the fourth try the tobacco caught and began glowing a bright orange.

He drew in a few puffs and just as quickly blew them back out. *Tastes like shit.*

The grass rustled again. He slowly put the striker and flint back in his pocket. Just as slowly, he gathered up his crossbow in his hands and gently eased the safety lever off. Despite the sentries' shouts that the only thing he was likely to shoot was himself, Listowk had cocked it and put a bolt in the groove.

The glow from the pipe blurred his vision, so he moved

the bowl to the side using his tongue on the stem. Squinting, he searched the grass, but there was nothing to see. The entire Forest Collective could have been camped twenty feet away and he wouldn't have seen them.

He sat still, drawing the occasional puff and listening, but no more rustling sounded. Bored and feeling slightly ill, he took the pipe out of his mouth and banged it against the wall. He watched the embers fall down to the moat and extinguish in the slimy mud at the bottom.

The sound of something crashing back in the castle was quickly followed by raised voices. Listowk wasn't sure, but he thought he heard Big Hog. He tucked his pipe back in the linen band.

"Time I checked in on the lads," he said, thumbing the safety back in place and un-notching the bolt. He swung his legs up and over the wall and around so that his back faced the saw grass. Easing his body forward, he reached out with his feet and found the wooden walkway. He jumped down, impressed that the walkway didn't sway. He had to give it to those mules; they built stuff to last.

More raised voices and the sound of running boots. Definitely time to see what they were up to.

He had just started walking toward the end near the watchtower when something hit the outside of the mud wall. He stopped and leaned over. An arrow stuck out of the mud right across from him. Were it not for the wall it would have hit him square in the balls. He froze, straining to hear or see the shooter.

He slowly turned his head away so that he used the side of his vision. Still nothing. He waited a few more flicks, then reached down and pulled the arrow out.

He ran his fingers along the shaft until he felt the fine grooves that had been cut into it with a knife. He didn't need light to see that they weren't random but mule runes. He had no love for the mules, but he'd grown to have a grudging respect for many of their ways. One was their skill at building. The other was their rune alphabet. You could convey a lot of information in a few runes.

Listowk rolled the arrow between his fingertips. He'd been right; the slyts were here and had Iron Fist under observation. He'd bet his left nut that they were sizing up the forts all over the valley, too.

He rubbed the shaft of the arrow against the edge of his rank shield until the runes were sanded away, then put the arrow in his quiver. More boots thudded on the ground and he caught a snippet that sounded like "you fucking bastards!"

He walked to the ladder and had just begun climbing down when the sentry poked his head out. "Figured you'd call it quits soon enough. All the action is in there."

"It does sound it," Listowk said, looking toward the barracks.

"I'd say come back again in broad daylight, but even then there's nothing to see out there," the sentry said, pointing toward the valley floor. "Been here three weeks, haven't seen a fucking thing."

"I believe you," Listowk said, resuming his climb down the ladder.

When he got to the bottom he paused. Bastard had shot it right at him.

"Good hunting, Wraith," he said, reaching into his quill and pulling out the arrow. As he walked into the camp he snapped the arrow in two and dropped it to the ground.

CHAPTER THIRTY

WRAITH WAITED UNTIL LISTOWK grabbed the arrow before turning and following after the two slyts who had been watching the camp. The slyts moved fast through the grass but made very little sound. Wraith had left his helm, aketon, and hewer in camp, taking only his short bow, a soft cloth quiver with thirteen arrows, and a hunting knife. Even then he was struggling to keep up with the slyts and keep quiet.

His awe at their stealth diminished when he reached the small animal trail they were using. Now he understood how they could move so fast and so silently. He stepped onto the path and crouched down. It was just a little wider than he was, and about five feet high. The slyts had woven the saw grass on either side to create walls and then carefully intertwined the tops in an arch, effectively hiding the trail from observation from above. It was simple and brilliant.

Even in the dark, Wraith could tell the path was well worn and had been used many times. As he followed the slyts down the hill he came across several paths that branched off from the main one. Small twigs had been stuck into the ground at the intersections, which he took to be markers. He was certain the paths would lead to the various fortress positions in the valley, but he'd have to confirm that later.

As Wraith approached the bottom of the hill he slowed. He knew there were dosha swamps there, which meant the slyts would be in the open. He crept the last few yards until he arrived at the end of the saw grass and the path. He looked out over the dosha swamp expecting to see at least the shadowy forms of the slyts, but they were nowhere to be seen.

Did they take another path?

Wraith eased himself back from the opening and began retracing his steps. After fifty yards and no sign of the slyts he stopped and sat down. Resting his bow in his lap, he closed his eyes and listened. Nothing. He opened his eyes and looked at the saw grass again. The weave wasn't neat, but it was solid. He put a hand down on the path and pressed on the dirt. It was compacted. A lot of feet had passed over it.

No closer to an answer, Wraith debated his next move. He'd been confident tracking the slyts would be possible. The idea of going back now and admitting to Listowk that he'd failed grated, but flailing about in the dark was stupid.

Reluctantly, Wraith followed the path back to the wall, nursing his wounded pride. He paused at the moat, then slid down it, stepping across the sludge in the bottom and scaling the other side. He waited for a sentry to call out, but none did. Slinging his bow, he reached up to the top of the wall and pulled himself up. He waited again for a sentry to shout an alarm but to no avail.

Thoroughly frustrated, Wraith walked the wooden gangway to the end and jumped down to the ground. He started walking toward Red Shield's barrack, then paused when he heard raised voices. It wasn't that he didn't like the other soldiers, but he found being in close quarters with them for any length of time created a sense of unease inside him.

He turned away, deciding to find a little place of his own to hole up for the night. He'd still tell Listowk that he failed, but that could wait until morning. It wasn't his pride that mattered; it was his sense of who he was as a man and a hunter. These slyts had outfoxed him. Had they known he was there? He didn't think so, but he'd keep at it until he could stay on their track or they found him.

He wasn't looking where he walked and his boot caught on a twig. *Fuck, I'm getting sloppy.* He stopped and looked down. Squatting, he picked up two pieces of an arrow.

Wraith held the arrow pieces in his hands. He rolled the shaft between his fingertips and gently brushed the fletchings. He looked toward the barracks, then stood up and headed off in a different direction. Behind him, the broken arrow rested in the dirt exactly as before.

CARNY STRETCHED OUT on the sailcloth hammock acting as his bunk and watched the festivities. He had to give it to the dwarves—they built quality stuff. Hammocks lined both sides of the barrack, strung between large bamboo poles sunk into the ground, which doubled as roof supports. The whole barrack reeked of mold, but the smell of the shield was already overwhelming it.

An aisle six feet wide separated the rows. Bamboo pegs had been hammered into the poles, giving the soldiers ample places to hang their gear. Woven grass mats were placed by every hammock. The dwarves had even dug fire pits every seventy-five feet in the aisle.

It was perfect. Well, almost. The reason for the current commotion was the dwarves' sense of height, or rather, lack thereof. The roof of the barrack, yard after yard of faded sailcloth, was only five feet off the ground. Carny didn't see it as all that big an issue. They'd had far less headroom on board the navy's *Daeskus* on the trip over.

"You loathsome little vermin did this on purpose!" Ahmy said. He was currently being restrained by Knockers and the fawn, Frogleg. Blood poured from a gash on Ahmy's head where he'd hit a bamboo cross-pole.

A group of ten to fifteen dwarves stood just inside the entrance of the barrack staring up at Ahmy with murder in their eyes. Carny knew he should be intervening. He was second-in-command, and with Listowk absent, he was command.

"Fuck it," Carny said, stuffing more Flower into his cheek. "Fuck all of it." He meant it too. Ahmy could damn well deal with his own shit. Let the dwarves kill him. It would save Carny a lot of heartache. Besides, the dwarves weren't staring daggers at him this time, which was a nice change. He squinted from his hammock, trying to make out the dwarves in the lantern light. They looked familiar, but then all dwarves looked alike. Still, these ones seemed particularly... obstinate.

"You want space above your head?" one of the dwarves said, stepping forward. "I will send you to your sky forest right now."

"LC, aren't you going to do something?!" Knockers shouted, struggling with Ahmy. Frogleg's heart was in it, but he was as scrawny as his namesake with about half the strength. The rest of the shield that were there were drunk or otherwise enjoying a few medicinal herbs. Ahmy, naturally, was sober, but that only made him more manic. It occurred to Carny that what Ahmy needed was a few drinks, a wad of Flower, and a snort of Sliver. Maybe, just maybe, he'd calm the fuck down.

Ahmy spit, because of course he would. The dwarf lunged, and the lantern nearest the door crashed to the ground. Shouts, grunts, and a single scream echoed through the barrack. Carny closed his eyes, the thumps of fists against flesh coming to him over a great distance, like the sounds of waves crashing on the beach. He missed the mountains.

High-pitched shouting rose up over the din and someone started blowing a bamboo whistle. Carny instinctively rolled to port, expecting the rag to bank, and fell out of his hammock onto the floor.

"Mercy sakes, all of you! Stop this at once!"

Carny pushed himself up from the floor and looked over his hammock. The lantern had been picked up and relit. It was officer so-and-so, the human in charge of the dwarves. He was barefoot, holding his trousers up with one hand and his hewer in the other, though it was still in its scabbard. Carny wondered if he realized that.

SL Listowk strolled in and looked around the room. Carny caught his eye and waved. Listowk ignored him.

"Shield Leader, thank the High Druid. I'm at my wit's end. I really am. I just—"

Listowk walked past the officer and to Ahmy. Without missing a beat he punched Ahmy in the gut, dropping him to the floor and taking Knockers and Frogleg with him. Carny had never really given much thought to the expression about hearing a pin drop, but in that moment he was convinced he could.

Listowk looked around at the members of Red Shield. "In your bunks, lanterns out, now. Where's Big Hog?"

"A few slyt villagers have a compound here in camp," Knockers said, getting to his feet. "They do the laundry and stuff. Big Hog went to talk with them about the land. Said if we're going to be here awhile he'd see about planting a garden."

"When he gets back, tell him he's now the LC." The soldiers looked over at Carny.

Carny shrugged. *Never wanted the fucking job.*

Listowk turned and faced the officer. "Sir, I suggest you take your men with you and call it a night."

The officer looked down at the groaning Ahmy, then at Listowk. "I can't say that I approve—"

"Now would be good, sir."

The officer paused. Carny could see the man's mind going through the scenarios. He was the highest-ranking soldier in the room, but when all was tallied that added up to fuck-all.

"Out," the officer said, turning and motioning to the door.

The dwarves shuffled their feet but didn't appear ready to leave.

"*Out! Out the… the fucking door now!*" the officer shouted, the veins on his neck bulging as if he'd swallowed a nest of snakes.

Carny made a half step toward the door before he realized the officer was talking to the dwarves. With a few glares, the dwarves turned and left the barracks. The officer took one last look at Ahmy and then turned and vanished into the night.

Listowk looked around the room. His face gave nothing

away, but Carny could feel the anger. He knew he should say something, but the damage was done.

"Get your rest," Listowk said, heading for the door. "Tomorrow's going to be a long day."

Quiet reigned in the barrack as Red Shield stood and looked at the doorway. Finally, Knockers broke the silence. "What do you think he meant by that?"

The answers weren't helpful.

As everyone went to their hammocks Carny sighed and walked over to the groaning form of Ahmist. He looked down at him for a long time. Finally, because there was nothing else for it, he dragged the boy down the aisle to his hammock and lifted him into it.

When Carny climbed back into his own hammock his happy feeling was long gone. He didn't bother with more Flower because he could tell he'd be chasing that feeling the rest of the night. As the lanterns went out, Carny lay back and stared up at the canvas roof. Of all the soldiers in Red Shield, he figured he was the only one wishing for the morning to come.

CHAPTER THIRTY-ONE

R ED SHIELD MARCHED the valley floor for a quarter candle, turning toward and then away from the eastern mountains. The peaks cast long, pointed shadows across the valley floor, creating the image of walking into a giant maw. Carny brought his boot down hard on the first shadow tooth he reached, daring the jaw to bite into him. He felt stupid, but if soldiers could wear amulets of the Sacred Tree and others with seeds and nuts from trees in their villages around their necks and tiny scrolls with safekeeping spells on them tucked inside their helmets, then he could and would kick these teeth.

The shield marched in silence. The events of last night coated everything like the dew on the grass. Ahmist walked with a calm, unwavering smile that Carny found disturbing. Big Hog refused to look at Carny, while Listowk remained near the front of the shield marching as if he'd been taken over by Sinte's ghost.

Carny expected Listowk to give them a break when they reached the Formaske River. They could all see the other shields that were fanning out across the valley and marching toward the jungle on either side. Several were stopped, their soldiers standing around talking, smoking, taking a piss. Carny wouldn't have minded all three.

Listowk, it turned out, had other ideas and instead of leading the shield over the low, wide bridge the dwarves had built, he turned left. Wraith moved to take ST and began searching the saw grass along the riverbank.

They were less than a mile from the northern end of the valley when Wraith stopped, turned to Listowk, and shrugged. Listowk immediately turned to the river and walked right into it. After a stunned few flicks, the shield followed, wading across in water up to their armpits, with their weapons held above their heads. It was cool, much more so than Carny thought it would be.

Soaking wet, the shield slogged their way across a series of untended dosha swamps instead of walking along the earthen berms that surrounded them. It was like walking through shit-colored snow. The dry top crust of the dosha swamp broke and they sank to their knees in fetid mud. The smell was vile. Carny gagged, but he hadn't eaten since yesterday so nothing came up.

They were being punished, that much was obvious, but to Carny's mind it was excessive. He brightened when Listowk took the shield out of the fifth dosha swamp and onto the berm. Finally.

A few flicks later, Listowk swerved and set off through a tangled mess of saw grass and bamboo. The long-silent shield began to grumble, but no one spoke loud enough to draw attention to himself.

The dew vanished and the air quickly became hotter and heavier. Sweat coated Carny in a wet sheen from head to toe. The insides of his thighs at his crotch started itching. He desperately wanted to grab some camphor out of his pack and rub it on, but Listowk's fast pace made that impossible.

Carny usually dreaded the tree line because it meant crossing over from open, safe space into the dark unknown. He didn't like it. He didn't understand Wraith's willingness to go into it alone, and at night. There was nothing friendly or inviting about the jungle the way there was about the forests back home. Everything here was overgrown, tangled, covered in barbs, and crawling with bugs that scared Carny more than rags.

By the time they reached the eastern tree line at the edge of the mountains the shield was a sweating, groaning shambles. With most—Carny included—suffering from the ill effects of their binge the night before, Carny doubted they could fend off a rabbit.

"Drink," Listowk ordered. No smile, no banter.

Carny forced himself to walk the few steps to where Big Hog had slumped against a tree trunk.

"So, could you plant corn here?"

Big Hog studied the water skin in his hands as if it were the first time he'd seen one.

Carny looked around, then back at Big Hog. "Look, I'm sorry. I didn't know Listowk would pick you."

"You mean you didn't care," Big Hog said, looking up from his water skin. "That's you, isn't it, Carny? Nothing matters. Not us, not the war, not the Kingdom."

"The Kingdom?" Carny said, cracking a smile. "You've been out in the sun too long."

Big Hog didn't smile back. "Yeah, the Kingdom. I know you think it's all one big joke, but I believe in it. I believe in what we're doing over here. It's messy, but that's what wars are. What do you think would happen if the Forest Collective took over? You think they are going to teach these people how to farm and make better lives?"

Carny looked around, but all he got were blank stares. "You're a farmer with more kids than cows on some piece of dirt in the backwoods. You really telling me you care about what happens here?"

"No, Carny, I'm done telling you anything," Big Hog said, slinging his water skin and pushing off the tree. He stood a foot away from Carny, looking down at him. "Drink your water, we've got a lot of climbing ahead."

Carny watched Big Hog's back as the soldier turned and walked over to Listowk. The rest of the shield started slinging their equipment and preparing to move out.

"Vooford was right, you know," Carny said, his cheeks flushing. "Every one of us here is a fool for fighting this war.

The king that ordered it is dead, and he wasn't even a real king."

Soldiers started walking past Carny as Listowk set off into the trees. Carny looked around him. He spotted Knockers and reached out a hand to grab his arm. Knockers pulled his arm away and kept on walking.

Carny stood there until he was the last one. He could probably walk back to the barracks and no one would care. *They'd like that.* He stood there a few flicks more, then kicked his boot across the dirt and followed after them.

SUBCOMMANDER PARMIK WATCHED the shields disappear into the eastern tree line from his vantage point atop cat 4 in Fortress Thunder II. He didn't envy the soldiers tramping through that jungle. They were little more than bait, at best hunting dogs sent to flush out prey for the cats. It looked like sweaty, dangerous work.

Parmik preferred working with the cats. He chose not to examine too closely the fact that they were huge. Parmik just knew that of all the duties in the service, chucking large rocks spoke to him. Yes, the danger of being crushed, or torn to pieces if a main brace exploded under pressure, was always present, but he'd take that any day over marching in that damn jungle.

A light wind from the north fluttered the map of the valley resting across his knees. He looked up at the flagpole on cat 4 to judge the speed. Of the three triangle flags on the pole, the lowest, made of blue silk, flapped fitfully. Above it, the yellow flag made of cotton barely moved, while the top flag, a red triangle of linen, was perfectly still. Parmik looked over at cat 3, positioned thirty yards to the south of cat 4; unlike cat 4, it currently faced toward the western mountains. Its wind flags were in concurrence with cat 3's.

Parmik opened the cover of his leather-covered notebook and wrote down the wind conditions and time of day. Unlike standard candle time, the artillerists used the position of the sun. He knew the wind would pick up as the day progressed, but for now there was no need to make a correction to the cats' aiming points. He traced his charcoal stick along the grids that marked the fire sector for cats 3 and 4 and the path the shields were going to take today. As long as the soldiers stuck to the plan, his cats would be able to support them with crushing fire.

Cat 4 trembled slightly and the sound of heavy boots vibrated up through the structure. "Master Magnolia," Parmik said, looking down from his perch at the climbing dwarf wizard.

"Commander Parmik," Magnolia replied, huffing as he negotiated the last few rungs and plopped himself down on the crossbeam beside Parmik. "A lovely morning."

Parmik looked back out at the valley. Fortress Thunder II sat on a low rise on the eastern side of the river a half mile from the southern end of the valley. It was surrounded by dosha swamps on all sides and topped with a patch of bamboo; it had taken the dwarves two weeks to build a wide-enough road to haul the cats into position and then another week to clear the top. The fortress wall of mud bricks was only three feet high, but Parmik had been assured the dwarves would be back to build it higher when the keep in Iron Fist was finished.

"It is that," Parmik said, unsure where he stood with Magnolia. "I wanted to thank you again for allowing twenty of your dwarves to stay here and help with the barrack." Parmik looked down at the squat, square structure placed in the center of the fortress. Unlike the large barracks within Iron Fist, Parmik had insisted that the fortress barrack have a wooden roof. He would have preferred stone, but what wasn't being eaten up by the keep was needed for shot for the cats.

"You think like a dwarf," Magnolia said. "You could easily put more logs and dirt on top of this roof, should that become necessary."

Had anyone else said Parmik thought like a dwarf he would have known it to be an insult. Coming from Magnolia he felt reasonably certain it was a compliment. "I hope it doesn't come to that, but I'd rather prepare for the worst."

"Wise," Magnolia said. After a pause he turned and looked at

Parmik. "Tell me, just how much worse might it get? They don't exactly tell us a whole lot."

"This valley is vital to the FnCs. Just by being here we've cut off their major supply route to their forces farther east," he said, pointing down at the Formaske. "They can go around of course, but that would add weeks to their journey and the army is moving to block those routes as well. This is the most direct and fastest way east. Without it, their forces will wither and die. They need to come take this valley back."

"I see," Magnolia said. "So we are, essentially, bait."

Parmik didn't like the sound of that at all. "No, more like an anvil. If the FnCs come they'll smash themselves to bits on all of this," Parmik said, motioning with his hands to take in all the fortress positions. He allowed himself some pride. "We have eighteen field cats, five boomers—oh, that's counterweight trebuchets—under construction, and fifty harrow throwers coming in this week."

"I'm not familiar with harrow throwers."

Parmik opened his book to a fresh page and began sketching. "They're light throwers, not like our cats. You know a harrow used in the field, to rake the soil?"

"Farming was never anything I tried my hand at," Magnolia said.

"Right. Well, it's really just a rectangle frame with rows of long spikes. Imagine you stood that on its side, and instead of spikes nailed in place, you had rows of bolts. One hundred fifty in total in five horizontal rows of thirty bolts each."

Magnolia nodded. "It sounds horrifying."

"Well, yes," Parmik said, feeling guilty but not knowing why. "They're a close-in weapon, really meant to protect the cats should the slyts somehow get this far."

"Another part of the anvil, then."

Parmik felt that Magnolia was accusing him of something.

"Yes," Parmik said, his answer curt. *I have no intention of having my head cut off by a slyt.*

"The world's a curious place," Magnolia said. "So much

effort put into killing each other."

Parmik had no answer for that.

The dwarf shifted on the wooden beam and smiled at Parmik. "My apologies, I have been told I get a bit too philosophical for my own good."

Parmik forced a smile. "It does make you think."

Magnolia sighed. "You know, we actually want the same thing, simply to be free to decide our own fate. The world is so obviously changing, and though we sit here on an engine of war, I hope the changes are for the better."

Parmik looked behind him toward Iron Fist. The dwarves were building a second infirmary so that their wounded could be housed separately from the men. Bear Battery had three more men on sick duty just this morning. He'd expected a few falls, some cuts, even runny bowels and sun vapors, but far and away the biggest injuries were black eyes, broken teeth, and bloody knuckles.

Parmik turned and looked back at the eastern mountains. He only grunted when Magnolia got up and bid him a good morning before climbing down. He sat on the beam and swung his legs as the sun came over the peaks. His map slid off his thighs and floated out past the fortress wall, finally landing in the muck of the dosha swamp.

He stared at it for some time. One corner snagged on some weeds and kept the map out of the filth. If he went down now he could probably save it. He stared at it some more.

Fuck it, I'll send one of the dwarves to go get it.

"IT'S A DISGRACE, is what it is," Dragonsmith Pagath said, picking up a handful of stone and holding it up in front of Vorly's face. "It's limestone. Limestone!" he shouted, crushing the rock into powder.

"I am aware," Vorly said, looking around at their roost. Jomkier was a palace by comparison. Without a quarry to commandeer in the valley, they'd settled for a rocky, sandy hill to the immediate north of Iron Fist. The mules had done an amazing job carving out a depression creating enough room for six flocks, but that still left four with nowhere to roost. Their solution, while ingenious, created a different set of problems.

"Would you rather be in the granite?" Vorly asked. Normally, the answer would be yes. Rags liked to roost with strong, heavy rock around them. Dense rock held the heat and helped the beasts maintain the tremendously high internal temperature they needed to prevent them from slipping into dormancy. Waking a sleeping rag was not for the faint of heart. The only granite to be found here, however, was in the sides of the mountains lining the valley. The downside, and it was huge, was that it meant slyts could sneak up on the roost from the jungle.

Pagath spit. "It's a damn disgrace is what it is."

"You mentioned that," Vorly said. "Look, no one is happy about it, but there's damn little we can do to change it."

Pagath looked up at Vorly. "They could stop building that keep for starters. All that stone could build some nice walls for my rags."

Vorly knew it was true. The commander of the forces in the valley, Commander Weel of the Second Legion, had taken the creation of Frontier Castle Iron Fist to heart. Mud walls weren't good enough for him. Instead, the majority of the mules had been set to work building a monstrous keep out of stone. Its walls already rose fifteen feet and the rumor was he was building just as deep belowground. Judging by the amount of spoil being hauled away from the construction and dumped into the dosha swamps, Vorly figured it was true.

"Well, I hear that Weel is trying to talk Modelar into drafting some of the rags to pick up some stone and fly it over to the keep," Vorly said, waiting for Pagath to explode. Hauling stone, wood, and other supplies was nothing new for rags. In fact, it had been one of the first things they'd been used for. Their rear claws were massive and powerful yet could hold a man without crushing him. Still, using prime Aero rags for ox work wasn't an option.

"That could work," Pagath said, tugging on the two braids of his beard.

Vorly shook his head. "That could work? If I suggested that you'd have my scalp."

Pagath let go of his braids and looked at Vorly. "If you said it it'd be because you thought it was a good idea."

"I'm lost."

"With Weel's permission, we fly over to the little quarry they're carving out of the mountain, pick up some stones, and fly them back. We drop one off at the keep and two at the roost."

Vorly reached up and scratched his head. "You, Master Dragonsmith, are one wily little bastard."

Pagath waved away the compliment. "It's a gift. Now get out of my roost and go get Weel's permission to rob him blind."

CHAPTER THIRTY-TWO

LISTOWK CURSED UNDER HIS breath and held up his fist for the shield to halt. They weren't a third of the way up the mountain and the sun was dropping behind the western peaks. If they didn't turn around now they'd be marching back to the camp in the dark, and he didn't know the area well enough for that yet. Holing up out here for the night was an even worse option.

It was his own damn fault. He was still pissed come the morning at their asinine behavior and had wanted to march them into the ground, Carny most of all. He'd succeeded, but now they were exhausted and barely moving. He'd let his temper get the best of him. He hoped it didn't cost them.

"Drink up, lads, catch your breath, and we'll start heading back," Listowk said, walking back down the path and smiling at the soldiers he met. "If you're nice and quiet I'll even take you over the new bridge." They were good lads. Young, stupid, and brash, but they had good hearts. He was SL now, and if he couldn't lead them any better than Sinte he'd eat his rank shield.

The mood of the shield rose as word spread that they were done climbing. And no more dosha swamps and rivers.

Listowk had reached the rear guard and turned to look back up the path when Wraith appeared at his side.

"We're being watched."

Listowk tensed. "How many?"

"At least two pairs, either side of the path."

Fuck. He motioned to Big Hog, who stood a few feet away, and filled him in on the situation. "I'll take the shield down. Big Hog, you hang back with six men and cover us. Once we're through you pull back and we'll cover you. The star arrow for the cats is red. When we reach the tree line I'll fire it and that should get us some cat shots if those boys aren't already half in the bag."

"You think they've got the distances all calibrated?" Wraith asked.

Listowk nodded. "They've been here for weeks. All they do is calculate distances." He could still see the cat shot that landed at his feet outside that little village.

"You don't want to engage them?" Big Hog asked. "Only four of them."

Listowk looked at the soldier. "You looking to earn a medal now that you're LC?"

Big Hog snorted. "Just tired of going up and down mountains with nothing to show for it but blisters on my feet. If we're here to fight, let's fight and get it over with."

Listowk understood Big Hog's frustration. He knew the soldier wasn't vainglorious. He was like most of them, sick and tired of marching and flying and more marching all over Luitox looking for an enemy who showed little desire to engage in a sustained battle.

"Battle will come soon enough," Listowk said, knowing he had to be the cooler head. "Let's just get the shield back to the barracks in one piece for today. Wraith, go do what you do and see if you have better luck this time," Listowk said.

If Wraith was insulted he didn't show it. Listowk turned and motioned for the shield to start moving. When he turned back to where Wraith stood the soldier was gone.

A buzz of whispers rose and fell as word was passed that they were being watched. Men buttoned up aketons and gripped their crossbows with far more intensity than before. Knockers began chewing on the stem of his pipe so hard the bowl bobbed in front of his face like a big fat bee.

"Easy now, my boys, we can do this," Listowk said, calmly speaking in a low voice as the soldiers moved past him. What he wanted to avoid above all else was a stampede down the path. If even one soldier spooked, the odds of the others bolting would increase. Who knew what the slyts might do then?

Listowk felt confident that there were no more than four slyts out there, but it wasn't absolute. The slyts had proven time and again to be a slippery foe. In all his time in the Lux he'd rarely seen a live FnC fighter. Usually, all he saw were charked remains. Worse, these slyts had eluded Wraith.

The shield leapfrogged down the hill, the rear guard passing through the vanguard and then reversing the process. It was slow, and hard on the nerves, but it gave them protection should the slyts decide to suddenly attack from the rear.

When the first arrow flew the shield was only twenty yards from the tree line. Listowk could see dosha swamps through the trees. The attack, however, came from the front, at the edge of the tree line. Listowk cursed his foolishness. With all his focus on what was behind them, he'd assumed that the closer they got to the valley floor the safer they'd be.

A soldier screamed. A whistle sounded in the jungle off to the left and was answered by one on the right. Arrows sliced through the foliage from both sides of the path and from positions between them and the tree line. The shield returned fire, the heavy twang of crossbows mixing with the sound of enemy whistles and the *fft* sound of arrows tearing through leaves.

"Stay low! Keep moving toward the valley!" Listowk shouted, looking into the jungle for something to shoot at. The slyts had to be close or their arrows wouldn't be making it through the foliage. He saw two arrows come in and stick into the ground at a steep angle.

"They're in the trees, shoot high!"

The shield became quiet as they shot and reloaded. The bowmen kept up a steady stream of fire throughout. Wraith was nowhere to be seen, but a slyt tumbled from a tree with an arrow in his right eye not five yards from Listowk. It was one of Wraith's arrows.

"Keep moving, keep moving!" Listowk ordered, slapping soldiers on the shoulder and even kicking a few to get them up and heading toward the valley. The fire between them and the tree line lessened as Wraith systematically cut down the slyts blocking their escape. Listowk estimated ten, no more than fifteen, slyts.

With nothing to shoot at, Listowk aimed his crossbow in a likely area and fired, then quickly reloaded with a red star. As he reached the edge of the valley he pointed his weapon in the air and shot again. The arrow flew skyward, trailing a stream of red smoke and fire.

"Skirmish line, form a skirmish line!" Listowk shouted as soldiers emerged from the jungle. He directed them to the left and right, counting them as they emerged. The berm of the dosha swamp provided good protection, although it was only ten yards from the trees.

"Wizard!"

Carny and Bard appeared carrying a third soldier between them. Two arrows stuck out of the soldier's chest. Listowk couldn't see who it was.

A booming clang sounded from somewhere in the distance.

"Fuck!" Listowk turned and saw a small dark objecting arcing through the sky. He'd panicked and fired the star too soon. Not all the shield were out of the jungle yet. Two of his men were still in there.

"Cat shot! Down, down, down!"

LEGION FLOCK COMMANDER Walf Modelar did his best to be pleasant, which he'd have been the first to admit was a peak he rarely summited. He looked around the main room of the keep and a sneer of contempt twisted his lips. *Looks like a Druid-damned whorehouse in a cave.* Woven mats of saw grass covered the stone floor. The ten-foot-thick stone walls were covered in carpets and tapestries. Burning lanterns hung from the eight-foot-high ceiling and along the walls, which was useful because there were no fucking windows. Not one. He shivered. Modelar looked up at the log ceiling and then down. Right now there was a solid six feet of logs, earth, and stone above his head. For a career rag driver used to the open skies, it was a nightmare.

"Nice little place," Modelar said, turning to Legion Commander Weel and doing his best to turn his sneer into a smile.

"In time it will shape up nicely, but for now we all must make do with what we have," Weel said.

"About that," Modelar said, not bothering with small talk. The sooner he got out of this death trap the better. "My rags are out in the open. I need the stone from that quarry to build the roost and put walls between my rags."

"And you're welcome to all you need," Weel said, sounding sincere, "once my fortifications are complete."

Modelar drew in a breath, ready to rip this pissant little fuck's head off, when a dull clanging sound reached him.

"What the fuck was that?" he asked.

A crippled soldier on crutches hobbled into the room. "Commander! One of the shields is under attack on the eastern slope!"

Commander Weel nodded. "I trust the artillerists are providing covering fire," he said, turning from the table to look at a large map spiked to the wall.

"Those rock jockeys couldn't hit a bell tower with another bell tower," Modelar said. "Tell them to stand down and I'll send in my sparkers. Too dangerous to fly with those rocks in the air."

"No," Weel said.

Modelar looked at him, trying to understand what kind of fool this officer was. "No? Laddie, I outrank you."

Weel smiled, which only irritated Modelar more. "Of course, my apologies. I should have been more precise. No, sir. I am in command of all ground forces here, including the artillerists, while you command the dragons," he said, his pronunciation of the word *dragons* sounding as if he'd just swallowed a bug. "The artillerists have strict orders to continue firing until they have used up their current supply of munitions."

Modelar started rising up on his toes and forced himself back down. "All their stones? Why?"

"Quite simple, really," Weel said, as if schooling a child. "This is the first attack by the slyts of any size. Our response will be… disproportionate. I want our enemy not just to be wary of us, but to truly fear us. They attack one of our patrols, we decimate an entire swath of jungle and everything in it."

"They kill ours and we kill their trees?"

"They're slyts, my dear commander. They may have come late to the Word of the High Druid, but they follow Dendrolatrism with a fervor."

"Most in the Kingdom are Dendros. You aren't concerned they'll be upset at all the dead trees?"

Weel rolled his eyes. "This is a blighted, filthy land. Have you seen the trees?" he asked, pointing up at the logs that made up the first layer of his roof. "It took the dwarves weeks to find enough straight ones to make this, and quite honestly, their reputation for craftsmanship is overstated. More to the point, High Command agrees with my approach."

Another soldier rushed in. "Commander! We have several shields engaged in battle. FnC forces on the eastern side are hitting all of our patrols."

Weel looked down at the large table in the room and studied the map of the valley spread out on it. Modelar wondered how the hell they'd gotten the table in there in the first place.

"Excellent. I want regular updates on the artillerists' fire. You see, sir," Weel said, looking up at Modelar, "demand for stones from the quarry is quite high. Priority must go to fortifying our positions and providing ammunition to the catapults. Building little homes for your dragons will just have to wait."

"Little homes… ?" Modelar said. His blood flowed so loud he heard it in his ears. The room grew fuzzy and a cold sweat covered his body.

"Commander, are you all right?"

Modelar shook his head and blinked. A rag was stepping on his chest. Druid be damned, it had never hurt this much. Mirina was right; his rage would kill him long before the enemy would.

"I need... just need some air," Modelar said, staring through Weel and his smile. "Good evening."

"And to you, Commander," Weel said, his expression one of bemusement.

Modelar turned and strode out of the room. Each step felt like he was walking along the edge of a cliff. By the time he climbed the stairs and reached fresh air the pain in his chest had subsided, although his left arm and shoulder were filled with that peculiar pins-and-needles feeling. Fourth time he'd had it in the last couple of years. Always seemed to hit him when he was dealing with a fucking ass.

He barely heard the cats firing as he got into the horse-drawn two-wheeled cart that had brought him over to Weels's fucking castle from the roost. The flockman driving the carriage helped him up.

"You feeling all right, sir?"

Modelar waved the question away. "Get me to the roost and don't spare the whip. Go!"

The driver saluted and hopped up into his seat, taking up the reins and shouting the horse into action.

Modelar wasn't sure how long the ride took. Most of it he couldn't remember. Hands gently lifted him from the carriage and carried him into the master witches' tent. The smell of herbs and potions was strong. He was placed on a cot. His boots were tugged off his feet and the collar of his jacket unbuttoned.

"Was he shot?" Flock Commander Astol shouted, bursting into the tent.

"Out! He needs peace and quiet," the witch said.

Modelar grunted and waved at Vorly to come over.

"Walf?"

Modelar rolled his eyes. "Damn humors got out of sorts... talking to Weel."

The tempo of the outgoing cat shots increased.

"What the hell is going on out there?" Vorly asked.

Modelar propped himself up on an elbow. "Shields being hit. Launch sparkers. Some of yours, too. They probably have wounded…" He fell back on the cot. Keeping his eyes open was becoming a struggle.

Vorly sat down on the cot and grabbed his hand. Modelar looked up at his friend and smiled.

"You know, you've always been a royal pain… pain in my ass." He closed his eyes. *Just need to rest for a bit.*

"Walf!"

Modelar opened his eyes again, but they wouldn't focus. *So damn sleepy.* "You're a pain in my ass, Vorly, you know that?"

"I've heard, yes," Vorly said. It sounded like he was miles away.

"Be a pain in Weel's for me. He deserves… your very… best."

Modelar closed his eyes. He was falling, and finally, blessed be the High Druid, he felt warm. *About… about fucking ti—*

CHAPTER THIRTY-THREE

THE FIRST CAT SHOT landed three hundred yards into the jungle. A series of heavy bangs told Listowk more were on their way.

Wiz ran across Listowk's line of sight toward the wounded soldier. Another group of soldiers emerged from the jungle as a salvo of cat shots fell. Pre-chiseled rock exploded on impact, shattering and sending broken shards in every direction. Listowk buried himself in the stinking muck of the dosha swamp as chunks of rock tumbled over his head.

"Wizard! I'm hit! Oh Druid, I'm hit!"

Listowk looked up. The tree line was a mess of shattered trees, rock dust, and leaves flying in the air. More whistles sounded, but these were off in the distance. A red arrow drifted skyward a thousand yards to the north.

Black Shield's in battle. Two stars sailed up to the south. The entire eastern side of the valley was engulfed. The slyts had waited for the patrols to begin their march back to Iron Fist, when the shields would be tired and it was getting dark. *Clever bastards.*

"Don't shoot until you have a target!" he shouted. It did little good. The shield was wild. Bolts flew into the jungle from inches above the ground to thirty feet in the air.

"Wizard! He's bleeding everywhere!"

"I'll get there when I can!" Wiz shouted. "Hold cloth on the wound and keep it there."

Listowk counted four soldiers down. Slyt arrows whistled over his head, but he ignored them. He had to get the situation under control. A soldier emerged from the jungle. It was Gulmich.

"Gully, did you see anyone else back there?" Listowk asked as the soldier ran to him and slid down the berm.

Gully rested his back against the berm, his chest heaving. He turned to look at Listowk. "I was the last one."

Listowk got up on his knees. "Big Hog, do we have everyone? Big Hog!"

Catapults sent in another salvo.

Listowk crawled out of the muck and onto the top of the berm. "Where's Big Hog?"

A few confused faces looked his way. "Last I saw him he was covering the trail," Knockers said, pointing back toward the jungle.

"Big Hog!"

"I'll go," Wraith said, getting into a crouch as he readied himself to run back into the jungle.

"The fuck you will! Stay put. Those rock jockeys are unloading everything they have," Listowk said.

More clanging booms echoed from behind them as more catapults joined the fray.

A new sound rose above the others. Listowk recognized it at once.

"Flat on your bellies! The slyts are shooting spinners!" No sooner had he said it than two of the whirling scythes crashed down in the dosha swamp twenty yards behind the shield. The whirling wooden blades cut into the dirt at speed, flinging the muck fifty yards in every direction.

"Cover your string!" Listowk shouted, arching his body over his crossbow. Clods of stinking mud hit him in the back. The shield's relatively safe position behind the berm was now less so.

More cat shot thundered in, tearing up entire trees and sending them cartwheeling through the air. Listowk could barely make out the tree line as mud, dust, leaves, and chunks of wood and stone clouded his view. Through it all, the shield kept up its fire and, even more startling, so did the slyts. How any slyt could survive the rain of rocks pummeling the jungle he didn't know, but arrows continued to fly out of the murk.

A second salvo of spinners slammed into the mud, this time seventy yards away from the shield. A couple of soldiers cheered, but Listowk didn't. As long as those damn scythes were falling, they were trapped out in the open, and night was coming.

Movement out of the corner of his eye toward the tree line drew Listowk's attention. He was about to shout at Wraith to get back when he saw it was Carny. Before he could yell, Carny disappeared into the cloud of debris and was gone.

"Hold your fire! Carny's in there and so is Big Hog. Hold your fire!" Listowk banged his fist against his crossbow. *Think, you stupid ass, think or you're dead.* "Stay alert, but do not shoot until Carny and Big Hog get back. The slyts can't hit us here, so stay low." He crawled along the top of the berm to where Wiz worked on the wounded soldier.

"How—" was all he said as he looked down at the pale, lifeless face of Frogleg. The Wiz's hands were red up to his wrists. He looked at Listowk. "He just kept bleeding."

"Not your fault. Go see to the others. I want everyone ready to move."

"What about him?" Wiz said, motioning with his hands toward Frogleg.

"We'll carry him with us. Now go!"

"Wizard! Big Hog's hit!" Carny shouted, emerging from the roiling cloud of destruction dragging Big Hog behind him. Carny had a grip on Big Hog's aketon at the back of the collar and was pulling him. Wraith darted forward, grabbed Big Hog under the arm, and helped Carny drag him the rest of the way to the berm, where they slid him down the far side.

"Where's he hit?" Wiz asked, scrambling over to Big Hog and patting his hands over his body. Big Hog lay still, his eyes closed, his mouth open. His breathing sounded slow but steady.

Carny pointed to Big Hog's head. His helm was severely deformed; a large dent the size of a fist marred the left side. Rock dust coated the dent.

Wiz grabbed the helm and tried to remove it, but it wouldn't budge. A single trickle of blood flowed down Big Hog's forehead.

"The dent is pressing against his skull. We need to get—"

"Wizard!"

Listowk pointed toward the call. "Go, we'll deal with Big Hog."

"Get his helm off, but do it gently," Wiz said, gathering up his bag. "If you see anything gray, just lightly wrap his head. Whatever you do, don't touch it!"

Listowk nodded and turned back to Big Hog. He'd been hit by a piece of cat shot. Listowk had called for support too early and this was the result.

"I don't have any cutters," Carny said, staring down at Big Hog.

"Cat shots!"

Listowk leaned over Big Hog's head to cover him. Carny leaned over his chest. The cat shots plowed into the jungle high up on the mountainside. A rumbling and cracking sound soon followed.

"They're rolling back down!"

A boulder as big as a man burst through the dust and bounded over the shield to land in the dosha swamp with a sickening wet thud. Two more rocks followed immediately after.

Listowk knew he had no choice. "Wraith, shoot a green star. Call off those cats. They'll kill us before the slyts get a chance."

Wraith had a star in his bow and fired a flick later. The arrow streamed green smoke as it arced skyward, but was blasted to pieces a moment later by a falling cat shot. Two more cat shots crashed into the jungle, though neither rolled back down. Listowk tensed, waiting to hear more whistling through the air. What he heard instead was worse.

"High Druid preserve us! Fucking sparkers!"

* * *

"STAY WELL BACK from the tree line, Blue Charger," Vorly said, flying Carduus high above the battle. "And keep your heads up!" For the moment, it was all he could do. The artillerists were chucking rock for all they were worth and until they stopped it was too dangerous for the bigger rags to go down. Truth be told, it was too dangerous for the sparkers, but they were nimble and certain they could dodge anything thrown their way.

"Always!" Blue Charger responded.

Vorly turned Carduus in a tight turn to port as they reached the north end of the valley. As they came around he could take in the entire scene. To his starboard, the western side of the valley was a quiet green shadow as the sun began setting behind its peaks. The eastern side, however, was a raging mix of dirt and dust and vegetation flying through the air. He counted six different pockets of battle dotted along the tree line. The sparkers were going to try to isolate the slyts in each one by laying down a line of fire behind them.

"I don't like this," Breeze said.

"What part? That the sparkers are going to run a gauntlet of stone? That they might burn more than just slyts? That we're all up here flying in a valley at dusk?"

"Yes!" Breeze shouted. "And I'm having trouble on plane."

Vorly glanced down at his sheet. It was a mess of interwoven colored lines. They pulsed and wiggled while dots winked bright, then vanished, only to reappear somewhere else on the sheet. Months ago that would have sent him running, but these days it looked fairly normal.

"Explain," Vorly said, catching movement out of the corner of his eye. He turned his head and stared. Buzzards were following his track. A flock of the carrion birds was circling the valley, keeping well back of Carduus. *Cheeky bastards.*

"I'm getting interference. The plane keeps shifting."

Vorly rolled his neck. *Perfect.* "An enemy thaum?" Their first and only encounter with one had nearly killed Jawn, and he was supposed to be a far more powerful thaum than Breeze.

Managing thaumics while flying on a rag was progressing

in leaps and bounds. There was a new discovery nearly every flight. Breeze and her cohorts had managed to increase the stability factor to the point that where the crystal was in the air mattered little in relation to its position in plane… or something like that. Vorly did his best to look like he was paying attention when Breeze or a visiting RAT presented the latest advancement in aero-thaumics and plane-shift calculation to the drivers so they'd know to take it seriously, but even when he did listen he understood about as much as would fill a thimble. He was relying on Breeze to give him a separate crash course on what he needed to know.

"Possibly, but I can't be sure," she said. Her voice was strong and if anything, she sounded angry. "I'm ordering all thaums off plane until I understand this better. You'll have to revert to hand signals," she said.

Vorly didn't protest. Breeze knew her thaumics and the others clearly followed her lead.

"Aye that," Vorly said, "your wish is my command. You know, never quite understood that phrase. If your wish is *my* command, then—"

"It's all right to miss him," Breeze said, cutting him off. "I am sorry he's dead."

"Who, Modelar? He was a loud, overbearing ass at the best of times."

"And your friend," Breeze said.

Vorly closed his eyes and let out his breath. He couldn't afford to think about Walf. You started thinking about the friends you lost along the way and it didn't stop.

"Breeze, for all that is holy, just drop it, please."

"You're right, I… you're right," Breeze said. "Sliding off plane."

Vorly looked down at his sheet and saw that it had reverted to being a plain, clear sheet of crystal. "Off plane, aye," he said.

"Here they come," Breeze said.

Vorly looked up. Five orange dots were rapidly growing in size as they fell toward the ground. The sparker drivers had their rags' air gills wide open, stoking the fire within. He nudged

Carduus to pick up his speed.

"Now, you listen to me, Carduus, and you listen good. You're about to see a lot of fire flying around. That doesn't mean you get to fire, got it?"

Carduus rumbled deep in his throat.

"Was that a yes?" Breeze asked.

Vorly hunched over and thumped Carduus a few times on the scales. The rag turned his head to the side and fixed Vorly with one large eye. They locked gazes for several flicks before Carduus looked straight ahead again.

"I dearly hope so."

CARNY STAYED BY Big Hog as the sparkers rolled in. From his position it looked like the rags were flying straight at him, their maws wide open, revealing the roiling inferno within. The cries and shouts of the battles dimmed. He became transfixed by the oncoming flame. He could still see Sinte charked to nothing but ash. He remembered the way the slyt bodies had shrunk so that they looked like children.

"Down! Down! Down!"

The darkening sky started glowing and then flashed with the light of five suns as the rags unleashed their flame. Carny's vision went white, then became a sea of vibrating dots. The roar of the flame sounded incredibly close, but unlike when they rescued the rag, the heat was little more than what it felt like to stand by an open hearth.

The jungle shook as the rags' flame tore into it. Maybe it was the damage from all the cat shots, or maybe these trees were drier, but whatever the case, the flames spread far faster than before.

"We'll be charked if we stay here!" the Bard shouted.

Soldiers were already standing up. Carny didn't see any more arrows in the air, but that didn't mean they weren't there. The sun was below the western peaks now and shadows flitted everywhere.

Carny looked down at Big Hog. He and Listowk hadn't been

able to get the helm off his head, so they'd wrapped a cloth around it and under his chin to keep everything in one place. His breathing was slow and his face was pale. They had to get him back to the witches, but deep down Carny was sure Big Hog was dead.

"I'm sorry," Carny said, leaning down until his lips were by Big Hog's ear. He grabbed his friend's hand and squeezed it. "I should be the one with a smashed skull, not you. You were right, I was only thinking about myself."

Big Hog's fingers curled around Carny's hand. "My head hurts," he mumbled.

Carny sat up straight. "He's talking!"

A couple of soldiers looked his way, but the raging fire captured most of their attention.

Carny looked around until he spotted Listowk. "SL, he just spoke! He's got a chance, but we have to get him out of here now."

"We all need to get out of here," Listowk said, pointing toward the fire. "I'm open to suggestions."

Carny looked back across the valley. It would take them a quarter of a candle to walk back to Iron Fist. They needed a rag. He looked back at the fire as a tree cracked and fell, scattering burning branches over the berm and into the dosha swamp.

"Does anyone have gloves?"

VORLY WISHED THE sheets were working. He wanted to congratulate Blue Charger on some beautiful flying. Five beautiful curving lines of fire stretched across the eastern slopes. It was amazing how well the jungle was burning.

"I see something," Breeze said. "Dead ahead, on the ground."

Vorly peered past Carduus's head. Sections of fire were moving away from the jungle and into a dosha swamp. As he got closer he saw that soldiers were carrying flaming branches.

"What the hell are they doing? They aren't going to cook out there, are they?" The sound of catapults still echoed in the valley.

The battle, as far as the artillerists were concerned, wasn't over.

"They're making some kind of sign with the fire," Breeze said.

Her voice sounded exceptionally clear and Vorly realized she was crouched right beside him.

"Get back in your saddle and strap in!"

"There, it's an X. See it?"

Vorly turned away from her. "Yes, it looks like an X."

"They want us to land there," she said.

"With those rock jockeys still in full swing."

"But look where they put the X. It's in the dosha swamp. The catapults are shooting deeper into the jungle. If we fly in low we'll stay under the flight of the stones."

Vorly turned to look at her. "Is that all we have to do?"

"I know it's risky, but they need our help."

Vorly realized she was as calm and determined as she'd been when she'd ordered the thaums off plane.

"Do you have any idea what a cat shot would do to a rag?"

Breeze shrugged. "I'm guessing we'd never know."

Vorly snorted. "You have a pair of balls on you. Fine, we'll do it. But if we explode, I'm kicking your bony ass all the way to damnation. Now sit down and strap in."

"HIGH FUCKING DRUID, it's working, they're landing!" Listowk shouted. *Son of a damn witch, Carny's idea worked.*

"As soon as that rag touches down get the wounded on board. The rest of us will hoof it back."

A salvo of cat shots rumbled overhead and slammed into the fiery slope, sending up geysers of flaming debris. The air was thick with smoke and visibility was getting worse by the flicker.

"Here it comes!"

Listowk buried his head in the crook of his arm as the wind swirled around him. He tried peering through the smoke but he couldn't see a damn thing.

"Did it land?"

"We aren't waiting around all day!"

Listowk knew that voice. "The rag is on the ground. Get the wounded to it now! Go!"

Soldiers sprinted through the smoke. Two wounded were able to hop and limp with some help, while Big Hog and Frogleg were carried. The arrows still stuck out of Frogleg's chest, but Wiz had wrapped them in cloth and secured them in place so they wouldn't move around. Listowk didn't know why Wiz had bothered, but he didn't say anything.

The wind blew the smoke away long enough for Listowk to see the rag. Soldiers were hauling Big Hog onto its back. Good. He turned to face the rest of the shield.

"All right, once they take off we're gone." No spinners had fallen for some time, but even if they had still been flying he'd have risked it. He wasn't getting charked out here. "We'll take the berm running west until we hit that stand of bamboo. Wait there until I get there."

Heads nodded.

"Get your heads down!"

Listowk ducked as the rag pumped its wings and crouched low on its hind legs before launching itself skyward. With a few beats of its wings it was several hundred feet in the air and, hopefully, out of the line of fire of the catapults.

Listowk stood up in a crouch. "Now it's our turn. Let's go! Run!"

CHAPTER THIRTY-FOUR

C ARNY HAD NEVER HIT a woman before in his life, but it was only Knockers clinging to his arm that restrained him now. He was still panting heavily from their run back across the valley, but though his head was spinning, he wasn't moving.

"We are not leaving him," Carny said, staring at the witch and daring her to say no again.

"I know, and I promise you he knows," the master witch said, her voice calm and her face showing genuine concern. "But I can't do my job if you are cluttering up my sanctuary, spreading ill humors about. You will only make what I have to do more difficult. Is that what you want?"

Carny let Knockers lower his arm. "You don't understand," Carny said, looking past her to where several witches were stripping Big Hog of his uniform and washing him down in what smelled like alcohol. "He can't die."

The witch placed a hand on his shoulder and held it there until he looked at her.

"I will do everything in my power to save his life. I can promise no more. Now, please, take your men and go get something to eat and drink. You've all been through a lot today."

"What are you going to do?" Carny asked.

"It's complicated, and it's messy."

Carny didn't budge, nor did Knockers or the Bard, standing beside him.

The witch shook her head. "Very well. We first have to remove his helm. I've sent for the proper tools and an expert to handle that. With his helm removed I will examine his skull and the wound. If my suspicions are correct he will have a fracture, perhaps several, that is pressing bone against his brain. If I don't remove that bone the pressure will continue to build until he dies."

"Then?"

"Then I drill into the skull to remove the pieces of bone and allow the damaged humors to leak out. This will, hopefully, rebalance his mind and body and begin the healing process. If that works, I will then cover the hole with a piece of tin."

Carny grew weak, his head fuzzy. He couldn't watch his friend be cut open. He turned and left the tent. This was all his fault.

He walked aimlessly with Knockers and the Bard in tow until he realized someone was blocking his path. He looked up and saw Ahmist.

"Is he still alive?"

"What?"

Ahmist held out his hand. It held a Dendro amulet. "It fell off him. I was hoping to give it back to him, and to pray for his soul."

Carny looked at Ahmist. The constant smile of earlier was gone. His face was filthy, his eyes red-rimmed, and his aketon was in tatters.

"He's still alive, so maybe you could pray for his body," Carny said.

Ahmist lowered his hand. "I can do both."

Carny raised his arm toward Ahmist. Ahmist flinched, but Carny smiled and patted the soldier on the shoulder. "Thank you," Carny said.

* * *

MASTER WITCH ELMITIA Bogston washed her hands thoroughly in a small stone basin while she kept watch on the soldier. His wound was obvious and complicated. A chunk of rock had caved in his helm to a depth of three-quarters of an inch on the left side in an area behind the temple and above the ear. Her first task was to remove the helm without causing any more damage. The soldier muttered a couple of times, so his humors were not yet depleted beyond the point of no return.

Dragonsmith Pagath entered the tent with a small bundle wrapped in leather. Elmitia nodded at him and motioned him toward the basin. When he walked over and she saw his hands, she shook her head. "I don't think we could get your paws clean if we had a week."

Pagath looked down at his hands. "Aye, the dirt does get ground in. But it's a good thing. Keeps the bad humors out."

The master witch let that go. She'd have a talk with him about hygiene another day.

"Well, proceed, but do not, under any circumstances, touch his head or any fluid that flows. Only the helm."

Pagath nodded. "Not the first one of these I've done you know," he said, following her as she walked over to the wooden table that was set up.

"Dragon husbandry is a whole other cauldron of newts. Now," she said, pausing as Pagath climbed up onto a stool by the table, "here's our dilemma. His helm is pressed tight against his skull. You can see the concave nature of the dent. Judging by the sign of blood and depth of the dent it's obvious there has been significant crush force to the bone."

Pagath looked at her. "So the poor bugger got hit in the head with a rock then?"

Elmitia massaged the bridge of her nose. "Yes. But we can't treat his wound until we remove his helm."

A witch draped a white cloth around Pagath's long beard and tied it behind his head. He leaned forward and looked at the helm. He studied it from several angles, nodding and muttering as he did.

"Well?" she asked.

"Same sort of thing happens with scales. Even had a chain get smashed into a rag's skull once. One of the links was right in there. Nasty business, that. It lived," he said, looking up from the helm. "Never flew straight again, mind you, always pulled to port, the daft bastard, but it lived."

"We don't need him to fly," Elmitia said. "Living would be more than enough."

Pagath nodded. "Right. So, I need you and you to hold his helm steady there and there," he said, pointing at two of the witches and then at the helm.

"And how may I assist?" Elmitia asked.

Pagath held out his filthy left hand and bent over the soldier. "You can start by handing me my talon shears. After that, look for the number-three chisel."

THE SOLDIERS OF Red Shield sat outside their barracks watching the sunrise. The smell of smoke hung thick in the valley and gave the dawn a faded look. Sparkers, two at a time, launched into the air. Their takeoff took them over the shield at barely two hundred yards.

Carny sat with his back against the mud-brick wall of the barracks and looked up as the first pair flew overhead. Their belly-armor plates were coated in dust and muck and even pieces of jungle. Several had scorch marks. Carny wondered if it hurt them.

A second and then a third pair launched. They began flying slow circuits up and down the valley. Carny watched them, waiting to see the telltale red glow as their sides heated up in preparation to fire, but they remained a dull gray.

"Slyts must have had enough for now," Longbowman Mothrin said.

Carny grunted and went back to studying the dirt in the V-shaped space between his legs. He drew furiously with his fingers, then wiped the drawings out and started over.

The Bard fiddled with his broken psaltery, a few out-of-tune chords sounding now and then as he tried to make repairs. Knockers whittled away at a new pipe, a pile of wood shavings between his boots. Wraith paced. He would stop suddenly and look out to the valley, then, after a few flicks, start pacing again.

Carny sifted the dirt between his fingers. He imagined Big Hog on his farm out plowing the fields, his beefy wife in a kitchen with a litter of kids about her. He threw the dirt down and brushed his hands on his trousers. He picked up his crossbow and began working the firing lever and checking the string for any frays. His fingertips left gray smudges all over the weapon.

Wiz rolled and unrolled a small ball of string. His aketon was covered in dried blood, but no one said anything. Ahmist got up from sitting on the ground and closed his Book of LOKAM. "Morning service is being held by the stables," he said. "I'm going... if anyone wants to join me."

"Say a prayer for all of us," Listowk said, ambling up to the group. Crossbowman Razchuts walked with him, his left arm in a sling. A few soldiers nodded at Razchuts and welcomed him back.

Carny looked up from staring at the dirt. "Any news?"

Listowk shook his head. "Nothing. Well"—he paused as he looked around at the soldiers—"they got the arrow out of Kistin's calf nice and clean. Looks like he'll keep the leg. Razzy here popped his shoulder bone falling down the berm. They gave him a couple of stiff drinks and popped it right back in place."

Soldiers nodded. Another time they might have cracked jokes, but not this morning.

"Frogleg," Listowk said, sighing as he did, "you already know about."

Wiz stopped rolling his string. "I did everything I could."

"That you did, lad, and we all know it."

Carny looked over at Wiz. The dried blood on his aketon now seemed like a mark, the way they would tar and feather someone. It wasn't always fair, but the mark stayed.

"Couldn't they tell you anything about Big Hog?" Knockers

asked, setting aside his pipe and knife.

Listowk sat down in the dirt and took off his helm. "I'll check again when I go back to the keep."

Mention of the keep drew some grumbles.

"So what's the great man think about last night? More medals?" Wraith asked.

"They're calling it a success," Listowk said. "Say we repulsed an FnC force three times our size."

Carny smacked his crossbow. "A success? Fuck him."

Listowk smiled and nodded slowly. "Commander Weel looks at the big picture. Iron Fist and all the fortresses are still here. The sparkers and the cats did their jobs and our friendly flock commander and his missus got the wounded to safety. Turns out after they dropped our boys off they made three more trips to bring in other wounded. So if anyone is getting a medal, those two deserve it."

Wraith said nothing. He started pacing again.

"So what, we just sit here and wait?" Carny asked.

Listowk slowly got back to his feet. He took his time to stretch and brush the dust from his trousers. He examined the bits of vegetation that still clung to his helm before putting it back on his head. "Weel wants to know how many slyts we killed."

Carny studied Listowk's face, trying to get a read on him. "Why?"

"It's a way to show the people back in the Kingdom that we're winning," Listowk said. "The FnCs aren't inclined to stand and fight, so whenever they do it's an event. It ain't like the old days when two armies took to the field of battle and whoever remained was the victor. It's messier now, and that means it's harder to figure out who's winning and who's losing. You've seen the criers that are over here now. They're supposed to chronicle what happens and then tell the people back home."

"So how do we do it?" Knockers asked.

"We count them."

Carny stood up, his crossbow clenched in his left hand. "He wants us to go back out there and count the bodies? And what about our dead? Does he want a count of those, too?"

Listowk looked around at the shield. His shoulders drooped and his voice was soft with weariness. "War isn't pretty, my boys. Most of it is awful. A couple of the sparker crews have offered to help. They'll take a couple of us back out."

"There's no room," Carny said.

"They're having some kind of trouble with their crystals, so the thaums won't be going. That means there's an open slot on each rag. I'm going to ride on one, so all I need is a volunteer for the other."

"I'll pass," Wraith said.

A few heads turned to look at Wraith, Carny included. The soldier volunteered for everything, especially when it was dangerous.

"I'll go," Carny said.

"If you both go, who's in charge?" Ahmy asked. "We need a new LC… don't we?"

Carny looked at Listowk. Listowk shrugged his shoulders and looked back. *He's not going to make this easy.*

"I'll LC," Carny said, tensing for the expected protest. None came.

Listowk nodded. "That's settled then. Carny, as you're LC, you stay back. Ahmy's right, we both can't be out there. So who—"

"I'll go," Knockers said. "I can't write, but I can count well enough."

"Done and done," Listowk said. "Carny, get these boys some food, then put them to bed. Knockers, follow me."

Carny tried to understand what he'd just done. Was it guilt over Big Hog? Maybe, but he couldn't worry about that now. Faces were turned to him, waiting.

"Anyone going to morning service with Ahmy, go now," Carny said. "When it's over, get back here and get some sleep. The rest of you, get inside and clean your weapons. I'll go get some food and bring it back. Questions?"

"I'm going to the infirmary to check on Big Hog," Wiz said.

"Help me get the food, then we'll both go over and check," Carny said.

Wiz nodded.

Carny looked around at the shield. "Barracks, weapons, food, sleep. Go."

They started moving. Carny turned, slinging his crossbow over his left shoulder as he did. "C'mon, Wiz, let's see what kind of slop they have in this place."

CHAPTER THIRTY-FIVE

"AND HOW'S OUR INVALID this morning? Any better?" Rickets asked, his voice growing louder as he walked into the tent Jawn had all to himself. It was small consolation for losing his sight, but Rickets had pulled some strings and gotten Jawn out of the large ward filled with sick and wounded soldiers.

"I thought you left," Jawn said, reaching out with his hands to find the jug of water by his cot. His fingers brushed the jug and he grabbed it. He drank straight from the jug. "Want some?"

"Thanks, no," Rickets said. There was the sound of boots on dried fronds, then the cot shook as Rickets sat down. A hand touched Jawn's shoulder. "You done feeling sorry for yourself yet?"

Jawn swung the jug at Rickets's head, or where he thought it was. He hit nothing, and the jug sailed out of his hand and hit the side of the tent.

"Fuck you," Jawn said, throwing himself onto his back on his cot. "If you're just here to torment me you've succeeded."

"We still have our mission," Rickets said. He didn't sound angry.

Jawn laughed. "You do. I'm a blind cripple." War wasn't supposed to be like this. You either came home a hero, or you came home a dead hero. Jawn had left no room for anything in between.

"The army thought so," Rickets said. "They were all set to

invalid you back to the Kingdom. You'd be released from the service and free to pursue whatever course you like."

Jawn heard the hitch, the subtle, telling use of the past tense that told him that Rickets was never to be taken at face value, even when you couldn't see his face.

"And what do they think now?"

The cot creaked as Rickets got up. "Now, well now they think it's time you got off your ass, off this pox of an island, and back to work."

"Why in the world would they now think all that?" Jawn asked.

Rickets cleared his throat. "Because I told them. I got the papers for you to be released from service, but I sent them back. Told them there was still some use to be had of you. They agreed. The Cow and Country Commission rides again."

With nothing to throw, Jawn shot out of his cot and lunged for the sound of Rickets's voice. This time, he connected, his left fist catching the crowny on the shoulder. The two men went down and rolled through the tent and onto the sand. Jawn punched and flailed.

"You fuck! You bastard! Why?!"

Rickets didn't punch back. No matter how hard Jawn hit, Rickets deflected his blows but never returned a punch. Finally, Jawn gave up and curled into a ball, sobbing.

"Fuck you, Rickets. Fuck you."

There was a long silence. Jawn had started to wonder if Rickets had left when the man spoke.

"I'm not wrong about you, Jawn Rathim. I wasn't when we first met, and I'm not now. I get being blind is a terrible fate, but unlike the men in those wards, you still have hope. You didn't get an arrow in the stomach or catch a disease that's slowly burning you up. You lost your sight, maybe not even forever, but even if it is… you're still alive."

Jawn waved at the air. "Don't forget my medal," he spat out. "I hear it's shiny, though I wouldn't know."

"Fuck your medal," Rickets said, his calm demeanor finally

cracking. "We both know you didn't risk your life for a medal. You can hate me all you want, but don't insult my intelligence." Rickets drew in a breath and muttered before continuing. "I'm flying out on a rag this afternoon. I'll swing by your tent before I go. If you're packed, we go. If not, well, then fuck you, too."

The sound of boots on the sand faded as Rickets walked away. Jawn lay in his own darkness, his fury so impotent he pounded the sand with his fist until it started to bleed, and then kept on pounding.

JAWN WAS READY when Rickets returned.

"I want to know why, Rickets. Why all of it? Why me?"

"You do ask the most interesting questions, Jawn Rathim. We don't have time for the big view, so let me answer the why that matters most—why keep a blind thaum in the service?"

Jawn waited for Rickets to answer, but the man stayed silent. Jawn opened his mouth to cajole Rickets, then paused. Why? Why would Rickets want to keep him? What skill did Jawn have that other thaums with eyesight didn't possess?

"I've gone deeper in the aether. I can control more processes. You know I've talked with Breeze."

"My dear boy, the RAT knows you've talked to her. High Command knows you've talked to her. I doubt there's anyone in Luitox or beyond who matters who doesn't know."

Jawn felt his cheeks flush. "If everyone knows... but they can't do it, can they?" he finished.

"That little wisp of a girl is the closest to you in ability on plane, and she's still miles behind. You know she and all the rest of the thaums at Bone and Thunder are off plane."

Jawn nodded. He didn't like the ominous name for the valley, but the moniker had stuck. Worse, though, was this new problem with the sheets.

"Might just be the air there."

"Or enemy thaums," Rickets said, giving voice to the more likely answer.

"Rickets, I don't know what it is people think I can do. Yes, I killed a thaum on plane, but I almost died doing it."

"That's just it, you didn't die. Your eyes are two red devils, and that's a shame, but the rest of you is fit as the day I met you. You know how many other thaums have managed to kill another thaum in plane and live to tell the tale? None."

Jawn shook his head. "Thaums are killed all the time."

"Yes, but never by another thaum straddling two planes. Never."

"Then send me to the academy. I can't study worth a damn out here. I'll need help."

"You'll have Breeze."

"I don't understand! Why the rush?"

Rickets's hand was on Jawn's shoulder again. "The Forest Collective has taken the bait. A bit more forcefully than anticipated. Massive columns of slyts are marching on Bone and Thunder as we speak. Thousands, tens of thousands. More have swung around the valley and cut it off from ground supply."

Jawn started to respond, but Rickets kept talking. "An even larger army of slyts is pushing its way east. Looks like the Western Wilds have finally had enough."

"Can we stop them?"

"Who knows? What I do know is that if Breeze and those soldiers out west are going to have any chance of getting out of this alive, they're going to need a miracle. And, Jawn, you're that miracle."

Jawn allowed Rickets to lead him out of his tent and toward the launch field, which he knew from before was really just a stretch of empty beach. As he climbed on board the waiting rag and cinched himself in, he saw himself as he was when he'd last boarded a rag here, heading off to Luitox and to war. Then, he'd fully believed that glory awaited. Now, as the rag flexed its wings and he sensed the power beneath him readying to launch itself skyward, he didn't have a fucking clue.

CHAPTER THIRTY-SIX

A FTER GETTING THE HERD settled with food and shooing them into their hammocks, Carny knew he couldn't sleep and went for a walk. He avoided the infirmary, having just been there with Wiz to check on Big Hog. Seeing the big farmer lying there, his head swaddled in bandages, hurt too much.

Wake up or be dead! But Big Hog hovered somewhere in between, leaving Carny lost for what to feel, and so he walked. He knew he had Wild Flower in his rucksack. A little vial of Sliver, too. The temptation to drown in them was strong, but he couldn't look down at another body of a friend and be responsible.

Soldiers from command ran past him, their uniforms neat and clean, their boots laced all the way up, and their helms polished. He watched them as they ran to the keep and disappeared inside. It was curious behavior.

"Carny! Whoa!" Bristom shouted, reining in his pony before it slammed into Carny.

Carny turned and came face-to-muzzle with Gallanter. He reached out and stroked the pony's mane. "Hi, Squeak. What's going on? You guys throwing a party?"

Squeak looked around, then leaned forward. "You haven't heard? Fuck, the slyts are coming."

Carny looked out at the still-smoldering eastern slope. "They're already here."

Squeak sat upright again. "No, I mean an army. Legions' worth. It's slyts from the Western Wilds. They're coming."

"That so?" Carny said. He knew he should probably be concerned, but the knowledge that slyts were coming to kill him didn't change his view on the world from a candle ago.

"Shit, are you high?"

Carny shook his head. "Haven't touched a thing since yesterday."

Squeak leaned forward again. "Oh, you're out. Look, I can get you a little, but the price is going up by the flick. If we really are surrounded it'll be a king's ransom for a quarter ounce of Sliver," he said. He sounded... gleeful.

"Naw, I'm good, you keep it," Carny said, giving the pony one more pat, then continuing on his walk.

"Look, if you ain't got silver I can spot you. In fact," Squeak said, spurring the pony toward Carny, "I could use a guy like you. I can't keep up with demand, and the way things are going, I'll be out of here soon. Work for me, and you'll have more silver than rain. And when things get crazy, I'll get you out."

Carny stopped and looked up at Squeak. "Out? There is no out."

Squeak shook his head. "That's the trouble with you boars— you don't think about the future."

Carny didn't react to Squeak calling him a boar. Soldiers wore the nickname as a badge of honor. Boars were tough, determined, and filthy. It suited soldiers like Carny just fine.

"This won't last; it won't even change anything," Squeak said, waving his free hand around. "You'll be back in the Vill someday and needing work."

The thought of going back to the Kingdom, taking a job, a family, all seemed like a dream to Carny. "Are they all going back to the Vill?" Carny asked, motioning to another group of command soldiers on the run.

Squeak snapped the reins and got his pony moving again.

"Everyone who can is looking to get a rag out of here before it's too late. If you change your mind, come find me... but don't take too long 'cause I ain't waiting."

Carny thought about that as he walked, finally arriving at the eastern wall. *Before it's too late.* He hoisted himself up onto the gangway, shouted a greeting to the sentries in the watchtower, then walked along the wall until he found a spot and sat down.

A pair of sparkers flew overhead, their passage like one of those strange warm winds that would sometimes blow in the middle of winter. He looked across the valley to where Red Shield had fought last night. The two sparkers Listowk and Knockers were riding were already skimming along the tree line.

"Count the bodies," Carny said to himself. He didn't understand it. Sure, a few soldiers did it. He knew Wraith put a notch in his bow for every kill, but that made a grim kind of sense to Carny. But why would the people back home care? The world had been so much simpler before the war. The king was the king, a battle was won or lost, and a man was either alive or dead.

Motion across the valley focused his sight. One of the rags was flying almost straight up, its wings beating in a blur. The one behind was climbing, too, but much more slowly. Smoke started pouring out of the rag's mouth.

Carny stood up on the wall.

Small blurs chased after the smoking rag. *Fuck, ballistas!* Carny was sure he saw two hit the rag. The second rag rolled over and dove, its maw opening wide as it let loose a torrent of blindingly bright flame on the jungle below. The roar of its fire reached Carny a couple of flicks later. Fire splashed and danced among the trees. The other sparkers in the air all turned and flew toward the fight while the smoking rag angled its way back toward the roost beside Iron Fist.

Carny wanted to feel guilty about this, too, but he had volunteered to go out and count the enemy dead, and Listowk had turned him down. As the sparker struggled to fly, a wave of despair swept over Carny. *Is that all this war is? We kill more of them than they kill of us?* He snorted at his own naïveté. That's what wars were *always* about. You kill enough of the enemy so that they can't or won't fight back. You kill them so they can't shoot the next arrow, launch the next ballista, and slit the next throat. You spill their blood until their comrades choke on it.

It was hard for Carny to remember a time when his life was about anything but how to kill and not be killed. Times had been hard growing up, but living life was always the reason. Now, fuck, now he really didn't care. He didn't live anymore. None of them did. They survived until they were wounded or killed. That wasn't life—it was simply a few extra candles added to your time before you were eventually snuffed out. Going back to the Vill was for soldiers like Squeak, who were only visitors in the war.

He looked up at the sun and closed his eyes. Carny knew he'd never see home again. He wasn't angry. If anything, he felt at peace. There was nothing left to worry about.

He lowered his head and opened his eyes as a bright orange flash over the valley changed his understanding of the war again.

"JUST PUT HIM down in the fields!" Listowk shouted to the driver. He raised his left arm to cover his face. The smoke pouring out of the sparker was growing blacker by the flick. The rag's scales creaked as heat poured through them. The heavy clay-soaked blankets designed to insulate the riders from the intense heat weren't enough.

"I can't!" the driver shouted. "He's keening bad. He won't stop until he gets back to the roost."

Listowk looked over the side. They were at least a hundred feet in the air and climbing. Jumping would mean almost certain death. He unhooked the restraint straps on his saddle and got into a crouch position. Sparkers flew hot even under normal conditions, but to stay on this rag much longer would be to roast to death. The string on his crossbow snapped, releasing the metal arms of the bow with a clang.

"We're going to burn!" Listowk shouted.

"I can get him back!" the driver shouted, turning to look at Listowk. Tears were running down his face. "I'm not leaving him. He's still got a chance!"

Listowk stared at the driver. *The stupid fuck is prepared to ride his rag to the end. He'll never jump.*

"Fuck that! Get him lower! I'm jumping!" Listowk shouted. He tore off his helm and aketon. The heat blankets were smoldering and the air shimmered, making it difficult to see. His lungs heaved with the effort to draw in the super-heated air and his skin began flaking and tightening on his arms and face.

"I'll try!" the driver said, swinging his iron gaff against the rag's neck. It bounced off the scales and seemed to have little effect.

Between wing beats, Listowk saw blurs of green and brown below. He wiped his eyes, but his vision would not clear. The heat enveloped him, roasting him where he crouched. He couldn't stay any longer.

Listowk stood up on his saddle, turned to the left, and jumped.

He cleared the wing by inches as it swung up on another stroke. The relief was instantaneous as he tumbled through the air. The rush of the wind cooled and soothed his skin. As he tumbled, his vision cleared and he saw the fiery nightmare the rag had become.

A feathery stream of flame gushed from a fist-sized hole beneath its left wing and trailed all the way to its tail. The air around the rag shimmered like shards of glass in a pool of blood. Several of the blankets were now on fire, revealing the heat-translucent scales beneath. The driver was no more than a blur in the heat, his arm still swinging the gaff.

A ballista spear wobbled through the air toward the rag. It struck the beast near the first hole and went all the way in. For a flick, nothing happened. Then the rag shuddered and vanished in a burst of white-orange light.

Scalding air slammed into Listowk as he hurtled toward the earth. He screamed, raising his arms to cover his face. Talons of fire reached down from where the rag had been and gripped his body in a searing embrace. The flames grew brighter as they fed off his flesh.

Listowk stopped screaming when he hit the ground.

CARNY GAGGED. EVEN though it was too far away, he thought he smelled burning flesh. Flaming chunks of the rag still tumbled through the air, but his mind could only focus on the falling figure and the fiery trail it left as it plunged to the earth.

A plume of inky black smoke boiled up into the sky, marking the end of the rag and its crew as the debris crashed into a stand of bamboo.

Carny jumped over the wall and started running toward the burning wreckage. Rags wheeled overhead making run after run along the jungle's edge, pouring down fire.

Squeak's words echoed in Carny's head: *Get out before it's too late.*

Carny kept running. He knew what Squeak didn't.

It had always been too late.

"DEAD?" THE BARD asked. He kept looking out to the valley then back at Carny as if somehow the news was going to change.

The shield stood around Carny. He'd just walked back from the remains of the rag. He didn't see any point in prolonging this. He held up Listowk's rank shield. It was marred by soot and still warm to the touch. It was the second time their Shield Leader had charked.

"The SL is dead. There wasn't much… him and the driver are buried out there," he said, motioning back over his shoulder.

Strained silence filled the air. None of them were new to death, but there were soldiers you knew would never die. They had that glow about them. Shield Leader Listowk was one of those soldiers. He wasn't supposed to die. It was just that simple.

Carny saw the despair. He felt it himself, but he could no longer indulge in that. "Bard, you're LC now. I want a weapons check of the entire shield in a sixteenth. Wraith, that goes for you and your bowmen, too. Strings, hewers, knives, all of it."

"Listowk's dead," Wiz said, his eyes misting. "We need some time to—"

Carny slammed his fist against the shield. "There is no more time. The slyts from the Western Wilds are marching. They don't like that we've taken their route east to the coast and they're coming to take it back."

The winch on the nearest cat began cranking. Others joined in. Carny pointed at Bard and then at Wraith. "Get your men up to the barracks, now."

Carny didn't wait to see if they complied. He started walking. "Where are you going?" the Bard called after him.

"To see a dwarf," he said. "Time we got some more firepower."

MINTER DHIST, SENIOR flock commander of the sparker rags, sat with Vorly on a wooden bench inside the limestone roost. Vorly had only known Minter a couple of years. He was young, tall, good-looking, and supremely confident in his abilities. That kind of thing could grate on Vorly, but Minter was also methodical and, above all, practical. He didn't take chances with his rags or his crews.

"Farro says they were crystal-tipped spears," Minter said. "Punched through the armor plate like it wasn't even there."

Vorly nodded. "Damn shame. Sorry about your man and rag," Vorly said. He'd heard one of the shields lost an SL riding along. He hoped it wasn't anyone he knew. He'd grown fond of the soldiers Carduus had been flying around.

"Yikson was a good man. And Windy, damn. He was the runt of the litter, but he threw fire hotter than any of them. Always trying to prove he was every bit as good, you know?"

Vorly did. Rag rivalries were every bit as intense as those

among people. It was one of the reasons they were separated within the roost.

Minter looked up suddenly. "Fuck, I'm sorry. I didn't even ask you how you're doing. I know you and the LFC were good friends."

Vorly waved away his concern. "Thanks. I'm fine. I miss the old bird, but with that temper of his, Walf was living on borrowed time."

"Scared the living hell out of me," Minter said. "Meanest son of a—sorry, no disrespect."

Vorly smiled. "He'd take it as a compliment." He leaned forward. "Listen, I wanted to talk to you about that. With Modelar gone, we lost our ability to go toe to toe with Weel. That's going to be a problem. We need a united front when dealing with that prick. We're both flock commanders, so—"

"Command is yours," Minter said immediately. "You've got way more experience and the thaums all think you're a visionary. It's my honor to serve under you."

Vorly patted Minter on the knee. "I appreciate that. Tonight, after all the rags are tucked in, let's get the flocks together. We'll have a few drinks, toast those we lost, and talk about how we're all going to make it out of this."

Minter turned to look at Vorly. "We're a long way from the coast."

"You saying the navy won't row up the river to come get us?" Vorly asked. Rumors were rampant; Vorly had heard the FnC's had invaded the Kingdom.

"Those pond ducks? They spend most of their time patching leaks in their boats."

"True enough," Vorly said, standing and stretching his back. "Now, let's go talk to our dragonsmiths and figure out what the fuck we're going to do about these crystal spears."

CHAPTER THIRTY-SEVEN

"**M**ORE FUCKING FAWNS," KNOCKERS said, pulling his unlit pipe out of his mouth and pointing as the fifth new rag landed.

Carny glanced up just in time to see a rag fly overhead. The flights had been coming in steadily for the last several days ever since the night of their battle on the eastern slopes. He went back to fiddling with his crossbow. It seemed wherever they went the enemy hid in the jungle. Arrows and bolts couldn't fly very far through that mess. They needed something stronger. He hoped his visit to the dwarves paid off.

"SL, the fawns. They're here," Knockers said, a little louder this time.

Carny looked up. There were indeed three new replacements standing in front of him. He laid his crossbow across his lap and leaned back against the barrack's mud wall.

"And who might you three be?" he asked, studying the newcomers. All wore new uniforms complete with greaves, and their aketons still had their sleeves.

"Crossbowman Vin Estow," the one on the left said, standing up straight.

Carny judged him to be in his late teens. He was tall, close to six feet, with broad shoulders, a dark tan, and a plain, flat sort of face that would probably look bored no matter what the occasion. Large, rough hands held his crossbow in a death grip.

"You a farmer, Estow?" Carny asked.

"Yes, sir. Pigs mostly."

Carny nodded. "Pig farmer. What about you?" he said, pointing to the short one in the middle. The boy looked fourteen if he was a day. His helm sat so low on his head Carny could barely see his eyes.

"Wizard Third Class Shamt Mosanbark, Shield Leader," Mosanbark said. Nothing fit the boy. The sleeves of his aketon hung down to his fingertips and his boots looked like they had room for a family of mice in each toe. "I was in the seminary when they asked for volunteers to learn wizardry and minister to the wounded."

"A druid in the making, just what we need. And what about you?" Carny asked, looking to the third soldier. The man stood easily, his crossbow slung over one shoulder. His equipment might have been new, but Carny could tell he was experienced in a fight.

"Crossbowman Targus Houff. Was a constable, night watch, Druid Edorlan's Alley," he said.

A couple of soldiers nearby whistled. Carny had been right. Dead End Alley, as it was known in the capital, was the center of the black market. Rumor was the king paid taxes to the Seven Families there to keep things calm.

"So you decided you wanted to try something easier then?" Carny said, smiling.

Houff didn't smile back. "Something like that."

Carny kept his smile, but he narrowed his eyes. Houff was going to be one to watch. "So, a pig farmer, a druid, and a king stick," Carny said, using the slang term for a royal constable. "Welcome to Red Shield. I'm your shield leader. Our barracks are right behind me here," he said, motioning with his head. "Grab an empty hammock and drop your gear. Knockers, get them set up, then show them around." He looked back down at his crossbow and started working on the string.

"Is it true? I mean, what they say about an army from the Western Wilds coming?"

Carny looked back up. Mosanbark was looking around, almost as if he expected slyts to pop up and start shooting.

"I don't know any more than you," Carny said. "Enough of the bastards are here already. Hell, you could be a slyt in disguise for all I know."

Laughter rang out as the rest of the shield enjoyed the show.

"I'm not a slyt... what's a slyt?" Mosanbark asked to more laughter.

Carny shook his head and turned back to his crossbow. "Knockers will explain it all. Now, off you go."

Carny kept his head down until the sound of boots faded away. He felt an anger bubbling up inside him. *Why did they have to send Red Shield another pig farmer?* It felt like they were trying to replace Big Hog, not just the soldier, but the man himself.

"Shield Leader?"

"What?" Carny barked, looking up. "Oh, Tryser, didn't hear you."

Dwarf Carpenter Tryser Abroma bowed. "Lightest dwarf on two feet. My shards call me Butterfly," Tryser said. *Shard* was the dwarf term for close friend, although it meant more than that to them.

A few members of the shield nearby snickered. Carny shot them a look and they quickly got busy. Butterfly, to Carny's surprise, didn't seem to mind the name or reaction to it.

"Were you able to come up with anything?" Carny asked, noticing the large burlap bag the dwarf had over his shoulder.

"Aye, I did indeed." He brought the sack down and opened it up, pulling out a crossbow that had clearly been modified. The bow arms were larger, the stock had been reinforced with metal plates, and the string was made from a thicker material.

Carny held out his hands and Butterfly handed it over.

"Heavy," Carny said.

"No way around it," Butterfly said. "I thought about hollowing out the butt, but best to live with it for now. Might try putting some cork in the butt, or that spongy stuff they've been melting and using. Got a nice bounce to it but it's solid. Could be just the thing to lower the weight and take some of the push when you fire."

Carny worked the firing mechanism. "Feels tight. Hell of a lot of stress on the wood," he said, looking up at the dwarf carpenter.

Butterfly took the crossbow out of Carny's hands and began turning a screw on a piece of metal plate he'd added to the main stock. "It's got to be tight. You're drawing almost double the weight now. Heavier string, reinforced bow arms and stock. You said you wanted to be able to hit through the leaves. This'll do it."

Carny nodded. He sensed eyes on him and looked up. Several soldiers from the shield were milling around, watching. Ahmist was front and center. Everyone knew his feelings about dwarves and where they ranked in his world, but to his credit, the soldier said nothing.

"Could you do anything with the bolts?" Carny asked.

Butterfly's eyes sparkled. "I think you're going to like this," he said, pulling a cloth-wrapped bundle out of his sack and placing it on the table.

Carny unwrapped it and saw ten standard-looking bolts with dark black points on the end of them. He picked one up and held it up.

"Iron? Some kind of stone?" The challenge with putting a tougher tip on a bolt was that the extra weight made the bolt nose down in flight, making it unstable.

"I thought to myself, *Now, what's tougher than steel but flies like a bird through the air?* Rags, of course. So I went over to the roost and nosed around and found these."

Carny looked closer. "Is that a piece of talon?"

Butterfly nodded. "I seen some flock sharders carting in big chunks of broken granite to use in the roost. Bit of a scrap going on about who gets stone out of the quarry, so ol' Maggs has a few of us keep an eye on what goes where. Anyway, I see them just toss the granite on the ground right in front of the rags. I figured they was going to eat it, but no, they start clawing away at it like it was a toy. Sparks flying every which way. But not just sparks, bits of broken talon, too. Turns out that's how they keep them great claws of theirs so sharp. So I did a little dealing and got me a bag full of the broken pieces. And let me tell you, that stuff is a pain to work with."

Carny smiled. Butterfly was a talker.

"You try it out?" Carny asked.

"Naw, didn't get the chance. You imagine if one of the higher-ups saw a dwarf out shooting a crossbow? They'd be screaming that the revolution is here."

While dwarves now enjoyed much of the same freedoms that men did, there remained several huge exceptions. A dwarf could serve in the army, but only in support roles. He could carry an axe, a pick, or a shovel but not a hewer, and definitely not a bow of any kind.

"You did a great job," Carny said, reaching into his pocket for his small leather bag of silver pieces.

Butterfly waved him away. "You hold on to that. I'm working on another idea. Not ready yet, but when it is, then we can talk silver." His smile was contagious.

"All right, you're on," Carny said, sticking out his hand to shake Butterfly's.

The dwarf held out his fist and Carny remembered dwarves "knocked the mountain." They bumped knuckles, harder than was comfortable for Carny, but he suspected Butterfly had held back.

"Best be on my way. I should have my new idea ready to show you in another day or two."

"Can't wait," Carny said, holding up his new crossbow. "Much obliged for this."

As Butterfly walked away, several members of the shield crowded around Carny to see the modified crossbow. The first to ask to hold it was Wraith.

"Didn't think you cared much for these contraptions," Carny said, handing the weapon over.

"I didn't; I don't," Wraith said, turning the crossbow over and getting a feel for it. "This is different."

"So it is," Carny said, sitting back and letting the soldiers examine the weapon. "Now we'll have to see how it works."

ARMS WRAPPED AROUND Jawn, and he felt a frizzy mane of hair in his face.

"Hello, Breeze," he said, patting her back. "I hear you're having some trouble on plane."

Breeze led him away from the rag, talking faster than a hummingbird about the latest developments with the sheets and the interference she was dealing with. Jawn listened, although not with great enthusiasm. He still didn't know what he could do.

"Did you hear what I said?" Breeze asked.

Jawn blinked. He'd drifted away again. He was doing that a lot these days. "Sorry. You were saying something about a mist?"

"We get a little fog in the valley most mornings, but I've noticed some way up around the peaks. It's been getting heavier, too."

"Change of seasons?" Jawn said, not really getting what this had to do with thaumics.

"I don't think it's natural," she said, although she didn't sound convinced.

"Don't know," Jawn said, not wanting to tell her she was being silly. "Maybe we could discuss it more tomorrow? I'm feeling a bit queasy after the flight."

Breeze squeezed his arm and began walking again. "Yes, of course. I'll take you to your quarters. We're putting you up with us, but I had them partition off one part of the barrack for you."

I wouldn't want to have to look at a cripple all day either, Jawn thought. "Thanks," he said, "that's very thoughtful of you."

CHAPTER THIRTY-EIGHT

CARNY CROUCHED BY FLOCK Commander Astol as the driver swung Carduus in a sweeping left turn. It was their third circle over the Codpiece and Carny hoped it was their last. He was getting dizzy staring down at the mountain.

"You see a red smoker yet?" Astol asked.

Carny shook his head as a salvo of cat shots slammed into the side of the mountain, tearing out patches of trees. "Nothing yet." The cat boys had been at it for over an eighth, pummeling the mountain with salvo after salvo. The first of the big trebuchets to be completed—Tall Terror—joined in, lobbing stones that looked as big as huts. The artillerists said they were going to soften up the mountain before the shields went in. Carny was fine with that. He preferred the cats be done with their work when he hit the ground.

"There!" Carny said, tapping Astol on the shoulder and pointing. A trail of red smoke sailed through the air and hit the mountain near its base.

"Sky Horse Leader to flock. The cats are done. Follow me in, clear."

A series of *aye-aye*s came out of the crystal sheet near Carny. He shivered. He knew it was just thaumics, but it was still unnatural.

"That sounded good, Breeze," Astol said.

"Jawn's been working the plane, finding me new paths. We're using an irregular slide shift. Every time one gets snarled he finds another," she said.

Astol looked at Carny and must have recognized the lost expression on his face. "I don't understand most of it myself."

Carny smiled. *Just get me down on the ground in one piece.*

"Prepare for landing!" Carny shouted, waving at the troops strapped in on Carduus's back. He looked to where Big Hog normally sat, then quickly looked away. The soldier remained trapped in a state between living and dead. It wasn't right.

Astol pointed toward the mountain as they descended to the valley floor. "You know, if those cats could clear a bit more brush, I could probably land you there instead of at the bottom. Save you a lot of climbing."

Carny saw the gap in the trees. It would save a lot of energy, but the risk would be high. "I'll keep that in mind," Carny said.

Carduus flared his wings as they approached the dosha swamp. Unlike previous landings, he came in at a gentle slope and then slid along his belly in the mud. It kicked up a ton of crap and smelled like hell, but it brought him right to the edge of the berm. Carny gave Astol a thump on the shoulder and jumped off.

The rest of the troops followed as the other rags began landing. A sparker rag wheeled high overhead but made no move to attack. For the moment, all was quiet.

Carny fanned the shield out into a skirmish line as it moved toward the trees at the jungle's edge. Stone dust and bits of leaves still fell through the air as they pushed through and into the jungle. Carny held his new and improved crossbow and wondered if he'd get the chance to use it. First, he had to navigate the torn tree trunks blocking his path.

"Bard, take your men around the left side of this mess. Wraith, you swing right. I'll go up the middle and we'll meet up at the other side."

Carny looked behind him. The three fawns were with his group. He wanted to keep an eye on them. The little wiz was glued to Carny's hip, while the former king stick, Houff, and Estow, the pig farmer, were toward the rear.

"Stay low, keep quiet, and keep calm," Carny said, turning back and raising a leg over the first log.

"Slyts!"

Whistles pierced the air. Arrows sliced out of the jungle to their front. Three hit the log right in front of Carny. He threw himself backward and fell on Mosanbark.

"You all right?" Carny asked, rolling over and getting to his knees. An arrow stuck out of the wizard's forehead above his left eye. Both eyes remained open, staring sightlessly up at the sky.

The twang of bowstrings and clang of crossbows brought Carny's attention back to the battle.

"Aim your fire! Look for the angle of the arrows!" Carny shouted, peering over the edge of the log. The arrows were coming in fairly straight, so the slyts weren't up in the trees.

"Rake the brush!"

The shield concentrated their fire low down, pumping bolt after bolt. Bard's group to the left looked to be pinned down, but Wraith's bowmen were advancing on the right.

"Keep it up, keep firing!" Carny shouted, running from log to log to check on the men. He found Estow and Houff behind a shattered stump, alternating their fire. "Good job. Keep it up."

He turned and started heading back down the line when he remembered he hadn't fired his new crossbow. He kneeled and thumbed the safety lever off. He saw movement thirty yards in front. He squeezed the firing lever. The bow arms flexed so much the force nearly ripped the crossbow out of Carny's hands. The bolt flew across the opening like it was being chased by a rag. He saw the bolt punch through the foliage, then heard a scream.

Wraith's group had now reached the far side of the smashed clearing and were shooting right into the side of the slyt line. More whistles sounded and the arrow fire to their front stopped.

Carny stood up and drew his hewer. "Follow me!"

He jumped over more felled trees and pushed his way through

the tangle of vegetation until he came to the slyt positions. It became immediately clear why the slyts hadn't all been killed despite the cats' doing their very best. Small, deep holes had been dug behind the trunks of trees on the upward side of the slope. The slyts must have hunkered down in those until the cats stopped, then popped out to fire at the shield.

Carny slowed, looking around for movement. He spotted three dead slyts on the ground. One of them moved, but before Carny could react an arrow pierced its skull.

Wraith appeared from behind a tree with another arrow already notched. "All clear on the right flank."

Carny nodded. He sheathed his hewer and bent down to cock his crossbow. He slipped the hook onto the string and grunted as he pulled up. When the latch caught the string he relaxed, taking a moment to catch his breath. He then put in another of Butterfly's talon-tipped bolts. The Bard appeared and signaled that everything was good.

Motioning with his hand for them to move forward, Carny stepped off, walking past the dead slyts. He saw his bolt sticking out of a tree trunk. The shaft was covered in blood. He traced its flight back to the slyt he must have hit. It was gruesome. The bolt had taken the slyt by the left shoulder joint and nearly ripped the arm right off. Carny could see muscle and bone through the blood. The slyt must have bled out.

"Got something here," Wraith said.

Carny looked up and walked to where Wraith stood. "Any casualties?"

Wraith shook his head. Carny nodded and then looked at what Wraith was pointing at.

A flat area ten feet by ten feet had been cleared. Logs and vegetation had been piled up around it, creating thick walls. The dirt floor was bare except for a crude wooden base with a single thick bamboo pole sticking out of it.

"Ballista stand?" Carny said.

Over the next eighth the shield found seven more positions of similar construction along with dozens of small holes and a cache of food, enough to feed the shield for a week. The biggest find, however, was the disassembled pieces for three ballistas.

Carny had the Bard write it all down in his journal. A rag call high above signaled it was time to pull back. Carny looked up the mountain. The slyts were planning on being here for a while.

"Burn it," Carny said.

Wraith fired a star into the pile, which immediately caught fire. Carny waited until the entire shield was moving before he turned and started back down the slope. He stopped when he got to Mosanbark's body. The two fawns were preparing to carry him down. Someone had pulled the arrow from his head, leaving a bloody hole.

Carny waited for them to pick him up, then followed after them. Seven dead slyts and three ballistas against one dead wizard. Somewhere other than where Carny was, he knew there were officers who saw that as a win.

MISKA WAS IN her glory. The soldiers were animated and talkative. Their barrack reminded her of a pub, complete with a cask of beer. From what she gathered, they'd successfully assaulted the mountain they called the Codpiece and destroyed several enemy weapons as well as killing two dozen slyts. She grimaced. High Druid, it was an ugly word. She still hadn't decided if she would include it in her stories when she got back to the Kingdom. You wanted to engage with people, not repulse them.

"What can you tell me about the wizard that was killed?" she asked, smiling sadly at the shield leader. He looked tired, and painfully thin, but there was an air about him that was dangerous. She found it very attractive.

Carny shrugged. "Didn't really know him. He was in the seminary, then volunteered to come out here. Try Estow or Houff. They flew out with him."

Miska nodded. That wasn't what she wanted to know anyway. She looked at his crossbow. "I understand a dwarf made that for you," she said.

Carny sat up in his hammock, startling her. "What do you know about it?"

"Nothing, I mean I just heard he made it. It looks different. Is it better than the others?"

Carny looked at her for several flicks before easing himself back down. "It's better. Shoots harder and packs a bigger wallop. Tore the arm off a slyt."

Miska nodded again. She bit her lip, debating whether to keep going, and decided she might as well or coming out here would be a complete waste.

"So... you get along with dwarves then?"

"Sure, they're like us really," Carny said.

"That's a very enlightened view, Shield Leader," Miska said.

"People are people, you know?" Carny said. He sounded genuine. There was no guile here, just heartfelt honesty. "I don't have a problem with dwarves, never have. Why should I? They've never done anything to me. People that have power and money, though, they're a different story. It ain't money that makes you good, it's what's inside."

Miska held her breath as he talked. Tears formed at the corners of his eyes. This was real. This was a man speaking a truth that she believed, too.

"But the LOKAM—"

"*Fuck the LOKAM!*" chorused the shield to a rousing round of laughter.

The soldier they called Ahmy stomped out of the barrack, but it did nothing to lessen the mood. They'd won today, even at a cost.

"Look," Carny said, propping himself up in his hammock. "I need to get some sleep. If you want to fuck, let's go out back and do it now, or leave me be."

Miska knew her cheeks were flushing. She started to get angry and walk away, but that was probably what he wanted. She stared at him and drew in her breath.

"Fine, let's fuck."

Carny's eyes widened. "Damn, I figured you'd just punch me."

Miska smiled. "Who says I won't do both?"

CHAPTER THIRTY-NINE

"I CAN'T BREATHE," CARNY said, only half joking. Miska straddled him, riding up and down on his cock. She was a big girl, and from Carny's position he got all of her as she drove down on his hips.

"Do you want me to slow down?" she asked, keeping up her rhythmic pace.

Carny grabbed her hips and pulled her down even harder. "Druid, no! I want to die like this!"

Miska squeezed and Carny heard angels.

"What was that?" she asked, stopping midbounce.

"My soul leaving my body," Carny said. He gave her ass a slap, but she remained still.

"I heard something," she said, twisting around to look behind her.

"Mercy, it doesn't bend like that."

"There's someone out there," she hissed.

Carny raised himself up on an elbow and looked past her body. They were in a secluded spot behind the barracks in a pile of sailcloth too tattered to use for roofs. "I don't see anyone or anything."

Miska turned to look back at him and leaned forward, her large, beautiful breasts enveloping Carny's face in a hot, sweaty puddle. He thrust his hips up, driving his cock as deep as he could. He truly could pass on right now and be entirely fine with it.

"Oh, Druid!"

WRAITH WATCHED THE SL and the crier for a few more flicks, then went on his way. He was disappointed that the woman had heard him. Not that he'd wanted to continue watching, but he had been sure he hadn't made a sound. No wonder he couldn't track the slyts. His stalking was letting him down.

He made his way through the camp, easily dodging the few sentries patrolling. The gray light of a waxing crescent moon cast muted shadows. He paused when he reached the wall. He could track the slyts all the way to the Western Wilds, but would it matter? He started climbing up the ladder. It mattered to him, and that was enough.

He slid over the wall and dropped down the other side. Without pausing, he jumped the moat and moved into the saw grass, angling toward the slyt path. Once inside he changed course and looped away from the path before coming back around to it. If any slyts were out here, they'd be looking for him at the wrong spot.

Wraith crouched low, straining to hear movement on the path, but other than the slow rustle of the grass by a light breeze, it was quiet. With just his bow, quiver, and hunting knife, he wasn't looking for a battle. He'd left his helm and aketon in the barracks, opting instead to wear just his tunic, trousers, and boots. Silence and speed were his allies, not armor.

Confident he was alone, Wraith was reaching forward to part the woven saw grass when the sound of wood on wood reached his ears. He froze. A shadow moved past him on the path heading east. A second and then a third went by him. He counted to twenty and then pushed aside the grass and stepped onto the path. He held his bow in his hands, an arrow notched and ready. No slyts.

He looked up the path to Iron Fist, then turned and began

following it down into the valley. He'd lost the slyts before when he reached the dosha swamp, but he was determined not to this time. As he got closer to the dosha swamp he slowed, his muscles tensing. By the time he could see the slight opening at the end of the saw grass he stopped. The slyts weren't there.

Wraith moved quickly to the opening and looked out. The valley appeared quiet. Then he saw them. Three small figures barely visible in the quarter moon. They were already across the berm and entering a patch of bamboo.

Bastards can move! He waited until the last one disappeared into the bamboo, then raced after them.

The next eighth was a trying one as Wraith drew deeply from inside to keep the slyts in sight. He understood now why he'd lost them before—they were fast. Far faster than he'd imagined. They moved from cover to cover like deer.

Wraith was navigating another berm when he stumbled and went down to his hands and knees. He let himself down to his stomach and froze. The third slyt stopped by a stand of saw grass and looked back. Wraith cursed his luck and waited. After several flicks the slyt turned and vanished into the grass. Wraith stayed where he was. It hadn't been more than ten flicks when the slyt popped his head out of the grass, several yards away from where he'd entered.

Following them into that grass was too risky. Wraith looked past it and spotted another patch a hundred yards away. It was the next significant piece of cover. He waited until the slyt disappeared again, then got up and ran for a position where he could watch the second area of grass.

He slid down the side of a berm near the grass and waited. Sure enough, the slyts emerged from the distant patch of grass and made for the one near him. The trailing slyt turned a couple of times and looked back the way they'd come, but his concern seemed to lessen the farther they got. When they reached the river they slipped into the water and quickly paddled across, their bows slung on their backs. Wraith followed suit.

Wraith started anticipating their trail across the rest of the valley, able to keep them in sight without directly following them. Two more times the rear slyt hung back and waited to see if they were being followed, but his comrades seemed to grow impatient with this and a series of rude hand gestures got the third slyt moving.

As they approached the tree line Wraith began thinking about his plan and realized he didn't really have one. He'd been so bent on proving he could track the slyts he hadn't given thought to what he would do after.

The slyts broke the last bit of cover and loped into the tree line. Wraith took after them. He'd come up with a plan later. For now, he'd keep following.

Once in the jungle the slyts slowed, giving Wraith a chance to catch his breath. They obviously felt safe among the trees. The Kingdom only attacked in daylight, its patrols always scurrying back to the safety of Iron Fist before nightfall. It was a predictability that worried Wraith, but for now, it was working in his favor.

The slyts climbed the mountain, winding their way among the trees on a path that Wraith wasn't sure he would have seen if he hadn't been following them. He lost track of time but figured they'd been climbing for a good eighth when the slyts came to a small clearing and stopped. Wraith moved off the path and swung around to the right. It was difficult to get a good look as there were a lot of plants blocking his view. He looked at the tree in front of him and made up his mind.

Slinging his bow, Wraith took off his boots and then knotted the laces and hung them around his neck. He grabbed a vine hanging down beside the trunk and pulled himself up until he reached the first branch. Slowly, with sweat dripping in his eyes, he scaled the tree until he sat on a branch twenty yards above the ground.

He wedged himself into a Y and then pulled some leaves and branches around him. From here he had a perfect view of the clearing and the path leading into it. The three slyts were now sitting in a small circle and talking softly among themselves.

Wraith leaned back in the tree and prepared himself for a long night. The leaves near him rustled. A moment later the furry head of a young marbled cat emerged, its amber eyes scanning the clearing. The small predator blinked, its ear tips leaning forward as it focused on the three slyts. It eased its body through the leaves but stopped short with the end of its long tail still shrouded in the shadows.

It lowered its body down onto the branch, settling down along the length of its chest and belly. The cat kept watch on the clearing, its eyes following the strange movements. Gradually, it brought its head down until it rested on its outstretched paws, its whiskers drooping to either side.

Wraith watched the cat with absolute fascination. Did the slyts do this every night? Was the cat waiting until they left to go check for scraps of food? Another movement caught Wraith's eye, and his fascination turned dark.

A foot and a half above the cat, a blood python lay strung out over several branches. Its reddish-brown splotches made it difficult to see. Only the python's flicking tongue tasting the air gave any indication it was there.

The python's obsidian orbs studied the cat. If the snake was aware of the slyts in the clearing it gave no sign of it.

For several moments, neither cat or snake moved, each absorbed in watching. Another breeze set the branches swaying. As the cat remained focused on the clearing, the python bunched itself, folding its body into a series of thick S's. It raised its head, its tongue testing the air one more time.

The python lunged, its jaws snapping open as its curved fangs sprang forward, ready to impale the cat. The cat looked up, its fur bristling and its eyes widening. It hissed, baring its own fangs, but it was already too late.

The fangs of the python had just brushed the tips of the cat's fur when an arrow sliced diagonally through the python's skull. The arrow continued its flight, burying its iron head into the branch just behind the cat's rear. The python's body continued its lunge, its heavy coils slamming into the much smaller marbled cat.

The cat wailed, jumping up in an attempt to grab another branch, but the weight of the python pushed it out into open space. The cat clawed wildly for purchase even as it fell toward the jungle floor. Wraith reached out, snagged its tail at the tip, and swung the cat in an arc, bringing it back toward the tree.

The cat landed claws-first on Wraith's tunic, its ears pinned back against its head, its amber eyes wide as it hissed its fear and fury.

"Shhhh, kit, shh," Wraith whispered, releasing the cat's tail and quickly placing his hand over its back. He pressed it close to his chest while keeping his head up and away from the swinging paws that were trying to gouge out his eyes. The claws dug into his flesh, but he gritted his teeth and kept the pressure on.

The slyts were standing up, looking in Wraith's direction. He cursed himself, but what was done was done. He readied himself to make a run for it, but more slyts suddenly entered the clearing. There was a greeting, a few motions toward the tree, then laughter. The slyts sat down again. Wraith counted seven now.

The cat hissed and scratched at Wraith's tunic. Wraith took the abuse and continued whispering to the cat, slowly bringing his head down so that he was staring directly into its eyes.

"You need to get smarter," Wraith said, his voice soft. "There are cold-blooded killers around here. They have no compassion and they can't be reasoned with."

The cat continued to stare at Wraith, hissing its anger at being held.

"Anger's good," Wraith continued, petting the cat with short, heavy strokes. "But you can't let anger control you. It's like wind in a sail, kit. If you let it, it will blow you onto the rocks. So you have to direct it, harness it and make it work for you."

The cat blinked and closed its mouth, its last hiss dying away.

"Good. You're learning."

The cat's racing heart and heaving lungs slowed down under his palm. Wraith lessened the pressure against it. The cat tensed its shoulders, pushing up against Wraith's hand. Wraith pushed down again, but gently. The cat relaxed once more and so Wraith lifted his hand.

The cat remained against his chest, its claws gripping the fabric of his tunic. Wraith brought his hand back down and stroked the length of its back to its exceptionally long tail. "Now, if you want to learn how to survive out here, you need patience. I'll wager that python had been sitting there most of the day. See those slyts out there? I've been tracking them most of the night." Wraith paused before speaking again. "Patience."

Wraith turned and settled back into the crook of a large branch. He rested his bow across his lap. The cat looked around, realizing it was free to do what it wanted. Wraith looked away, surprised that he wanted the cat to stay.

The cat unhooked its claws from his tunic and stood on his thigh. Wraith grimaced as the cat tensed, its claws digging into his skin through the worn cloth, and then leaped. It landed gracefully on the branch below where the snake hung dead from the arrow in its skull. The cat looked up at Wraith once, then hunched down by the snake and began to gnaw at its flesh.

Wraith watched it for a while, studying the movement of its jaws as it pulled and tore at the carcass, delicately stripping away the scaly skin to get at the succulent meat underneath. He'd let the cat get its fill before carving up the rest. He'd grown to like the taste of snake since he'd been in the Lux.

With the sound of the cat chewing, Wraith returned his attention to the clearing. More slyts arrived and joined the circle. They came in twos and threes, and it dawned on him that these were small scout patrols that had been in the valley and were now coming back with their reports.

A blur of fur and the cat was on his lap. It looked up at him as if to say, *The snake's all yours*, then curled up in a ball and began licking its paws.

Wraith reached down and gently ruffled the cat's fur. The cat looked up at him, then went back to licking. A new group of slyts arrived, but this time coming down from the mountain. Wraith leaned forward. *I'll be damned. It's a shift change.* The first group of slyts rose from their circle and greeted the new group. The numbers appeared to be about the same. They talked briefly and then split, the original group heading up the mountain, the new arrivals heading back down into the valley.

Tracking the slyts farther up the mountain crossed his mind, but he quickly killed it. He'd found out a significant piece of information that the army should know about. His duty now was to get back to Iron Fist. He looked down at the cat and nudged it with his hand.

The cat hissed and buried its head in its paws. Wraith nudged it again. "Sorry, but I have to go."

The cat dug its claws into Wraith's leg and got up, arching its back as it did so. It turned and looked Wraith in the eyes, and for a moment he thought it might pounce, but the cat hissed one more time and then bounded to another branch and disappeared into the shadows. Wraith watched it go, rubbing his thigh as he did. He forgot about the python and quickly shimmied down the tree, putting his boots back on at the bottom.

He stood up and stretched and the cat landed on his shoulder, hissing. Wraith spun around and reached for the cat but it was already bounding away. An arrow meant for Wraith's head hit the trunk of the tree in front of him. Wraith dove toward the shot, pulling his hunting knife from its sheath and slashing at the shadows. His knife hit something solid and warm liquid splashed his hand.

His momentum took him forward and he crashed into the slyt, and both fell to the ground. Wraith pulled his knife from its chest and drove it under the slyt's jaw, severing the large vein there. Blood gushed into Wraith's face and he leaned back, wiping at his eyes with his free hand.

The slyt made a gurgling sound, then lay still. Wraith gasped, his heart pounding. He looked around, expecting dozens of slyts to come pouring out of the trees, but none did. Knowing that every flick he didn't move brought him one flick closer to being found, he sheathed his knife, retrieved his bow, and, grabbing the body by its tunic, lifted it up onto his shoulder and carried it into the jungle. He walked several hundred yards before finally setting it down.

In the little bit of light coming through the leaves, he studied the slyt. He was young, probably just a teen, but he'd heard they lived longer than men, so who knew. He wore a uniform—tunic and trousers—made of a dark green fabric that felt like cotton. A simple rope belt, a bow, a quiver, and a small hunting knife were his only items. It occurred to Wraith that this had to be the slyt who had almost seen him earlier. And like Wraith, he had decided to go out hunting alone.

Wraith sat on his haunches, staring at the body. He'd have to leave it here. He stood up and kicked some leaves over it and walked away.

CHAPTER FORTY

VORLY STOOD LOOKING AT a map of the valley drawn by the longbowman. It was pinned to the wall of Vorly's tent and fluttered and moved like a living thing with each takeoff and landing of a rag.

SFC Minter, along with Breeze, the blind thaum Rathim, and the shield leader for Red Shield, stood around in a semicircle. All, save Rathim, stared at the map as Wraith explained what he'd seen the night before.

"They meet here, in this clearing."

Minter leaned closer. "I know that area. We could hit it no problem in the daylight, but in the middle of the night? Not a chance."

"It only works if you hit it when they're there," Wraith said.

"Why not use the cats?" Shield Leader Carny said. "They've got the range."

"But not the accuracy," Wraith said, tapping the map. "These slyts are fast. The moment they heard the first cat fire they'd scatter."

"You tracked them," Vorly said, amazed the soldier had. "Couldn't you lead your shield there and then hit them when they show up?"

Wraith shook his head. "I barely tracked them, and they almost got me. They'd hear the shield a mile away."

"I want to help," Minter said, "but I can't do it at night. Our rags are skittish enough as it is. Flying them in the dark in this valley would be a nightmare. I'm sorry."

Breeze tapped Vorly on the arm. He turned to look at her. She raised her eyebrows but said nothing. Vorly understood. He turned back to Wraith. "You're sure? Absolutely sure that they meet here every night?"

Wraith paused before speaking. "No, but I'll go out again tonight, and as many nights as is needed to confirm it."

Vorly nodded. "What did Weel say?"

At this, Wraith and his SL shared a look. "About Weel…"

"You didn't tell him," Vorly said. "I understand. Right, as it happens, we have flown at night, and while it's not our favorite thing, it can be done. We won't be able to see that clearing though. We'll need it marked, and that'll mean someone has to be there to light the marker."

"I'll be there," Wraith said.

"Wraith, wait a flick," Carny said. "Even if this works according to plan, you're going to be in the middle of a lot of slyts with rag fire pouring down."

"If I put the marker right in the clearing, you can hit it?" Wraith asked, turning and looking at Vorly.

Vorly nodded. "Aye, we can."

Wraith shrugged his shoulders. "Just tell me how many more times you want me to watch them then."

Vorly reached out and placed a hand on Wraith's shoulder. He got the immediate impression that he shouldn't have, but he kept it there. "Son, we'll go tonight. Every day those slyts watch us they learn more." He turned to Carny. "You all right with this, SL?"

Carny looked at Wraith and then back at Vorly. "Not really, but Wraith's sure, so he has my blessing."

"Then it's settled, we launch tonight."

JAWN HELD ON to Breeze's arm as she led him back to his quarters. "Why'd you bring me? I had nothing to offer." He knew he sounded like a petulant child, but he didn't care. Breeze had made him look like a fool.

Breeze stopped suddenly. "And whose fault is that? You just stood there like a lump on a log."

Jawn raised his hands. "Breeze, I'm blind. I can't see a damn thing."

"I know, but you can slide between planes. You can feel your way through the aether in a way I can't. I want you on plane tonight when we launch."

Jawn finally understood. "I'll aid you in whatever harmony you need, of course." He turned, expecting her to start walking, but she remained standing. "What?"

"That's not what I meant. If this goes as planned, a lot of slyts are going to be dead, and their command is going to be wondering what happened. If they have thaums—"

"Then they'll be on plane searching to see if thaumics were involved," he said, finishing her thought. A glimmer of pride welled up in his chest.

Her hand squeezed his arm. "You have value, Jawn. You can help—just believe in yourself." She started walking again.

They walked in silence. Jawn still wanted to be upset at Breeze, but she'd given him something to do that was real. It wasn't out of pity. No one could do what he did on plane. He lifted his head as an idea began to take shape.

Yes, there is a way forward.

CARNY DIDN'T BOTHER to watch Wraith leave Iron Fist as the sun sank behind the western peaks. Only a few people knew what he was doing, and Carny preferred it that way. Not that he suspected spies, but the less Weel knew, the better.

"You don't need to fly with us," Flock Commander Astol said, coming around the far side of Carduus and patting the rag's head as he did. Carduus rumbled and closed his eyes. Carny supposed that was purring. "It's not going to be like a day flight. Rags aren't great in the dark, especially with mountains around."

"One of my men is risking everything tonight. I'm coming," Carny said. He looked over at Knockers and Wiz. "And they're coming, too."

Vorly shrugged. "We have the room. We launch in a sixteenth, so don't go anywhere," he said, turning back to Carduus.

Carny turned to Knockers and Wiz. "Last chance to change your mind."

Knockers shook his head. "He'll be in the jungle alone. We have to make sure he doesn't get left out there," Knockers said, staring hard at Carny.

"No one's being left," Carny said, surprised at Knocker's intensity.

"I know," Knockers said, adjusting his crossbow slung across his chest.

Carny looked at Wiz.

"If something goes wrong, I need to be there," Wiz said. He lacked Knocker's suppressed energy, but it was clear his convictions were just as strong.

"Let's hope it doesn't," Carny said.

WRAITH CHOSE A tree a hundred yards to the left of the one he'd been in the night before. It offered a good view of the clearing while giving him ample cover within its leaves. He didn't climb it right away but circled around the entire clearing, searching for signs of a trap or any indication that the slyts knew what had happened the night before. They obviously knew one of their scouts was missing, but if he was prone to going out on his own like Wraith they wouldn't be too worried yet. Assuming they hadn't found his body.

He had a short debate with himself on whether to check on the body or not. In the end he decided there was little to be gained and so didn't. He'd know soon enough if the slyts had changed their routine.

Satisfied no slyts were in the vicinity, he approached the tree.

He scattered a few twigs around the base before climbing. If any slyts did come looking he hoped he'd hear them.

He settled into a crook of three branches, bringing his bow up to ensure he could shoot without getting caught on anything. His quiver was filled with six star arrows.

The number of things that could go wrong was immense, but Wraith saw no point in worrying about them. This was their best chance to disrupt the slyts in advance of whatever they were planning.

The whisper of paws on a branch was the only warning Wraith got before the marbled cat leaped onto his lap. Its claws dug in and Wraith winced.

"We're friends now, are we?" Wraith whispered, reaching out and petting the animal. It twisted its head to the side and closed its eyes as Wraith rubbed the inside of an ear. "You're going to want to get out of here soon," he said, but didn't try to shoo the cat away. He appreciated the company of another hunter.

"I'm going to call you Ugen," he said, leaning back in the tree to wait.

CHAPTER FORTY-ONE

THE COOK FIRES AND lanterns visible in Iron Fist and the fortresses dotted across the valley proved invaluable as Vorly urged Carduus into a spiraling climb. Without them he wasn't sure he would have been able to orient himself. Volunteering to fly this mission had been rash, and as they leveled out at six thousand feet he wondered why he'd done it.

Minter had been wise to pass. The man knew the limits of himself and his rags and had turned it down. Truth be told, Vorly wasn't all that convinced Carduus was any more suited to flying at night, but the rag had done it, which meant he could do it again.

Vorly reached behind him and patted the rucksack on his back. Breeze had insisted they pack supplies in case something went wrong. Vorly appreciated her concern, but if something did go wrong a couple of mangoes, an extra water skin, a loaf of bread, and a small wheel of goat cheese wasn't likely to rescue the situation. Still, there was some comfort in having along two well-armed soldiers and a wizard.

"All clear on plane," Breeze said, her voice coming through the tube at little more than a whisper. "Black Star is reporting a clear plane as well."

Vorly clicked his tongue twice to acknowledge her. Yet one more thing they'd refined. He turned in his saddle and looked past Breeze to the three soldiers accompanying them. He had to remember to pass along his condolences. They'd lost two shield leaders in a matter of weeks, both charked. The new one seemed solid. Vorly hoped he lasted.

There wasn't much thermal to catch so Vorly put Carduus into a series of slow climbs and long glides. It kept wing noise down to a minimum. Most important, however, was that it would keep Carduus calm and cool. The beast knew something was up. His chark meal had been huge, double what he'd normally get for a flight. Rags weren't the sharpest pricks on a rose, but they'd learned that extra chark meant some kind of break from the norm. The warmth coming up through the heat blankets was tolerable, but only just. Additional blankets had been tacked to Carduus's sides to hide the glow, and Pagath had even painted a thin layer of pitch on Carduus's wings over the major arteries to dull the light of the rag's molten blood. Vorly and Breeze wore sparker uniforms loaned to them by Minter's crews. Extra layers of protection would shield them from the worst of the heat. Additional heat blankets had been provided to the soldiers to wrap themselves in.

A movement by Vorly's elbow made him turn. Shield Leader Carny crouched down beside him. He moved around on Carduus with a lot more assurance than he had on his first flight. *The boy might have a little mule in his bloodline.*

"I thought I saw lights," Carny said. "North and east, other side of the mountains."

"Villages maybe? There are a few around here," Vorly said.

"Maybe," Carny said, though he didn't sound convinced. "If there's a chance, I'd like to check it out after."

"Let's focus on one thing at a time. If this does work, every slyt in fifty miles will be up. Might get a bit unhealthy up here."

Carny nodded and went back to the other soldiers. Vorly thought about swinging Carduus a little wider on the next turn so he'd be a little farther east but then quashed it. He needed to be as close as he could to the clearing when that soldier fired those stars.

Vorly brought Carduus around in a wide, lazy turn and

began his next run up the eastern side of the valley. The jungle appeared as a ruffled black blanket below.

The clang of a hammer on sheet steel rang out, marking the midnight candle. Carduus growled, his head turning toward Iron Fist. Vorly snapped the reins and brought his head back. He looked at the lights below and calculated they were about two thousand yards out from the clearing.

Vorly gave Carduus the glide kick and the rag immediately stretched out his wings. As he started to drop, Vorly flicked the reins and Carduus rumbled, dropping his head as he picked up speed. So far, so good. Now it was all up to one soldier on the ground. If the slyts were there, he'd fire the stars.

WRAITH COUNTED FIFTY-THREE slyts in the clearing. That was more than the night before. He looked down at the newly named Ugen curled in his lap and nudged it with his hand. Ugen lifted his head to hiss, then dropped it back down. Wraith tried again with the same result. Finally, he grabbed one of the star arrows and poked Ugen with the tip. The cat sprung up hissing. Wraith held up his hands.

"Sorry, but it's time to go," he whispered. "You don't want to be around for this anyway, trust me."

The cat flexed his claws, digging in a little deeper into Wraith's thigh, then proudly hopped off his lap onto a nearby branch and trotted into the shadows, his tail held high.

Wraith made sure he wasn't sneaking back, then turned his attention to the clearing. Now all he needed was the midnight candle to sound. He held his bow in his left hand while his right held the first star. He was no more than thirty yards from the clearing, close enough that he could put a star into a slyt, but he decided against it. If this worked, the rag would take care of the slyts.

He wiggled his butt on the branch and focused on his breathing, slowing it down to a nice, even pace. He thought of it as a big, slow waterwheel. In for ten… hold for ten… out for ten… hold for ten…

Thoughts and distractions faded. His world narrowed to the group of slyts ahead. He practiced notching the star in quick, fluid motions, making sure his elbow didn't hit anything on the draw.

The first clang of the midnight candle rang out. They'd agreed that on the seventh clang he'd fire. By then the rag would be approaching the clearing, needing only the light of his stars to guide it in the rest of the way.

Wraith notched the star. Weighing five ounces, it was almost twice as heavy as a standard arrow and so required the shooter to aim higher to compensate for the extra weight.

As they had the previous night, the slyts paid no attention to the distant clangs and chatted softly among themselves. On the fifth, Wraith drew back on the string. Unlike a longbow, the draw on this smaller bow was light and didn't require massive effort.

When the hammer hit the sixth time, Wraith held his breath and sighted down the arrow. Wings on the wind told him the time had come. He released the string as the hammer struck seven. The star shot from his bow and began trailing a tail of red sparks. A slyt turned. Wraith notched the second star and drew, aiming in the same direction. Spots floated in front of his eyes after the first shot and he cursed himself for not closing his eye when he released. The second star flew, its path veering slightly to the right of the first.

Shouts rose up from the clearing. A rumbling roar grew on the air as the night took on a red glow.

Several slyts had their bows in their hands, arrows notched. The two stars burned in the clearing as more slyts rushed toward them. And above them, a brightening reddish-orange light descended.

Wraith dove from his perch, caught a lower branch with one hand, dropped to another, then jumped down to the jungle floor, rolling as he did so. He got up running, not bothering to look back. His way forward appeared in stark relief as the flame from the rag plunged into the clearing and tore the night apart. Heat slapped him in the back and he gasped as the air around him turned searing. He crashed through the foliage, no longer trying to move quietly. His bow twisted in his hand and he knew the string had snapped. He kept running.

A sharp pain hit him in the lower back and he screamed. The stars in his quiver had ignited. He reached around as he ran and ripped the quiver from his body, flinging it away. The pain was beyond anything he had ever experienced in his life. He stumbled and fell to the jungle floor. Heat washed over him in a roaring wave. Leaves withered and caught fire. He crawled, his voice one long scream as demons plunged a white-hot knife into his back.

Wraith reached out for a log or something to grab on to and pull himself forward and found only air. He tumbled several feet into a small depression. He landed on his back; lightning exploded inside him and everything went black.

EVERY FLICKER OF flame that Carduus poured down on the clearing was his life cut shorter. When Vorly kicked Carduus and pulled up on the reins to stop him, he figured the beast had just given up a year. They banked to port and raced down the side of the mountain before Vorly urged Carduus to climb.

Carduus roared with joy. Vorly recognized the sound and it brought a tear to his eye. Smoke streamed from Carduus's nostrils, and sparks twinkled as they flew past Vorly and vanished in the night.

"Good boy! Good boy, Carduus!" Vorly shouted, pounding the rag's plates.

Carduus roared again and began to turn back toward the clearing.

"Once was enough," Vorly said, snapping Carduus back.

Flares of color assaulted Vorly's eyes, and the small section of his face that was open to the air in his helm felt tight and hot. He looked back at the mayhem they'd caused and whistled. He couldn't see the peaks of the mountains for the glare of the fire. In addition to the clearing, flames had surged along paths that led to it, creating the effect of a fiery spider on the slope. He immediately thought of the soldier and wondered if he'd made it.

"Breeze?" he asked, talking into the tube. He tapped the tin cone and it fell off and flew away in the wind. He looked down and saw that the tubing had melted.

"Breeze?" he asked, turning this time. She was bent over her sheets and didn't hear him. He started to reach back to touch her, then remembered how dangerous that could be.

"Breeze!"

Her head flew up.

"I just wanted to check that you were all right," he said. He looked past her to where the soldiers had already slipped off the blankets and were staring at the fire.

She nodded. "Fine! Much better than the last time."

Vorly smiled, then realized she couldn't see it. He gave her a thumbs-up and turned forward. Shield Leader Carny was at his elbow again a moment later.

"Were you on target?"

"I saw the slyts in the clearing. Your man did a great job," Vorly said.

"He would have made it out of that, right?"

Vorly paused before answering. "He knew it was coming, and he knows how to move around the jungle. I think so."

"We can't just leave him out there," Carny said.

Vorly nodded. "If he's not back by daybreak, and we aren't tasked with other missions, I'll fly you to the clearing myself. If it's safe to land, we will."

"Thanks." Carny started to get up, then crouched back down. "Those lights I saw on the other side of the mountains are still bothering me. Could we take one flyover?"

Vorly reached up and took off his helm. "Boiling my brain in that thing."

"Too late," Breeze chirped.

Vorly held up a hand and gave Breeze a rude gesture. "I'm not keen to be flying around up here in the dark, but Carduus is still pretty excited, so trying to land him right now wouldn't be fun. Sure, let's go check those lights."

Vorly reached for his whistle, then thought better of it. The slyts knew a rag was in the air, but he didn't want to give them any help in finding them. They were flying the western side of the valley, so Vorly eased Carduus up until he was above the peaks. They flew through a layer of mist that was surprisingly cold. It clung to everything it touched and made Vorly uneasy. A flick later Carduus broke out into a clear night sky leaving the mist and the feeling behind.

"You feel that, Breeze?" Vorly asked, noticing vapors of steam swirling away from the trailing edge of Carduus's wings.

"Yes. Getting more interference on plane again, too," she said.

Vorly looked over at his crystal. Instead of a clear black field that appeared to have no bottom, it looked gray around the edges and blurred for a flick before clearing up again.

"Thaums?" he asked.

"Not that I recognize. I'm going to go a little deeper in plane with Black Star, so if I don't answer right away don't worry."

"Be careful," Vorly said.

"What village is that?" Carny asked, pointing west.

Vorly looked. A collection of lights was gathered less than a mile from the mountains. "There are no villages to the west, only to the east. Everything west of here is the Wilds."

"It's the Forest Collective," Carny said.

Vorly began picking out more lights in the jungle. He counted several thin strands that led to the mountain chain. Ignoring his own caution from earlier, he turned Carduus west so they'd fly over the lights.

"Tell your boys to make sure they're strapped in. We might do a bit of flying here in a flick," Vorly said, pushing Carduus into a gliding dive.

The wind picked up at once and Vorly squinted, hoping against hope that this was something other than a slyt army.

A volley of ballista spears flew up in front of Carduus, their tips twinkling as if they'd been dipped in diamonds.

"Hang on!" he shouted, pushing Carduus into a steeper dive. Carduus raced over the treetops and across a clearing twenty times the size of the one they'd burned. Thousands of slyts looked skyward as they passed. Arrows began flying. Vorly readied Carduus for a steep climb, then changed his mind when he saw a highland plain of saw grass.

"Motherless Druid!" Carny said.

Thousands of slyts marched through the grass, their lines surprisingly neat and straight, guided by lit torches every fifty yards. Carduus roared and opened his air gills, preparing to fire. Vorly was tempted to let him, but thicket after thicket of arrows filled the sky. Every flicker they stayed here, the chance of getting hit increased. More of the crystal-tipped spears flew up at them, and they were getting closer.

"Thaum!" Breeze shouted. "We're being tracked!"

Vorly looked down at the sheet. Four separate red lines were converging on the single blue one that marked them.

"Carduus, climb!" Vorly shouted, spurring the rag at the same time.

Carduus, excited by all the commotion, reacted as only a young bull could and went from horizontal to vertical flight in a flick. Immense pressure slammed Vorly against Carduus's back. Vorly reached out and grabbed Carny just before he flew off into space. The crystal sheet beside Vorly tore away from its easel and was whipped away in the wind, trailing a snake of braided copper cable.

Carduus climbed like a boulder rolling down a mountainside. Every wing beat was a thunderclap of stunning force. The heat emanating from him became scalding as he pushed for the stars.

Vorly tried and failed to sit up. Carduus's acceleration kept him pinned. His vision grayed as color leached out of his sight. He recognized the dangers and knew that if he didn't get Carduus leveled out now the rag would keep climbing while his passengers blacked out.

"Lev… el!" Vorly shouted, although it was barely a gasp.

Carduus pumped his wings twice more, then adopted a

glide as his momentum carried him still higher. Vorly's vision widened and the colors returned. The weight crushing him slowly lifted and he struggled to sit upright again, pushing up on the shield leader, who groaned.

"Breeze?" Vorly shouted, turning as soon as he could.

"We're still being tracked!"

"What do you need me to do?" he asked, glancing past her again to check on the soldiers. Blessedly, they were still on board, although looking significantly more disheveled than before.

"Take us back to Iron Fist. Black Star and the other thaums are working up a process!"

Vorly turned back and gathered up the reins. "Roost, Carduus, roost!"

Carduus rumbled his approval and went into a turn. Vorly didn't spur him to make it any tighter as he wasn't sure he was up to the flight forces after the climb.

"Thanks for grabbing me," the shield leader said.

Vorly slapped him on the shoulder. "Can't have your shield losing its third leader," he said, then immediately regretted it. If the shield leader took offense he didn't show it.

"Lost my damn crossbow," he said.

"Carduus is rambunctious, and he's not fully grown yet."

The shield leader shuddered.

"We have to warn Weel," Carny said.

Vorly motioned behind him to Breeze. "Done. Right now we have to focus on getting back in one piece. Go check on your boys and get strapped in. I'm hoping we won't have any more moments like that, but I can't promise."

As the shield leader got up and made his way back, Vorly looked down. The lights were smaller and he guessed they were at ten thousand feet. Carduus was a monster. That thought made him smile.

Using small nudges, Vorly steered Carduus toward the north end of the valley. He wanted to cross over the mountains at a different location in case the slyts they'd already overflown had a surprise waiting.

A deep-throated boom shook the sky, followed by a brilliant white bolt of lightning. It struck the top of a mountain. Vorly couldn't be sure, but it looked awfully close to where they'd crossed over earlier. Carduus hissed and banked away from the valley.

"Damn it, Carduus!" Vorly shouted, reefing as hard as he could on the reins to pull him back.

Carduus shook his head and chomped on the bit, swinging away from the valley again. A second thunderclap filled the night sky, followed by two lightning bolts. These bracketed the same mountain peak. Vorly was certain it was the one they'd flown over. It occurred to Vorly that things were happening in reverse. Usually the lightning hit and then you heard the thunder.

"Are those thaums?" Vorly asked. When Breeze didn't answer he turned. He could see her hunched over the sheets, a light blue glow outlining her. He turned back, leaving her to her work. His job was to get them to the roost.

"Look, you flying furnace, we need to get back to the roost. You hear me? We do not want to be up here with lightning, especially when it's being aimed at us."

Vorly doubted Carduus got all that, but the word *roost* was powerful. Carduus turned back toward the valley.

"That's a good boy," Vorly said, patting his scales. "We'll swing well to the north and come in that way. We won't cross over any mountains."

It started raining. Steam roiled off Carduus as if he were a hot spring in winter. Despite his fear of burning alive, Vorly started stripping off layers. It was either that or cook inside the uniform.

Three more thunder bursts preceded three lightning strikes along the western mountain peaks. Carduus growled and snapped his jaws, but as Vorly was flying him at an angle away from where the lightning was hitting, the rag kept to his course.

"They're no longer tracking us," Breeze said.

Vorly turned his head partway. "That lightning was for us then?"

"Yes. Black Star created a diversion, a presence on plane

that translated to a place out here," she said. She sounded tired but pleased.

"How's the poor bastard see?" Vorly asked.

"He still doesn't, not out here. But on plane, well—"

"I know," Vorly said, interrupting her, "it gets very complicated. We're almost to the north end of the valley. If all goes well I'll bring Carduus straight in. He's had a long night in a short time."

"I'll stay on plane until we land," Breeze said.

Vorly made one last check on the soldiers, then turned all his attention to getting Carduus back down safely. He imagined he'd be talking with Commander Weel sooner rather than later and didn't relish the thought. With Walf dead, Vorly was acting overall commander of the Aero forces, but he doubted Weel would afford him the same respect that he had Walf. Then again, Vorly doubted there'd been much respect afforded between the two from the outset, so it probably wouldn't matter.

The looming shadow of the Codpiece appeared and Vorly tightened his grip on the reins. It was dark, the valley was surrounded by the enemy, thaums were casting lightning bolts, and it was raining for good measure. He rolled his shoulders and leaned into the rain pelting him.

"Breeze, get Black Star to find that crowny Rickets and have him waiting for us at the roost," he said.

"Should I say why?"

"No, I wouldn't want to spoil the surprise." He leaned forward and gave Carduus a few good thumps. "All right, boy, get us down in one piece and I'll personally chark the biggest, juiciest brorra you've ever seen."

CHAPTER FORTY-TWO

"UNACCEPTABLE!" WEEL SHOUTED.

Vorly stood at ease in the heart of Weel's keep and reminded himself that this little fuck wasn't the reason Walf was dead, he was only part of the reason. Vorly hated the bastard, but he'd stop short of putting his fist through Weel's face.

"I'm sorry you feel that way, Commander, but I chose to exercise my prerogative and attack the enemy," Vorly said. "A successful attack, I might add, and in the course of returning to the roost we discovered the arrival of the main Forest Collective force, not to mention their use of thaums."

Weel glared at Vorly from across the large table. "What you succeeded in doing was nothing short of gross insubordination. You have no authority to conduct missions without my approval."

Vorly smiled. "I understand your confusion. I do have the authority. What I didn't do, for which I do apologize, was to notify you in advance."

"I outrank you," Weel said, pulling out what he probably thought was his trump card.

"Yes, sir, but as I've been temporarily granted command of all Aero Service, your rank doesn't really matter." Vorly expected Weel's head to explode, but the man suddenly calmed, as if all his rage had been whisked away, or clamped down into a little ball hotter than the insides of a rag.

"Commander, you Aero Service types are all alike. Your former boss, he was much like you. A proud, impetuous man with little regard for authority or procedures."

Vorly's smile wavered. *Hit him and you're done. Breathe.* "We believe in taking the fight to the enemy," Vorly said through clenched teeth.

"Indeed," Weel said, placing his hands behind his back and staring at Vorly with absolute contempt. "But in your zeal to prove yourself you overstepped. Those soldiers weren't yours to command. High Command has been alerted to your breach of conduct."

It had, in fact, occurred to Vorly that this would be a problem. He turned and looked to his most unlikely of saviors. "Crown Representative Rickets has something to say about that."

Rickets stepped forward, beaming from ear to ear as if there were no other place in the world he'd rather be. Vorly wondered if it wasn't an act and the man actually lived for this kind of madness.

"Commander Weel, I must say this is a lovely keep you're building here. Thick walls, deep in the ground and well away from the wall and the fighting. Sort of a like a gopher hole, really."

Weel's nostrils flared and his hands came flying around from his back. "How dare you talk—"

"Shut the fuck up, Arthuw, before I have the flock commander here feed you to one of his rags."

Weel was so taken aback his mouth hung open for several flicks. When he finally regained it he sputtered with rage. "You... you're finished. Your career, everything! It's all over. You understand that?"

Rickets shook his head sadly and pulled out a sheaf of papers and laid them on the table. Vorly knew they were his Cow and Country Commission papers and that they were so much bullshit. Was Rickets really going to rely on bluffing Weel? Vorly suddenly questioned his reliance on Rickets, but it was too late to change course now.

Weel looked down at the papers, reading the title. He laughed.

"If you think that gives you authority to—"

Rickets reached into his tunic and pulled out a small black shield that fit in the palm of his hand. He casually tossed it onto the papers. It landed with a thud.

Weel and Vorly leaned in for a closer look. Vorly had known Rickets was up to no good the moment he saw him, but he'd had no idea until now just how right he'd been.

"Mother of the Sacred Tree. You're a Dark Ranger," Vorly said, whistling softly. "And all this time I figured you for some simple spy with a crooked streak."

Rickets nodded his head. "I have… many talents."

Weel stood transfixed, his gaze riveted on the shield. "I… that's not… how do I know it's real?" he asked, finally looking up. He'd gone white, and his eyes darted about looking for something that wasn't there.

Rickets shrugged. "Officially, you don't. But tell me, Arthuw, what does your gut tell you?"

Vorly realized that was the second time Rickets had used Weel's first name. It shouldn't have been a threat, yet Weel seemed to think it was.

"There are witnesses here," Weel said, pointing around the room.

Rickets didn't bother looking. "In a Frontier Castle surrounded by the enemy? Witnesses are only useful if they're alive."

Vorly's joy at Weel's destruction vanished. Rickets was a Dark Ranger. Forget the bland exterior, the smile, the banter; the man was a killer for an organization renowned as much for its ruthlessness as it was for its secrecy. If Rickets wanted someone to disappear, Vorly had no doubt he could make it happen.

Weel looked utterly lost and Vorly found himself pitying the man against his better judgment. Yes, Weel was a prick, but Rickets was a diabolical prick on a scale Weel—and Vorly—was only just beginning to comprehend.

"What do you want?" Weel finally asked.

"Peace in our time," Rickets said. "Alas, I don't see that happening in the near future. So instead, why don't we all focus on working together to see that our heads don't wind up as ornaments in a slyt hut?"

Weel nodded.

"Wonderful," Rickets said, pocketing the shield, and rolling up the papers and stuffing them in his tunic. "Now, we need to talk about how we're going to save our skins," Rickets said, walking around the table and looking at the map of the valley on the wall.

Weel stood up straight. Some of his former arrogance had clearly returned. "We have the Forest Collective exactly where we want them. They will wreck themselves on Iron Fist and limp back to the Western Wilds, and the war in Luitox will be over."

Vorly stared. "You understand we're surrounded," he said. "And outnumbered."

Weel smiled. "Gentlemen, this," he said, pointing to the map, "is my field of expertise. The plan has always been to lure the Forest Collective into a fight and then destroy them. We had to offer them a tempting enough target, and with enough incentive, that they would have no choice but to attack us. Being surrounded is but a part of the plan. All it really means is anywhere we choose to attack, we will find slyts to kill."

Vorly looked at Rickets, who seemed more bemused than anything else. "And what if this plan of yours doesn't go exactly as envisioned? The FnCs are moving everywhere. The army isn't coming to our rescue any time soon."

Weel waved away Vorly's concern. "A minor inconvenience at best, although when we do defeat the Forest Collective here, and I assure you we will, our victory will be all the greater because we did it alone."

"Are you hearing this?" Vorly asked, turning to Rickets.

"I am," Rickets said, "and I hope, for all our sakes, that Commander Weel is right. I suggest you two work out your differences. I have other matters to attend to," he said, nodding and then turning and walking out.

Vorly watched him go, then sprinted after him. He caught up to Rickets in the stairway. "That's it? 'I hope'? That's the best you've got?"

Rickets looked up at Vorly. "I quashed his desire to court-martial you. I think you will agree that his mind is now firmly focused on the coming battle and his glorious victory. What else would you have me do? Of my many skills, commanding legions in battle is not one of them."

And there it was. Rickets, snake that he was, was right. He'd done Vorly a great service, but only just. There was still a battle to be fought.

"What was with using his first name?" Vorly asked. "He turned white when you said it."

Rickets looked blankly at Vorly. "Some things are better left unknown," he said, moving to head up the stairs.

Vorly reached out and grabbed his arm. "Fuck that. I want to know."

Rickets looked down at Vorly's hand, then up at Vorly. "Arthuw isn't his first name, it's Narcus. Arthuw is his son's name. Lad just turned two last week."

Vorly let go of Rickets's arm. "You'd kill a child to get what you want?"

Rickets's expression never changed, but his voice deepened so that Vorly felt it as much as heard it. "Do you know the oath I swore, that all Rangers swear? It's 'For the Greater Good.' Sounds nice, right? But they left a word implied at the beginning, deliberately." He leaned in until his face was only inches from Vorly's. "Do you know what that word is?"

Vorly shook his head. He'd broken out into a sweat and found the keep walls were starting to close in around him.

Rickets leaned back, an affable smile on his face. He was the chatty, harmless crowny again. *"Anything."*

CHAPTER FORTY-THREE

"HE'S STILL OUT THERE, Shield Leader," Knockers said. "We have to go get him."

Carny stood in front of the shield by Watchtower 7 on the southern wall. The sun was barely up and the valley was already a hive of activity. Fog obscured the valley floor while a lingering mist clung about the peaks. Rags were taking off constantly. Sparkers had already set five different fires as they attacked slyt forces coming over the mountains. So far they had managed to destroy every spinner and ballista the FnC had hauled up the far side of the mountain, but based on what Carny saw last night he doubted they could keep up the pace.

The cats positioned in Iron Fist banged out another salvo, making it impossible to talk. A dwarf wagon train hauling stone shot from the quarry rumbled through the gates, adding to the mayhem.

"Look, I'm as worried about him as you are. I asked the flock commander to have all his drivers keep an eye out for him, but they've got their hands full," Carny said. "If anyone can make it out there on his own, it's Wraith."

"If he's not back by tonight, I'm going after him," Knockers said. He was shaking, but he held Carny's eyes and didn't look away.

As much as Carny admired Knockers's loyalty and

determination, Carny couldn't risk the shield to look for one man, not when the slyts of the Western Wild were here. "Knockers, I haven't forgotten, and I want him back, too, but we just have to stay put for now. I'm sorry, but he's going to have to fend for himself for a little longer."

Knockers didn't nod. "No one gets left behind," he said, then turned and walked away.

Carny looked around and caught several soldiers turning their heads away as he looked at them. Damn it, there wasn't any other choice. They had their orders and Carny's job was to keep as many of them alive as he could. On top of everything, they were currently sitting around while the other shields were marching to battle. The Sixth and Eighth Phalanxes were pushing through the southern end of the valley in an attempt to open up the river while the Ninth and Tenth Phalanxes were doing the same in the north. Meanwhile, the Seventh was assigned static defense of Iron Fist and the fortresses.

"He's awake!"

Carny looked past the shield to see Wiz running toward them. Carny's first thought was *Why wouldn't Wraith be awake?*, then he realized who Wiz was talking about.

"Big Hog?"

The shield crowded Wiz as he ran up. He was flushed and breathing heavily, but the smile on his face said everything.

"He… he woke up this morning. Asked what all the racket was," Wiz said to much laughter.

The bastard's awake! Carny turned away to brush a tear out of his eye.

The shield started moving en masse toward the infirmary.

"Where the hell are you all going? Get back to your posts. We'll see that layabout later. Right now we're guarding this wall."

The looks on their faces couldn't have been sadder than if he'd just kicked a puppy.

"Druid, give me strength. Fine, you can go visit Big Hog, two at a time."

There were groans, but Carny immediately cut them off. "It's that or you all wait until we're relieved."

The shield quieted.

"Bard, I'll let you choose who goes first. I've got to go see a dwarf again."

Carny left as the shield crowded around Bard. *I'll be damned, he pulled through.* More tears came to Carny's eyes, but he didn't bother to wipe them away. He looked up as another salvo of rocks thundered overhead. A chunk from one split off and landed at his feet. He bent down and picked it up, weighing it in his hand. Good four pounds.

He looked up to the sky again and heaved the chunk of rock after the salvo.

"Fuck the Lux," he said, smiling like he'd just learned how.

"WE WERE LUCKY," Jawn said, holding on to a clay mug as he sat at the communal table for Obsidian Flock. "The FnC thaums overplayed their hand. If they hadn't, I don't know if you would have made it back."

Chair legs scraped and he heard the other drivers and thaums get up from the table. Breeze must have been shooing them away.

"Yes, they're gone," she said, as if reading his mind. "Why are you doing this? You saved our lives. The only one who doesn't seem to know it is you."

Jawn knew she wouldn't understand. "I was lucky, Breeze. Don't you see, that's not enough. Luck runs out."

She placed her hand on his. "Jawn, you're more than lucky. You plane-shift like the very wind. None of us can keep up with you. It's nothing short of amazing. Your power is—"

"Reckless," Jawn said, needing her to hear him. "Breeze, I can plane-shift the way I do because I don't care. I go deep because I don't expect to ever come back."

"What are you saying?"

"I'm saying I chased those thaums and then drew them away because... because part of me wanted them to catch me. It was thrilling, and I was sad when they gave up."

Breeze pulled her hand away. Jawn tried to imagine her expression and settled on a mixture of contempt and shock. He was surprised when her hands enveloped his again.

"Jawn, I won't insult you by saying I know what you're going through, because I don't. What happened to you is terrible, and I am so sorry that it did. I also know that despite what happened, you are still you."

Jawn started to protest but Breeze wouldn't let him.

"No, Jawn, I'm not buying it. You were a thaum of exceptional ability before, and you are one of even more ability now. But what really matters is that you are the kind of man who is willing to risk his life to help others. That's who you were, and that's who you still are. Eyesight or not, you are a man who cares, and a man who cares doesn't throw away his life. Especially not now when people who care about him need him."

"Breeze, I—"

He felt her hair against his forehead and then her lips kissed his. "You make your own light, Black Star."

Jawn sat at the table holding the mug long after Breeze left. He was lost. Only last night he'd been ready to end it all, taking on four enemy thaums in a duel that he was certain would have been his end. Now... fuck, what the hell now?

He heard footsteps approaching and waited for them to pass. When they didn't, he turned.

"Jawn, it's Hyaminth."

"Hi, Hy," Jawn said, smiling at the inadvertent cuteness.

"The mist isn't burning away, it's actually getting thicker. And there are thunderclouds forming to the north. If the skies close in the rags won't be able to fly."

The slyts weren't stupid. They saw the great advantage the Kingdom possessed with its flocks of rags. If you couldn't kill the beasts, at least not easily, then take away their sky.

Jawn let go of the mug and stood up. "Then I guess I'd better get to work," he said, holding out his elbow for Hyaminth to take, which she did. As they walked out of the mess hall Jawn considered that the answer had been with him all along. He did care and would do whatever he could to protect those he cared about. That, he was surprised to realize, included himself.

CARNY WAS STILL smiling as he rounded the corner of the main dwarf barrack in Iron Fist and came upon a group of dwarves surrounding a single dwarf. The group turned to look at him. The glares were similar to Carny's initial meeting with the dwarves on the coastal mountain.

"Morning, gents," Carny said, choosing to ignore the outright hostility. He recognized Tryser, the dwarf weapons expert he'd come to see, as the one being singled out. "Lovely day in the Lux."

Master Pioneer Black Pine, the clear leader of the group, turned and faced Carny.

"Keep walking," he snarled, his clenched fists like sledgehammers.

"It is a morning for a walk," Carny said, continuing with his bravado. *Fuck you, you little shit. You scared me last time, but not again.* "In fact, I think I will. I just need to borrow Tryser there."

"You deaf? Get the fuck out of here."

Carny reached to pat his crossbow and remembered he'd lost it last night. It was the reason he was coming to see Tryser. He settled for scratching his balls. "That's not going to happen. Not now, not ever." Knowing the only way out was advancing, he took a step forward. "Time you fellows were on your way. Lots going on and I'm sure you have jobs to do."

The dwarves around Black Pine shuffled their feet. This wasn't going the way they'd expected.

"You think I won't hit you?" Black Pine said.

Carny noticed that despite the threat, he didn't step any closer. *Got you, you fuck.*

"You hit me, I kick your teeth down your throat, and the slyts come and gut all of us because like fucking idiots we're fighting among ourselves. Doesn't really make much sense."

"We've got more in common with the slyts than we do with

you," Black Pine said. "They just want to be free. Ain't no slyt ever owned a dwarf. But here you are with your very own pet," he said, pointing at Tryser.

Carny's confidence took a hit. "Pet? I think I see the problem. You seem to think that you're not part of this army because you've had it hard, is that it?"

Black Pine's eyes narrowed. "What the fuck would you know about having it hard? Ever been a slave? What the fuck kind of hardship have you suffered?"

Carny's eyes misted, but for a wholly different reason than before. "They killed my mother, you piece of shit. That enough fucking hardship for you? We were this close to starving, living off scraps. She found a deer carcass that a poacher had killed and took some meat. She didn't even kill it, just took some fucking meat. King's wardens took her and said pay a fine or go to prison. We didn't have shit. She caught the consumption in prison and died. All for taking some scraps of deer meat from a fucking carcass!"

Several of the dwarves had backed up. Any interest they might have had in taking on Carny vanished.

"You know—" Black Pine said, but Carny took another step and shouted, "Fuck you! Fuck you and your fucking attitude! Either take a swing or get out of my sight. I'm done with this," Carny said, taking another step. "Like it or not, you're just as much a part of the Kingdom as I am. We both have reasons to hate it, but you know what? The slyts will put an arrow in your heart as quick as they will in mine if they get the chance."

Black Pine stood glowering at Carny but made no move. Carny wasn't going to wait around for him to regain his footing.

"Tryser, I need to talk to you. The rest of you, get back to your posts, now!"

A dwarf started to walk away. Black Pine turned and looked at him. The dwarf shrugged and kept walking. Others joined him and soon the group was moving. Carny pointed at Tryser and motioned for him to move. Tryser did, leaving Black Pine standing alone. Carny turned his back on the dwarf and started walking away with Tryser beside him.

"You're crazy, you know that?" Tryser said.

Carny blinked and wiped the tears from his eyes. "I always suspected. You going to tell me what that was about or do I already know the answer?"

"Black Pine just can't let go. He found out I was doing some work for you and said I was a traitor to our people."

Carny shook his head. "But he thinks being in league with the slyts is better?"

It was Tryser's turn to shrug. "In his mind, he does. Like he said, slyts didn't enslave our people."

Carny recognized a delicate area and decided to avoid it. "I lost my crossbow. I was hoping you could modify another one for me."

Tryser looked up at Carny. "How'd you lose it?"

"Long story. Can you modify another one like that? It worked like a charm."

Tryser smiled. "I knew it would. Not to worry, I finished the next one. Was on my way to tell you when you found us."

They walked to one of the few stone buildings in Iron Fist other than the keep and went inside. It was the armory. The smell was hot and acrid, but unlike in the roost, it was mellowed by the scent of wood. Carny was surprised to see a mix of men and dwarves working together.

"It's all about the steel in here. None of that bullshit you saw outside," Tryser said. A few men and dwarves nodded Tryser's way, then went back to work. Carny saw an array of metal and wood machines that both amazed and unsettled him. A few more lanterns and this place could be a dungeon.

"Black Pine doesn't have a problem with this?" Carny asked.

Tryser huffed. "There's very little in this world that Black Pine doesn't have a problem with. Out there, he'll do his best to make your life miserable," Tryser said, pointing with his thumb. "He actually tried coming in here once and making a stink."

"What happened?"

"These are my shards, and I'm theirs, dwarf and man. Black

Pine and his crew got a little bit more than they bargained for. They haven't been back."

Carny nodded. "So you built a new crossbow."

Tryser walked over to a workbench. It was built lower to the ground than the ones the men were using, so there was no need for a step stool.

Tryser pulled a leather cloth off a crossbow the like of which Carny had never seen. The two steel bow arms had been cut down the middle to create four. Each set of arms had its own string that looked like steel thread. One set of arms loaded above the stock, the other below. More intriguing, there was a brass rectangular box fitted into the stock just forward of the firing lever. Cogs were visible inside it through gaps in the metal sheet.

"What does it do?"

Tryser lifted the weapon and placed it in a vise, which he then screwed tight. "It reloads," Tryser said, working the firing lever. He stuck a steel spike inside the mechanism, which held whatever it did in check while he slowly manipulated the action. "Top bow fires first. As it does, the residual energy winds a spring inside the box. That draws the second string, but only about three-quarters. To get it all the way you grab this lever here," Tryser said, pointing to a new lever in front of the firing lever that Carny hadn't noticed and pushing it forward, then back. "That cocks it the rest of the way."

Carny watched, his mouth agape. "How did you make this?"

Tryser looked at him. "Using this," Tryser said, pointing to his head. "But that's not the best part. I hollowed out the length of the shaft. It'll take six bolts. Unfortunately they're shorter than regular bolts by a good four inches. However, every time you cock the lever to set a bow to full draw, it inserts a bolt into the firing groove." He demonstrated. As the string was pulled all the way back, a bolt from inside the stock dropped into the lower firing groove.

"That's amazing! Tryser, do you know what you've done?"

The dwarf nodded. A few of his fellow armorers had gathered

round. "Well, credit where credit's due. Jeefer there came up with the double bow, and Sowk built the crux gear that works the reloading," Tryser said, pointing to a man and then a dwarf.

"Still say it should be called the Sowk gear," Sowk said, to much laughter.

Tryser pointed to a small maker's mark engraved on the brass gearbox. "We had a vote, and despite a protest we settled on MON Manufacturing." There were smiles all around, save from Sowk, and a general swelling of chests.

Carny played along. "MON?"

"Middle of Nowhere," the group said in unison.

Carny nodded. "I like it," he said.

"Wait until you try it," Tryser said, handing Carny a quiver of cut-down bolts. Carny noticed brass parts piled on Tryser's bench, enough for several more of the modified crossbows. "You going into business?"

Tryser looked up as another salvo of stones whistled overhead. "Six shots," he said.

"You're deaf," another dwarf said. "That was five."

Tryser shrugged. "What were you asking me?"

Carny pointed at the brass parts. "How many of these are you making?"

Tryser gave him a wry smile. "With this modification you'll be able to shoot eight bolts in the time it took to shoot one. I figure that'll become popular. And what's popular is good business."

Good business? Carny's stomach soured. "You wouldn't charge the troops, would you?"

The armory grew silent. Hammers hung in midair as all eyes turned to Carny.

"No," Tryser said, his voice even, "but I sure as fuck plan to charge the army."

Carny hung his head, his cheeks flushing. "Damn it, Tryser, I'm sorry. I don't know why I said that."

Tryser punched Carny's left biceps so hard that Carny's hand went numb. "It's all right. You grew up getting fed a lot of shit about dwarves so it stands to reason a little of it's going to trickle

476

out now and then." Tryser looked around the armory. "What are you lot staring at? Get back to work!"

The armory bustled to life as Carny rubbed his left arm. "Why do you dwarves have to punch all the time? A polite *fuck you* is fine, you know."

Tryser balled his fist as if he was going to hit Carny again then opened it up and patted Carny's arm. "Habit. It's how you know your *sharder* is solid, you know?"

"So am I?" Carny asked.

Tryser smiled. "You ain't diamond, but you ain't sandstone either."

Carny could live with that. "Can I see the crossbow now?"

Tryser handed it over. Carny was immediately struck by how light it felt despite the modifications.

"Hollowed out the butt as well," Tryser said. "It won't fire as far or pack as big a wallop as the other one, or even the original model, but it's still lethal, and with eight bolts in the air you'll hit a lot more."

Carny held the crossbow like a newborn babe, afraid to make any sudden moves. His eyes kept coming back to the strings. "Is that steel?"

Tryser looked around the room before answering. When he did, he kept his voice low.

"You know what happens to a rag after it dies?"

The image of the exploding rag Listowk was flying flashed in his mind. "I've seen it."

"No, I don't mean when they die, I mean after. Sort of like slaughtering a cow or a hog. They cut up the parts and use them," Tryser said.

"I thought rags turned to stone or something after they died," Carny said.

"Eventually the metals and minerals in their bodies do crystallize, but if you get to them right when they die, you can butcher a lot. And if you know what you're doing, you can keep the bits pliable."

Carny looked at the string again. "So this is…"

"Sinew," Tryser said. "Left foreleg. Hind leg or butt is stronger, and wing shoulder is best, but this is still damn good."

Carny was sold, which brought up a question. He'd promised to pay Tryser, but after putting his foot in his mouth he wasn't sure how to proceed. "I'm a man of my word," he said, not sure what to say next.

"Never doubted it," Tryser said. He motioned for Carny to lean in, which he did.

"Here's the thing: me and the lads have been talking and we think there might be some real opportunity here, so we decided on one percent."

Carny stood up. "I don't understand."

"You had the need, we came up with the solution. Like I said, we wouldn't charge you lads. But, when this battle's over, we're going to put together a proposal for the army to reequip with this," he said, pointing to the crossbow. "We're cutting you in for one percent of the profits."

"I don't know what to say," Carny said. He'd never been in business in his life.

"All you have to do is sign," Tryser said, handing Carny three sheets of paper with dwarven runes on them. Carny looked at them but couldn't read what they said. He could see, however, that all three looked the same.

"All very standard," Tryser said, handing Carny a quill that had already been dipped in ink. "Just sign your name on each page at the bottom, or an X if you prefer," he added quickly, "and then a drop of your blood in each circle by your name."

"Drop of my—ow!"

Sowk had leaned forward and jabbed Carny's thumb with a needle.

"All very standard," Tryser said again. He showed Carny where to sign, and then took his thumb in his hand and pressed it on the circle, leaving behind a small drop of smeared blood. Tryser then signed each piece of paper, pricked his own thumb, and deposited his blood by his name. After blowing on the ink and blood he folded up one sheet and handed it to Carny.

"Don't lose this. When we get out of here that's your ticket to the good life."

Carny held the crossbow in one hand and the sheet in the other and wondered which was more dangerous.

"One question," Carny said, realizing he had hundreds. "This whole business thing only works if we win, right?"

Tryser patted him on the arm. "Unless Black Pine is right and the Forest Collective welcomes us with open arms. But not to worry, our money's on the Kingdom."

Carny felt reassured, mostly. As he left the armory and tucked the sheet into his tunic he did his best to banish the thought that Tryser and the MON crew had more contracts ready to be signed, only written out in slyt.

CHAPTER FORTY-FOUR

P ARMIK SUCKED AT THE splinter in the heel of his right hand as he walked away from cat 3. The crew had been lax in keeping the torsion ropes free of anything that might cause fraying, and so a quarter candle had just been lost replacing seven lengths of rope.

Truthfully, ropes frayed, and it was bound to happen with the number of shots they'd been throwing. Parmik's real annoyance was that Weel would be calling him to his damn keep to explain why cat 3 had been out of service.

"He can kiss my ass," he said out loud. It felt good to say it.

The distinctive heavy beat of a rag drew Parmik's gaze up. A single sparker was climbing, no doubt going to fly the valley to look for slyt targets. *Better you than me*, Parmik thought, watching as the rag flew north. That infernal mist was back and thicker than ever. He knew now it wasn't fog, but something the slyts were concocting. It remained high enough that it didn't really affect their ability to sight the cats, but he'd heard rumblings from the roost that it was playing havoc with the rags and their use of thaumics.

The sky grew darker as he walked. A storm was brewing. Now that would affect the cats. He stopped and turned. *Better tell cat 3 to oil their ropes*.

A lightning bolt darted across the sky and hit cat 3. Everything in front of Parmik froze in stark relief as if painted on a canvas using only black and white. A flick later, the world around Parmik exploded in a burst of red and orange. Something unseen picked him up and tossed him ten yards in the air. Wood and metal shrieked as they tore apart. The twelve crew members on cat 3, still getting the first shot ready since the repair, made no noise at all, their bodies vanishing in a blinding flash of light.

Bleeding from his nose and ears, Parmik rolled over and looked at where cat 3 had stood. Only a towering column of fire and smoke remained. Thunder boomed and the ground shook. Another lightning bolt lashed down and delivered the same fate to cat 4.

His head buzzed as if filled with bees. Every part of him grew heavy. Parmik didn't understand. He struggled to push himself up higher. Propped on his elbows, he looked down the length of his body. He was completely naked, his body peppered by splinters of wood. It took him several flicks to understand something else was different.

Everything below his knees was gone. Tendrils of greasy black smoke rose from the stumps of his legs. The rest of his legs were several yards away. Improbably, his right leg and boot stood upright. The smell of roasted meat hung in the air.

Pain, like a roaring, tumbling avalanche of razor-edged rock, raced up his body and buried him in agony. He screamed. His back arched until he thought it would snap. He writhed and shook. His vision blurred and then began to darken, but even as he slipped into unconsciousness the agony of his body was supplanted by something more horrifying; if he lived, he would be shorter than a dwarf.

"CALL HIM BACK now!" Vorly shouted, running through the closed flaps of the crystal tent the thaums had named the Black Palace. The first thing that struck him was how cold it was inside despite the heat of midday.

Hyaminth and Breeze sat at a simple wooden table, each with

a crystal sheet in front of her. Copper braids snaked from each sheet, some to the floor and others up through the roof of the tent. The sound of the shattering of cat 3 still echoed in the roost.

"We're masking him, but we're having a hard time staying in touch with Growler," Breeze said, referring to Minter's RAT. She didn't turn around, but kept her head bent over her sheet.

More thunder and lightning boomed in the valley. "I don't care what you have to do, call him back!" Vorly shouted, turning and running back out of the tent. He sprinted to the east wall of the roost and scrambled up it, joining dozens of flockmen and rag crews already there.

"Sir, did you see that cat go up?" Rimsma said as Vorly stopped and caught his breath. "Just shredded it."

Vorly knew men and dwarves had just been killed on that cat, but his concern right now was with Minter. He looked north and quickly spotted the lone rag flying along the jungle edge. Lightning bolts slashed down all around it.

"What the fuck is he doing out there?" Vorly asked. Minter hadn't said anything about flying to him that morning. They'd been very careful with their flights of late as the mist and lightning had become increasingly dangerous.

"I was there when he launched," Rimsma said. "Faery Crud were spotted all over the northern end of the valley, in broad daylight no less! He said there was no way he was going to pass up a chance like that."

Vorly understood, but it didn't make him feel any better.

"It's not worth risking—" was as far as Vorly got when three lightning bolts converged on Minter's rag. White shimmering light radiated out in waves followed by roiling clouds of red and orange flame. The sound of the explosion reached them on the wall a few flicks later.

The remains of Minter, Growler, and his rag scattered over the valley floor sending up geysers of dirt, smoke, and flame. No one on the wall said a word.

* * *

VORLY SAT WITH his back resting against a pile of saddles in the dark. The slyts were now all over the north and eastern slopes of the mountains facing the valley floor and the fucking lightning had all but pinned Vorly's rags to the ground.

A lightning bolt crashed into one of the hastily erected stone pillars constructed around the roost. He barely flinched. Each pillar was topped with an iron rod as thick as his arm and six feet long. Between the efforts of the flock thaums and the rods, the roost remained protected from the increasingly frequent lightning strikes the slyt thaums kept conjuring. Vorly snorted and waved at the air in front of him.

"Pardon me, not conjuring, directing via a complex thaumic process involving a whole lot of bullshit I could give two fucks about," he muttered, and lifted the wineskin to his lips and had another drink.

He was grateful for the thaums' efforts. His animosity—and it had grown to massive proportions—was directed at the slyt thaums. They were trying to destroy his rags with lightning! They had them penned in, unable to fly because of their damn, fucking lightning! It wasn't just unfair, it was downright contemptible. The whole notion of fighting from somewhere hidden rubbed him as cowardly.

"Come out and fight like a man… or a slyt, or somebody," he said, talking to no one. He was alone in a shed for harnesses and other tack. It was dark, it was raining, and he was, he'd admit to himself if no one else, thinking about Walf and Jate and poor damn Minter.

"Fool," Vorly said, saying it to himself and to Minter.

There was no chance of going out to recover what parts they might find of his body, which only made it worse. The slyts were everywhere.

Vorly put the wineskin to his lips and emptied it. He was drunk, and it didn't help one bit. The pain remained. Death after death, and for what? A fucking valley in the middle of beyond nowhere?

Another lightning bolt crashed into a pillar, turning the night white. Vorly raised his arm to cover his eyes. When he lowered it again a figure stood in the opening of the shed.

"I thought I'd find you here," Breeze said, walking toward him and sitting down opposite him.

"You're a bright one," Vorly said, bringing the wineskin up to his lips, then remembering it was empty. "You wouldn't have anything to drink on you, would you?"

"You've had enough," Breeze said.

"You know... ," Vorly said, struggling to sit up, then giving up and slumping back against the saddles. "You know, you might be right."

"Jawn was able to open a plane through the interference. A rescue column is headed for the valley. The Forest Collective invasion of Luitox is driving deeper and all forces are needed to defend our positions along the coast. We have to hold out until they get here and we are pulled out. That could be as early as the day after tomorrow."

"Day after tomorrow," Vorly said, mulling it over. "Help will arrive... day after tomorrow."

"I know it's too late for Minter, and all the others, but it's not too late for those of us left," she said.

"You're right," Vorly said, knowing he should feel buoyed by the knowledge but unable to. "Reinforcements arrive, the slyts melt back into their jungle, and the Kingdom rejoices." More lightning crashed outside. Vorly counted five strikes in succession. "I think those thaums have other ideas," he said. A new anger blossomed in his breast. "What the fuck good are you anyway? Their thaums keep us trapped like rats while all our RATs can do is send messages? Where's our fucking lightning? Wait, don't tell me," Vorly said, his voice dripping with contempt. "It's complicated."

"I know you're upset," Breeze said, her voice tight. "I know this hasn't been easy—"

"Easy? That's all it's been. Just sitting here with nothing to do while all around me burns. Couldn't be easier."

"We're all doing our best, you know," Breeze said, anger giving volume to her voice. "Everyone is trying. Half the thaums are blooded and two nearly blinded themselves like Jawn trying to find the slyt thaums."

"But they haven't, have they?" Vorly said, unable to contain his own anger. He sat up, his head a vortex of rage and sorrow. He pointed to the sky. "You know how I know? Because I'm not up there flying!"

"Jawn's found the thaums," Breeze said.

Vorly blinked. His stomach churned and he felt like he was going to be sick. He closed his eyes, counted to five, and the feeling passed. "What?" he asked, opening his eyes and breathing.

"He knows how to locate them. They're constantly on the move. It's one of the reasons it's been so difficult to find them. But he found a sign, a way to track them."

Every hateful thing Vorly had just said to Breeze filled him with bile. He turned his head, then vomited. When he was finished, he wiped his mouth with the back of his hand and turned back to her.

"Breeze… there are times when I'm… a fucking ass. I know you're doing your best, you all are."

"I never wanted to let you down, not ever," Breeze said. "From the first time we flew together my only goal was to prove to you that I… that what I do has value."

Vorly doubted he'd ever felt hollower and more pathetic in his entire life. "Breeze, I've never said this, but I am proud of you. Before you showed up and became the biggest fucking thorn in my side I couldn't imagine flying with anyone. Just me and Carduus. That's all I wanted. That's all I needed. And now… now I don't mind so much that you're back there."

Vorly peered into the darkness and took a good look at her. He realized she was crying.

"Bloody High Druid. Don't do that."

"You can be the biggest ass, Vorly Astol," she said, wiping away the tears. "And then you go and prove yourself to be the sweetest."

"Well, you're still the biggest thorn in my ass."

Breeze shook her head and blew out a breath. "Men. The only thing worse is your absence."

"Right… I guess," he said, not really following her train of thought. "Let me get my feet under me and we'll go get these thaums."

Breeze brushed her hair out of her eyes and looked at him.

"It's not that simple. I'm worried he's going to sacrifice himself in order to kill them," she said.

"What do you mean?"

"He will find them and keep them engaged while we close in on them and destroy them."

Vorly remembered something about this from the thaum Jawn killed before. Only then he'd done it on plane.

"He can't do what he did before?"

"They have four thaums working in what we call an entanglement." Breeze looked at Vorly and continued. "Think of it like a briar patch, all intertwined."

"Sure, I can picture that. But we have more thaums than they do. Why can't all of you tangle up and beat them at their own game?"

"Because their thaums will never untangle. They joined on plane and will never be able to separate. That's why we've been having such a hard time finding them. There aren't four distinct signatures; it's one that's spread out but still connected."

"And you can't do that?" Vorly asked, still holding on to the crux of their conversation, but only by his fingertips.

"Our best guess is that their thaums are in a deep sleep they'll never come out of. They're dying, slowly. But while they're alive they remain on plane and lethal."

Vorly thought he understood. "You're right. I want to fly, but not at the cost of you and the others killing yourselves."

Breeze smiled, but it was forced. "But Jawn will. He alone has the ability to meet them on anything like even terms. He won't be able to defeat them on plane, but as long as he's engaged with them, I'll be able to locate them for us to strike."

More memories from Jawn's fight with the thaum came back to Vorly. "But if he's engaged with them when we kill them, he'll die too, right?"

Breeze nodded.

"Can't you warn him to disengage before we hit them?"

"I'll try, but even if I can, I don't think he'll listen."

"You like him," Vorly said.

"Of course I like him," Breeze said.

"No, I mean you really like him. In a way you don't feel for Rimsma." Vorly waited to have his head taken off, but Breeze only sighed.

"Yes, I like him. A lot."

Vorly finally got it. "Breeze, we're all scared. We've all lost people we care about. We're cut off and far from home with an army of slyts closing in who want to kill us. None of us want to lose anyone else, but time isn't on our side, Breeze. This shiny little anvil is turning into a sucking pit that will take us all down with it before those reinforcements get here if something doesn't happen, and soon."

Breeze didn't say anything. Vorly tried to read her face in the dark, but it was too difficult. He was starting to nod off when she finally spoke.

"He'll be ready tomorrow night."

"Then so will I."

Breeze nodded. She placed her hands on her thighs and stood up. As she walked to the door she paused and turned.

"Does this valley really matter that much? Is it worth the cost?" Breeze asked. "I mean, all the work, all the sacrifice and even if we win, we're going to walk away from it."

"It isn't about the valley," Vorly said. "Maybe Weel thinks it is, but he's wrong. It's about you and me and Jawn and that shield leader Carny and everyone else. The criers can tell the people back in the Kingdom we're fighting for ideals and philosophies at odd sounding places on a map, but what we're really fighting for is each other. Our sacrifice out here isn't for this valley—it's for them."

Breeze stood in the doorway and seemed to think about what Vorly had said. "Get some sleep, Commander," she said, and walked out the door.

Vorly stared after her, then eased himself down on the saddles. "No one else is dying if I can help it," he mumbled, closing his eyes and drifting off into a dreamless sleep.

CHAPTER FORTY-FIVE

"FORTRESSES ELEVEN AND THIRTEEN have fallen. We have to hold this line!" Carny shouted, walking crouched over as he moved along the hastily constructed skirmish line. Red Shield was five hundred yards outside Iron Fist, strung out along a dosha swamp berm. Black Shield was on their left flank, and Gray Shield held their right. Cats 7 and 8 were providing a constant barrage of stones a hundred yards ahead to block the path of the oncoming slyts. The bastards had taken the eastern mountains, the river, and now controlled most of the valley floor.

"I've got movement!"

Carny squinted in the dark. Several figures were running across a dosha swamp and making their way toward Iron Fist.

"Hold your fire!" Carny shouted, standing up on the berm for a better look. He started to yell for Wraith to shoot up a star but remembered the soldier was still missing. "Bard, put a star up."

The hiss of the burning arrow lit up the night as it flared a dazzling white. The running figures were revealed.

"This way!" Carny shouted, motioning for the survivors of the fortresses to come over to the skirmish line. "Watch out for the stakes," Carny said, pointing down at the bamboo stakes driven into the north side of the berm. He'd hoped to have prick vine, but they'd had to make do with what they could scrounge.

The first soldier reached the berm and threw himself over it. He was shirtless and wild-eyed. Fifteen more soldiers suddenly appeared and came over the berm. Wiz collected any who were wounded and led them back to a stand of bamboo where he'd set up a makeshift infirmary. The rest gathered around Carny. He counted eleven, nine men and two dwarves. Only three had weapons.

"Those with crossbows fill in on the line. The rest, there are axes and hewers by the bamboo. Cut the bamboo down and make stakes four feet long."

Carny looked at the faces as they walked past. He drew in his breath when he recognized the dwarf Black Pine. He let him walk past and stopped the last soldier walking to the bamboo. "Which fortress were you in?"

The soldier looked at him for a few flicks as if he couldn't remember. "Thirteen. I knew it was unlucky, but Raester said that was just superstition."

Carny didn't bother pointing out that Fortress 11 had also fallen. "What happened?"

"They just didn't stop coming. Our cats tore holes in their line big enough to drive a team of oxen through, but more just took their place. Kept up a wall of arrow fire. Our cat looked like a porcupine. We were pinned down and couldn't get to the stones. Everybody that tried got killed."

The soldier shook, his hands grasping at nothing. Carny realized he should direct this soldier to Wiz, but the man wasn't finished.

"That's when the mules saved our asses."

"What?"

"Without those stones, we was done. We had a bunch of them mules from the pioneer company with us. They were setting up those harrows, only they never got time before the slyts attacked. So they ran to the stone pile and got us enough shot to keep firing. There were twenty of them. That one they call Black Pine, he was like a demon. He threw rocks nearly as hard as a cat. Saw him take a slyt's head clean off."

Carny turned to watch Black Pine. The dwarf grabbed one of the hewers and set about cutting down the bamboo. "You go see Wiz," Carny said. "He'll give you something for your humors."

The soldier shook his head. "I'll cut bamboo if it's all the same to you." He was shaking so hard now Carny feared he'd fall over.

"Here," Carny said, reaching into his haversack and pulling out a ball of Flower. "Tear off a chunk of this and give it a chew. It'll help," Carny said.

The soldier looked at it, then at Carny. "I know what that is. LOKAM says not to."

Carny leaned forward and put the ball of Flower in the soldier's hand. "Fuck the LOKAM."

The soldier seemed to consider that, then tore off a piece of Flower and popped it in his mouth. He started to hand the rest back to Carny.

"You keep it. I think I got all I could out of it."

"Much obliged," the soldier said. Carny wasn't positive, but he thought his shaking had lessened.

"SL, we just got more reinforcements," Knockers said, pointing toward Iron Fist.

Carny turned. Two wagons pulled by brorra were making their way across the dosha swamps. Dwarves, dozens of them, were helping to pull the tarp-covered objects on the wagons.

"I'll check it out," Carny said. "Tell Bard to make sure he has someone keep tabs on our flanks. I don't want one of the other shields hightailing it and leaving us holding our pricks in the wind."

Knockers nodded. He took his unlit pipe out of his mouth and pretended to knock burnt tobacco out of it. Carny wondered if the soldier really thought there was tobacco in it.

"Wraith's still out there," Knockers said. "The bridge across the river is just over there. I could sneak across and get to the other side and—"

Carny put a hand on Knockers's arm. "That's your death, and you know it. Slyts are everywhere. You wouldn't get fifty yards."

"Wraith would look for us," Knockers said.

Carny wondered about that. *Would he?* He honestly didn't know. "And we will look for him, but not now. I need you here. If we don't send these slyts packing we won't be of much use to anyone. Besides, odds are he's curled up snug as a bug in some tree."

Knockers put his pipe back in his mouth and nodded. "I have your word then. We won't leave him behind."

Carny's respect for Knockers grew. The boy was willing to risk his life for a soldier who probably hadn't said four words to him. Carny held out his hand. "You have my word."

Knockers reached out and shook his hand. His grip was firm though his hand was cold.

"Shield Leader?"

Carny released Knockers's hand and turned. Captain Tiffanger of the dwarf pioneers was walking toward him.

"Sir," Carny said, nodding instead of saluting. No point in giving the slyts a better idea of who was in charge.

"Well met on this terrible night," Tiffanger said, extending his hand. Carny was surprised but took it. Tiffanger's grip was even stronger than Knockers's.

"I'm guessing that's not roast brorra you've brought us," Carny said, pointing to the wagons.

"No, although they'd be useful in kebobing them for the fire," he said.

"Kebobing, sir?"

"It's a—best left for another time. No, I've brought you something better." The tarps were pulled off, revealing six harrows.

"Nasty looking," Carny said, walking over as the dwarves lifted the first machine off a wagon and began setting it up along the berm. With its rows of arrows it reminded Carny of a porcupine. He walked in front of it for a better look.

"No!" Tiffanger shouted, grabbing Carny by the arm and yanking him back.

"What the hell, man?" Carny asked, shaking loose.

"So sorry," Tiffanger said. He let out a breath and shook his head. "We never, ever, walk in front of one of these. Never. The trigger mechanism is a bit… delicate."

Carny looked back at the rows of arrows and briefly pictured himself impaled by them. It was… messy.

"That's probably the first thing you should mention," Carny said, unable to get the number seven out of his head. It was, he calculated, the approximate number of arrows that would have pierced his cock and balls.

"Yes, again, I am terribly sorry. I have no doubt we'll get the trigger problem solved, but in our current circumstances it seems best to use them as is, with all precautions taken of course."

"The slyts are that way," Carny said, pointing north.

"Indeed," Tiffanger said. "I'll ensure the harrows are properly positioned."

Carny forced a smile. "Please do." He nodded again to Tiffanger and walked back along the skirmish line. The Bard met him coming the other way.

"Are those the harrows I've been hearing about?" he asked.

Carny shuddered. "Yes. Stay well clear of them and under no circumstances walk in front of one. Tell the men that, too."

The Bard nodded. Carny waited for him to broach whatever was on his mind, but he seemed hesitant to.

"Were you looking for me?" Carny asked.

The Bard sighed. "Knockers is gone. Just took off. He was stuffing saw grass in his aketon one flick and the next he vanished. Kept going on about Wraith being out there alone."

"Fuck," Carny said. No wonder Sinte and Listowk had looked like old men. Running a shield was an endless line of problems.

"What do you want me to do?" the Bard asked.

"He made his choice, there's nothing we can do," Carny said. "If he makes it back I'll kick his ass, then put him in for a medal."

The Bard nodded. He looked at Carny and Carny noticed for the first time that the soldier was clearly upset. Carny reached out and patted him on the shoulder.

"Look, if we live through tonight and the relief column gets here, I'll lead the search party myself."

"That's not it. Aw, Carny, I'm sorry. I didn't want to be the one who told you. Big Hog's dead."

Carny dropped his hand from the Bard's shoulder and stepped back a pace. "What?"

"I heard it from Wiz. He sent a couple of soldiers to the infirmary and one of them came back with supplies and told him."

The world around Carny crushed down into a very small, very quiet space. "When?"

"Earlier tonight. I would have told you sooner but—"

Carny waved off the rest of the Bard's explanation. He'd put off going to see Big Hog, saving the reunion as something to look forward to. The vision of seeing his friend again was the oxen pulling him through this nightmare.

"They say he just went back to sleep and that was it," the Bard said.

Carny nodded. "Keep on the flanks. I don't want us losing contact with the other shields when things get going."

"I'm on it."

The two men stood silently. The sound of distant battle ebbed and flowed. Finally, the Bard raised his hand as if to salute, thought better of it, turned, and walked away. Carny flexed his grip on his crossbow and stared over the berm.

The slyts were coming.

He squeezed the crossbow hard until his hands hurt.

The slyts were coming.

JAWN SAT IN his den, a small burrow dug ten feet into the ground, then given a roof of logs and dirt. It was damp, chilly, and pungent smelling, but he loved it. He couldn't tell day from night down here, and he loved that, too. He was isolated, yet with the panels of crystal sheets at his fingertips, he was more in touch with the world than he'd ever been in his life.

A knock sounded on the piece of wood Jawn had asked the dwarves to place by the opening to his den. There was no door, only a piece of sailcloth draped over it.

Jawn didn't answer, hoping his visitor would leave. He had a pretty good idea who it was.

Miska, the crier woman, had already been there early that morning. Jawn knew it was dawn because she told him, among many other things he had no interest in. When it became apparent that what she really wanted were his views on the cultural shifts taking place in the Kingdom, he quickly bid her good day.

The knocking came again.

"I must ask that you leave. I am engaged in work and cannot be disturbed."

"Well that's a lot of bullshit," Rickets said, tromping down the roughly hewn stairs. "I figured you were shacked up down here playing wizard with that crier woman."

"Miska?" Jawn said. "Odd duck."

Rickets coughed. "One way to put it. Spinsterhood seems to have affected her more than most."

Jawn chuckled. "All she really wanted was to talk about social relations between the races."

"Did she ask about thaumics?" Rickets asked.

Jawn shook his head. "Don't think she cared the first thing about it to be honest. Bit insulting, but not everyone's a fan." Jawn expected a laugh in reply from Rickets but didn't get it.

"How are you, Jawn, really? You've been spending almost all your waking candles in the aether. The other thaums talk as if you're becoming part of it."

"I'm great, Rickets. I know this hovel of mine isn't much to look at, but it connects me. Down here, I'm the earth. Do you know what I mean?"

"Not in the least," Rickets said.

Jawn wanted Rickets to understand. The two of them had been through a lot together and despite his uncanny ability to annoy Jawn, he was also his friend.

"It's amazing. I don't know, maybe it's because I lost my sight, but I'm refinding myself in thaumics. I slide through planes in the aether with an ease and understanding I never imagined I would possess. Rickets, it's as if the secrets of thaumics were opening up like flowers after a spring shower. All I have to do is be there to witness the beauty and the power."

"You reading poetry in there—or is it *out* there?" Rickets asked.

Jawn shook his head and slowed his breathing. He was getting himself worked up just thinking about what was possible.

"I wish I could make you understand! Rickets, it's our future. Not just mine, but all of us." He struggled with the words. *How do you express everything?* "I knew I was dead. I mean, I absolutely had accepted that I would die in order to defeat the enemy thaums. That was the way it had to be. But now, that's no longer my future. Given another week I think I could take them on myself and destroy them. The academy is going to be astounded when I show them what I can do."

"The RAT is well aware of what you've been up to," Rickets said. He sounded... dejected, though Jawn couldn't figure out why. "Your accomplishments are the talk of the highest of circles."

Ah. Jawn now understood Rickets's lack of enthusiasm. He smiled and turned to face his friend. "Not to worry, I'll make sure all due credit is given to my partner in the Cow and Country Commission. Truthfully, Rickets, if not for you I wouldn't be who I am today." Jawn reached out his hand. It hung there in the air. Jawn started to pull it back, then Rickets grabbed it and shook it.

"Sorry, my mind's been wandering lately," Rickets said.

"You're the sharpest mind I've ever known, Rickets. I've learned more from you than I think I did at the academy." Jawn meant it.

"You're probably right," Rickets said, being gracious instead of insulting. "I think I'm just getting a little old for this job," he said.

He did sound tired. "We'll get through this, Rickets. I'm more sure of that now than ever. The thaumic processes I can conduct are staggering, even to me. And it's not stopping. I see potential everywhere and in everything. When this is over, oh, Rickets, it's going to be amazing."

Rickets squeezed Jawn's hand, then let it go. "You are special, Jawn Rathim, I knew that the moment I met you. But don't get ahead of yourself. We still need to make it through tonight."

As if to emphasize the point, lightning crashed down outside.

"Trust me, Rickets. We will win this battle," Jawn said. He'd never been more confident than he was right now.

"I'm sure you're right," Rickets said, his voice taking on a more upbeat tone. "I'm about ready to get out of this place anyway. I don't think the Lux suits me anymore."

CHAPTER FORTY-SIX

CARDUUS ROARED. HE WAS scared, and Vorly didn't blame him one damn bit. He was terrified as well. They were over the valley and climbing up through the mist shrouding it. Lightning bolts lanced through the night sky, kinking and changing direction as if looking for something, or someone. Vorly knew they were hunting him, Carduus, and Breeze.

"Keep climbing. The other thaums are creating diversions on plane and Black Star is going deep. Once he tracks them I'll have their location and then steer you to them," she said.

Vorly jumped as a lightning bolt darted down just twenty yards in front of them. Carduus bucked and veered hard to starboard. Vorly didn't yell at him or yank on the reins. The air smelled burnt as they flew through it, unlike the sulfer-tinted air Vorly was used to.

A strong wind began buffeting them. Vorly hunched over, thankful for once for the heat coming off the rag.

"How in blazes can a wind be cold here?"

"It's complicated!" Vorly said with Breeze in unison. They both laughed. It was forced, but it still felt good.

The sound of battle drifted up from the valley floor. Before they'd climbed into the mist Vorly had gotten a good look and wished he hadn't. Most of the fortresses were gone, overrun by the slyts. In their place, ballistas and spinners had been erected.

Vorly missed the days when arrows and spears were the only things you had to worry about. At least those made sense to Vorly. Now he was chasing lightning, and dealing with the aether and thaumics. His entire world had been turned on its head inside of a few months.

A cat salvo, the first one he'd heard in some time, echoed off the mountains. The Kingdom's territory had dwindled to a perimeter of a thousand yards outside Iron Fist that included the roost and one fortress. The little quarry had been lost yesterday, which meant the supply of stones for the cats would soon run out. Vorly snorted. Would Weel allow them to take stones from his precious keep to continue firing?

"Black Star just slid through four planes!" Breeze said. The awe in her voice was apparent. "It's like watching water. No matter the resistance, he finds a way under, over, or through."

"Let's hope he makes it back," Vorly said.

"HUG IT!"

Carny dove for the berm, pressing his body against it as hard as he could. An arrow volley whistled down and quilled the dosha swamp. Screams and curses rose up. Not everyone had found cover in time.

Slyt whistles rose above the din, signaling another attack. The sound worked its way into Carny's ears like an ice pick. He shivered.

"Wait for the harrows, then pick off the survivors!" Carny shouted, finding a courage he thought he'd long ago used up and peering over the berm.

Slyts ran toward him. There were hundreds, and these weren't the peasant rabble they'd tangled with before. These were slyts from the Western Wilds. All part of the Forest Collective, but they had more in common with Carny and Red Shield than they did with the Luitoxese.

They were disciplined, moving on the sound of the whistles, halting and launching a volley of arrows with nothing more than a hand signal from a leader. Carny would have admired them if they weren't trying to kill him.

The slyts came on, stepping over the bodies of comrades from previous attacks. They had to know what was in store as they approached the shield skirmish line, yet they didn't waver.

The distinctive whirr of spinner scythes added a new violence to the air. Three sailed well over the line and crashed into the mud of the dosha swamp, kicking up gouts of stinking filth. The fourth, however, slammed into a harrow by Black Shield.

The machine flew apart, its mass of bolts let loose as the tension they were under prior to firing was released. Arrows went up, back, to the sides, and forward, killing and maiming slyt and soldier alike.

Carny turned away. He didn't want to go like that, his flesh torn and riddled with splinters of wood. He knew how he wanted it. A single arrow, one with a crystal tip, right between the eyes. Quick and hopefully painless.

"Fire!"

The remaining harrows released their bundles of arrows, flinging the missiles forth when the slyts reached the kill zone thirty yards away.

The whoosh of wind as the arrows took flight was followed by the wailing cries of those not immediately killed. The entire slyt front line was down, their bodies a bleeding, shredded mess.

Carny found himself wondering what Big Hog would have had to say about it. Would all that blood help the crops grow next season?

"Hug! Hug!"

Carny ducked. An arrow glanced off his helm and his ears rang. More screams. *Fucking bastards!* The slyts were learning. They'd caught the crews reloading the harrows.

The whistles shrieked as a new wave of slyts came on. Carny looked down at his crossbow and flicked off a piece of something wet. He told himself it was mud.

"Check your string! Hold your fire until you have a clear

target. Stay calm and stay low," Carny said, pushing himself away from the berm and walking in a crouch behind his men.

Arrows flew constantly overhead now. The slyts weren't waiting. Carny tripped on something and fell to his knees. An arrow knicked the lobe of his left ear. He yelped and twisted his head as a second arrow slammed into his chest.

Carny fell backward, his breath knocked out of him. He landed on his back, his free hand reaching for the arrow in his chest, but grasping only air. Carny looked. The arrow wasn't there. He lifted his head. His aketon was torn and one of the metal plates sewn into it was gone. Son of a witch.

"Oh, that stings," Carny said, sitting up and rubbing his chest and then his ear. The sounds of battle came back to him and he got back to his feet. He ran in a crouch along the berm until he got to a gap where two soldiers lay crumpled in the muck. He reached down and turned the first one over. It was Evost, the pig farmer. He'd taken an arrow to the neck, tearing out his throat.

Carny stepped over his body and grabbed the shoulder of the second soldier. He was covered in blood. As Carny began to turn him, Ahmist sat up, his hewer in his hand, ready to strike.

"Fuck! Easy, Ahmy, it's me," Carny said. He looked at Ahmy for wounds but didn't see any. "Where are you hit?"

Ahmy lowered his hewer and looked down at his body before looking back at Carny. "I thought I was, but I think all the blood is his," he said, pointing to Evost.

Carny knelt down and patted Ahmy, checking his limbs and torso. "You're good."

Ahmy patted his own chest, then looked up at Carny, his face panic stricken. "Where's my amulet?"

"Fuck that, the slyts are coming," he said, pushing Ahmy to the berm and joining him there. Crossbows fired, knocking down a few slyts, but not nearly enough. Carny judged the distance and got up on one knee. He flicked the safety lever and squeezed, firing the first bolt. It took a slyt in the thigh. He used the cocking lever and fired, hitting the same slyt, this time in the shoulder. He cursed and cocked again, trying to find a rhythm.

The third shot hit a slyt who was leaning over the one wounded in the stomach. Carny fired again, hitting the second slyt just in front of the left ear. He cocked a fifth time and the lever stuck.

"Fuck!" He looked down and feverishly worked the lever back and forth to unstick it. He could see bits of mud falling out of the bronze gearbox. "Ahmy, fire, my bow's jammed."

"I need my amulet!" Ahmy shouted, firing.

Carny reefed and the lever moved freely, loading the next bolt. He looked up and fired, hitting a charging slyt in the mouth.

The slyts were only ten yards away now. The shield was dropping them one after the other, but it wasn't enough.

"Prepare your blades!" Carny shouted, firing one more time and then reaching for his hewer.

This was it. The slyts just kept coming. *Fuck them all*. Carny gripped his hewer and vowed to kill as many of the bastards as he could.

The crash of a trebuchet shot five feet in front of Carny knocked him on his ass. Rocks fell from the sky like giants tearing down mountains. Three more came in, stitching a neat line in front of the berm and flattening slyts.

A ragged chorus of cheers rose up from the skirmish line as the slyts turned and ran.

"How's that for timing?" Carny said, shaking his head and reaching down to grab his crossbow. He felt something and picked it up. "Hey, Ahmy, found your amulet," he said, turning and holding it out to him.

Ahmy lay slumped over his crossbow, a single arrow sticking out from between his eyes. Carny looked down at the amulet in his hand. He held it between his fingers, rubbing the outline of the Sacred Tree as he contemplated Ahmy's body. Finally, he bent down and gently rolled Ahmy over onto his back. With a tenderness he never would have shown the soldier in life, Carny leaned over Ahmy and placed the amulet on his chest.

"You were always a fucking prick," Carny said. He looked up and knew that this defensive position was no longer tenable. They'd beat back the slyts, but the harrows were out of commission and the boulders in front of the berm now blocked their lines of fire.

He considered waiting for new orders but killed that idea on the spot. These men were his responsibility, and even if every one of them was doomed, he wasn't going to make it any easier for death to claim them.

"Grab your gear and leave nothing behind for the FnC. We're moving to the last line outside of Iron Fist. Fall back!"

CHAPTER FORTY-SEVEN

J AWN SLID ON PLANE and left his body behind. He gloried in the cold that engulfed him. He'd always fought to keep a grasp on who he was when he entered the aether to conduct a process, but that was before. Now he knew he could fly from plane to plane and return to his body whenever he wished. Breeze worried about him, he knew that, but she didn't understand. He was… more.

The academy taught a thaum how to conduct processes, but what none of Jawn's instructors had told him, perhaps because they themselves didn't know, was that a thaum *could* go beyond the conducting of processes to actually become a process. Cross-planing was everything. Jawn had been taught to fear it, but now he understood it was the key.

Losing his sight had felt like the end of everything, but no longer. In the aether, he was king. He dove deeper, letting the cold clarify his mind. He left the imaginary mountain peak that centralized his being and allowed himself to disperse, entering plane after plane. The thrill of fear gave him pause, but he quickly brushed it aside. He understood now. Two planes, ten planes, it made no difference. Once you grasped the importance of letting go, you could be everywhere in the aether.

The tangle that was the four slyt thaums loomed before him. It was bold, tying four minds together and in so doing, four planes. Jawn had marveled at what they had done, but now he pitied them, for they had sacrificed everything to gain this power, at the cost of their lives. He appreciated the irony. He had been prepared to sacrifice his own, but now the planes opened up before him like new vistas to be explored. He could do what they could not.

He dove deeper still, cascading his existence all around the slyt thaums, slowly sealing off their escape routes one by one. They lashed out, aware of his presence. The heat of real pain reached him in the deep, and he remembered that though he could now cross-plane with abandon, he was still mortal, and could still be killed.

Jawn dispersed himself over more planes still, accepting the burning cuts as minuscule parts of himself were destroyed. It hurt, and he knew the price would not be cheap when he returned to his body, but that no longer mattered. This was where he wanted to live!

Growing frantic, the slyt thaums coursed energy through the planes, trying to follow him, to pin him down and set him adrift, but he was too fast, too adept. He took their blows, all the while weaving a net around them. He focused all his energy on one shining point and drove it deep into their presence, like a stake into a heart. Their screams reverberated through the aether as they writhed. Specters of energy surged from the cold and coiled around his presence. He had trapped them, but they in turn had him.

Now Jawn did feel fear. It was no longer up to him whether he lived or died.

Breeze, I have them.

"WE'VE GOT THEM! They're on Codpiece!" Breeze shouted. "They're on the south face, just below the peak."

Vorly looked. "I can't see it! The damn mist is too thick to the north."

"They're there. Jawn has them," Breeze said.

Vorly looked down at his crystal. The sheet was alive with lines twisting and pulsing like a nest of snakes.

"I believe you, Breeze, but I can't fly Carduus straight at a mountain I can't see."

"We have to attack!" Breeze shouted, her voice growing frantic. "Black Star has them engaged, but he can't hold them on his own for long."

"How the fuck I am supposed to attack something I can't see?" Vorly asked, wondering if he'd made a fatal mistake in agreeing to this. *Maybe*, he realized, *but what choice did I have*? Between the mist and the lightning, his rags might as well be oxen for all the good they were doing. If the enemy thaums weren't destroyed, the valley was certain to fall.

Vorly eased Carduus into a turn to port, letting their height slip in the hopes of seeing a path through the mist. "Breeze, without a marker, I can't see anything. Can you do that lightning-bolt thing and hit them?"

"No! That's a whole other process and, oh, fuck it! We have to burn them with Carduus. It's the only way, and we have to do it now!"

Vorly reefed Carduus into a turn to starboard, looking for a glimpse of the Codpiece. A lightning bolt lit up the sky as it sliced down at them no more than fifteen yards in front of Carduus. The rag howled and veered to port. Burnt air stung Vorly's nostrils as they flew through its wake. Another bolt landed fifty yards to their starboard, briefly revealing the mountain peak it hit in a spray of flame. Vorly knew that, if not for the other thaums back at the roost working to shield their flight from the slyt thaums, Carduus would have been hit by a bolt long ago. As it was, the bolts were getting damn close.

"I have a terrible idea!" Breeze shouted. "I'll get Hyaminth and the others to quit shielding us. We'll navigate by the lightning bolts!"

"Woman, are you mad? They're the only thing keeping us in the air!"

"I can guide you. Every bolt shows up a couple of flicks on

plane before it strikes. I can tell you what to do to avoid them, but you have to do exactly what I say."

Vorly sat up in his saddle and twisted his back. A string of three bolts plunged down a hundred yards to port, momentarily ripping away the veil of mist and darkness to reveal the valley below.

"Do it!" Vorly shouted, gripping the reins tight in his gloved hands. He glanced down at the crystal, not sure what to expect.

"Climb, climb, climb!"

Vorly tore his eyes away from the sheet and pulled back on the reins. Carduus responded and drove his massive wings down in a violent show of force. It sounded as if the very air itself had been torn asunder.

"Fuuuuuuck!" Vorly grunted as a suffocating weight enveloped him and his vision grayed. A lightning bolt sliced diagonally beneath Carduus, but Vorly was unable to see a thing. Not waiting for Breeze's next command, he kicked Carduus with what strength he still had.

Carduus slowed his wing beats and began to level out.

"Dive, dive, dive!"

Vorly snapped the reins and threw himself forward in the saddle as Carduus flicked his tail, heeled over onto his port wing until he was nearly upside down. In a move as graceful as it was terrifying, Carduus arched his long neck up and over Vorly until his head pointed toward the valley floor and then dropped like an avalanche.

Vorly's head pounded, as if it was being pumped full of hot water. The wind screamed in his ears as Carduus began shaking, his scales clattering in the growing turbulence. Vorly turned his head to the right to check on Carduus's wing and then quickly looked back. The membrane was vibrating so hard it was difficult to tell if the wing was even still there.

Vorly was about to pull Carduus out of the dive when a dazzling burst of ball lightning stitched the sky all around them. Every cardinal direction was ablaze with crackling white fire. Only Breeze's order to dive had saved them.

"The Codpiece!" Breeze shouted. "Go left! Port, go to port!"

Vorly spurred Carduus to port, allowing Carduus to twist and contort his body as he flew through the ball lightning. Vorly looked up and the peaks of the northern mountains were clear in the burning light.

Two more lightning bolts stabbed down at them. Vorly kicked Carduus into a series of quick turns and rolls, climbing and diving as they approached the peaks. Another bolt hit, missing them and lighting up a peak ahead.

"There!" Vorly shouted, pointing. For a brief flicker the outline of Codpiece was visible.

"Now!"

Vorly looked down at his sheet. The screen was a mess of angry red lines. He looked back up and then took his helm off and tossed it away.

A bolt hit a peak just to Carduus's starboard wing, not fifty yards away. Shards of the lightning flared out and hit his wing, setting it on fire. Carduus roared.

Vorly saw the fire out of the corner of his eye but ignored it. There was the Codpiece, dead ahead. This was working! The lightning was providing him the light he needed.

"How far down the peak?" Vorly shouted.

"No more than a hundred yards! We have to hurry!"

Vorly loosened his grip on the reins and shouted at Carduus. "The bastards throwing lightning bolts at you are sitting on that mountain! Get ready, my boy, get ready!"

Carduus angled his body so that he began to arch skyward as they approached the peak of Codpiece. His air gills opened and wind roared into them, churning the fire inside Carduus into a maelstrom.

Vorly gasped as the heat built. "Breeze, get ready to slide off plane! Tell Jawn to do the same!"

The clouds and mist above the valley flashed and shook as lightning and thunder ripped through them. More bolts stabbed down at Carduus, but the rag flew unwaveringly at the peak.

"They have us! I can't shield anymore! The next bolt will kill us!" Breeze screamed.

Vorly closed his eyes and made the sign of the Sacred Tree. "Fire, Carduus, fire!"

A heat unlike anything Vorly had experienced before on Carduus enveloped him. Even with his eyes closed his vision turned white.

"My crystals!" Breeze shouted.

"Slide off, now!" Vorly shouted, holding Carduus on course.

Risking blindness, Vorly peered through the fingers of his gloves covering his face. A roaring pillar of pure white fire flew out of Carduus's maw and plunged into the jungle on Codpiece.

The very top of the peak shimmered and then shattered, scattering rock and trees for hundreds of yards into the air. Carduus's fire continued to hammer the mountain. Vorly watched it all, terrified and amazed at what he'd set loose.

"Vorly, we're going to die here!" Breeze shouted.

Vorly tore his eyes away from the destruction. She was right. They couldn't survive this kind of heat.

"We'll jump!" he shouted, unbuckling his harness. He turned and grabbed her, lifting her out of her saddle and holding her in his arms.

"We'll die!" she shouted.

He looked into her bloody eyes and smiled. "Maybe, but we're not charking!"

As Carduus carved the mountain with his fire, Vorly took a step to the side, closed his eyes, and jumped.

IT OCCURRED TO Carny as the slyts came across the dosha swamp and closed in on Red Shield's final skirmish line that he had never made a last will and testament. Not that he really had anything of value, except maybe the piece of paper he'd signed with Tryser for the crossbow. Still, it seemed wrong.

"Bard!"

"SL?" the Bard shouted, lifting his head from his position along the berm ten yards away.

"If I die, you can have my things!"

"What?"

"He said," Wiz shouted, running past, "if he dies, you can have his things!"

"Oh." There was a long pause as the slyts fired another volley. "I guess you can have mine if I die then."

"What the fuck am I going to do with a psaltery?" Carny shouted, standing up and firing a quick couple of bolts, then ducking back down.

"Well, what I am going to do with... what the hell do you have?"

"Nothing really!" Carny shouted, reaching into his quiver and pulling out his last three bolts.

"So if you die, I get nothing?"

Carny thought about that as he reloaded his crossbow. "Yeah, I guess so. Never mind!"

Carny recocked his crossbow and was preparing to fire when a series of lightning bolts lit up the sky to the north.

"Better there than here," someone said.

Carny was looking down his bow, searching for a slyt leader to take out, when the sky grew lighter. Suddenly, white light tore the darkness away. Carny could see the slyts as clearly as if it were daytime.

The Codpiece lit up like a torch. The entire valley became a dizzying landscape of vibrating light. A flick later, the entire peak of the Codpiece exploded. The roar of the flame reached them a flick later, rumbling across the valley. The force of the sound shook Carny's chest from the inside.

Carny squinted and saw a shape pass in front of the mountain, then disappear in the glare reflecting off the mist. It reminded him of a comet among the stars, but instead of falling, this comet was climbing higher into the sky and picking up speed as it did so. In that moment, two smaller objects fell past the comet's tail and disappeared into the jungle.

An arrow wobbled past Carny's head and he brought his gaze back to the field of battle. The slyts massing in front of the shield's position were milling about in confusion, but despite the thunderous explosion on the Codpiece they weren't retreating. In fact, they were quickly sorting themselves out for another attack.

Even Carny could do this math. They were massively outnumbered. One more slyt charge would finish them. Whatever happened on the peak of the Codpiece wasn't going to help Red Shield.

"Prepare to volley!" Carny shouted, turning and pointing at his men. "Fuck tomorrow, let's make tonight forever!"

Carny took a step forward, ramming the last of his bolts into the feeder mechanism. The sound of cocking bows filled the night. Soldiers moved up beside him. Red Shield, what was left of it, leaned forward, waiting only for his command to unleash their final volley.

Carny gritted his teeth, knowing these were the remaining moments of his life and realizing that there was nowhere else he'd rather be. As the slyts formed ranks and took aim, Carny smiled. He wouldn't die alone, and he wouldn't die in vain. He was with his brothers, and that was everything.

"Fire!"

Red Shield and the survivors from the destroyed fortresses that had joined them let loose with a howl that drowned out all other sound. The front row of the slyts facing them crumpled as bolts and arrows tore through them. It was a horrible sight, but Carny only had eyes for the following rows of slyts moving up to take their place. With the last of his bolts spent, Carny slung his crossbow and grabbed his hewer. He raised it high in the air and then pointed it forward.

"Make it count!"

Men and dwarves charged forward, their voices raised in fury and fear. Shadow and light raced across the battlefield like windswept flames, turning everything in front of Carny into a jumbled mess. The slyts, caught off guard by the charge and the flashing light, were unprepared when Red Shield crashed into them.

Carny swung his hewer down, cleaving the arm off a slyt

bowman. The force of his swing sent Carny stumbling past the slyt and headlong into another one, bowling him over and taking Carny to the ground with him. The slyt's hand flew up and grabbed Carny by the throat. Carny kneed the slyt in the stomach then brought the handle of his hewer down on the slyt's head. There was a loud crack and the slyt's hands fell away.

Two more slyts appeared to Carny's right. He raised his hewer and using a backhand stroke sliced them across their chests. Without armor, the blade bit easily into their flesh and bone.

The flashing light grew brighter, turning the battle into a dance of shadows. Carny got to his feet and swung his hewer around his head, unable to determine slyt from shadow. Heat wafted over him, as if a fire had been lit.

A knife blade flashed out of the melee aimed for his neck. He turned, already knowing it was too late as the slyt lunged forward. Carny opened his mouth to scream as a rock flew past his ear and caved in the slyt's head.

Carny wheeled around to see Black Pine standing a few feet away, another chunk of rock in his hand. He had his arm cocked back ready to throw. Carny dove for the ground as Black Pine heaved. The rock sailed over Carny and took another slyt in the chest, slamming into his rib cage with a sickening crack.

Unsure if Black Pine was throwing at him or the slyts, Carny rolled and got up in a crouch, facing the slyts. He raised his hewer, prepared to swing it for the last time when the blade glowed red and became hot.

"Fuck!" he shouted, dropping the hewer as the sky above him erupted, spewing white light into the ranks of the slyts. He dropped to the ground and curled up in a ball, cringing for the moment the flame would burn him. A roaring wind blasted the field of battle, threatening to pick him up off the ground and fling him into the sky. The heat around him rose and then subsided, as did the sound.

It took Carny several flicks to realize the nightmare was gone and he was still alive. He raised his head, blinking. Smoke and ash drifted in the air. The slyt frontline was no more. In its place were smoldering bits of charred flesh. Further back, those slyts not caught in the fire were running.

"Did you see that?" the Wiz shouted. "Look at him go!"

Carny looked up into the sky. The comet he'd seen earlier was ascending into the night, its glowing body trailing a wake of twinkling sparks. The rag rolled its body as it climbed, as if it were playing. Carny imagined it could reach the very stars and keep going.

A single trebuchet shot landed among the slyts, but it was unnecessary. Their screams of terror grew more distant by the flick as they stampeded to flee the valley.

A new sound filled the night as rag after rag launched from the roost and took to the air. The mass of fires burning around the valley gave them more than enough light to fly, and the lightning, Carny realized, had stopped. More fire poured down onto the retreating slyts, drowning their screams in molten death.

The Bard walked up to Carny and stopped. His eyes were wide, but he had a grin on his face. "That was fucking amazing!"

Carny smiled and looked up to follow the rag's flight. The mist choking the valley was evaporating. He could already see some stars in the night sky.

The sound of hooves made Carny turn.

Weel appeared astride a white horse. His helm gleamed and he held his hewer in his right hand, swinging it above his head. Squeak, astride Gallanter, rode up beside him. The messenger looked miserable which brought a smile to Carny's face.

"We have them on the run!" Weel shouted. "Now it's time to finish them off! Charge!"

His horse reared, then took off at a gallop across the dosha swamp and after the retreating slyts. His coterie of staff, their horses shying and whinnying, eventually followed suit. Squeak and Gallanter remained in place. Carny walked over to Squeak. Squeak started to smile, but it froze on his face when Carny reached out and slapped Gallanter's rump. The startled pony bolted into the night after Weel carrying a screaming Squeak along with him.

No one said anything. Carny stared after the impromptu

cavalry charge long after he could no longer hear the hooves, or the screams. Carny finally turned and faced the shield.

Red Shield was a terrifying sight. Bloodied and blackened, what was left of their uniforms hung in tatters from their bodies. Almost every soldier sported a bandage cloth soaked in blood and filth somewhere on his body. Many had several. Even now, the Wiz was tending to a fallen soldier, dressing his wounded arm.

Carny wished Sinte and Listowk could be here to see them now. Sinte, because it would drive that bastard crazy, and Listowk, because he'd be so damn proud.

"Are we going after him?" the Bard asked.

"Fuck him. Let him count the slyts himself," Carny said. He cradled his crossbow in his arms, gently rubbing his fingers along the wood and metal, checking for damage. Amazingly, the strings hadn't snapped. Carny didn't care how Tryser got it, but he wanted rag sinew for every bow in the shield. "Wraith and Knockers are out there somewhere. We don't go anywhere until we find them."

There were grunts and nods. Carny set off, walking with purpose toward the jungle. The Bard fell into step beside him. Carny glanced over his shoulder. Red Shield followed close behind. They spread out, bows facing in different directions, covering all angles. Carny knew they were exhausted—he was too—but he also knew they'd follow him to the Valley of Fire and Damnation and kick the gate in when they got there.

Carny turned and started walking backward. "Red Shield. Take a drink, check your string, and grab bolts and arrows as we go.

"I have no idea what we'll find when we get in there—only the LOKAM knows."

"Fuck the LOKAM!" roared Red Shield in response. Carny smiled and turned and began walking forward again.

The Bard started to pull out his psaltery, then stopped. "Sorry, SL, guess this isn't the best time."

Carny looked around at the carnage and the flames. Cries

and groans drifted on the air. The smell of blood mixed with the smoke and left a stain inside him he knew he'd never be able to clean. "Actually, this is the perfect time. Play one of those new songs you've been working on. You know, something that tears through the shit and the haze like that rag just did. Something," Carny said, clenching his fist, "that roars like the very wind is on fire."

The Bard smiled, his teeth flashing in the night. "I've got just the thing," he said, raising his right hand high in the air and bringing it down hard across the strings.

A reverberating wail went up, assaulting Carny's ears and making him wince. He looked over at the Bard.

"Too loud?" the Bard asked. "I had that dwarf make some modifications to it."

Carny grinned. "Fuck no. Louder. I want the High fucking Druid to hear it. Red Shield!" he shouted. "Let's go get our boys!"

JAWN SLID OFF plane, his body shaking and drenched in sweat. He fell out of his chair and onto the dirt floor. He vomited, gagging for what seemed an eternity before his stomach stopped heaving.

He'd done it. The slyt thaums were dead and he was alive. At the last flick he dispersed himself throughout the aether, slipping through the slyt thaums' grasp. Tears rolled freely down his cheeks. The arrogant young man who had been so concerned about glory and battle was gone. This was his true purpose. The possibilities that his thaumics had to offer would change the world.

Breeze would be fine, he knew it. She was strong, she was smart. Of course she'd slid when they fired. It was the prudent thing to do. He'd rest for a few flicks, then get back on plane and find her.

Footsteps thudded on the steps.

"Who's there?"

"It's me," Rickets said, walking into the room.

"Rickets! We did it. It worked. The slyt thaums are dead." Jawn forced himself to his feet.

"I know. Their army is pulling back," Rickets said "That rag really put on a light show."

"I saw it," Jawn said, pointing to his head, "in here. It was... amazing."

"And you did it all on your own," Rickets said. "That's... that's incredible."

He still sounded tired and dejected, but Jawn wasn't having it.

"Rickets, we all did it. I told you that."

"I know."

Rickets's hand fell on Jawn's shoulder and the two men embraced. Jawn wished he could look into Rickets's eyes, but the moment was perfect all the same.

"You're two breaths from passing out," Rickets said, easing Jawn back onto his chair. "You need to rest."

"Just a few flicks, then I have to get back on plane." Jawn smiled. "Looks like the Cow and Country Commission came through in the end." Silence greeted Jawn's statement. "C'mon, Rickets, that's funny."

"You're right, I'm sorry. But you did it. You defeated them." Rickets didn't sound happy.

"I had help," Jawn said.

"Do you understand the power you now have?" Rickets asked. "You're more powerful than any king."

Jawn frowned. "I told you, it isn't like that. The power isn't mine. I only use it," Jawn said.

"A distinction without a difference," Rickets said. "You know, when I first met you, I thought you were the most insufferable son of a witch I'd come across. If you'd taken a slyt arrow in the heart, I wouldn't have shed a tear."

Jawn smiled. "I wasn't fond of you either."

"You really are exceptional, you know that?" Rickets said. "The more I realized that, the more I wished it wasn't true."

"It took me a while to accept that you weren't a complete asshole, too," Jawn said, wondering if Rickets had been drinking.

"But we can compliment each other later. You promised me a story about Ox and Crink, and I think I've earned it."

"I suppose you have at that," Rickets said. "I told you I met them, years ago."

"I remember," Jawn said. "I wish I had been there."

"All their adventures, all those stories they told…" Rickets said, then trailed off.

Jawn heard the sorrow in Rickets's voice and suddenly didn't want to know any more. "Look, on second thought, I—"

"I wish it all could have been different," Rickets said, cutting Jawn off. "Truly, Jawn, I want you to know that," Rickets said.

Jawn heard Rickets's clothes rustle and knew he'd stood up.

"Save your story," Jawn said, realizing now why Rickets had been so hesitant to share more about Jawn's boyhood heroes. "It doesn't matter, it really doesn't. We're Rickets and Rathim. Our adventures will surpass theirs a thousandfold." Jawn stood, holding out his arms to embrace his friend again.

Something hard and cold jabbed into Jawn's chest below his heart. He gasped, understanding it was a blade. It slid out and his knees buckled. He fell to the floor, slumping sideways until he leaned against his chair. He tried to get up but his body wouldn't cooperate.

"Rickets… ?"

"Why? Why the fuck did you have to be so good?"

Jawn heard him crouch down beside him. He tried to reach out a hand, but he could only make his fingers twitch.

"I don't… understand."

"I know you don't," Rickets said, stroking Jawn's hair. "It was never really about the crystals. It's always been about what someone like you can do with them. The other thaums, their skills are impressive, but not like yours. When you lost your sight, you became something else. That scared people, Jawn."

Jawn slid a little farther down the chair. Why was it getting so damn cold?

"You… fucking… coward," Jawn said, forcing out each word. He could taste blood in his mouth. "I only want to help people.

I'm no… no threat."

"But you are, Jawn, you *are*. The fact that you don't see it is what makes you even more dangerous. Those in power don't understand altruism. They can't fathom why someone would pursue power and then not use it to their advantage."

Jawn gasped for breath. Rickets gently lifted his head and cradled it in his arms. Jawn wanted to move away, but he had no strength.

"And so… they ordered… you to kill me?"

There was a pause. Something warm and wet dropped onto Jawn's cheek and trickled into the corner of his mouth. It was a tear. "They actually left it up to my discretion. I… I couldn't take the chance."

"Killing me… doesn't change a damn thing," Jawn said. He gritted his teeth and forced the words out. "I'm not as special as you think. There will be others… others like me."

Rickets stopped stroking Jawn's hair, gently laid his head down on the floor, and got up.

"I know, Jawn. That's why there are others like me."

Footsteps sounded and then faded, and Jawn was alone. He struggled to get up but began coughing blood. He saw the planes before him and started sliding. He moved effortlessly, his mind as free as the wind. He was invincible on plane. He was—

CHAPTER FORTY-EIGHT

VORLY OPENED HIS EYES. All he saw was black, so he opened them again. This time, his eyelids parted and he saw light. It was morning. He was on a ship. No, sailcloth, but not a sail. He was in a tent. He heard hushed voices. He breathed in and smelled the mix of herbs and lime and knew where he was.

"Oh, High Druid save me," he groaned, lifting his head and then giving in to the pain and letting it fall back down.

"He lives," Master Witch Elmitia said, coming and standing over his bed.

"I'm not sure I agree," Vorly said, lifting his head again and holding it there for a few flicks. Elmitia shook her head but reached down and fluffed his pillow, allowing his head to stay propped up. He looked around the tent. It was filled. There were men and dwarves in cots and on the floor.

"Now he's a witch," she said.

"I hurt."

"That's what happens when you jump off of dragons and into the jungle. Why you're not dead is a mix of all the foliage you fell through and dumb, idiotic luck."

"I hurt. A lot," Vorly said again, in case Elmitia wasn't fully clear on the concept.

"Your humors are so mixed at the moment I really don't know how you're alive. And you have two broken legs."

Vorly nodded. "I thought it felt like my humors were a bit out of sorts."

"I'll give you something for the pain shortly. For now, just lie there and don't try getting up."

"You know, from this angle, you are a very charming woman," Vorly said, staring up at her breasts.

Elmitia bent over until she was staring him in the face. "It's good you tried jumping off a dragon first. When you heal, and then I get ahold of you, you'll be lucky to crawl." She stood up and walked away, leaving Vorly aroused and scared.

"Oh, Vorly!"

Vorly turned his head as Breeze ran into the tent and buried her face in his chest, hugging him.

"My ribs. My back. My neck."

She lifted her face and released him, sitting down on his cot. Her face was puffy from crying. A huge bandage covered her right ear and part of her head, but she seemed to have survived their plunge into the jungle better than him.

"I'm so happy to see you," she said, and started sobbing.

"Takes more than that to kill me," he said. He forced his left hand to move enough to touch her leg. "Breeze, it's all right. I'm going to be fine. How are you walking? I have two broken legs."

Breeze kept sobbing. "You broke my fall."

Vorly winced. Bits of his last moments on Carduus and the ensuing jump into the night came back to him.

"I couldn't lose you, too," Breeze said, struggling to control herself.

"What are you talking about?"

Breeze wiped the tears from her eyes and caught her breath. "He's dead. Jawn's dead. He was stabbed in the heart."

Vorly closed his eyes. *That fucking snake. It had to be Rickets.* Vorly knew he couldn't trust that bastard but still hadn't expected this. He opened them again and looked at her. "I'm sorry, Breeze, I am so sorry."

Breeze nodded. Vorly wished he could do more, but the pain coming from his legs was making it difficult to think.

"I know he meant a lot to you."

Breeze nodded as she kept sobbing.

"Greatest thaum I've known, except for you," Vorly said.

Breeze looked up and tried to smile. Her eyes widened.

"Carduus!" she said, startling Vorly.

"I miss him, too," Vorly said. "Poor bastard deserved better. They always do."

Breeze shook her head. "No, no. He's alive! He kept on flying. They said he looked like a shooting star going across the sky. After attacking the mountain, he flew into the valley and fired on the slyt army, then he headed west. That was the last anyone saw of him. But... he was alive."

Tears came to Vorly's eyes and he didn't try to hide them. His entire body shook as he cried. He looked up at Breeze, her image blurry through the tears.

Breeze grabbed his hand and squeezed. Vorly did his best to squeeze back.

"The daft bugger did it," Vorly finally said.

"Did what?" Breeze asked.

"You said he looked like a shooting star," Vorly said. "That's the fire molt. Maybe one in a thousand survive it, but those that do . . . oh, Breeze, Carduus will be legend. We have to find him."

Breeze nodded. "We will, but right now you need to rest."

"I think you're right. Please call Master Witch Elmitia over. I'd like to drink myself back into oblivion."

"That's something we need to talk about when you're better," Breeze said, regaining some composure. "You drink entirely too much."

Vorly nodded. He was in so much pain he'd agree to anything. "You're right. But for the moment, I could really use a little shot."

Breeze looked at him, then stood up. "I know, but after you're out of here, things are going to change."

Vorly watched her walk away and then closed his eyes. Between Elmitia and Breeze they just might shape him up into something halfway presentable. A man destined for greater things.

"But not if I can help it," he mumbled.

EPILOGUE

RICKETS DIDN'T LOOK BACK, not once. He knew from past experience that there was no gain to be had. Enough ghosts followed him, their eyes looking questioningly at him, wondering why. He didn't need more. He couldn't afford more. He'd done what needed to be done. "For the Greater Good."

"Anything," he muttered, looking down at his hands. He wasn't sure how long he stood there, but the sun was rising over the eastern peaks when he finally came to his senses.

"You're getting too old for this shit," Rickets said, looking around at the jungle. It was time for a change. He headed east, deciding to climb up and over the mountains instead of risking the southern route. He could see the relief force already pouring through it. They wouldn't know to look for him yet, but all the same, he wasn't taking chances. He hadn't lived this long by making mistakes.

He wiped sweat from his brow with his hand and then dried his hand on his tunic. *Fuck, it's hot.* The climb was tougher than he expected. He'd let himself get a little flabby, but a fighting-fit crowny who only pushed a quill drew too much suspicion. Still, he thought the climb would be easier as much of the eastern slope was charred ash. Now that he was here, however, he saw that while much of the vegetation had been burned, twisted vines and trunks remained, constantly tripping him up.

He made his way through a piece of relatively untouched jungle and then stopped on the far side at a clearing. The blackened bodies of slyts lay everywhere. He remembered the soldier who had volunteered to go out and signal the position of the clearing where the slyts congregated. This must be the place.

His hand casually slid into his tunic and grabbed the hilt of his knife. That soldier was still missing. Rickets looked around, careful to make as little noise as possible. He quickly decided that even if the soldier had survived he'd be long gone from—

"Who are you?"

Rickets spun around and threw his knife. A soldier stood between a pair of trees just ten yards away at the edge of the clearing. He was covered in leaves and grass, blending in so well it was like he was a tree himself. Rickets's knife hit him square in the chest with a heavy thunk. The soldier stumbled back a few paces, his mouth open in an O before collapsing without a sound.

"Fuck," Rickets said, crouching low and grabbing for his second knife. He took a few breaths and calmed himself down. He waited, looking for any sign the soldier would get back up. Motion overhead made him look to the sky. Vultures were starting to circle above the clearing.

Realizing he couldn't stay here, Rickets got up and slowly walked toward the soldier. The boy was one of the bravest he'd ever known. He'd come out here alone to track the slyt scouts and survived the rag attack, too. Just damn bad luck that he had to spot Rickets. Well, his family would get a medal and a small stipend and the thanks of a grateful Kingdom for his service. It was something.

A twig near the soldier moved. Rickets froze. A small jungle cat lifted its head and looked at him. The tufts of its ears were singed and it was covered in soot. Poor thing had been through hell the last few days. Rickets judged it to be a few pounds at most. Not much, but maybe a couple of meals. He walked closer, lowering the knife to his side. He smiled.

"Are you all alone?" he asked, moving toward the soldier and not directly at the cat so as not to spook it. "Was he your friend?

Was he keeping you company out here?" The cat was curious, turning its head one way and then the other as it watched him. It gave no indication it was going to run.

"I'll be your friend," Rickets said, getting to within a few feet of the body. "It's what I do. I'll be your friend, I'll make sure nothing and no one hurts you, and then, when it's time, I'll end it."

He flexed his fingers on the knife handle and prepared to throw. He made a note to remember to retrieve his other knife. A branch snapped off to his right. He turned his head. Another soldier stood there. Instead of an aketon, he'd wrapped several broad leaves around his torso which he clutched in obvious pain. He had a bow in his left hand, but he was using it as a staff for support.

Rickets started walking toward him, offering the soldier a warm smile. *Do it, and go.*

He raised his arm to throw and caught motion out of his left eye. He turned.

A group of Kingdom soldiers stood at the edge of the tree line. They were bloody and battered and seemed more specters than men. They stared at him, each man locked on to Rickets with a determination that bordered on the insane.

Rickets let the knife slip out of his fingers, but it was too late; their arrows were already in flight.

Rickets sank to the ground, his arms and legs going limp. He would have fallen forward onto the arrows protruding from his chest if not for the arm that caught him around the waist and steadied him. He fought to breathe, gasping in the humid morning air.

Wind blew in Rickets's right ear and it took a moment for him to realize it was someone whispering.

"What?" Rickets said, his lips barely moving.

"Some days you fuck the Lux, and some days it fucks you."

The arm released him. Rickets slid to the ground and slumped against the trunk of a tree. He fought to breathe, forcing his body to work. The soldier walked around him and over to the body. The other soldiers crowded around. None said a word.

"Knockers? Knockers?" the soldier asked. He pulled the knife from the body. It made an odd squeaking sound as he did. He tossed the knife to the side and bent over the body again.

"You in there?"

The body sat up. Knockers blinked his eyes and then clutched his chest.

"He threw a knife at me!" Knockers shouted, his eyes wide in surprise. "Did you see that, Wraith? A knife!"

"We all saw it," Wraith said, motioning to the other soldiers. "That pipe you've been whittling saved you."

Knockers fished around in his aketon and pulled out a chunk of ironwood partially carved into the shape of a pipe. "There's a great big crack in it. It's ruined."

"What were you doing out here?" Wraith asked.

Knockers looked up at him. "Looking for you. I told the SL we weren't leaving you behind."

Rickets fought to breathe, desperately trying to move his body, but a weight like iron pinned him to the ground.

Wraith patted Knockers and gingerly stood up, then helped Knockers to his feet. The cat returned, bounding through the debris to rub up against Wraith's trouser leg.

"You came out here for me?" Wraith asked.

"Of course," Knockers said. "We don't leave anyone behind."

The certainty of his voice struck Rickets. No doubt, no hesitation.

Knockers looked over at Rickets. "What about him? Carny," he said, turning toward the shield, "what do we do with him?"

The one called Carny walked a few paces and looked down at Rickets.

Carny stared into Rickets's eyes. Rickets looked for a trace of compassion... something, anything that would give him the edge to make it through the next few flicks. He'd been in dire situations before and he'd come out alive. It wasn't too late, even now. He just had to find a way. He noticed a couple of soldiers wore the pendant of the Sacred Tree. "The... the LOKAM says—"

"Fuck the LOKAM!" the soldiers shouted, their voices ringing in the morning air.

Carny smiled at Rickets. "You know, I think we'll let the Lux decide what to do with you," he said.

Wraith bent down, groaning as he did so, and scooped up the cat, which perched on his shoulder. Without looking back, the shield turned and started walking down the slope.

Rickets opened his mouth to call out, but the effort hurt too much.

"Hey, Carny?" Knockers asked, their voices growing distant.
"Yeah?"

"What happened? I saw all the lightning and the Codpiece explode."

"We held," Carny said. "Drove the slyts out of the valley." There was no joy in the statement. "Squeak found us this morning. Little fucker said Weel and his staff are up for medals on account of their charge." Hoots of derision greeted this statement.

"Is the fighting over then?" Knockers asked.

"For now. Squeak said we're pulling out, as soon as Weel counts the bodies."

"Pulling out? Who's taking our place? I saw more troops arriving."

"No one," Carny said. "We're all needed back by the coast."

"No one's staying?" Knockers asked.

"Only the dead," Carny said.

"So… we won?" Knockers asked.

There was a long silence and Rickets thought he would hear no more; then their voices came to him from far away.

"We didn't lose."

"Is that enough?"

There was another long pause.

"It's something."

Rickets choked, spitting blood. His mind raced. There was still an out. There was always an out. There had to be.

Motion in front of him focused his eyes. A blur of black feathers filled his vision as a condor landed a few feet away.

The bird splayed its wings wide as it settled on the ground, momentarily blotting out the sun. It fixed a beady eye on Rickets and opened its beak, issuing a series of abrupt hisses.

"Go, eat," Rickets whispered, doing his best to motion with his head at the charked remains of the slyts strewn about the clearing. "You'd only choke on me."

The condor cocked its featherless head to the side and stared at him with an unblinking eye. It ignored the dead slyts and continued to stare at him.

"I'm not dying," Rickets said, gritting his teeth as he pushed himself up a few inches. His entire body shuddered with the effort, but it was worth it. He wasn't dying, not here, not like this. He coughed, spraying blood into the air. The condor opened its beak, still staring at him.

More motion drew Ricket's gaze skyward. The birds circling above him were slowly descending toward the ground.

Unable to keep looking up, Rickets lowered his eyes. The condor remained where it had landed, still watching him.

"Fuck the Lux," Rickets said, holding the bird's gaze.

The condor stared back, and waited.

ACKNOWLEDGMENTS

Thanking those who offered their skills, friendship, and encouragement while I wrote this book is a privilege I treasure. I am especially indebted to my first readers: my brother, Michael Evans; my parents, Robert and Barbara Evans; my indomitable fellow warrior in all things writing, Deb Christerson; and the exceptional kindness and professional counsel of my friends Chris Schluep, Bill Takes, and, especially, Shelly Shapiro.

My agent, Don Maass, who suggested I write a fantasy based on the Vietnam War, and my editor, Ed Schlesinger, who unwaveringly ushered the idea into reality, providing expert guidance and sound advice that kept me on track (and sane) through the writing process —I thank you both!

I'd also like to note my respect and admiration for Louise Burke, President of Gallery Books, and Vice President Jen Bergstrom, for their trust and support, as well as the fantastic job done by the many people at Gallery Books who turn my writing into novels I am proud to share with you. These passionate champions of books are noble stewards of the written word and I count myself fortunate to collaborate with them.

Not forgotten are my intrepid mates in Morior Invictus / Rebellorum Draco alliance in the Hobbit: Kingdoms of Middle-Earth online game. Our battles are as legendary as our comradeship. An equally deserved tip of the hat goes to the many publishing and writing folks in the Drinklings of New York City.

Finally, I wish to acknowledge and commend all the veterans I have known over the years. These men and women, whether they fought in Normandy, Khe Sanh, Fallujah, Helmand province, or any number of battlefields around the world, did so knowing that they risked their lives so that we might live and enjoy a world free from the violence and death they faced. To thank them is hardly sufficient. And so I honor their service, and I remember them.

Chris Evans, New York, NY